"An inspiring and compassionate 21st century epic adventure, part *Paradise Lost* and part *Wizard of Oz*.... An evolutionary and cultural vision that blends the grim equations of survival and extinction with the regenerative powers of courage and hope."

—Thomas Allen Nelson, author of *Kubrick: Inside a Film Artist's Maze*

"This book should firmly fix John Weiskopf's star in the heavenly constellation of great authors. He is more than just a master writer: he is a healer. While *The Ascendancy* has all the makings of an epic tale, it is a story that heals with hope that can be transported from its pages into the very hearts of people everywhere. This book should hold a place of honor on any book shelf, preferably between *Harry Potter* and *Lord of the Rings*."

—Reverend Ronald D. Culmer,
Rector of St. Clare's Episcopal Church, Pleasanton

"Since the 9-11 tragedy there has been a great need for healing of sadness, anxiety and anger; this 'historical myth' *The Ascendancy* truly helps to fill this need. John Weiskopf's magical mixing of history and legends could only come about from an author with the creative genius of a filmmaker, cinematographer, English teacher, religious seminarian and a participant first hand in shamanic rituals, who has experienced nights in the mountains of Machu Picchu. This novel will captivate you and assist you in working through our national trauma in ways that only the power of a myth can do."

—Michael M. Lydon, MSW, ACSW, CGP Licensed Clinical Social Worker

"Nightmare utopias are by now pretty standard fare—from *Brave New World* to *1984* to *Fahrenheit 451*. John Weiskopf reverses this with *The Ascendancy*, which offers a more hopeful vision of the future than even the Biblical Armageddon. How will this come about? 'Compassion,' Weiskopf writes, 'will be the key.'"

—Paul F. Cummins, Executive Director of New Visions Foundations

"*The Ascendancy* is Soul Centered. It expands our consciousness about the changes coming in all of our lives. As we learn to accept and embrace our differences, a true global community is possible. With humor, compassion and great love we see the past through the present, and create a NEW FUTURE."

—Dr. Ann Josephine Ullrich, Th.D.,
Author of *Fairy Tea*, a children's fairy tale

"Like C.S. Lewis and J.R. Tolkien, John Weiskopf puts us in a fantasy world which intertwines astronomical science, historical experience and Native indigenous spirituality. With the challenge of choice directed toward his characters, the author challenges us to live in reality rather than the fantasy of our present world which offers us such an illusion of security. *The Ascendancy* speaks of hope and possibility. The illusion of security only leads to destruction."

—Rev. John S. Wintermyer, ret. Chaplain, Washington Hospital Center &
Physician Assistant, Unity Health Care, WDC

"A New Age remake of 'Jack and the Beanstalk', *The Ascendancy* takes America's post-September 11 angst, and wraps it up in a fairytale with characters worthy of Lewis Carroll. Throw in an Inca prophecy and the imminent turn of the Mayan epoch in 2012 and you get a metaphysical fantasy whose flights of imagination leave you clinging to the green leafy twists of the beanstalk arising from the ruins of New York's Ground Zero."

—Carlos Aranaga, SciFiDimensions.com

"John Weiskopf is the master storyteller of the 'information age'. Let go and climb 'The Beanstalk' with him. Like a laser beam, through an amazing mixture of cultures, times, and dimensions, he reveals the essence of humanity in *The Ascendancy*. Life won't be the same after encountering Potter Sims!!"

—Sandra Secunda, International artist & cultural promoter, Teacher of
French and Latin at Basis Scottsdale

"With diverse influences including The Brothers Grimm, L. Frank Baum, Lewis Carroll and Jared Diamond, John Weiskopf deftly weaves a fascinating tale of courage, compassion and hope. Interlacing current events with South American mysticism and history, *The Ascendancy* proves to be an electrifying page-turner, driving humanity toward a plausible future. I'll follow Jack, Caitlin, Gandor and Potter Sims up the Beanstalk anytime they choose to venture."

—Jake Hamilton, Writer/Musician

"*The Ascendancy* blends fairy tale, history, fantasy, and science fiction. Join Jack, a gifted musician & Caitlin, an astronomer-scientist on a modern day *Jack in the Beanstalk* adventure as they travel through time and space. A page turner, this powerful book will educate and intrigue you until the very end!"

—Nancy Varljen, Principal, Mountain View Elementary

"A thought-provoking novel, *The Ascendancy* takes you on a mystical journey through the past, the present and the future, showing how all of mankind is connected and how one man can make a difference. Loosely based on *Jack and the Beanstalk* and taking events from current history, *The Ascendancy* shows us an incredible new world filled with wildly imaginative people and places. This isn't your father's fairy tale."

—Kirsten McDonald, ITC, The Center for Early Education

The Ascendancy

The
Ascendancy

A Novel

John M. Weiskopf

iUniverse, Inc.

New York Lincoln Shanghai

The Ascendancy

iUniverse books may be ordered through booksellers or by contacting:

iUniverse
2021 Pine Lake Road, Suite 100
Lincoln, NE 68512
www.iuniverse.com
1-800-Authors (1-800-288-4677)

This is a work of fiction. All of the characters, names, incidents, organizations, and dialogue in this novel are either the products of the author's imagination or are used fictitiously.

ISBN-13: 978-0-595-40920-4 (pbk)
ISBN-13: 978-0-595-86418-8 (cloth)
ISBN-13: 978-0-595-85283-3 (ebk)
ISBN-10: 0-595-40920-2 (pbk)
ISBN-10: 0-595-86418-X (cloth)
ISBN-10: 0-595-85283-1 (ebk)

Printed in the United States of America

For my children Caitlin & Sebastian
and
For Jude, my wife and best friend

For the victims of September 11, 2001
and
Their families who sacrificed so much

"Pachakuti is the name given to the millennial moment when one world perishes and the next begins. It means, quite literally, the over-turning of space-time."

—William Sullivan, *The Secret of the Incas*

AUTHOR'S NOTE

There is a profound change that is taking place on our planet. Millions of people across the earth are feeling it. It is a universal sociological phenomena. It is political; it is religious. It is spiritual. It affects every aspect of every society on our planet, and will gather increasing momentum as our world approaches 2012.

THE ASCENDANCY first began as a screenplay years before the events of September 11, 2001. The characters, the plot, the central images and the locations were essentially unchanged when I wrote the novel, but since the world had drastically changed since September 11, the way the novel was perceived, by fact, had also changed. In essence, reality had colored and dramatically changed fiction. As an author, who is passionate and committed to the theme of my novel, I decided that I had to preserve the story with its characters, locations, conflicts and symbols intact, as I had originally written it long before that horrific Tuesday morning, September 11, 2001.

Years of research, as well as several journeys to South America, went into the information contained in *The Ascendancy*. The Yamqui Drawing, or Jack's dream, is an actual manuscript of chronicler Juan de Santacruz Pachakuti Yamqui Salcamaygua. It is the cosmological diagram of the Incas as the chronicler drew it four hundred years ago. The prophecies of the Hopi and the Incas, the mathematics of the Mayan Calendar, the documented fall and subsequent collapse of the Inca civilization in Cajamarca, the discovery of the Bible Code by Dr. Eliyahu Rips, the Keck Observatory on Mauna Kea in Hawaii, the architecture of Machu Picchu in the Andes of Peru, all of these are based upon extensive research of historical events, scientific theories, and ascendant locations of our Earth.

What is remarkable is that the oral and written prophecies of diverse indigenous peoples, who were separated by centuries and thousands of miles, are similar, if not, in some cases, identical. What may be even more remarkable is that the knowledge derived by these peoples from listening to the earth and the universe leads us to the same conclusions obtained from the scientific research of quantum physics, string theory, mathematics and archaeology using the most sophisticated computers. These different indigenous cultures have collectively left a powerful message for us at the brink of the 21st Century.

Just as there is a diversity of cultures and governments on our planet, there is diversity in how humankind derives it information. They are all valid.

Out of the death and debris of September 11, 2001, there is a great hope, if we are willing to see it and we are willing to ascend.

—John Weiskopf

Jack's Dream

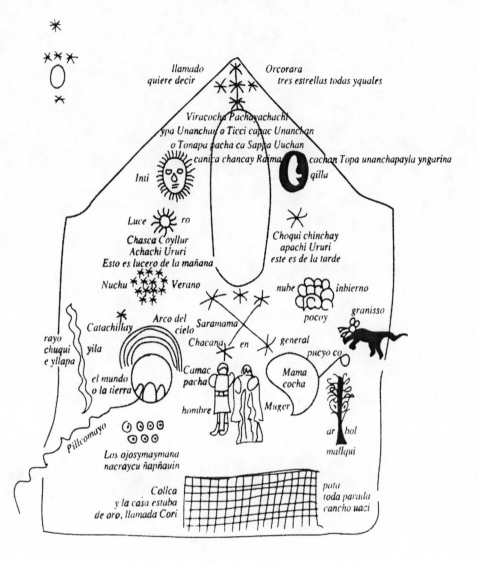

The Drawing of Juan de Santa Cruz Pachakuti Yamqui

CHAPTER 1

⚜

MAUNA KEA 2001 C.E.

Her jeep teetered at 4,200 meters on the edge of the world. It was the first time in Dr. Caitlin Bingham's life that she felt deeply troubled. She did not know why. As a scientist and a woman of enormous ambition and courage, it was an unsettling feeling completely foreign to her. Something was very wrong.

The red volcanic cinders struck her windshield with a fury creating a scratchy and unnerving hiss. She squinted around each sweep of the windshield wipers, but the view was nearly impenetrable as the wind churned up cinders in the light cut into the night by her headlights. She was worried. Next to her was a seven-hundred-meter drop into the darkness. She could barely make out the narrow road that was only a tiny ribbon meandering upward through the treeless Martian summit. All she wanted to do was get to the Keck.

As her jeep approached the summit, she breathed easily. The moonlight illuminated the alabaster and stainless steel structures that poked above the landscape. Beyond, moonlight reflected off the huge white clouds, which extended to the horizon making them fat and aloof beneath the black sky stuffed with billions of stars.

Caitlin ruled her life by intellect and logic. Though it was anything but rational, she felt that the Mauna Kea Summit on Hawaii was at the rim of the world. She liked the paradox that something so barren, desolate and unpredictably turbulent was Earth's observation post. As she neared the summit, Caitlin caught glimpses of the thirteen giant telescopes through the swirling cinders that sandblasted her windshield, yet the hostile landscape gave her comfort and belonging. A faint smile pursed across her lips. She was home. Thirteen telescopes, she thought, from eleven countries on four continents.

For her, the Keck was one of man's greatest achievements. Its huge cylindrical eye looked out to the endless black sea of the night and uncovered the origins of the universe from billions of years long gone. That glimpse into the ancient skies excited Caitlin; it made her life worthwhile.

She drove her red jeep up sharply next to the moonlit alabaster Keck dome, got out and slammed the door, but the sound was sucked into the vast emptiness. The volcanic particles stung her cheeks, as she ran inside.

Inside the Keck dome, two scientists monitored their computers. Caitlin saw them through the glass window. As she walked by the giant telescope, the three hundred ton Keck rotated into position creating a deep steady hum that echoed through the volume of the dome. Caitlin walked into the computer control room with a self-assuredness that comes with being the youngest archeoastronomer in the world, twenty-seven and already famous.

Caitlin examined a binary on her video monitor. Puzzled, she stared at the screen. She fed the printout rapidly through her fingers, reading the binaries printed in columns down the white paper. Her eyes opened wide. The two other astronomers in the room were preoccupied with their own calculations. They hardly noticed her.

"Where's *Pachakutek*?" her voice pierced the room's academic composure.

"What are you talking about?" one of the astronomers responded, his voice detached.

Dr. Wilson never took his eyes off his own monitor, as he continued jotting notes down on a pad. He was the senior astronomer.

"I can't find it! It's gone!" Caitlin blurted out.

Dr. Wilson cocked his head arrogantly; he was too busy for this. After dozens of publications in astronomical scientific journals, Dr. Hugh Wilson now sixty was comfortable in his chair at the Keck. Caitlin was too brassy, a thorn in his side. After all, he had earned the right for an unruffled retirement after his Supernova discovery at the Cerro Pachon observatory in Chile.

"Did you hear me? Pachakutek is gone!" Caitlin repeated.

The third astronomer, Dr. Wayne Miyashiro from the University of Hawaii, looked away from his monitor. He walked over to Caitlin to examine the binary. He glanced at her calculations.

"It is there. You just missed it," Dr. Wilson countered, his monotone hung in the air, like a dead weight. "It is three degrees and twenty-seven minutes from

Maia in the Pleiades!" He monitored Wayne Miyashiro in his peripheral vision, as Miyashiro checked Caitlin's notes.

Caitlin was infuriated. She could feel the blood heating up in her cheeks, as Wayne Miyashiro rifled through her calculations. She was frozen hard in place as she stared at Wilson. How dare this has-been question my work! She thought. An anger grew inside her stomach, where it became a taut ball of arrogance, but outwardly she restrained herself. She would be quiet for a few more seconds, but then she could no longer contain herself. Who does he think he is?

"Look, I discovered this planet!" she shouted, "I know more about it than you do, and I'm telling you it is gone!"

Perturbed, Wilson pushed his chair back away from his desk, so that the legs made a screeching sound across the tile floor. Caitlin thought what an obstinate gesture. He is such a child.

Wilson stood up. This interruption is a complete waste of time, he thought. It is costing money. Lots of it! With his shoulders slightly hunched and eyes cast slightly downward, he saw Caitlin glare at him in his peripheral vision as he walked over to her calculations, which Miyashiro held jumbled loosely in his hands. The university is paying $100,000 a night for the opportunity to be here! Wilson thought. He stared at the binary numbers on the computer printout, then looked at Caitlin's monitor. For ten seconds, he was still like a stone. Caitlin and Wayne Miyashiro watched. Though Caitlin knew she was seconds away from vindication, it did not matter to her. What mattered was that Pachakutek was nowhere in the universe, and that fact was physically and astronomically impossible. Struggling to hide his skepticism, Hugh Wilson walked calmly over to another monitor, typed on the computer keyboard and read the binary that spilled across the screen. A baffled look flushed across his face. He returned to Caitlin's computer and rifled through the printout that was lying in a pile on the green tile floor. Seconds passed. He looked up at the giant Keck with his mouth dropping slightly open.

"This is impossible," he said.

CHAPTER 2

ANCIENT WATCHER OF THE STARS

It was three hours before the sun would rise. It was cold. While his people slept, Juan de Santacruz Pachacuti Yamqui stood alone on the temple. His Incan people had chiseled the temple of Intihuatana out of one piece of granite. To hitch and hold the sun, a thick post rose out of the center of smooth granite platform. Yamqui rubbed his hands together, his fingertips and toes were numb from the cold, but he was used to it. He stared at the nearby mountain Huayna Picchu. He knew her every jagged edge and curve, her cool and stately presence under the full moon. He knew the mountain when the sun was at its highest point. She threatened. Her curves and her vertical slopes and sharp protruding rocks attracted, yet warned with a raw feminine beauty.

Yamqui's eyes slowly scanned the star patterns that sparkled in the Great River of Stars above his village. Tonight was the winter solstice, the most important night of the year for Yamqui and his Inca people. Yet Yamqui did not know that the night was June 19 of the year 1503, as he watched stars arch in a dance across the night sky, time merely flowed through his life and those of his people like the stars above flowed through the Great River of Stars. He knew the pattern of the stars intimately, as he knew his wife and son. He knew that the planting and harvesting of the crops depended upon the prophecy of the stars, which had become his companions in the night. He would interpret them for his people. He was a master astronomer, though he knew nothing about classifying the stars by type or spectrum or magnitude.

Yamqui was fifty-two years old, an Inca Shaman, descendant of the Q'ero line. Toiling the earth over many years and hiking the Andes over many miles had painted Yamqui's face with the hues of the soil. Though the sun tanned his skin, it made his face radiant, oddly preserving his youthful appearance even into old age. He was a watcher of the stars.

For forty years, Yamqui stood on the same spot during every solstice. Near Machacuay, the Great Serpent in the night sky, Yamqui watched as a dark spot, which he and his Inca ancestors referred to as the fox, chased the dark spot of the llama across the billions of stars that flooded the Great River of Stars. Yet, tonight Yamqui's visionary insight told him that something was wrong. He turned and looked at Urcuchillay, it was unusually bright tonight, he thought.

Years of stellar observation taught him that tonight was different, unlike any night that he had seen before or any that would come after. Yamqui was apprehensive. The stars did not follow their usual predictive path. When the fox chased the llama, the Nuchu Verano, or Stars of Summer, were supposed to rise in the East just before sunrise, but they did not. They were gone. That glitch in time was a moment the visionary shaman did not understand. It was by all reason impossible. He knew that it prophesied a great historical event, and it made him uneasy.

Moments later, Yamqui's eyes glazed over and his muscles stiffened. It was as if he had been struck by lightning. In a nanosecond, a flash image appeared in his inner sight. This was not just an image, it had the concrete, three-dimensional solidity of the real world. He could see it. He felt it. He smelled it. He had a burnt taste in his mouth.

Yamqui saw the planet Earth, but he was miles above it. He saw blue oceans covered by white swirling clouds and land masses of mottled red and brown and green. Suspended above the colorful great ball in the great blackness where the stars lived, he saw a large white bird with great strange and square wings. It was gliding effortlessly. He knew by his instinct that this great white bird was not of his time, but many, many years into the future. The large white bird did not flap its stiff wings, as it floated above the blue, brown, and white great ball, while looking down upon the majestic ball that floated in the blackness.

Yamqui surrendered to the vision. He licked his lips with his tongue, the taste was acrid, and then a brilliant flash covered his vision, glazing his eyes over with white, red, and orange flames. Standing in the cold stillness of the mountain, Yamqui felt his skin burning. He looked down. The hairs on the back of his hand were singed off. He touched his hand with his fingertips. The ground shook and he saw a Great Island City with buildings that ascended to the sky with thousands of people running through the streets. Two Great Towers of stone and metal were collapsing, their huge girders crumbling, the massive concrete blocks were pulverized into dust, and pointed iron archways like cathedral buttresses crashed to the ground. A cloud of smoke and ash filled Yamqui's vision. It rolled through the narrow city streets like a great beast, a giant black cat devouring people as they ran for their lives. The enormous black and purple-gray cloud mushroomed over the Great Island City blotting out the sun and the once cloudless morning blue sky. Yamqui could hear his own heart beating, merging with the rapid heartbeats of thousands of people who scrambled through the narrow streets to escape the falling debris and ash. Some of the people were on fire; some dusted gray completely covered in ash; others screamed with their mouths opened wide in terror, but no sound emerged between their lips.

As quickly as it came, the vision vanished. Yamqui could hear the beating of his own heart in the mountain silence. For minutes, he stood there without moving a muscle. He licked his lips, the singed taste of ash on his tongue was gone. Humbly, the Q'ero shaman lowered his gaze from the billions of stars to look upon his village.

CHAPTER 3

MACHU PICCHU

As Yamqui looked down upon Machu Picchu, he knew that his vision was somehow related to the village, but he did not how or why.

Machu Picchu had been his life. He had grown up there since he was a young boy of six years old, when his Shaman father took him and his mother and left their village of Chua Chua that was nestled into the mountains at 4,420 meters in the Andes to travel by foot to the new village. The young Yamqui did not know distances; all that he knew was that the trip was long and arduous. However, he remembered it being the greatest trip of his life, better than all of the trips combined, which he took with his father into the surrounding Andes. He remembered that the sun came up and set twenty-eight times and the moon was full the day before they left the Qero community of Chua Chua, and it was full again the day they arrived at Machu Picchu. Machu Picchu was his new home, and it was 450 kilometers from the village, where he grew up.

When the young Yamqui arrived at the Inca stone city of Machu Picchu, he was overwhelmed, even at six years old, by its sheer beauty. It seemed to him raw and majestic at the same time, built on the edge of a mountain. Though he did not know that Machu Picchu was 2,350 meters above the sea, the city's ascendancy filled his being. He was part of the mountains, and like a great soaring Condor, which he had watched soaring in the Andes, so many times in his six years, he felt that he could look down upon the earth from here. It was much closer to the ground than Chua Chua, but inside he felt that was good because it linked the land to the mountains and to the sky and to the stars above. Now during the Inca rituals, the shaman Yamqui would draw sacred parallels between the Urubamba River, which flowed around his ancient village and the Great River of Stars, which meandered through the night sky. Yamqui kept a vigilant nightly eye on the stars. As spiritual seer for his people, he knew the stars prophesied their destiny. As a wise shaman, he accepted the cards, which the stars dealt to his village because Yamqui had a deep faith in nature's design and balance.

Tonight the balance was disturbed. He knew by the stars that it was a short time before sunrise on the night when the sun would rise over the eastern Andes and cast a shadow over the stone post in the center of the Temple of the Sun. It was the winter solstice. Yamqui kept staring at the eastern horizon hoping to see the Nuchu Verano, Stars of Summer, but they were still nowhere in the night sky. He was most confused and concerned. He fidgeted, something he rarely did, for he would often stand for hours motionless with his eyes tracking the stars. He turned to the West to see the Cross, *Cruz Calvario* setting. Then, he turned to the East. Where are the Nuchu Verano, the thirteen Stars of Summer? He wondered. They should be rising there. No heliacal rise? Every solstice, Yamqui watched the Nuchu Verano as they rose just before sunrise, when the sun's light obliterated their starlight. For Yamqui and his village, it was the heliacal rise, a sacred moment of Andean truth that told the Incas when to plant their crops, and when to reap.

For the first time in his life, Yamqui stood on the mountaintop in complete disbelief, shaken to his soul and marrow. Though he did not know the date, he knew the meaning. It occurred on the winter solstice June 19, 1503, when the heliacal rise of the Nuchu Verano never happened. It was an impossibility. The stars were simply gone, a fact that the wise shaman and master astronomer could not explain.

CHAPTER 4

THE SON OF YAMQUI

Yamqui had been up all night during the winter solstice waiting for the thirteen stars of Nuchu Verano to rise. It was early morning and the sun shone brightly over Machu Picchu. Usually Yamqui walked with music in his stride, but today he plodded. He was tired from the emotional toll the night had extracted from him. He walked slowly from the Main Temple up the stone steps toward Intihuatana, the highest sun temple in the village. As he stood with his back to Intihuatana looking down over his village, the responsibility of being their patriarch and protector deepened in him.

He watched the threads of smoke from morning fires spiraling up from the Inca houses; in the quarry, he saw stonemasons splitting rock, as dozens of men shouldered an enormous twelve-sided stone that would become part of the village's Main Temple. He stepped to the other side of Intihuatana and watched the Inca women washing their clothes at the fountain. On their backs, they carried their infants swaddled tightly in colorful woolen bundles, called *pachas,* dyed the colors of the rainbow.

As Yamqui looked down upon his people, his heart was heavy. He had seen much during the night. A wave of care and protectiveness flowed through his being, as he thought, How will I protect my people? How will I tell them what to expect from the coming years, when I myself am not sure? As Yamqui watched his people going about their daily tasks, he thought perhaps maybe he should not tell them about the vision and the stars falling out of place in the sky. It would frighten them. They would not understand. How could they? For the first time in his life, Yamqui would hold the truth from his people and that bothered him greatly. There was nobody for him to talk to except his spirit guides and the gods of the mountains, which had guided him throughout his life.

After several minutes passed, Yamqui walked down the many steep stone steps from Intihuatana toward his home. As he walked through Machu Picchu, many villagers greeted him with smiles and respect; they revered Yamqui. He smiled and exchanged warm greetings with them hiding deep within himself what he knew could change the life of every man, woman and child in the village.

When Yamqui entered his home, his wife Ch'aska Naira Pachakusi saw him and immediately knew that something was wrong. She had never seen her husband so weighty, so worn. His childlike enthusiasm was gone. She left the hearth where she was preparing breakfast and walked over to him.

"What has happened?" She spoke in Quechua.

"I cannot talk about it, so please do not ask me," he said.

Ch'aska was taken aback by her husband's abruptness and his change. Yamqui saw her withdrawal from him; though she did not back away, it was in her eyes.

"When I understand, I will tell you," he said gently. "Please say nothing about my disposition to the people." Ch'aska nodded her head.

Yamqui walked to the stone table and poured a cup of water. He drank it standing up scanning the room and lost in his thoughts. Ch'aska watched him, as she returned to the stone hearth, where she was preparing breakfast. Yamqui, his wife and son lived in a simple stone house with a thatched roof, like an idyllic stone cottage in a fairy tale forest. The furniture was simple, even austere. In the center of the hut, there was a smooth granite table with four thatched wooden chairs.

Yamqui turned to his wife, "Where is Sebastian?"

"Up on the terraces."

Yamqui set the cup down, gave his wife a kiss on the cheek and left. He walked up the cobbled stones toward the upper level of Machu Picchu, where the llamas grazed near the vertical terraces. In the distance, clouds were gathering over the mountains. Yamqui paid no attention as he walked up the terraces toward his eighteen year-old son.

From the time Sebastian was ten years old, his father Yamqui had taught him everything about the Incas, rituals passed down by the ancient ones, ways of tracking the stars and constellations, methods of farming on the vertical terraces, how to use herbs for healing, and the immense responsibilities of a master shaman and leader. One day, he knew that his only son Sebastian would become the new shaman of Machu Picchu village. Sebastian would become the Inca tribe's shaman, healer, and sage.

Sebastian, now eighteen years-old, sat atop the ledge near the Watchman's Hut playing a zampoña and watching the village below. His music echoed off the surrounding mountains and carried over the village. Sebastian had acquired a reputation among the villagers, who claimed that his music had so much power that it made the flowers brighter, the sky a deeper blue, and the sun more radiant.

Sebastian Juan de Santacruz Pachacuti Yamqui was taller than most Incas, nearly six feet. His skin was tinted with the color of the rich fertile land. His eyes sparkled with the light of the stars. His hands were large and strong, his lips full, and his hair black as the Andean night sky.

As Sebastian played, he watched an Andean Condor, the sacred bird of the Incas, glide over Machu Picchu. The condor's wings spanned twelve feet from tip to tip.

Finally, Yamqui reached the Watchman's Hut, he sat down next to his son and together they looked down over the village. Many minutes passed in music, and then Sebastian stopped. A silence hung in the crisp Andean air.

"I've watched you and recently you seem discontent. Is there something bothering you?" Yamqui asked.

Sebastian was slow to speak. "Father, I am leaving tomorrow."

Yamqui was not surprised. He knew that this moment was coming, but this was not a good time for the master shaman to lose his son; however, Yamqui never let on.

"I want to see what is beyond our village." Sebastian spoke with certainty. "I have thought about this for a long time, but I did not want to say anything until I was certain."

"Where will you go?"

"I don't know."

"I always thought that you would become a great Inca shaman," Yamqui said to his son with sadness in his voice. "I felt that the day was not far off, when you would lead these people. I saw it so clearly, but I also saw your discontent." Yamqui was very much perplexed. He stared off over the village as he spoke, "But your leaving is not clear to me yet, so I do not understand. And that is more bothersome to me, that I cannot see it, though I know you have decided to leave."

"I am sorry, father."

"What will be, will be, my son, and I will accept it."

Yamqui embraced his son tightly and Sebastian was comforted. Yamqui turned and walked down the vertical terraces toward his home in the heart of Machu Picchu. Sebastian watched his father with mixed emotions.

Between the distant mountain peaks, there was a deep rumbling. A thunderstorm was approaching. Behind Sebastian, the sky was darkening and the clouds were closing in. On the vertical terraces, the llamas sensed the approaching danger. They were jittery. It began to rain. The mountain rumbled deep with thunder, as the skies got darker. The mountain peaks surrounding Machu Picchu flashed with lightning. A lightning bolt struck the mountain Una Picchu, whom the Incas referred to as the child mountain.

Another lightning bolt struck behind Machu Picchu mountain. The llamas scattered, so did the villagers as they retreated to the safety of their small *qolgas*. The rain fell harder. As if from the hand of a powerful sky god, a lightning bolt cracked through the air down toward the village. The air above Sebastian split and then compressed all around his body, as a sudden burst of wind slapped his skin with a powerful sharp smack. The thunderbolt cut a jagged path out of the hollow of the deep dark clouds and lightning struck Sebastian impaling his left shoulder. The crack of the air, the blinding burst of light, and the deafening roar of the strike all unfolded in a millisecond. The bolt hurled Sebastian twenty feet across the agricultural terraces.

A hush fell over Machu Picchu. Sebastian's body lay lifeless on the garden terraces soaked by the violent rain, burnt by the fire from the sky. In the rain, above the terraces, an Andean Condor glided over Sebastian's body.

CHAPTER 5

‹❦›

THE MAKING OF A SHAMAN

It was a clear bright morning. The sun shone through the trapezoidal window of the Yamqui home. Sunlight fell gently across the folds in the blanket covering Sebastian, who lay in bed. Much of his hair was gone. What was left was singed. The ends were melted together in small charred knots. Blisters were painted over with an herbal medicinal paste that covered his face and hands, and a bandage wrapped around his left arm from his shoulder to his wrist. Under the bandage, his skin was badly burned and disfigured. Sebastian's eyes were open, but he was clearly dazed, as he lay motionless. His mother gave him soup, which he sipped slowly.

Next to Sebastian's bed, there was a table upon which lay a colorful woolen cloth of repetitive design, triangles with interwoven stripes of red, green, brown and yellow. Upon the opened cloth were thirteen stones called *khuyas*. Each stone came from a mountain in the Andes and carried with it the power of that mountain's spirit, *apu*. The stones varied in color, size and texture. One was granite shaped like a mountain; one was green with brown speckles; one was deep blue like the sky just before night; one was flat, like a stone one would skip across a pond, its color was a green and slate gray with slight ridges like the skin of the land. And there were others, each with its own color, shape and power. Each khuya held the power of the apu.

Yamqui arranged the khuyas in two circles upon the cloth, called the *mesa*. One inner circle of stones with three khuyas, the ten khuyas of the outer circle surrounded the inner ones. Then from a simple woolen brown and white bag that hung from his side, Yamqui took a shiny reddish-clay earthy stone with black inclusions, a simple beautiful khuya shaped in a triangle like a small mountain, smooth to the touch and comfortable to the palm. He placed the red khuya in the center of the circle upon the mesa, where it was surrounded by the three inner khuyas. Yamqui closed his eyes and held his hands over the mesa and the khuyas. He blessed the khuya, and with utmost purity and intent, he invoked the power of the apu. From his bed, Sebastian watched. After several moments passed, Yamqui removed the smooth glossy-red khuya, walked over, and stood next to his son. Holding up the red earthy khuya for Sebastian to see, Yamqui spoke.

"This is the power of apu Machu Picchu. It is from the very spot where you were struck by lightning, my son. For days, I prayed that you would live, but I would have accepted whatever was written for you. Destiny has carved your path out of the sky. You have been chosen to be a great shaman. I have much to teach you. But first, you need to close your eyes and dream."

Yamqui placed the glossy-red earthy khuya into his son's open palm. Sebastian looked at his father with tears in his eyes, closed his fingers firmly around the khuya, and then closed his eyes. As he slept, hundreds of dreams filled him up.

Twelve months passed as Sebastian healed. Every night dozens of dreams sustained his spirit and made him wiser. After a year, marks of that eventful night on the terraces remained imprinted on his body, marks from an instant that changed his life forever, an instant that he could not even remember. A discolored burn that twisted and stretched his skin extended from his left shoulder down to his wrist. Red and brown blotches covered the back of his left hand into the webbing of his fingers, and gave them a rubbery look. Pits and indentations covered the helical folds of his ear, similar to a boxer's cauliflower ear. His skin was stained with a reddish mark that looked like a river winding its way from just above his left ear lobe down to just below his jaw.

It was night. Shaman Yamqui knew this night's importance. It was when the influence of the light and dark were in perfect balance, it was center to Inca balance. Though they did not have a modern semantic for the time, it was September 21, 1504 C.E., the Vernal Equinox. By the moonlight, Yamqui, his wife, and their nineteen year-old son Sebastian left their home and walked across the ancient stones toward Intihuatana. At dawn, Sebastian would be ordained an Inca shaman.

The sky turned from deep bluish-black to pink. During the final minutes before the sunrise, the Nuchu Verano disappeared just above the horizon. It was the heliacal rise. Yamqui alone ascended Intihuatana, while Sebastian walked around to the opposite side, where there were seven stone steps, each step corresponding to one of the seven charkas within his body. Sebastian knew that these seven steps were the paths of the shaman, each step symbolizing a state of spiritual holiness and healing power necessary to protect and guide the people of Machu Picchu.

The time had come. When the sun peeked over the Andes, its warm rays falling over the village, Yamqui signaled Sebastian, who began his ascent up the seven steps of Intihuatana. Sebastian took each step slowly allowing his spirit to be filled with the colors of the rainbow and the spiritual grace that would open his being.

When Sebastian reached Intihuatana, he closed his eyes. He could feel the sun shining brightly on his eyelids. He saw red. He felt surging passion and connection. The sacred moment was consummated. The sun had christened Sebastian Juan de Santacruz Pachacuti Yamqui shaman, healer and sage of his people.

CHAPTER 6

PROPHECY

The following night shortly before dawn, the father and son shaman stood atop Machu Picchu looking at the star patterns, which traveled along the same path that it had for thousands of years. Astronomers would later call the path the ecliptic. The moon illuminated the village bordered by the mother-mountain and child-mountain, Huayna Picchu and Una Picchu. The night sky was clear; the air was brisk.

"As long as my father, his father before him, as far back as the Inca mind can remember, the stars spoke to us," Yamqui said. "Many, many generations of fore-fathers ago, over thirty ages past, on the day of the year, when the sun casts a shadow over the post in the Temple of the Sun, our shaman great ancestor watched all night, but the Nuchu Verano did not rise. Right there," Yamqui pointed to the spot in the sky where the Nuchu Verano would rise. He contin-ued, "In the same way, the night before you were struck by lightning, I stood on the mountain all night, but the Nuchu Verano also did not rise. It has only hap-pened twice." That night which Shaman Yamqui spoke of was June 21, 650 C.E.

"How is that possible?" asked Sebastian.

"I do not know. I just know it was." Yamqui answered.

"What does it mean?"

"I understand why. It was a prophecy." Yamqui looked at his son, and then turned his eyes toward the horizon. "It means there is a great change coming," he said.

Sebastian was mystified.

"You've heard me speak of Pachakuti?" Yamqui asked his son.

"Yes."

"Pachakuti is Inca prophecy. It means there will be a Great Shaking, a quaking of the earth. It is the moment in a millennium when one world ceases to exist and the next begins."

"I have never felt an earthquake," Sebastian answered.

"I had a vision. There was a great white bird in the sky. I felt a great rumbling in the earth, and then a great fire consumed the mountains and villages and the land as far as I could see."

"When will this happen?" Sebastian asked.

"During a time and place far from us, but it will have a great effect upon everyone."

"What kind of effect?"

"It will be a time for the world to rise and become a great beacon in the heavens or burn out like a dying ember and disappear from existence."

"You know this for certain?" asked the newly initiated, young shaman.

"With all my heart." Yamqui answered. He looked up the stars and scanned the Milky Way. "There are some things that we know with certainty, Sebastian. This is one." Yamqui said as he looked into his son's eyes.

Sebastian was disturbed by his father's words; Yamqui saw it in his eyes. "Many, many years from now," Yamqui continued. "There will be one day, one single day, when the leaders and people of the world must choose between two paths. It will be a great historical event that will determine the life or death of the world. I know this with absolute certainty."

Yamqui's words had a great effect upon Sebastian, who stood motionless.

"Compassion will be the key," said Yamqui.

A long silence lingered in the cold mountain air, as they both stared at the stars and constellations.

CHAPTER 7

LIFE FINDS A WAY

Hurrying along the streets of Manhattan's East Side, Jacob Tott hugged the buildings to keep from getting soaked. His friends called him Jack, but his father called him Jacob when he was angry with him or simply wanted to get the upper hand.

Jack was twenty-six years old, had a sparkle deep in his hazel eyes, bushy eyebrows. His light brown, thick hair that dropped down his forehead and dripped water into his eyes as he ran through the rain. Torrents of rain fell on New York City as it had never fallen before. The city was more than dark; it was foreboding. Thunder rocked the towering Manhattan skyscrapers to their foundations. Every window shook, every wall, every locked and bolted door. This was an assault aimed at the great city, aimed to feed the fears of its people. Lightning pierced the black skies down to the streets. With three small beans, a map and a violin bridge tucked securely in his pocket, Jack dashed through the flooded streets. Suddenly, he saw a taxicab.

"Taxi!" he yelled.

But the taxicab drove on. Jack's summons were muffled by the torrential rain as he stepped out into the center of the street. He screamed, "Hey, taxi! Hey!" The cab's brake lights glowed red. The taxi made a quick U-turn and pulled up to Jack, who jumped into the cab.

Inside the cab, Jack gathered himself.

"Where to?" asked the cabbie.

"Wherever it's dry."

"Nowhere around here, bub," barked the cabbie. "I've been driving a cab for nearly thirty years, born here. Never seen any storm like this."

"Me neither," replied Jack with a wet furrowed brow. He looked out the back-seat window at the city pelted by rain.

"Vesey Street near the World Trade Center site," Jack said to the cabbie.

"Buckle-up."

In lower Manhattan, the lightning illuminated the gigantic hole, where the World Trade Center Towers once stood. They drove one block from the World Trade Center site. Outside of the cab, everything moved in slow motion for Jack. Heavy curtains of rain fell obscuring the volume created by the gigantic hole. It was a wet wasteland of death and ruin.

Jack yelled to the cabbie, "Stop the car! I'll get out here!"

The cabbie turned incredulously toward Jack, "Are you kidding? It's Noah's flood out there, bub!"

"I'm already wet."

"Your dime, bub. Wanna get struck by lightning? Be my guest."

The cabbie shook his head and stopped the cab. Jack paid him and stepped out of the taxi into the pounding rain. The cab drove off. Jack walked a half a block in the relentless rain and stopped at the fence. Near one corner of the gigantic hole at the World Trade Center site, a giant crane, draped with an American flag, stood solemnly in the rain overseeing the hole. While staring out at the desolate hole in the ground, Jack reached into his pocket and took out three beans. He did not look at them; he merely rolled them around in his hand, as he stood in the rain looking out over the World Trade Center landscape. Suddenly, a lightning bolt forked through the dark clouds above the excavation site and struck the huge crane. Like a welder's arc, sparks shot out from the crane's cross-hatched arm. Jack thought the lightning was meant for him, but somehow missed. *Sins of the father passed to the son*, Jack thought. The ground trembled. He quickly pocketed the beans and raced off in fear, anxious to get home. This was no ordinary storm.

Jack trotted through the lower Manhattan streets hugging the buildings. His hair was matted to his head, his clothes were soaked, his body chilled to the bone. Lightning blinded the city. Walking toward Vesey Street, he felt the ground shaking beneath him from each roll of thunder; it felt like the earth was angry. His eyes met the eyes of a few passing strangers. In an instant, he saw the dark light of fear in their eyes. He thought that they were caught together in a city besieged by events far beyond their control. In an instant, Jack felt camaraderie with them; yet, he knew that he would never see them again.

Ten minutes later, Jack entered his home at 36 Park Row, the Potter Building. It was a distinctive terra cotta Victorian skyscraper with ominous gargoyles, which sneered in the torrential rain. Even though the storm raged, Sam the doorman was there to greet Jack warmly.

"Good evening, Mr. Tott, bad night, isn't it?" greeted the accommodating bellman.

"Frightening, Sam." replied Jack.

Sam forced a smile. He was a quiet student of people. His job was to hold a door and greet the thousands of people who walked through it, to say goodbye, and to wish them well. Twenty-two years of doing it had given Sam time to learn how to read people in a matter of seconds. Since September 11, 2001, Sam had seen much sadness and worry in people's eyes, but knew that all he could do was smile, hold a door, and offer a gentle hand.

Sopping-wet, Jack walked through the lobby and headed to the elevator. Jack stepped into the elevator, as the doors closed he looked into the lobby. It was desolate. As the elevator ascended, Jack became lost in the hum as he rolled the three beans around his palm. Then the elevator door opened, and he stepped into his three-bedroom apartment; the walls shook and trembled from the thunder.

Inside his apartment, he found his mother Mattie sitting on the living room couch, holding Natalie, his sister. They were both terrified. Outside, the storm raged. As Jack entered, a bolt of lightning flashed and the ground rumbled shaking the entire apartment building.

Mattie was forty-nine, attractive and colorfully dressed. She had rosy cheeks and sparkling green eyes that made her look like a feisty wench in Elizabethan England. Around her neck hung an unusual twenty-four carat, sun-shaped amulet with wavy rays and etched symbols on the sun's face.

"This is terrible!" Mattie cried out.

Jack approached his mother and Natalie. In the next room, his Amazon parrot Peekaboo screeched between thunder blasts "Get a Life! Get a Life! What are you doing? Peekaboo! Peekaboo!"

"Did you sell the violin?" Mattie did not see the Stradivarius violin in his hands. Jack was silent trying to figure how to tell his mother.

"Where is the violin?" Mattie persisted, this time with worry in her voice.

"Mother, listen to me—" Thunder rocked the apartment. Mattie's eyes were wide with fear, but she kept her attentions focused upon the whereabouts of the Stradivarius.

"Did you sell it?" Mattie yelled above the din and flash.

"Yes." Jack was hesitant and Mattie picked up a slight ring of uncertainty hidden in his voice.

"How much?"

"I didn't get money for it." His fingers touched the unseen beans in the darkness and secrecy of his jacket pocket.

"You didn't get money! Where's the violin?" Mattie was impatient, nervous.

Jack was silent, as the rain pounded upon the windows.

"Where is the violin, Jack?" With eyes wide open, dread written on her face, Mattie screamed at Jack. Natalie watched silently. Lightning cracked and thunder rolled through the apartment shaking everything like a great earthquake.

"What did you get?" Mattie walked toward Jack, who backed away. "Jacob Tott, what did you get for the violin?"

From his pocket, Jack took out the three beans. He held them out in his palm for his mother to see.

"What's this?" Mattie exclaimed. She got closer. "Beans! Beans!" Mattie could not believe her eyes. "Does this look like a fairy tale to you, Jack?" she screamed, as she pointed around the room.

"Mother, they're magic beans—" Jack tried to explain, but before he could finish Mattie cut him sharply off.

"Magic? You mean you gave away a rare Stradivarius violin, which has been in our family for four generations? For beans!" Mattie's voice was cacophony of disbelief and fury.

"These aren't just any—"

"Have you lost your mind?" Mattie screamed above the storm; she was in a fury. Neither Jack nor Natalie had ever seen their mother this angry. Mattie's fury frightened Natalie more than the storm itself.

"Mother, I saw the most incredible things at this shop. A man named Murland called me this morning." Trying to be calm and convince his mother of his sincerity, Jack tried to explain his encounter with Mr. Murland.

"I don't understand what happened, but I know it happened," Jack continued.

Mattie was numb with disbelief and fear of the future. She did not hear him. Her mind was a jumble of scattered thoughts, frantic with questions of survival wrapped in fear. How are we going to live? How am I going to keep Natalie alive? She wondered, and then she yelled at her only son, whom she thought would never in a thousand years make such an unimaginable foolish mistake. "These are our lives! This is real! What about your sister?" Mattie grabbed Jack and shook him.

On the couch, Natalie began to cry, disturbed by her mother's anger. Natalie was Jack's fourteen-year-old sister. She had leukemia. Doctors had given her less than one year to live. She had lost much of her hair; her eyes were dark and sunken.

Just then, there was a great bluish-white lightning bolt, which struck just outside their building. It shattered the living room window into thousands of pieces of glass. The lights went out. It was pitch black. Then, a lighting bolt cut across the room hurling glass everywhere, it covered the hardwood floor. As rain poured in, a great thunderbolt rocked the apartment. It was as if the apartment was at the epicenter of a 6.0 earthquake. The wind blew through the open window into the apartment. In the room swirled rain, wind and rage. When the shaking stopped, lightning flashed repeatedly creating an eerie stroboscopic light show in the battered apartment.

"What about your sister?" Mattie screamed. Natalie watched helplessly in the fetal position on the couch.

"I'm sorry, I made a mistake!" Jack yelled. Mattie saw the shame on his face and his lowered head only when the lightning flickered.

Peekaboo screeched, "What are you doing? What are you doing? The sky is falling! The sky is falling! Peekaboo!"

"Let me see them," Mattie yelled. The lightning flashes cut through the room.

Jack opened his palm briefly displaying the three beans between lightning flashes. Mattie grabbed at Jack's palm taking the beans. She hurled them in fury across the room. A series of lightning strobes flashed illuminating the beans as they flew across the room. Two of the beans hit the apartment wall, and like marbles rolled across the hardwood floor. One bean flew out the open window. A brilliant flash illuminated it as it sailed out the window. Thunder rumbled shaking the apartment building to the core.

"Mother!" Jack screamed, as he ran to the shattered open window. All he could see were sheets of rain falling from the black sky. Rivers of rainwater washed debris down the streets. It was a torrent eroding a path through the lush garden of the Potter Building, a garden pruned and tended religiously every Monday morning. One bean rolled down the muddy trench into the street, where it joined Popsicle sticks, dead branches torn from oak trees, decorative stones, leaves, jagged pieces of rock, cigarette butts, beer bottles, cans, condoms, street litter, and tire hubcaps once collecting in curbs. It was an avalanche of urban debris. It rolled like a raging river toward the great hole where the World Trade Center Towers once stood.

The earth at World Trade Center's ground zero was a muddy gray. Torrents of water rushed into the mud caverns created by the twisted metal and smashed concrete. Swept into the heart of the World Trade Center excavation site, the bean tumbled over a concrete slab into a waterfall of rain. At the bottom of the waterfall, debris was scattered everywhere. The bean settled firmly into the gray primal clay. Thunder rocked the ground. The city trembled. The bean quivered.

CHAPTER 8

HOME IN THE SKY

Caitlin looked out the window of the Cessna Citation X at the sunset sky streaked red and orange with finger-like clouds. At 27,000 feet and one hundred and ten miles southwest of Baltimore, Maryland, she picked up the radio microphone, depressed the microphone button, "BWI, this is Citation Three-Niner, say active and conditions."

Though she was a professor of archaeoastronomy at Colgate University in New York, a child prodigy in mathematics, and an author, flying was her passion. She was a crackerjack pilot, so exceptional that NASA had sought her out to become an astronaut. She began flying when she was ten years old. Her father, Timothy Wallmark Bingham, had taught her.

A voice crackled back over the cockpit radio, "Citation Three-Niner, this is BWI tower, winds are 275 degrees at 8 knots with a fifteen mile visibility."

Caitlin studied the rosy-fingered sunset. Simply beautiful, she thought. Her degrees and fondness for penetrating academic dialogue had not stripped her of a love of the simple. She marveled at the world. She stared at the fiery sky as she banked the jet.

"Citation Three-Niner, land on runway 04/22, do you copy?"

"Roger, BWI. Runway 04/22, this is Citation Three-Niner out."

"Roger, Citation."

Caitlin's eyes zeroed in on the heading as she banked. No matter how overloaded she became with work, she would never give up the sky. Flying made her free as a bird. She watched the runway as it slowly came up to meet her. The jet skidded on the runway spitting out puffs of blue smoke. A satisfied smile trickled across her lips. She exited the Cessna Citation jet and got into a waiting black Lincoln Town Car. The car sped down the runway.

CHAPTER 9

ഇ⁂ഉ

A PLANET IS MISSING

It was now 10 p.m. in Greenbelt, Maryland at NASA's Goddard Space Agency. Caitlin stood at the head of a large conference room table, which was full of scientists and executives: Dr. Frederic Chatke, the director of the Keck Observatory, the Chief Information Officer for NASA Pat Bennington, NASA project scientist Dr. George Glechkler, and U.S. Army Brigadier General Mark Finnett. Caitlin gave a presentation, referring to the large projection screen behind her. On the screen was a detailed chart of our solar system, which included planets and their moons and the Kuiper and the Asteroid belts.

"This photograph was taken exactly one day before the new planet *Pachakutek* disappeared," Caitlin said as she pointed to a dot on the star chart.

Dr. George Glechkler asked, "Have you calculated an orbit for the planet yet?"

"Yes," responded Caitlin. She hit the button on her MacBook Pro, which fed the Power Point information into the data projector. Overlays of colored orbits for each planet, moon, asteroid and comet popped onto the image of the solar system. With a red laser pen, Caitlin traced the orbit of the recently discovered planet *Pachakutek*.

"*Pachakutek's* orbit here was plotted one day before the planet disappeared. We can only be certain of the accuracy of *Pachakutek's* orbit to within a 1.053 degree deviation because we have only been observing the new planet for two-and-a-half years. Now, this image was taken two days ago." Caitlin hit a key

- 26 -

on her MacBook Pro. "Notice the projected orbit of *Pachakutek* here," Caitlin traced the dotted orbit of the newly-discovered planet, but there was no dot on the screen where the planet should be. "However, you will notice that *Pachakutek* is gone." Caitlin turned to the scientists and administrators at the conference table.

Dr. Frederic Chatke, the director of the Keck Observatory, pointed to the chart, "Is it possible, that the new planet is hidden by magnetic interference from another planet or is shadowed by another planet's orbit?"

"No, we checked everything." Caitlin was confident. "We used continuous images from the Hubble. There are no other planets eclipsing *Pachakutek's* orbit nor is there any magnetic interference. There is nothing anywhere near *Pachakutek*."

"What about your calculations on *Pachakutek's* orbit—could they be wrong?" asked Dr. Glechkler. His thick crop of grey hair accented his dark, deep-set eyes, which stared directly at Caitlin, but she was unflinching.

"Our calculations based on astrometry, radial velocity, and the planet's transit all support this orbit. There are no mistakes."

Pat Bennington, NASA's Chief Information Officer spoke up, "So, why has it disappeared?"

"I don't know," said Caitlin. "I've never seen anything like it."

Baffled, the scientists stared at Caitlin, just as U.S. Army Brigadier General Finnett did, but he was silent as he evaluated her.

Nothing more needed to be said. After many silent seconds had passed, Caitlin broke the silence, "Maybe, it is so mystics will link this to some historical event."

Brief chuckles spread through the conference room.

Even though Caitlin had studied the rituals and religious ceremonies of ancient cultures, she was a scientist, who believed only in empirical evidence. She did not believe in superstition, in spiritual forces that carved out destinies, or in prophecy.

CHAPTER 10

THE FIRST ENCOUNTER

In the Tott apartment, lightning outlined Jack's guilt-ridden face, as he looked down at his sister Natalie, who was shaking on the couch. Jack leaned down to hug her.

"Leave her alone! You've done enough!" screamed Mattie as she yanked Jack away from his sister. Lightning flashes revealed the fury in her face. Jack fell backwards in a heap upon the floor, as a thunderclap violently rocked the room. Ashamed, and unable to look at either his sister or his mother, Jack fled the apartment. On his way out the door, he glanced at the floor to see if any of the beans were visible, but they were gone. All he wanted to do was get away. He raced down the hallway to the stairwell, and yanked the door open. As fast as his legs would move, he clambered down the five flights of stairs.

At the World Trade Center excavation site, lightning flashes illuminated the eerie scene. In the mud and dirt, a green halo rimmed the bean, which rolled off to the side. In a crinkle and snap of its tough shell, the bean broke open. It curled out, twisting its way through the rubble, guided by a 500 million years of lessons in survival, determined to make its mark, to survive. The torrential rains fell drenching the enormous American Flag, which hung from the giant towering construction crane whose black iron arm jutted out above the bean.

Jack ran onto Park Avenue into the pouring rain. The streets were nearly desolate. It was as if some supernatural force had waged war against New York City. Terrified, he ran into a nearby wooded park. In the wet and the dark, lightning created haunting silhouettes out of the tree branches. Jack stopped and curled up on a bench beneath a large oak tree. Suddenly, the air above him split. With a crack, the air compressed around Jack's body. Woof! A violent crack exploded in brilliant white light above him. A bolt of lightning reached up from the ground to meet the sky only twenty feet away. It split the large oak tree in two, as the ground rumbled.

Terrified that he would be struck like his father, Jack wondered, why was the storm chasing him?

Even though Jack did not adhere to one religion or spiritual creed, he believed that Karma did exist and that life extracted some measure of cosmic justice. However, at this moment, he was confused. He had done nothing wrong.

To escape the storm, Jack ducked into a public restroom. It was dark, except for the irregular stroboscopic bursts of lightning that followed Jack into his hideaway. The lightning flashes illuminated the urinals and the graffiti-plastered walls. Jack huddled in the corner of the dirty restroom in a fetal position. He wanted to get as far away from the restroom door as he could. He closed his eyes. The lightning was too bright. He hunkered down, curled up tighter. I must sleep! He told himself. Sleep, I must sleep.

Over the next several minutes, Jack began to nod off. Years of musical training had taught him how to filter out noise at will. He would ward off the storm by ignoring it. Though the storm raged, his head bobbed. Sleep was the only escape.

Suddenly, from outside the restroom, he heard a loud flapping of wings. It frightened him. He jumped up off the grungy cement floor, walked to the restroom door and stared out into a thick cluster of trees. The flapping crackled through the din of the rain pelting the tree leaves, even overpowering the roar of the thunder. The flapping got louder. From the restroom doorway, Jack heard tree branches cracking. Curious, he walked toward the sound of the splintering wood near the cluster of trees, stopped and looked up into the trees. Raindrops fell into his eyes. He blinked away the water dripping down from his bushy eyebrows. The tree limbs were thick and dark, while the images fleeted between the lightning flashes. Gigantic black bat wings, fast and powerful, swept through the trees; their wings extended twenty feet from tip-to-tip. Jack wondered how this could possibly be as he dashed in and out of the dark and lightning flashes. Were these harpies? Jack thought. Relics of the ancient Greek myths here in the 21st Century? He had read about them and had seen pictures of harpies in a college

Greek mythology course, but this was impossible. Harpies were not real. He stared up into the treetops, while he chased the gigantic flapping black wings that blended into the crackling storm. Relentlessly, Jack tracked them as far as he could until the ancient creatures disappeared into Central Park's darkest shadows.

Jack searched for the creatures, but they were gone. He stood in the forest and listened. Only the patter of raindrops splattering on the leaves between the cracks of thunder filled the forest. Baffled, he walked back to his restroom sanctuary.

As Jack entered, he stopped abruptly at the door and stared at the end of the restroom. The lightning flashed outlining a figure sleeping in a fetal ball in the corner. He saw himself curled up. *Am I dreaming?* He walked hesitantly over to his body, his body lying on the filthy restroom floor. He stood next to it, afraid to touch it, afraid to think it was his body. A great rumble of thunder shook the park and the restroom.

From nowhere an enormous man stepped into the doorway, as lightning outlined his colossal form. Ten feet tall! Jack thought. The creature's silhouette stuck Jack to the quick. It was as if this creature was born out the chaos and fear of the city. Jack looked down at his body still crumpled in a fetal ball, and then he looked at the colossal form who staring at him. The giant man took a few menacing steps toward Jack. The deep resonance of the giant's voice made the plumbing rattle and shook the fixtures in the tiny dank restroom, when he spoke.

"Quite a night, isn't it?" asked the giant.

"Yes," answered Jack nervously.

"Are you frightened?" The giant took another step.

"Yeah, I am."

"Times are changing, you should be," the man said in a sepulchral voice that rang with foreboding. In three steps, the colossal man was nearly on top of Jack, towering over him.

"Are you sure?"

"Am I sure of what?" Jack trembled with fear. He glanced down at his sleeping body curled up in the corner. I'm dreaming, I've got to be dreaming, Jack repeated to himself as his mind raced. He was sure that this creature could not hurt him. It had to be a dream.

"Are you sure?" The colossal man pressed Jack once more.

"Am I sure ..." Jack faltered. Murland said the same exact words, Jack remembered. "Am I sure of what? Murland said the same thing!" Jack was fishing for anything that made sense, any connection.

"Do you know Murland?" Jack persisted.

The colossal man ignored Jack's question and repeated his same three words. This time he emphasized each word. "Are … you … sure?"

"I'm frightened," Jack's voice quivered. Then he thought, how could a dream frighten me? Dreams frightened people all the time, he argued with himself.

Silence smothered the air in the dirty restroom.

"One last time. Are you sure?"

Thunder howled and growled all around. The lightning outlined Jack's frightened, confused face. He wanted to wake up, but this was so real. Jack wondered anxiously, what if I am awake? He looked down at his body again. It was motionless, oblivious to it all. He was sleeping. But could he possibly be asleep through all of this?

"I don't know what you want." This time Jack's tone was belligerent. After all, this was a dream and dreams could not hurt you. The colossal man poked Jack in the shoulder with his index finger. It was stinging, sharp. *Dreams were not supposed to do that.*

"Be sure," the colossal man's voice rang with finality. Lightning flashed illuminating the room. Jack got a close-up flickering look at the man's face. His eyes were golden yellow with a rich brown corona around them; they were deep with evil. Even though his face had chiseled features with sharp cheekbones, there was an elegance and charm about him. He wore a long white gown with long sleeves from which protruded huge hands with grasping long fingers. Outside, the thunder rolled more, as it shook the walls of the restroom. Between flashes, the colossal man disappeared into the brilliant lightning and darkest shadows of the night storm. Jack ran to the restroom door, where he watched. He waited for another lightning strike. Eyes wide, he willed his eyes not to blink. He had to be sure that this evil man had gone. A series of great thunderclaps and lightning flashes lit up the entire park. The man had disappeared. Jack relaxed, so he walked back into the restroom. He looked down at his sleeping body. Wake up! He told himself. Wake up! Jack stooped down. He nudged the shoulder of his sleeping self, but the body did not budge. Tired, Jack slumped down resting his back against the wall. Slowly, he leaned his shoulder until it rested against the shoulder of his sleeping self. He would doze off, then wake up and this would all be over. The night noises filled his imagination with fear. He was confused because the dream was too real. Sometime during the long dark hours, when the rules of the real world and the events of imagined world converged, Jack convinced himself that he was awake and safe, so he drifted off to sleep.

In the morning, huddled against the wall, Jack slowly opened his eyes. He awakened to silence, which was disturbing, for he expected there would be some noise, any noise. He looked down, but his sleeping body was gone. In the fleeting seconds of silence that hung stale in the bathroom, Jack wondered. Was last night real? Jack stared at the restroom door. Slowly, he pulled himself up off the dirty concrete floor. He wiped his filthy hands on his pants.

"Somebody must've don' sumpin' awful wrong, I taught we wuz goners!" A voice by the urinals startled Jack.

An old homeless man was sitting on a urinal smoking a wet brown cigarette butt. The man had been watching Jack.

"That makes two of us," replied Jack as he straightened himself out, trying to distinguish himself from this pathetic man, who looked like he had led a hard life for many years. "Did you see that giant man in here last night?" Jack asked him.

"I dunno know, whad he look like?" the homeless man answered, but his reply suggested he was teasing Jack, who just stared at the man wondering whether he was just being resentful because of his situation in life or if, in fact, he was part of something. Jack was not making sense. He was sure now that last night was a dream. It had to be.

"He was big, and scary," Jack explained to the homeless hobo. Jack watched every twitch, every blink the man made, so he could understand and put to rest the uneasy feeling that he had in his stomach.

"Got nottin' to tell ya'," the hobo said as he smiled, exposing his decayed and crooked teeth.

Jack took one last look at the homeless hobo. As he neared the restroom door, he looked back at the urinals. The man was watching him and he had an impish grin on his face. Jack quickly fled to the outside world.

CHAPTER 11

A DAY DAWNS GREEN

The sun shone brightly. The sky was deep blue and clear. Groggy and wet, Jack looked around the park. It was beautiful, serene. As he walked slowly through the park, he looked at the bright green foliage. It was still wet. There was a fresh green smell in the air. Then, he heard urban sounds invading the pastoral scene— helicopters, people screaming, and horns honking, but it was not the normal urban squalor. There was a hysteria in this screaming, which Jack had heard not long ago on the morning of September 11. He ran through the trees to the edge of park. He could not believe his eyes. Rising from the area of the World Trade Center and soaring miles above Manhattan was a gigantic green thing. Thousands of people were running through the streets of lower Manhattan in a frenzied mob toward the huge green thing whose branches sprawled everywhere across and above the city.

Jack stopped on a corner and stared at it. He hyperventilated as he watched the thousands of people screaming and running through the streets of Manhattan. All he could think about was September 11. Thoughts flew across his mind like lightning. His mind traveled back to that Tuesday morning in September, he recalled all of the images, the pandemonium. His mind was a jumble. Then, flashes of the strange meeting with Murland popped into his mind. Beans. The Stradivarius. Lightning and thunder. The great storm. The demonic giant in the park restroom. Is this a dream? With chaos unfolding all around him, Jack realized the great green thing was a Beanstalk. That Beanstalk story. This can't happen. There were thousands of New Yorkers, who were all living and sharing this communal moment; they were running in hysteria through the streets of Manhattan. Jack knew this was too real to be a dream.

Some New Yorkers stood on the sidewalks a comfortable distance from the Great Beanstalk. They had no intention of racing to the World Trade Center site and the Beanstalk. They were too apprehensive.

The Beanstalk rose where the World Trade Center Towers once stood and disappeared into the swirling clouds that hovered miles above the city. Dozens of its enormous green branches spiraled down, disappearing into other sections of the puffy clouds. Huge, arched green tendrils dipped into the Hudson, as hundreds of other branches navigated their way through the side streets of Manhattan, turning corners, growing down alleys at a speed that a police radar gun would have recorded as 12 m.p.h. The tendrils grabbed onto buildings. Like ivy, they climbed the outside walls. Some reached into open office windows, prying their green fingers through the office spaces toppling desks, chairs, and filing cabinets. People fled for their lives. The Beanstalk's leaves were enormous, some hung over the roofs of office buildings. The Beanstalk dwarfed New York City. News helicopters buzzed the Beanstalk.

New York was in total chaos. Thousands of people massed near the Beanstalk. Jack was again part of the thousands, running down the street. Some New Yorkers stood dumbfounded staring up at the Great Green Beanstalk covering their mouths with their hands in astonishment. Most were paralyzed in awe and fear. Many raced like moths to a flame toward the Great Green Beanstalk. The NYPD worked frantically to cordon off ten-blocks in every direction from the Beanstalk and the excavated World Trade Center site. However, thousands of people had already gathered inside the yellow barrier at the base of the Beanstalk. It was nearly impossible for the police to remove the thousands who had flocked to lower Manhattan's excavated site.

Underneath the city, the subway lines were in shambles. Enormous brown and white roots punched through the ceilings and walls of the subway tunnels, especially those beneath the World Trade Center. Trains had derailed and crashed; and, people by the thousands were walking though the subway tunnels to the nearest exits.

At the World Trade Center site, people thronged around the Beanstalk, as the NYPD tried to keep order and cordon it off. Police cars and fire engines pulled up from every direction. News crews were frantic. Helicopters competed for airspace.

One drunk moseyed up to a police officer who was trying to keep people at bay behind the yellow police barricade. The drunk raised a bottle, "It's the end of the world!" he said as he toasted the air.

The Potter Building, the luxury condominium building on Park Row, where the Tott family lived, was splintered and barely standing. Despite the inherent dangers and warnings, tenants of the building stood on their balconies, watching the activity unfold at the excavated World Trade Center site.

In Manhattan, Jack raced through the streets with a wild mob toward the Beanstalk. While the police struggled to control the surging crowds, Jack ducked under the barrier on Park Avenue. He ran along a building toward his home. There was so much frenzy and chaos everywhere that no one noticed him. Jack maneuvered his way around the fallen splintered trees and partially collapsed buildings toward the front entrance of his home. Bleeding and injured, some people were hobbling out of the building. The Beanstalk had ripped out and replaced one entire side of the luxury condominium building. It was surprising that the building was even standing. He looked for the doorman Sam, but Sam was nowhere in sight. *Is Sam all right?* As Jack dashed through the foyer, he glanced across the once luxurious lobby to the shattered ruins of tables and chairs, a smashed grand piano, broken sculptures and torn paintings in beveled gold frames. He looked beyond the rubble to the great round green mass. It was the Beanstalk. The Beanstalk's trunk rooted hundreds of feet deep under the city and above ground covered several city blocks in every direction. Enormous green branches, some twelve feet in diameter, split off the trunk and dipped down, crashed through the concrete streets and pulverized buildings, as far as six blocks away from the World Trade Center Plaza. One immense branch had cut a vertical path directly through The Potter Building. In the noisy chaos, Jack paused to look at it. He marveled at its size and its greenness. The screams and sirens interrupted his thoughts, so he dashed toward what was left of the stairs. He ran up.

CHAPTER 12

NEWS TRAVELS

At the White House, Chief of Staff Andrew Spade was at a desk speaking on the telephone to an official in New York. As he spoke, he watched a wall of television monitors where every network and cable news station showed the melee' at the Beanstalk.

On the opposite side of the globe, in a television studio, a Japanese game show was interrupted. On screen, a journalist excitedly described events in New York. Over her shoulder, the Beanstalk towered nearly three miles over the city; it dwarfed the Manhattan skyscrapers.

In a Moscow news station, a wide-eyed Russian anchorman spoke rapidly to the camera. He gestured over his shoulder to a television monitor showing the bedlam in Manhattan. A horizontal scroll rolled across the bottom of the screen with text of updated information.

At the London Stock Exchange, trading had come to a halt. People stood transfixed staring up at the television monitors scattered about the room. Reduced to a small image at the bottom of the enormous Beanstalk, a BBC anchor recapped the events as they unfolded in New York, while behind him, dozens of planes and helicopters buzzed around the Beanstalk.

CHAPTER 13

THE ASCENT

Outside of his cage, Peekaboo sat on a railing in front of Jack's apartment. As Jack entered, Peekaboo screeched.

"What are you doing? The sky is falling! The sky is falling! Peekaboo!"

Jack grabbed Peekaboo, and he entered his apartment. The giant green Beanstalk had demolished the Tott home where one third of the living room had been swept away by this green force. Mattie and Natalie lay dazed on the couch with Mattie holding her daughter, who appeared weak and sickly. They were both nearly in shock.

"Mother!" Jack yelled as he approached her.

"It was the beans," said Mattie, dazed. In disbelief, she repeated herself, "It was the beans."

"Was the beans! The sky is falling!" Peekaboo mimicked.

"Are you okay?" Jack tried to help his mother and Natalie.

"No, I am not!" She was in tears and near hysteria. "What is happening?"

Jack did not answer his mother, because he did not know himself. He did not understand any of it.

"Nat, are you all right?" He took her hand in his.

"I don't know." Natalie responded weakly.

Outside the window, a ladder from a hook and ladder truck was being raised to the Tott apartment. Below, a police bullhorn bellowed, the words echoing off the building.

"Evacuate the building! This is the police. Evacuate the building!"

"We've gotta get out of here," Mattie said moving toward Natalie.

"I can't, Mother. I'm going up." responded Jack.

"Climb up there?" Mattie pointed to the hole in the roof, where the Beanstalk spiraled over three miles above the city and disappeared into the fluffy white cumulous clouds. "Are you crazy?" Mattie said staring at Jack.

"Get a life! Get a life! Peekaboo!" the Amazon parrot shrieked.

"Mother, I have to go up there! If Natalie is going to live, I have to go up there! Murland is responsible for this! Don't you understand?" Jack pleaded for his mother to understand.

"No! No, I don't!" Mattie responded confused, scared.

Just then, the giant ladder rested against the window frame of the Tott apartment. Jack saw it. He lifted Natalie off the couch cradling her into his arms.

"What are you doing?" yelled Mattie.

"What are you doing? What are you doing?" Peekaboo blurted out.

Jack carried Natalie over to the window. The New York firefighter waited on the ladder. Jack kissed Natalie tenderly on her cheek, then handed her carefully out the window to the firefighter, who put Natalie on his back with her arms wrapped securely over his shoulders. He clutched her two wrists together tightly just below his neck.

"I love you, Nat." said Jack. Natalie had tears in her eyes, as the firefighter began descending the rungs.

"I love you, Jack," she yelled back.

Mattie stood behind both of them watching anxiously.

The firefighter yelled to Mattie, "Lady, you next! I'll be back in a minute!"

Jack watched the firefighter take Natalie carefully down the ladder. On the ground, Jack saw thousands of people massing in the street all around the base of the Beanstalk. It was bedlam. The NYPD and NYFD struggled to keep order.

"Evacuate the building! Evacuate the building!" The police bullhorn bellowed out again.

Jack returned to the giant branch of the Beanstalk.

"You're not climbing that Beanstalk!" Mattie stepped in front of him.

"Yes, I am."

Jack skirted around Mattie, and began to climb, but his mother pulled at him. Jack tried shaking her off, but Mattie pulled harder.

"Stop it!" Jack yelled struggling to free himself.

"You are not going!"

Jack jumped off the Beanstalk and faced his mother. "Listen to me, Mother. I have no choice. Murland, the man who gave me the beans for the Stradivarius, told me that somewhere up there is a way to save Natalie, make amends with Dad, and there's something else. I don't know what it is, but I can feel it."

"No, Jack!"

"Mother! I must go up there! I know this in my heart!"

Mattie was struggling to process everything that was unfolding. She had lost her husband by lightning strike during a picnic. She knew that she would soon lose her daughter to leukemia. She did not want to lose her son.

"I can't lose you, Jack! I've lost my husband! And—" Mattie looked down to the splintered floor, and she began to cry as she thought about Natalie, Gage and her family. Jack takes her into his arms and hugs her.

"I promise you that I will be back!"

Mattie held onto him, and then lifted her head up and stared deeply into Jack's eyes. "You be careful up there, do you hear me?"

"Trust me, mother," Jack said as he looked into her green eyes that were red with tears and wide with fright.

Just then, the firefighter standing on the hook-n-ladder returned to the windowsill. He yelled at Mattie and Jack. "Come on, let's go!"

"I love you, mother." Jack held his mothers cheeks with his hands and kissed her on one, then turned, and climbed onto the Beanstalk, gripping the tendrils that jutted off the massive green branch. Jack pulled himself skyward.

"Hey! What are you doing?" The firefighter yelled as he watched Jack climb the massive green Beanstalk.

Peekaboo screamed, "What are you doing? What are you doing?"

Crying, Mattie screamed at Jack. "Wait!"

Jack stopped and looked back. He saw his mother removing the gold necklace with the 24-karat sun amulet from around her neck. Stretching as high as she could on her tiptoes, she reached up for Jack. He leaned his head down toward her. He hung the gold necklace with the 24-karat sun amulet around his neck. She hugged him tightly with tears flowing down her cheeks. "You come back to me. I can't lose you!"

As the firefighter stepped over the windowsill into the room, Jack climbed.

"Hey, you can't go up there!" The firefighter yelled as he charged at the Beanstalk, which Jack climbed hastily.

"What are you doing? The sky is falling!" Peekaboo screeched.

As Jack climbed the Beanstalk, the firefighter grabbed Jack's pants leg. The firefighter pulled; Jack pulled. The firefighter tugged harder; Jack tugged even harder. Mattie grabbed a splintered piece of 2x4 on the floor and began whacking the firefighter on his NYFD helmet, but the firefighter would not release his grip upon Jack's pants leg.

"Let him go! Let him go!" Mattie yelled as she walloped the firefighter repeatedly on the helmet.

"Stop it, lady! Stop it!" The firefighter yelled as he swatted Mattie's arm that was wielding the 2x4, while still tugging on Jack's pants leg. Trying to keep his balance, the firefighter yelled up to Jack, "You get down! Get down now!" The firefighter became more frustrated. "Stop it, lady! Stop it!"

"Climb, Jack!" Mattie yelled.

"Climb, Jack! Climb, Jack!" Peekaboo screeched.

Mattie whacked the NYFD firefighter two more times, then dropped the 2x4 to the floor and grabbed the firefighter's heavy asbestos coat to pull him away from Jack. She yanked hard on the firefighter; the firefighter yanked on Jack in a tug-of-war. Jack tried to climb the Beanstalk, but he could not move, and Mattie was unable to pull the firefighter away. Finally, with her fists clinched tightly around the firefighter's asbestos coat, Mattie fell hard to the floor using her body as a weight to bring the firefighter down.

"What are you doing, Lady? Stop it!" The firefighter struggled to shake off Mattie, who was crumpled in a twisted heap on the floor. She tugged heftily on his thick asbestos coat with her clenched fists. Frustrated and weakened, the firefighter lost his grip on Jack's pants leg. Suddenly, Jack was free. As the firefighter fell to the floor in a clump on top of Mattie, Jack scrambled up the massive green Beanstalk.

"Climb, Jack!" Mattie yelled toward the immense splintered opening in the ceiling.

From the floor, Mattie watched her son as he climbed up the Beanstalk and disappeared through the great hole in the demolished roof.

Outside, thousands of people massed around the Great Green Beanstalk. The hook-n-ladder extended up the Beanstalk toward Jack, who nimbly climbed ahead of it. A firefighter was perched atop the ladder's top rung. News and police helicopters flew around the Beanstalk filming both of them.

On the ground, as the hook and ladder climbed into the sky only feet away from the Beanstalk, spectators surrounded the firefighters and their trucks. With batons, the police pushed the crowd back, as they cheered enthusiastically for Jack. "Go! Go! Go!" they yelled. Their cheers got louder and louder.

The world watched on the network and cable news stations as the events unfolded in Manhattan. The image of Jack climbing the massive Beanstalk had everyone riveted to the television. News helicopters were squeezed into every inch of television sky. As Jack climbed, the ladder moved into position. The higher Jack climbed, the higher the ladder followed him. The firefighter at the top of the ladder yelled to Jack, as the ladder climbed closer, but the news helicopters were too far from the Beanstalk. Suddenly, Jack slipped and fell. Dozens of bright green tendrils that corkscrewed over one another like an enormous spider web caught Jack as he plunged toward Manhattan below. Flailing in the tendrils, Jack grabbed the edge of an enormous leaf and hoisted himself up with his feet kicking wildly in the air hundreds of feet above Manhattan.

People pointed to Jack hundreds of feet above them as he clutched the Beanstalk for his life. On another street, protesters carried signs and chanted, "The end-of-the-world is near!" Evangelists preached. Frenzied people swarmed the fire truck.

Looking down on the mob below, Jack hung on for his life, as the ladder closed in. The NYFD firefighter leaned over the rung of the ladder as far as he could to reach Jack. Hovering just behind the two was a CNN news helicopter. As the firefighter leaned, he slipped and nearly fell to his death. Jack was scared; he too was losing his grip. The firefighter struggled, but with his legs kicking and his arms swinging to distribute his weight, he regained his balance. Though Jack was only six feet from him, it was clear to the firefighter that it would take too many minutes to maneuver the huge ladder close enough to Jack and the Beanstalk. Jack was on his own, so at that moment, he swung his legs up and wrapped them around a Beanstalk branch. He secured a seat on the branch. Once stable, Jack and the NYFD firefighter exchanged looks. Holding onto the branch, Jack looked down at the swarms of people beneath him. Jack and the NYFD firefighter looked at each other. The firefighter touched the brim of his fire hat as if to salute Jack; Jack saluted him back. The firefighter lowered the ladder and once again Jack climbed the Great Green Beanstalk. From below, cheers rang out in the streets of Manhattan.

In the boisterous crowd, one British man yelled as he watched Jack dangle, "Two quid says the bloke doesn't make it!"

"Don't you know the story?" a man in the crowd below said to his friend.

Nearby, a woman interrupted, "He's going to climb the stalk and kill the giant!"

"Giant? The giant is probably a terrorist! You can bet on that!" said another onlooker. "Anyone want to bet that he comes down with the golden eggs?"

"And that his name is Jack!" exclaimed the first man.

Just then, on a portable television set which an onlooker was holding for everyone to see, the CNN correspondent reported, "We've just gotten information about the man on the Beanstalk. His name is Jacob Tott, but friends and family call him Jack."

Cheers erupted at the base of the Beanstalk.

At the World Trade Center Plaza, everyone's eyes focused upward on the Great Beanstalk. People chanted. "Jack! Jack! Jack! Jack! Jack!" The police did everything that they could to squelch the unruly crowd. Rioters tried to climb the Beanstalk; the firefighters hosed them down. The madness unraveled.

CHAPTER 14

AN UPSIDE-DOWN WORLD

Three miles above the city, Jack climbed the Beanstalk. The only sounds that he could hear at this height were his own labored breaths and heartbeat. Tired, Jack sat on a large green branch, where the air was thin and difficult to breathe. The skyscrapers looked like toy blocks. One hundred feet above him were thick, swirling clouds into which the Beanstalk disappeared. As he rested, he heard a distant rumble. Jack searched the sky in the direction of the rumbling. He squinted. Far off, he spotted two faint specks.

Flying swiftly toward the Beanstalk, just feet beneath the turbulent cloud layer, were two metallic objects. The rumbling got louder. Nervous, Jack watched as two silver-gray specks sped toward him. Suddenly, the rumbling became a deafening roar. It was two F-16 fighters.

From the cockpit of one of the F-16 fighters, the pilot saw Jack clinging to the Beanstalk. As he flew by at nearly Mach 1, the pilot pushed a button on his flight stick. High-speed cameras beneath the F-16 clicked-off dozens of photos in rapid succession. Jack clung to the Beanstalk. The air around him shook with a deafening roar. The F-16 fighters split, each to a different side, as they peeled off around the Beanstalk. As the jets passed, a voice resonated deep and strong out of the fading wake of the F-16 jet roar. "Fee Fi Fo Fummm."

Jack heard it. As he watched the F-16 fighters disappear on the horizon, he looked around. Where was this voice coming from? He composed himself, and then climbed toward the strange swirling clouds above him. Reaching up, his arm disappeared inside the clouds. His hand struck something wooden. He climbed a little more up the Beanstalk until his head and torso disappeared into the swirling clouds. Inside the clouds, Jack saw a great wooden door, twelve feet long and seven feet wide, its wood nicked and marred with cuts and hammer marks. Two huge iron hinges held it solid against a wooden frame that was obscured by the thick rolling clouds. Opposite the hinges and bolted to the door was an old rusty iron latch and a massive iron handle. Jack reached up inside the thick white clouds, grasped the iron latch, turned it and grasped the massive handle. There was a heavy iron click that echoed through the swirling clouds. He pushed the great door open and the hinges creaked.

Carefully, Jack stepped higher on the Beanstalk to see what lie beyond the great wooden door. He hung upside down from a cave ceiling. In this world above the Great Green Beanstalk, gravity was inverted. Hanging upside down, he peered around the cavern like a bat. Below him, inside a misty cave room, thousands of stalactites hung from the damp ceiling and hundreds of stalagmites grew upward out of the muddy wet floor. A flowing stream glowed with a turquoise phosphorescence, as it meandered through the center of the cave and disappeared around the bend. Ripples of watery light fluttered and danced across the reddish-brown cavern walls. It looked most curious. Jack carefully inched himself farther upward to see more of the cavern, but the gravity sucked him in and he dropped with a thud to the hard cavern floor and was knocked unconscious.

CHAPTER 15

CHOSEN FOR THE SKY

Elsewhere, in the skies above the Potomac River in Washington D.C., a Boeing CH-47 Chinook 66-19138 helicopter owned by NASA banked sharply over the river to land at Reagan National Airport. Inside the helicopter, the only passenger was Dr. Caitlin Bingham. She stared out at America's national monuments—the Jefferson and Lincoln Memorials, the White House and the Capital, as the helicopter made its approach.

"We'll be landing in a few minutes, Professor." The captain's voice rang crisply through the loudspeakers in the cabin. As she reflected on the past events, they flew on approach over the Pentagon. Caitlin stared out the window at the Pentagon. She saw September 11 all over again, black smoke rising from Pentagon. Fire. People running, screaming. Caitlin's face was blank; she was seeing the images of that horrible day play out like a movie in her mind. This was the first time she had been approved to fly over Pentagon airspace. The Chinook helicopter banked to set down at Reagan Washington National airport.

In the Department of Defense, a large insignia hung on the wall in a conference room. Men and women who were representatives from the military, government, astronomical observatories, and the U.S. Congress sat around a mahogany conference table. Senator John McBane, Senator Hillary Clendon, Dr. Frederic Chatke, the director of the Keck Observatory, the Chief Information Office for NASA Pat Bennington, NASA project scientist Dr. George Glechkler, and U.S.

Army Brigadier General Mark Finnett were also present. Caitlin sat at the head of the table. Dr. Kenneth Arnolds, director of the committee, led the interview.

"Archaeoastronomy is your field of expertise, Professor?" asked Dr. Arnolds.

"Yes," Caitlin answered confidently.

"Can you explain to us, Dr. Bingham, what is archaeoastronomy?" asked U.S. Senator John McBane.

"Yes. It is the study of ancient cultures, the Mayans, the Incas, the Hopi, the Aborigines, or the Egyptians to understand how celestial phenomena directly influenced every part of their culture, their planting and harvesting cycle, how they designed and constructed their cities, their social and political structure, pretty much everything."

Pat Bennington asked, "Is there a direct relationship between these cultures and the stars or the planets?"

"Our research," Caitlin replied, "indicates that there is a correlation between a star system's cycle and the life cycle of civilizations at a particular moment in their history. In every culture around the world, man has always given the stars the power of prophecy. We read about the influence of stars and constellations in cultures' religions. We have the myth of the bright star that guided the three Wise Men to the Christ Child's manger in Bethlehem; there are countless references to the stars by poets and writers in every culture. We see cultures that have designed their cities and worship sites based upon the movements of the sun, the moon, and the stars—Stonehenge, Machu Picchu, Pyramids, and the Caracol of Chichén Itzá. Consciously and unconsciously, we are linked deeply to the stars and planets."

Dr. Glechkler interrupted her, "Dr. Bingham, what you are saying is that you think there is a link between the stars and what is happening right now on our planet, in particular the Beanstalk in New York City?"

Silence preceded Caitlin's response. Everyone knew that this was a loaded question, including Caitlin, so she took her time to respond.

"I suspect that there is, but not in the way that you are asking me. I am a scientist not an astrologer. This is not astrology. I think this has more to do with a cycle or pattern. Because these events are unfolding right now, it is difficult if not impossible to deduce any significant meaning or explanation. When we have the luxury and comfort of a hundred or even a thousand years of hindsight, it is quite different." Dr. Glechkler relaxed back into his chair. He liked her answer.

Senator Clendon spoke up. "Dr. Bingham, I understand that you gave a presentation a few days ago about the planet, *Pachakutek*, which you discovered. Is that correct?"

"Yes, it is, Senator."

"And this planet has mysteriously disappeared?" asked the Senator from New York.

"That is correct."

"What does that mean?"

"Do you mean is this a prophecy of some kind?" Caitlin wanted to avoid misinterpretations of any kind.

"No, I am asking how could a planet simply disappear?" Senator Clendon shot back smartly.

"We don't know."

There was silence in the room.

"Does that mean that the disappearance of this planet is something that you expect will be explained in time?" Senator Clendon asked.

"We don't have enough data. That is all that I can tell you."

A U.S. Army Brigadier General Mark Finnett interrupted, "Excuse me, Dr. Bingham. I am a military man, so I don't know what happens on some star millions of light years away or in some tribe deep in the Amazon rain forest, but I do know about strategic military operations. And that seems to be why we are here."

Caitlin had a quizzical look on her face. General Finnett continued.

"Do you know anything about strategic military operations, Dr. Bingham?'

"No, sir, I don't."

Irritated, General Finnett challenged the distinguished body gathered around the conference table. "Then, why are we here? What in God's green earth makes you think you can handle something like this?"

"I'm not sure I understand your question, sir." Caitlin asked innocently.

"This committee is here to evaluate whether you should become part of a Special Forces team to deploy to the top of the Beanstalk," Director Arnolds said.

Caitlin sat back in her chair. *Should I consider this opportunity?* Deployment would demand that she postpone her current research.

"I see." Caitlin's voice was tentative.

"Does that make you uncomfortable?" asked Senator McBane.

"No, sir, I'm honored. It is just that I am processing it. I have two projects at critical stages, right now."

Everyone in the room scrutinized her, as she considered her response. After minutes, she spoke with total confidence.

"I am not sure why they would need me, but if I am selected, I will give it my best."

"Your best?" General Finnett blurted out. "What are we running here? This is highly technical operation, and with all due respect, Dr. Bingham, your place is in a university classroom and an observatory."

Dr. Glechkler quickly spoke up. "Dr. Bingham is one of NASA's top recruits at Houston's astronaut training program."

General Finnett became noticeably quiet.

"Dr. Bingham, do you feel that you are qualified for this?" asked Senator Clendon.

"Yes, senator, I do."

"One last question," Dr. Arnolds asked, "Why do you think that there is a link between the disappearance of the planet and the appearance of this Beanstalk?"

"I never said that," Caitlin defended herself with a perplexed tone.

Dr. Arnolds picked up a piece of paper with typed notes. "Dr. Bingham, we have a transcript of your presentation to NASA at Goddard. In it, you say, and I quote, 'mystics will link this to some historical event.'"

The room was silent, as they all looked at Caitlin.

"I was being facetious," responded Caitlin, amused by the reference.

"Under the current circumstances, would you still be facetious?" asked Dr. Arnolds.

"No, the circumstances have changed significantly." Caitlin realized then that in twenty-four hours her life might change radically, forever. Dr. Arnolds broke the quiet, "The team from McGuire Air Force Base will deploy in six hours. Do you agree to be part of that team?"

"Yes, sir."

Dr. Arnolds adjourned the meeting.

CHAPTER 16

EARTHROCK

Ten days before the Giant Beanstalk had turned the world upside down, the beginning of the 21st Century was an era of rapid change. It was a time of alliances. It was a time of mistrust. Above the earth, the incomplete International Space Station, orbited over North America, South America, Africa, Europe, the Middle & Far East, and Australia. From space, the earth looked exactly as the astronauts had described it during their first trips into space, the big blue marble. Blue oceans, white clouds, sandy deserts, the red and brown plains, green fertile fields, raised purple, white-capped mountains, all remarkable colors and textures and patterns seen from space as diverse as the nations living upon it.

The International Space Station orbited over the East Coast of the United States. Miles below the rain pummeled New York City's Times Square. Thunder rocked the unyielding steel and concrete skyscrapers, as lightning cracked through the night air.

Ten days before Jack ended up alone and unconscious on the wet cave floor in a bizarre unknown world, he was in Greenwich Village. Outside of the Earth-Rock Cafe, people covered their heads with newspapers as they scrambled through the city into cafes and office buildings. Like a bomb, a roll of thunder rocked the windows of an eclectic jazz club called The EarthRock Cafe. Inside the club, people were jammed wall-to-wall, shoulder-to-shoulder, people of all kinds—blue collar and white, younger hipsters, and middle-aged managers; they were white and black, Hispanic, Indian, Arab, and European. The room vibrated with a new music. It was a blend of organic and synthetic.

On the small EarthRock Cafe stage, Jack and four other musicians played an assortment of odd instruments, which looked like leftovers from a bizarre garage sale. There was a large synthesizer, some drums, old Church organ pipes, flutes and stringed instruments from different countries. Glass bottles, sheets of metal, pieces of wood and pipes, and bells dangled from huge coat frames. Everything dressed the stage like a weird thrift shop. Taped to the walls of the café were mementos from the World Trade Center tragedy—photos, poems, badges from fire and police departments across the United States, and a few miniature flags representing the countries of the remembered World Trade Center victims. The room pulsed and throbbed with life.

As leader of the band, Jack stood in the center playing a Korg Triton synthesizer. His fingers flew across the keyboard. Passion flowed out of the speakers and bounced off the walls of the club like thunder in the Grand Canyon. It was like no music these people had ever heard. Jack was mesmerizing. With every note and musical phrase, he moved deeper into his music, into a place where he lost himself, where every muscle and pulse surrendered to deep unknown memories of his past. Dressed in a silk black shirt, Levis, black Lucchese cowboy boots, and multiple piercings, sweat dripped down his cheeks into his dimples as he rocked to the music he created.

The door to The EarthRock Cafe blew open bringing in the blowing rain along with a gentle white-haired man dressed in a conservative suit, who looked nearly like Santa Claus. The man shook out his umbrella. Using it like a cane, he maneuvered his way to a lone seat at a small circular table in the back. He watched Jack on stage. The old man got caught up in the music. He tapped his foot on the sawdust floor and rapped his fingers on the tabletop, as he drank in Jack's every nod, hop, and bob.

On the stage, Steve the percussionist rolled his sticks in a flash across the electronic drum pads. His eyes connected briefly with Jack, and nodded in the direction of the white-haired man.

"That's the man who was asking about you!" Steve yelled.

Squinting, Jack looked out to the audience at the white bearded man in the black suit who was now rocking slightly in his chair.

"Who is he?" yelled Jack.

"I think he's an agent or something. He's definitely important," Steve said as he rolled his sticks in a blur across his sparkling Ludwig drums.

Jack looked over at the amused white-bearded man nestled comfortably in the crowd and nodded. The man returned the nod and raised his umbrella in salute and approval. The band cut loose. The room became electric. People swayed. They patted their hands on their knees, some clapped, while others tapped their toes on the sawdust floor. The EarthRock Cafe was a musical spectacle as Jack led the band and the crowd in a whipped-up frenzy. After the crescendo, Jack turned to Steve.

"What time is it?"

Steve said, "Who cares!"

"What time is it?" Jack insisted.

Steve checked his watch. "Eight o'clock!"

"Damn!" Jack exclaimed in surprise and disgust.

Jack glanced briefly at the man with the white-beard, and then stopped playing. The band picked up the slack, as Jack leapt off the stage into the audience. Confused, the white-bearded man stared at Jack, who by now was fleeing for the front door weaving his way around the tables. Some people smiled and patted him on the back, while others watched curiously. The band members were mystified, as they watched Jack grab a suit bag hanging on a coat rack near the front door. As he left the club, Jack's eyes caught the eyes of the white-bearded man.

Outside The EarthRock Cafe, it was ominously dark. Rain pounded the city. With his suit bag draped over his shoulder, Jack stayed close to the café wall to keep from getting soaked. He wiped the water dripping into his eyes and scanned the street for a yellow cab. The streets glistened brightly with a myriad of color from city lights. Frantic, Jack stepped into the street and flagged a taxi.

"Taxi!"

A taxi pulled over to the curb, where Jack stood getting drenched. Jack opened the door and got in holding his suit bag. He slammed the door and the taxi sped off sloshing through the water.

Even with the windshield wipers beating at their fastest speed, it was nearly impossible to see out the front window. Jack watched the wipers swish back and forth, he liked the incessant, steady beat that they made. The taxi driver's eyes darted back and forth from the rain-battered streets to the rear-view mirror, where he could see Jack in his back seat doing something.

"Late for a date?" the cabbie asked curious about what Jack was doing.

"Something like that." Jack responded indifferently.

Jack removed his boots and unzipped his fly. He lay down across the back seat and struggled to pull his drenched Levis down his legs. The taxi driver watched somewhat nervously in the rear-view mirror, as Jack continued to struggle with his wet Levis. Finally, Jack uncurled the Levis from around his ankles, unbuttoned his black shirt and peeled it off his chest. The cab driver watched every move that Jack made. The cabbie was curious and unsure. Too many things had gone wrong in his cab, and he easily read the panic on Jack's face. Nevertheless, the cabbie sped his taxi through the darts of rain and the drenched city. Sitting half-naked in his jockey shorts and black socks, Jack unzipped the suit bag and took out a tuxedo, a white shirt, and a black bow tie and put them on. One by one, Jack removed each piercing from his ears, nose, eyebrow and tongue. He took off his rings and bracelets. He stuffed them into a small black suede pouch, which he promptly zipped and slid into the inside pocket of his tuxedo coat. Then, he straightened himself.

CHAPTER 17

CARNEGIE HALL
RE-VISITED

The taxicab pulled sharply up to the curbside entrance of Carnegie Hall. The hundreds of lights from the hall's five canopies reflected brightly in the wet street and sidewalk illuminating the entire Carnegie Hall entrance. Holding the suit bag high above his head, Jack exited the taxicab and slammed the door. Dressed in his tuxedo, his piercings gone, he ran through the rain to the front door and entered. The taxicab drove away over the reflection of the Carnegie Hall lights shimmering in wavy pools of street water.

Jack entered the Carnegie Hall lobby. Standing upon the plush carpet beneath an enormous chandelier, he stopped for a few seconds to listen to the solo violin music, which filled the air of the great hall.

Jack grabbed an usher, "Please check these for me." He handed the usher his suit bag. Before the confused usher could utter one word, Jack raced across the lobby to the far side entrance and ran down the outer side lobby of the concert hall toward a backstage entrance, where a police guard stood. The music of the New York Philharmonic resonated in the great hall. The guard stopped Jack.

"Let me in," Jack insisted.

"No one's allowed back here." The guard stood firmly with his arms crossed.

While Jack waited at the steps, he listened to the sweet violin music rising in the great performance hall. A man dressed in a dark suit with a pocket kerchief, a man of some apparent authority, approached. His name was Sanders and he was the stage manager. Over the years, Jack and Sanders had developed a dislike of each other. On repeated occasions, Jack told his father that Sanders "had it in for him", but Jack's father dismissed Jack's claims as inconsequential and told Jack "you'll just have to toughen up and not let him get to you." You could tell by Jack's silence that he did not like Sanders. When Sanders saw Jack, a sneer wrinkled his lip and a look of disgust passed across his face.

"Let him in," the stage man instructed the guard.

The guard unlocked his arms and stepped aside. Jack leapt up the three steps into the backstage area. Without even acknowledging the stage manager, Jack walked by brushing Sanders' shoulder with his own. Jack quickly maneuvered around the backstage tables, pulleys, ropes, and props. From behind the red velvet curtain, he looked out at the New York Philharmonic playing to a packed house. The crowd was spellbound by the music. It was Bach's *Concerto for Two Violins in D Minor, Third Movement.* Loren Fazcel conducted.

Standing in the center of the Philharmonic, a concert violinist played. He was a handsome man with graying hair, who had celebrated his fifty-fifth birthday just three days before. He cradled his Stradivarius violin as if it were a child. His name was Gage Tott, and he was Jack's father. Gage's passion and grace were seasoned with age; it showed in his face. His passion not only filled the great hall, but it commanded respect.

Gage Tott grew up in Kansas. He began his study of violin at nine years old, when his mother drove him twenty miles for a one-hour lesson in Topeka with the man who was first violinist with the local community symphony. He practiced two hours a day, after completing his after-school farm chores. At sixteen years old, Gage left his Kansas farm to study violin on a scholarship to the Julliard School of Music. He never returned to Kansas.

Gage's notes transcended the revered space in Carnegie Hall; they transcended this moment in time. Fearful of the criticism that he knew that his father would heap upon him, Jack stood to the side of the stage and watched his father, a legend, play.

With his father's violin calling him, Jack walked backstage, where a violin lay on a table. Jack opened the case and took out the violin. Confidently, Jack walked behind the rows of plush curtains, and quietly plucked the strings making minor tuning adjustments. When he was finished, he stopped and listened to his father's solo performance. With one sweep of his hand, Jack straightened his hair, took a deep breath and strode confidently onto the stage with his violin at his side. Some of the New York Philharmonic musicians looked up in shock. How disappointed his father must be. He was never responsible. While weaving the baton through the air, Loren Fazcel's eyes hurled angry darts at Jack, who positioned himself directly across from his father. As Jack raised the violin to his shoulder, he watched his father's eyes looking for some eye contact, for recognition, even anger would be acceptable, but there was no look, not even a glance. Gage ignored his son, his partner in music. Jack shifted his eyes to Loren Fazcel, who waited for the perfect moment, and then nodded. Jack joined in with his father. The notes blended. The music rose sweetly in the great hall. During Jack's entrance upon the stage, not one musician lost a beat.

Spellbound, the sell-out crowd listened to the father-son duo, as the music soared like a bird in flight. Jack had settled in. His fingers flew across the strings with a grace and sophistication that told of years of study and practice. The Philharmonic played in perfect sync with the father and son duo. The performance was the stuff of the gods. In the brief caesuras, you could hear the hiss in the air, not one person moved in their seats.

Echoes of the performance floated out of Carnegie Hall and rose above the city, above the horns of the traffic, above the people shuffling to and fro. The music hovered above humbly, like a gathering of angels looking down.

In a luxurious condominium in lower Manhattan, only blocks away from the World Trade Center site, the Bach Concerto resonated through the living room on a media center that covered nearly one entire wall.

In a back bedroom, with an intravenous tube in her arm, Jack's sister, Natalie rested in a home hospital bed while she listened to her stereo. Her eyes sparkled.

Sitting on the bed next to her was Mattie. She held Natalie's hand gently weaving her head ever so slightly to and fro in the air, while listening to her husband and son perform.

Sitting on the bed, Mattie and Natalie were captivated by Gage and Jack's performance. As the music rose toward a finale, mother and daughter sat holding hands, as the father and son played.

On the Carnegie stage, Gage leaned his head and violin into the music as it built to a crescendo. Beads of sweat collected on Gage's forehead. Jack's fingers were a blur as they flew across the stings. Cutting his baton through the air, Loren Fazcel led the Philharmonic through the final pages of the concerto. The musicians' eyes darted from the sheet music to the conductor to the father and son duet. For everyone in the hall, time was held in suspension. With a rousing finale, they played the last note. It was an unprecedented performance. After three seconds of silence, there was uproar as the applause and bravos rose to a sustained, almost deafening crescendo. The audience rose to its feet. Loren Fazcel held up his hands in the direction of the father and son duo, and then directed the attention to the orchestra. He exhorted the audience to applaud for Gage and Jack. As he did, he locked eyes with Jack. The conductor was still mad. Jack and Gage took repeated bows, which extended far longer than was comfortable for either of them. The Philharmonic musicians applauded, the stringed musicians rat-tat-tatting their bows repeatedly upon their instruments.

Caught up in the moment, Jack looked at his father. Gage glared at him. This was the first look that Gage had given his son, since Jack walked onto the brightly-lit stage. Gage's look stung his son, and Jack's smiles crumbled into disappointment. He had hoped that his performance would quench his father's anger, that the music would have softened him, or at least given his father an excuse to temporarily forget and forgive his son. But it did not. Now, Jack knew that nothing could do that, but time. No matter how brilliantly he played, Jack had not only let his father down, but now he was back in the real world, in his father's world.

Philharmonic orchestra members packed up their instruments. Some musicians congratulated Gage, but nobody spoke to Jack. Conductor Loren Fazcel walked over to Jack.

"This is the second time you've pulled this. You are never playing here again," The conductor's eyes showed his loss of respect. It affected Jack deeply.

"I'm sorry," Jack lowered his eyes.

"You have a great talent, Jack, but I'm finished with you," Conductor Fazcel finished and walked away. He approached Gage.

"It was a great performance, Gage." Loren Fazcel patted Gage on the back.

"Thank you," replied Gage, "and I'm sorry."

"What's done is done. Perhaps your judgment was in error, but you picked up the slack."

Loren Fazcel left the stage, as Gage packed up his Stradivarius violin.

The Manhattan streets glistened with a rainbow of colors from the city lights. The rain had stopped. A black Lexus drove down the street. Inside, Jack stared out the window lost in the passing wet light of the city, while Gage drove.

"Do you know how many hoops I had to jump through to arrange this?" Gage glared at his son, partly in anger, partly in bewilderment. Jack had a brilliant talent, yet he was wasting it, Gage thought. He wanted desperately to understand his son, but lacked the patience to listen. His professional expectations had always been high and unyielding, sometimes too much so.

"I didn't ask you to arrange this. It was your idea," Jack said.

"This was a lost opportunity."

"An opportunity for one thing, to show off what a gifted musician you've raised!" Jack countered.

"Don't you talk to me like that!" Gage yelled, and then bit his lip. Moments passed as he stared out the windshield at the passing lights of the city. "Lorin knows how good you are. I do not have to convince him. Your virtuosity has done that!" Gage was trying to persuade his son. "I'm not going to be around forever, you know. One day, you could become the Phil's concert violinist, if you want it."

Jack did not want to talk about it any further. He would hear no more. Matter-of-factly, he said to his father, "I am sorry, but I am not 14 years old anymore. I've simply lost my interest in violin."

Gage and Jack locked stares. After a few anxious seconds, Gage watched the unstable formless reflections in the wet street, as the Lexus drove through the city.

CHAPTER 18

TWO DISCONNECTED WORLDS

Ten minutes of silence passed as the father and son sat staring out at the passing city. The constant muffled sound of the tires swishing over the wet streets was the only sound that pierced the thick air in the Lexus. The car pulled into the circular driveway of the Potter Building and stopped under an emerald green awning. The Potter Building was once part of Manhattan's famous legacy called Newspaper Row.

A doorman promptly opened the passenger door. Jack stepped out, as the door buzzer sounded.

"Good evening, Mr. Tott," greeted the doorman.

"Hello, Sam," replied Jack in a warm friendly tone.

The doorman walked around the car and took the keys from Gage.

"And how are you this evening, Mr. Tott?"

"Fine, thank you, Sam."

"And how did the performance go?"

Gage hesitated, glanced at his son, then responded, "I guess it went as fine as could be expected, Sam. Thank you for asking." Gage walked on mumbling, "Fine. It went fine."

"That's good," replied Sam as he smiled politely. He knew that it did not go well. Sam had known that something was not right between this father and son for a long time, but he recognized that tonight he sensed a resignation in Gage, and that concerned him because he liked Gage Tott.

Gage and Jack entered the lobby of the condominium carrying their violins. They waited at the elevator in silence. The elevator door opened. Once inside, Gage and Jack stared straight ahead at the polished brass elevator door.

Gage turned to his son. He could see his own reflection in the gold panel where the floor elevator lights glowed. Jack's reflection was blurry.

"You have a rare talent, Jacob. All I am trying to do is get you to use it."

"I am using it."

"In that club?" Gage caught a glimpse of Jack's blurred reflection moving in the gold plated panel.

"How would you know?" Jack confronted him. "You've never come to listen, not once, in all these years."

"No, I haven't," Gage said, his tone neither regretting it, nor implying that he would go to the club and listen. It was simple, he despised alternative experimental music.

The elevator door opened and they stepped out into their three-bedroom Manhattan condominium. Jack walked ahead of his father toward the foyer. In the background, a parrot screeched at regular ear-piercing intervals. The bird was Jack's Amazon parrot, Peekaboo.

Mattie Tott waited for Jack and Gage in the foyer. She kissed Gage, as Jack tried to squeeze by them.

"Just a minute," she reached out and grabbed Jack's shirt as he tried to slide by.

As he walked toward the living room, Gage heard Peekaboo screeching. His cackle echoed through the entire apartment, "What are you doing? What are you doing? Peekaboo! Peekaboo!"

Gage stopped.

"Will you please shut that bird up?"

Mattie stood directly across from Jack, "Not that it makes any difference, but I want you to know that you embarrassed this family today on national radio," she said. "And you hurt your father terribly."

"I never meant to embarrass anyone," Jack said.

"That's it?" she waited for Jack to say something else, anything that could even remotely help her understand what he did.

"I'm sorry."

"Sorry? That is sad, Jacob. No, it's more than sad, it's pathetic." More than angry, Mattie was disappointed.

"Don't you get it? Violin isn't my voice anymore! I didn't want to do Carnegie Hall today, he did!" Jack nodded toward his father. "Classical music is <u>his</u> music, it is no longer mine! I've outgrown it!"

"You arrogant ..." Gage was so angry that his bottom lip quivered. Jack noticed. "Nobody outgrows classical music!" Gage said. Jack stared into his father's eyes, calmly turned away and walked down the hallway. In the background, Peekaboo screeched loudly adding to the mounting tension in the Tott home.

CHAPTER 19

NATALIE'S WORLD

Natalie Tott was sitting up in her home hospital bed, as she typed on a keyboard that rested on her lap. She studied a large computer monitor mounted on a swing arm above her legs. Her eyes sparkled. Opposite her bed, the HDTV screen and stereo system were off. Two enormous walnut bookcases filled with books covered the adjacent wall.

When Jack entered her room, his demeanor changed. A huge smile blossomed on his face; his eyes lit up when he saw his sister.

"Hi ya, kiddo!" he said as he plopped down on the bed next to her and gave her a peck on the cheek. His manner was subdued because of the fight with his father. Natalie knew it the second that he walked through the door, even though she was busy typing. She could read Jack in a glance.

"One second," she said, as she continued typing as if what she was doing was, for the moment, more important than anything else in the world. Her words filled up the colorful website. Jack watched. After a few minutes, she took her hands off the keyboard, rested them at her sides and smiled at Jack.

"Did you hear the concert?" Jack asked.

"I heard it. In fact, I timed it. You missed eighteen minutes, almost the whole first movement."

"Thanks," Jack shook his head. He had hoped to have at least one ally. He thought that his sister would understand because she had heard his music in the village and liked it.

"Hey, lighten up," Natalie kicked him under the covers with her foot. "There are worse things, you know." With her arm that had an intravenous tube in it, she swung the computer around for Jack to see.

"Read it," she said. She typed on the keyboard and scrolled down the website. Jack read the words that filled up the computer screen.

"I was just talking to this girl," Natalie said. "Her name is Melanie. She's seventeen years old, pregnant and was diagnosed three days ago with inoperable terminal cancer. They gave her twelve months to live."

Natalie named her website "Got Talk?" She designed it, setting up links to physicians, child counselors who specialized in childhood terminal diseases, church intervention programs, and multiple chat rooms. Nearly seven hours a day, or until she got so tired she could do no more, she chatted and advised boys and girls between six and eighteen years old during the last years, usually months, of their lives.

"Let me see," Jack said as he moved the keyboard in front of him, punched some keys and scrolled down the page. He read some of the desperate emails and heartfelt responses written to his sister by total strangers. Natalie watched him.

"Do you see why it's absurd to get upset because you and Dad didn't get to play eighteen minutes of violin together?"

Jack grinned, embarrassed. He stroked Natalie's arm gently.

In the background, Peekaboo started screeching again. "What are you doing? What are you doing? Peekaboo! Peekaboo!" Just then, Gage and Mattie walked into Natalie's room. Jack moved down to the end of the bed and sat in the wicker chair. His father seemed calmer now, though he did not look at Jack.

"Hi, Butterfly." Gage kissed his daughter and gave her a hug.

"Daddy, I loved the concerto—even the part that Jack missed."

Jack scoffed at Natalie, especially after their conversation. That was Natalie, the fly-in-the-ointment; Jack loved that about her. He wanted to smile, but would not give his father the satisfaction of seeing it.

"The concert was for you, Butterfly, every note." Gage was proud of his daughter.

"Your father and I were talking," said Mattie, "How about going on a picnic tomorrow?"

Gage asked Natalie, "What do you say, are you up to it?"

"Duh? What do you think?" Natalie smiled widely.

Gage turned to Jack. "If we leave at 9 o'clock, do you think you can wake up in time?"

"That's funny." Jack looked at his mother, turned and left the room.

Mattie's eyes caught Gage's eyes. She was not pleased with him; he was picking a fight with Jack. For quite sometime, she knew that this was more than a battle of egos or a clash of two great artistic temperaments. It was an age-old battle. It was a father struggling to hang onto a son, who was on the verge of rejecting his way of life, and a son who was struggling to free himself from his father's expectations and assert his own individuality. Her glare at her husband showed her disapproval. Mattie knew this obstinate side of Gage too well; he had always been like this.

CHAPTER 20

———— ❧ ————

MATTIE

Mattie Joe Flingit grew up in Austin, Texas, where she was considered the best pianist her high school had produced in years. At nineteen years old, she fell madly in love with a talented rock musician, who painted his face and arms with serpent scales. She married him three months after their first meeting and left him ten months later because he had an insatiable appetite for other women. She moved to New York, where she earned a BA in music from NYU's school of music. Two years later, she met Gage Tott, a concert violinist.

On their third date, she took him to a rock club in Greenwich Village, where a new, electronic-blues-rap-rock group from Austin was headlining. She loved the music; Gage hated it. Thirty minutes into the performance, he stood up and took her firmly by the hand.

"Let's go, we're leaving."

"What are you talking about?" she said baffled.

"I am not going to listen to this," Gage insisted, as he walked toward the front door. Mattie shuffled reluctantly behind him.

Outside, they stood in the street and argued, as passers-by watched.

"This was <u>my</u> date!" Mattie yelled.

"I will reimburse you. That is not music. It is an atrocity. And I won't condone it with my presence." Mattie's mind flooded with flashes of her former husband, playing guitar on stage. She loved his music; she did not love his lifestyle. She also loved Gage's music.

"I disagree with you. I find that music stimulating, intriguing." Mattie contested.

"Music should uplift the spirit, not denigrate it. This is music in a spastic search for a home." Gage's words rang with finality. Mattie knew it. She could push it, but she knew that she would never see him again, so she took his hand and they walked down the street.

Gage and Mattie married one year later.

Now in Manhattan, over twenty-five years later, Mattie became lost in recollections of her past. After minutes, she turned her attention to Gage sitting on the bed talking with their daughter, but she could only think of Jack, who left the room without saying a word.

CHAPTER 21

JACK'S SACRED SPACE

Jack entered his bedroom. A large black iron cage stood in the corner by the window. Colorful parrot toys hung in Peekaboo's cage. Perched on a swing was Peekaboo, who was a birthday gift from his mother at his eight-year old birthday party.

"Peekaboo, Peekaboo, what are you doing? The sky is falling!"

"You got that right, Peek." Jack said, as he set the violin on his chair and walked over to Peekaboo. The parrot skittered snappily along his perch toward the opening of the cage making clicks with his mouth. Jack took Peekaboo out of the cage. He laid down in his bed with Peekaboo skittering across his chest.

"Peekaboo, Peekaboo!" the bird screeched.

"Shut up," Jack said as he took his thumb and index finger and gently clamped down on Peekaboo's beak. The bird shook his head, but Jack would not let go. Jack liked playing with him this way.

The walls of Jack's room were covered with posters of Mozart and Beethoven and a photograph of Albert Einstein with a quotation taken from The New York Times Magazine on August 2, 1964. It said, "The unleashing of power of the atom bomb has changed everything except our mode of thinking, and thus we head toward unparalleled catastrophes." On another wall was a poster of Charles Darwin on the *H.M.S. Beagle*, plus *National Geographic* charts of star constellations and galaxies. A large glossy color poster of Machu Picchu hung on another wall near Jack's bed. On the bottom of the photograph, there was an inscription written in gold ink, "'To My Son on his 13th Birthday—Nosotros tuvimos muy buen tiempo juntos!' All My Love—Dad." Jack stared at the poster.

Jack had been thirteen with thick, wavy brown hair, a strong physique, and a broad smile that showed off the braces, which sparkled and filled up his young mouth. Next to him, his father Gage walked excitedly, eyes open wide and using huge strides over the granite stone walkway. Jack kept pace with him. Before them was the entrance. The sign read: Parque Nacional Machu Picchu. Gage bought two tickets at the stone house to the famous Inca ruins. With dozens of other people walking in front of and behind them, they passed through the turnstile.

Together they walked down the stone walkway toward a main gate, a trapezoidal arch made of huge stones carved by the Incas. Framed by the arch entranceway, they saw Huayna Picchu Mountain, green, rocky and foreboding in the distance. She was majestic; she had a curving ascending form. Neither spoke as they passed though the stone gateway into the immense ancient ruins, but their eyes were riveted to the mountain. As they walked farther, there was a six-foot high stone wall on their left. Above it, they saw gigantic, steep terraces of stone and dirt built upon a vertical slope of the mountain. The terraces extended up the side of the mountain, blocking the view of the top. They followed the terrace next to the stone walkway to where it ended. Gage stopped. Jack stood by his side.

"My god," Gage exclaimed in a tone that whispered sacred and a quality of being humbled.

"It's so big," the thirteen year-old Jack said.

"Isn't it magnificent?" Gage said as he put his arm around his son's shoulder and looked at him.

"Yeah." Jack never forgot the moment. It was a grand moment of connection between him and his father. It was the same feeling that he had when they stood at the edge of the Grand Canyon for the first time and felt its enormous volume inside.

Before them was Machu Picchu. They saw Huayna Picchu mountain towering over the village, the main plaza with its calming bright green grass, flanked by hundreds of stone houses, to the left in the distance, an open stone area that looked like a temple. Just beyond was a small pyramid-shaped hill, where dozens of people were climbing the steep stone steps. On top of the pyramid knoll, people were gathered around a stone structure. With people swarming over it taking pictures, Jack thought that from a distance that it had the appearance of a great monument, like the Lincoln Memorial or the Washington Monument, but this stone monument did not stick its head far above the stone platform that it seemed to grow out of. Jack remembered after learning that it was the highest point of Machu Picchu besides the surrounding mountains. It was Intihuatana, the point, where the Incas symbolically hitched the sun to their earthy village on the solstice. Even at thirteen years old, Jack knew that it, like the Inca people who had lived five hundred years before him, ascended to the sky.

Together, with their backpacks mounted securely on their backs, Gage and Jack combed the ruins of Machu Picchu for hours. As the sun began to set over the Andes and the sunlight painted a soft warm glow over the ancient cold stones of the village, a magic silence filled the air. The thousands of tourists who swarmed over the ruins were gone, on their trains heading back to Cuzco, only about fifty people remained, scattered everywhere over the enormous village to see the sun set over the ancient city.

"Come with me," Gage said as he moved quickly retracing his steps to Machu Picchu's entrance. Jack walked briskly behind him to keep pace. Once outside the main gate, Gage went directly to the gift shop, which was closing. He convinced the man at the door to let him in to make a quick purchase. Jack shadowed his father curiously. Gage grabbed two zampoñas and took them to the register. He paid for them, and as quickly as they entered the gift shop, they left. They hurried through the entrance, flashed their hand stamps to the Nacional Parque guard, and walked through the Main gateway toward the center of Machu Picchu.

The sun was setting. A yellow and orange swathe of color airbrushed a glow over the ruins. They walked up the steep stone steps next to the vertical terraces, where there was a quaint stone house open on one side. Behind them was the ceremonial rock and Machu Picchu Mountain, the male mountain, which overlooked the ancient village, as if to protect it. Gage walked on the grass over to the edge of the hill that sat opposite Huayna Picchu and the entire village. He sat down on the wall, and Jack sat next to him. Gage handed Jack a zampoña and Jack smiled. Gage raised the flutes, each pipe bound together with a cord woven from a rainbow of colors, to his lips and played. He blew gently over the pipes, it was sketchy at first, sometimes no sound came out but a whoosh of air, then a note, here and there, sporadic and choppy, but the notes soon flowed softly. He adjusted his lips creating the right angle and the right flow of air. Gage learned quickly. Jack watched him, and then raised the zampoña to his lips. He learned quicker than his father. It was if Jack somehow already knew how to play. Both were accomplished musicians, so the language was natural to them.

The sun had just set over the Andes and all around the stone buildings and temples of Machu Picchu and the surrounding mountains that celebrated the ascendant ancient ruins glowed with reds, oranges, yellows, deep indigo blues, and purples. Gage and Jack played on their zampoñas, their music intertwining and creating harmonies with each other. Like a steady gentle breeze, the notes echoed off the stone walls and temples of the great city, and off the rocky crags and walls of the mountains surrounding them. Just above them, the Pleiades, known to the Incas as the Nuchu Verano, were rising, but the father and son did not notice. Together, they were filled with their music as it summoned the Incas who had once lived in the stone houses and worshipped in the temples. Little did he know, but it was a singular moment in Jack's life, a birthday that he would remember to his dying breath.

Lying on his bed in his Manhattan apartment, Jack stared at the poster of Machu Picchu.

Near the Machu Picchu photograph, there was a framed signed photograph of his father with composer Leonard Bernstein, when his father performed "The Lark Ascending" before a capacity crowd at Carnegie Hall. On another wall was a laminated 30"x 14" photo of the World Trade Center before September 11, and on the opposing wall was a laminated 45"x 24" photo of the World Trade Center's recovery site with several large cranes and New York City Firemen combing through the piles of rubble.

Jack grabbed a handful of assorted nuts from the end table, and placed them upon his chest. Peekaboo walked around on Jack's chest breaking the seeds open one-by-one. Balancing himself on one claw, he clasped the nut with the other claw. He rotated his claw clockwise and lifted it to his beak. Crack. The shell broke open. Jack watched Peekaboo crack nuts, then turned his head toward the Machu Picchu poster and stared at it. Out the window next to the poster of the ancient Inca ruins, the stars shined brightly. Gazing out the window at the stars, Jack's eyelids began to droop. Slowly, his eyes closed.

CHAPTER 22

THE GOLD AMULET

Jack lay across his bed asleep. Peekaboo had flown back into his cage, where he stood still on his perch, his tiny black eyes closed. The cage to his door was wide open. In the night sky, as bright moonlight hovered over Jack's eyes, whispers and random clicking sounds filtered down the hall into Jack's bedroom. Slowly, he awoke and squinted at the full moon outside. It hurt his eyes to look directly at the moon. He heard whispering down the hall. Curious, he rolled out of bed, walked over to Peekaboo's cage and closed the birdcage door. He tiptoed down the hallway following the noises.

In the kitchen, Gage and Mattie sat at the table speaking in low voices. Bills and papers cover the table. Tape from an adding machine trailed across the table and down onto the patterned linoleum floor. Gage scrolled the adding machine paper through his fingers and examined the numbers printed down the tape.

"Look, I can get a job," Mattie said. She fidgeted with the gold amulet on the necklace, which hung around her neck.

"If you get a job, we'd have to hire a nurse," Gage said. "She needs one of us here with her."

Barefooted, Jack tiptoed on the hardwood floor down the hallway wall toward the kitchen. Stopping ten feet from the corner, so his parents were unaware of his eavesdropping, Jack listened while leaning against the wall.

"In one month, our insurance runs out, what are we going to do?" asked Mattie.

"We will sell everything we own to keep her alive."

Mattie thought for a moment, then slowly reached up and grabbed the twenty-four karat gold amulet of the sun that hung on her necklace. Mattie had a resigned look on her face.

"I will sell this." She clutched the gold amulet in the palm of her hand.

"No, you won't. It has a long history."

Gage's surname was Tott, which he got from his father, whose ancestors had their roots in Yorkshire, England and centuries before in Sweden, but the ancestors of Gage's mother were from South America, the Cordillera de Vilcabamba region in Peru. His mother's name was Maria Josephina Cucho.

It was in the 15th century that a humble Inca artisan Ch'uya Anqasmayu Quri crafted gold necklaces, amulets, and bracelets of remarkable Inca design. Family legend had it that the amulet, which Mattie wore around her neck, was a gift of love from Ch'uya to an ancestor of the Cucho family, who was a powerful female Inca shaman. The necklace was subsequently passed down for generations until it fell into the hands of Gage's mother, Maria.

Gage was quiet and deeply thoughtful. This was a different side of Gage. He allowed Mattie to take his hand in hers. She ran her fingers gently along his.

In the silence of the night, Jack heard the surrender in his father's voice, the deep worry over a problem that might not be solvable. He had never seen or heard his father like this.

"We'll find another way," Gage said in a low voice. "No matter what you do, you never trade the past." He was steadfast. Mattie knew it by his manner. She knew that she would never convince him otherwise. They sat at the table staring at the pile of bills and the adding machine tape in silence.

Leaning against the wall in the hallway, Jack listened. He was motionless as his parents' conversation stopped. It was so quiet in the still of the night that Jack could hear the hiss of the air. He walked past his own room down the hallway and stopped at the closed door of Natalie's bedroom, entered and shut the door silently behind him.

Natalie was asleep. Next to her bed, chemicals illuminated by the shimmering moonlight dripped out of a translucent bag into her arm. This drip every three seconds kept her alive. Jack tiptoed across the room. He moved the wicker chair next to her bed and sat. He watched his sister lit by the cool moonlight. Her breathing was deep. He laid his head on Natalie's bed, only inches from her fingertips, stared out the window at the stars, which sparkled over New York City, and closed his eyes.

CHAPTER 23

DESTINY'S WHITE FINGER

Slumped in the wicker chair, Jack awoke in Natalie's room. The sun was shining in through her bedroom window. Jack moved the chair back into the corner and quietly tiptoed out of the room. As he neared the door, Natalie called out.

"Thanks for keeping me company."

"You were awake?" Surprised, Jack turned around.

"Off and on." Natalie's voice was groggy.

"You okay?"

"Better than … we're going on a picnic," Natalie smiled.

Jack walked over to the bed, leaned over and gave Natalie a kiss on the forehead, then left.

Walking down the hallway, Jack passed his parents' bedroom. Their door was closed. Jack tiptoed passed their room and entered his bedroom. He closed the door silently. With his clothes on, he collapsed on top of his bed, closed his eyes, and dropped instantly off to sleep.

Suddenly, there was a loud knock on the door. The door opened. Gage poked his head into the room.

"Jack, we're leaving in fifteen minutes." Gage said as he left the door cracked open slightly and began to walk away.

"I'll be ready." Jack answered. The door eased open and Gage stuck his head back in the room.

"I'm looking forward to all of us being together. It's been a long time." Gage looked at his son and cracked a faint smile.

"Me, too," Jack said.

Gage nodded, turned and walked down the hallway.

The sun shone brightly over the Catskill Mountains. The trees were bright green. The sky was deep blue. A white van curved its way through the mountains. Gage drove, Jack sat in the passenger seat, while Mattie tended to Natalie in the backseat. Classical music filled the van. It fit the scenery. With her near-bald head bundled under a ball cap, Natalie drank in the mountain scenery. Out the window, she saw the bridges of the Shawangunk Kill River, and the towns of Crawford, Gardiner, and Shawangunk nestled into the Shawangunk Ridge. Natalie was at home. Her entire being was at peace.

After winding through the Catskills, Gage followed a narrow paved road to a spectacular overlook on top of Slide Mountain. He stopped the car. Together, the Tott family unloaded the van on the perfect picnic spot overlooking the Catskills. They picnicked on a blanket spread out on the pastoral mountainside. They talked, as they ate. Natalie lay on a futon, as Gage sat next to her. It was rare moment in time, and they all knew it.

"You know, we should do this more often," Gage said.

"When you and Jack find the time." Natalie poked her father's arm. "And you're not practicing or you're not thinking about your next performance or flying to Europe or lecturing."

"I get the picture. I get it." Gage said acquiescing.

Jack stared at Natalie. "You are the only one who could get away with that," Jack said. "Not even Mom could." Gage noted Jack's comment with a raised eyebrow.

"I often want to get away, it's just difficult." Gage defended himself, while he gingerly spread a piece of brie over a slice of French bread.

"I wasn't talking about getting away," Jack countered.

Gage spread the brie methodically over the bread. "I am often too critical. And I don't take criticism well. I know that about myself." He took a bite of the bread. "But I am working on it," he said matter-of-factly looking at Jack, then to the rest of the family.

Everyone was quiet.

"All right, so maybe I should be more PC, I guess that's how it is today, isn't it? I'll make more of an effort. Promise." They did not believe him. It was in their eyes.

"Just as long as you and Jack don't have to bicker before we do this again," said Natalie. "We are here because of what happened between you and Jack yesterday."

"Not so," Gage argued.

"So," Jack countered.

Gage was surprised at Natalie for dredging up yesterday's father-son conflict. He nodded his head so slightly, revealing little agreement, and surely not enough to lower his pride. "How does a fourteen year old girl become so wise?" Gage asked.

"When she has less time," Natalie answered matter-of-factly.

Silence hung in the mountain space all around them. In the serenity of the greenness and the spatial greatness of the mountains for a few sweet minutes, they forgot about Natalie's imminent death, so her comment stung like a slap in the face. It brought them instantly back to their life and her waning life. Gage and Mattie looked at each other. Mattie fought off the tears.

Natalie had no pretenses, as she spoke in a calm voice, "Why hide? I am dying. I accept it. I am wiser because leukemia has forced me to be. I will not be sorry for that, in a strange way I am grateful for it."

An intimacy flowed through the Tott family. They admired Natalie so. They felt humbled by her. Just then, Gage spotted a bright blue butterfly twenty feet away from the picnic blanket fluttering over some wild flowers.

"Look over there, it's a Karner Blue," Gage said as he pointed.

"They are endangered," Jack said in awe.

"Pine Bush is nearby," added Gage.

"What's Pine Bush?" Natalie asked innocently.

"Pine Bush is where the few surviving Blues nest and breed." Jack's tone was somber.

"How do you know that?" asked Mattie.

"I read an article published in *Nature Magazine*," Jack responded, "And I've hiked at Pine Bush, it's about thirty miles that way."

Jack pointed toward the south over the Catskill Mountains.

"I'm impressed," said Gage watching his son. That moment, Gage was proud of his son, and Jack felt it.

"When was the article published?" Gage asked.

"About five years ago, in the October issue," Jack said. "See there's a lot of things other than violin music that you don't know."

Gage bit his lip; he did not want another fight. Mattie looked a dart at Jack to head off any inciting comment. Jack got it. He looked over the mountainside.

"Seven years ago, there were so many Karner Blues," Jack said as he pointed. "I saw about three or four dozen Karner Blues right there. They were just standing on this patch of sand. Their wings were erect and closed. The undersides of their wings were pale blue with dark dots and orange spots. When I got closer to them, they all fluttered into the air. Their upper wings are a beautiful sky blue. They looked like white and blue clouds fluttering all around."

"Why would anyone kill them?" Natalie asked.

"People don't kill them, Nat, we destroy their habitat, and they have nowhere to go." Jack said.

"Daddy, why do you call me Butterfly?"

Understanding that this was not only an extremely rare moment for his family, but also that the words which he chose during the next two minutes would affect his daughter for the rest of her life, Gage took his time. Music had taught him that timing and playing the notes and musical phrases with the perfect execution brought out the greatness of a musical score.

"A butterfly is born a caterpillar. The threads of its cocoon have the strongest tensile strength known to man, but one day this plodding earthbound creature miraculously breaks through millions of strong silk threads to emerge as this exquisite winged creature, which lights upon the world. The butterfly symbolizes the poetry of metamorphosis and evolution. It is the best that we become. That is why I call you butterfly."

Natalie's eyes filled with tears. Mattie was crying, and Jack was visibly moved; his cheeks were flushed. Gage leaned over, gave Natalie a tender kiss on her forehead, and without saying another word, he took his Stradivarius violin from the case and walked over to the edge of the mountain. He stood beneath a Great Black Oak tree. He raised the violin to his shoulder and played. It was an excerpt from Beethoven's *Pastoral*. The notes echoed through the mountains.

From the picnic blanket, Jack, Mattie, and Natalie listened and watched as Gage played. The moment was magic, the first in many years for the Tott family.

"Why don't you go over there?" Mattie said leaning toward her son hoping to heal the rift between father and son.

Jack stood up and walked quietly over to his father, who was playing under the enormous tree. Jack stood several feet behind his father, so he would not interfere with his playing or distract him from his musical space. When Gage finished, Jack approached. They stood under the Great Black Oak. They looked out over the magnificent valley. Gage held up his million-dollar Stradivarius violin.

"One day this will be yours," Gage said to his son. He waited, but Jack was silent.

"Dad, I am very grateful for everything that you have done for me, but I don't want any pressure."

"I'm not pressuring you," Gage quickly retorted.

"You are."

"Jacob, you have a rare talent. Don't take it for granted."

"I don't. It is just that you and I see music differently."

"What does that mean? I honestly do not understand. I taught you how to play. I gave you the love of classical music." Gage struggled to understand.

Jack looked into the iris of his father's blue eyes, "You gave me a love of music. You showed me how to put passion into the discipline. But Classical music is not a part of me, like it is you."

"You're better than I was at your age!" Gage said.

"It is not about being better!"

Gage stepped back, and took a slow breath. They looked at one another in silence. Gage struggled to keep himself under control.

"Okay, Jack. Then, what do you want?"

"I want to be connected to people with my music."

"You don't feel connected, when you're playing the violin?" said Gage in disbelief.

"No." Jack's answer was like a steel door slamming shut.

"Malarkey!" Gage screamed in anger and despair. He could not believe what he was hearing. "I've watched you when you performed solo for thousands of people!"

"I feel passion, but not connection," Jack spoke slowly. He was deliberate, as if he was watching himself play before two thousand people who anticipated every note. He was controlled and methodical. He wanted his father to understand what he was feeling, what was in his plans, but Gage was too emotional and filled with disbelief.

"Violin is too singular, it is too isolated."

"Too singular? Goddamn it!" With his toe, Gage kicked a small stone across a patch of dirt and rocks, where it disappeared into some weeds and brush. It was like denying himself, his own connection to music. His own son, a world class concert violinist at twenty-five years old, was renouncing not just this classical music tradition, but it was as if he was also rejecting the time and love that Gage had painstakingly devoted to his son for over twenty years.

From the picnic blanket, Mattie watched her husband and her son drawing up sides, preparing for battle. It made her anxious, and helpless.

"When I play violin I feel …" Jack searched for the correct words. Gage waited, hoping that Jack would say something positive that he could build on.

"I feel stiff and alone," Jack continued.

"Enough!" Gage takes two steps backwards away from Jack. "What's happened to you?"

Jack saw that his father was close to the edge, but Jack would not stop.

"Look, when I play at the Club for 200 people, I feel more connected to the world than if I was playing violin for two thousand people sitting breathless in Carnegie Hall!"

"You think you are going to make a living out of experimental music?" Gage was frustrated and enraged.

"Do you remember for my thirteenth birthday, you took me to Machu Picchu and we sat on that stone wall and played the pan flutes together?" Jack asked with hope sparkling in his eyes.

"I remember it well," Gage answered.

"That music made a deep imprint on me. The music that I compose and play at the club grew out of that magical experience. Ironic, isn't it? You handed me the zampoña. You introduced me to a music that would cause me to question my commitment to being a classical violinist."

Gage was stunned. The silence of the mountain filled the air. Only the wind rustling the leaves of the Great Black Oak said anything. After a few reflective moments, Gage turned to his son. "Perhaps I was wrong, maybe I should have come and heard you play."

"You should have." Jack was unflinching.

"I will make you a promise. I will come and hear you play at the club, but I want you to keep your heart and mind open about violin. Don't block it out completely."

Jack was not sure if his father had heard anything he had said. The two men just stared at each other. Then, resolute Jack said, "I am going to do what I have to do."

Gage sighed long. It was a breath of frustration. "Listen to me, Jack. I know that you love this music. But you also have a life-changing opportunity here as a guest concert violinist with the New York Philharmonic, for Christ sakes. If you don't take it, I guarantee you that it will blow away with the wind."

"Why can't you hear me? Why can't you accept me?" Jack's tone was calm, as if he was begging.

"I am not asking you to give up your music, I am merely asking you not to give up the violin."

Jack was silent. He felt that his father was manipulating him. He knew that his father was good at that. Always getting what he wanted, but this time Jack was not going to relent. Neither spoke for nearly sixty long seconds, as they looked out over the Catskills. The wind blew through the leaves on the sprawling branches of the Great Black Oak that towered above the two men. Father and son, both artists, listened to the music composed by the rustling leaves. It was a moment that Gage and Jacob shared with total unspoken understanding. Gage turned to his only son with longing in his eyes, pleading in his voice.

"Would you play one song for me?"

The shared moment had passed. Jack considered for many seconds. He looked out over the grand space of the valley below them. He thought long before he looked into his father's eyes.

"*The Lark Ascending*?" Gage begged his son one more time. "I love how you play it." He held out the violin toward Jack, but Jack would not even look at the Stradivarius. "Please," Gage said one last time.

The silence between them thickened, as Jack took his time.

"No. You always ask me to play just one more song, one more concert, one more … one more. It stops now. No." Jack said. Nothing would change his mind, and Gage now angry and sad knew it.

"Jacob, do you think I was always sure? That there was some voice whispering in my ear?" he asked humbly. "If I have learned anything, it is that life is uncertain, especially now. I have known that for a long, long time. What is precious about life is not tomorrow or next week or five years from now, it is about this moment. It is the love and commitment that we make in this moment."

Gage's meek tone surprised Jack, since he had never heard his father quite like this before. Jack still nevertheless tried to defend himself. "That's what happens when I play at the club," he said.

"You're not understanding, Jacob, you're not listening," Gage spoke softly to his son. His anger was gone. "I've played solo at the Pyramids, for the Pope, and in Germany when they tore down the Berlin Wall, but those were rare events. Most of the time, we just fumble along, hoping that we are making the right decisions."

"I must be a terrible disappointment to you," said Jack.

"In some ways, you are, but in some ways it is my fault because I think that I really don't know you as I should, and that bothers me the most. If I said that I was sorry, I would not know even what I was sorry for. So I don't know where to begin."

Gage's eyes began to tear. He tried to hide his tears, but could not.

"I am older. I should be thinking about retiring, or writing a book, or traveling around the world with your mother, who has been waiting every week for years for me to come home after concerts, trips abroad and social engagements," Gage was somber. "But instead of a secure happy end to my life, which I have worked so hard for, I find myself frightened and insecure. The entire planet is crumbling all around us, and we are helpless to stop it. I am losing my son to a music that is a contributor to the downfall of classical traditions, which, I believe, reflects the deterioration of our society. I am losing my daughter to leukemia. She will probably die before I do. And, I can't do anything to stop any of it." Gage stared out over the mountains. Silence weighed the air down between them.

"Please, I need to be alone for a few minutes." He turned away from Jack.

Awkwardly, Jack walked back to the picnic blanket wondering if he should have said anything at all to his father to ease his disappointment. He looked over at his father standing alone beneath the Great Black Oak with his Stradivarius violin dangling loosely by his side. Lightning struck on a mountain far away. Gage watched it. A storm was quickly approaching. An eerie still silence hung in the air. There was a loud, quick crackle. The air compressed all around Gage, Jack, Mattie and Natalie's bodies. A great wind slapped against Gage's skin. The air above his head split. Instantly, there was a blinding flash of light. A great blue-white finger of lightning reached down through the blue sky and impaled Gage like a spike. The thunder ripped through the mountains shaking the Great Black Oak to its core. Gage Tott's Stradivarius violin was hurled fifty feet through the air, as if the hand of destiny had reached down and cast it violently away from him. The Great Black Oak split in two, right down the middle.

"No!" Jack screamed and he heard it echo through the darkened mountains.

CHAPTER 24

A LUCID DREAM

It was a bright sunny day. The sky was blue, and there were birds chirping in the trees. A slight wind blew through the leaves. In every way, it was the perfect day, except that this day Jacob "Jack" Tott was burying his father. On the pea-green lawn, hundreds of mourners gathered around Gage Tott's casket. Loren Fazcel, the conductor of the New York Philharmonic, members of the orchestra and friends stood solemnly with folded hands staring at the bronze casket, which glistened in the sunlight, as the minister prayed. Jack held his mother's hand, while Natalie sat next to them in a wheelchair. Jack had his other hand around her shoulder. The ceremony ended and everyone walked solemnly to their cars.

In Manhattan's Potter Building in the Tott family home, Jack and his mother Mattie sat stunned, somber and emotionally exhausted at the kitchen table. The sun had long since set. Dishes, coffee cups and saucers, and plates of partially eaten food were piled high in the sink and covered every inch of counter space in the kitchen. The mourners had left. The condolences were over. The tears had stopped for the moment.

"He didn't have a life insurance policy," said Mattie. "I don't know what we're going to do."

"We're going to sell the Stradivarius," responded Jack.

Mattie was wild with disbelief.

"No!" Mattie screamed. "Your grandfather gave him that violin, and his father gave it to him. That violin's staying in this family!"

Jack was calm, as he spoke to his mother. "On the mountain, Dad told me that one day, it was mine. So, now I'm claiming it."

"Jack, you listen to me. You are <u>not</u> selling it!"

"We need the money," he countered.

"It makes it easier to turn your back on classical music, doesn't it?"

"That's a cheap shot, mother."

"Call it what you want, but it's the truth." she stared at him. "Your father's not here, so who's going to stop you?"

A silence filled the room. Then Jack spoke with no inflection in his voice. He wanted his mother to understand what he was saying was lucid and rational, clouded with no emotion, only fact. "If we keep the Strad, Nat dies. Fate has made the decision for us."

Mattie could not even look at her son. A sad and heavy resolve hung in the air, as Jack stood up. He kissed his mother on the cheek and left the kitchen. With tears running down her cheeks, Mattie sat alone clutching the gold sun amulet, which hung from her neck.

Jack walked into his room. He took Peekaboo out of the cage. The green Amazon parrot immediately started talking. "Peekaboo, Peekaboo, hello. What are you doing?"

Peekaboo walked up Jack's arm.

"Am I doing the right thing, Peek?"

"Right thing, right thing!" responded Peekaboo as he walked up and down Jack's arm and shoulder.

"I sure hope so," said Jack. His voice was somber and shaded with doubt. He walked over to his dresser, where a violin case lay covered by the soft warm light from a nearby Stiffel lamp. He opened the case, inside was his father's Stradivarius violin. Gently, he lifted the centuries old violin into his trembling hands. He turned it over in his hands examining it carefully; he looked closely at the burnt violin bridge. Tears overflowed in Jack's eyes and streaked his cheeks down to the corners of his mouth. He stood alone, humbled and confused, holding the Stradivarius violin, while his mind conjured up images of playing violin with his father, watching his father perform in concert before thousands of people, and their final afternoon on Slide Mountain under the Great Black Oak tree. Jack laid the violin tenderly down on the dresser, just beneath the lamp next to its red satin-lined case. He turned the lamp off and walked to his bed. Moonlight shone in through the window illuminating the room. Jack rolled back his bed covers, removed his shoes and his clothes and lay down. He grabbed a handful of seeds from a bowl near the end table, and held out his open palm. While Peekaboo pecked at the seeds, Jack lay in bed staring at the Stradivarius violin illuminated by the soft moonlight. Many minutes passed, until Jack's eyes slowly closed and he nodded off.

The seeds were all eaten; Jack was asleep. Peekaboo flew across the room into his cage, where he landed on his perch. He blurted out into the silence of the moonlit room.

"Peekaboo, Peekaboo. What are you doing? The sky is falling!"

There was no answer. After a few whistles and clicks, Peekaboo settled down on his perch for the night. In bed, Jack did not budge. Hours passed when Jack's eyes began to move back and forth beneath his eyelids, as he tossed. He was in R.E.M. sleep. Jack dreamt.

It was a lucid dream, unlike any that Jack had ever dreamt in his life. He was inside and outside of his dream simultaneously, walking through a maze of uneven angled and contorted walls. Jack could feel the room. It was like a presence within him. When he turned his head ever so slightly, his head spun like vertigo. His dizziness blended in with the uneven angled walls and sharp corners. Jack played with it, surrendered himself into it. The corridor transformed into a brilliant white floating space that had no boundaries. Everything in the room floated in the white space.

In the white space were enormous shapes and holographic images varying in height from ten feet to fifty feet. Some shapes aligned on the left, others on the right, which was itself very disorienting, since the white space had no walls, no ceiling, and no floor. On the right, a woman dressed in a colorful robe and gold jewelry faced Jack, but she did not acknowledge him. Near her was a great tree over fifty feet high. It towered above Jack. The branches sprawled out in every direction into the white space. There were thousands of bright-veined, green leaves and hundreds of colorful balls and geometric, colored boxes, which hung from the branches. Between the woman and the tree was a deep turquoise blue lake. Jack walked to the lake's edge. He put his foot into the turquoise blue water and saw an aquamarine translucence. High above the lake, suspended in the white room, were great white cumulous clouds, an evening Star, and the crescent Moon. Just to the right of the lake was a huge female Jaguar. Snarling and growling, the Great Jaguar eyed Jack. The cat's red eyes glowed and tracked Jack he walked around the white space. Jack was cautious, but strangely, he was not afraid. This was no nightmare.

Opposite the woman stood a man, dressed in a colorful robe made of the finest Alpaca wool. A gold Inca necklace hung from his neck.

To the left of the man floating in the white space were seven brilliant stars. Jack knew that these were the stars of the Pleiades, the Nuchu Verano also called the stars of the Summer, above which was a globe with an azure blue sky and snow-capped mountains with a blue river flowing from them, and then disappearing as far as Jack could see into the horizon of the white space.

Above the great globe shined a rainbow, which arched halfway around the world. Jack walked through the rainbow. He could feel the colors. As Jack passed through it, a great bluish-white lightning bolt struck just to the left of his ear; it startled him. Still in the dream, he flinched in his bed.

Jack moved deeper into his lucid dream. He tilted his head up toward the brilliant light that sparkled in the upper regions of the white space. It was a large oval; it radiated golden light everywhere. He started to come out of his dream, but tilted his head ever so slightly to get the dizzy sixth sense feel back. He noticed a cross of stars above the golden oval. Jack started to loose his balance. He felt like a skydiver freefalling. As he turned, he watched the shapes and worlds all around him. At the grounded bottom of the whiteness, he saw a series of crosshatched earthen vines intersecting at perpendiculars. It was world of earth, a maze of twisted vines with knots.

Aloud, he cried out in bed, "Maze! Life maze!"

Suddenly, there was ringing. It grew out of the white space. The ring got increasingly louder. Jack's dizziness faded. He tried to get it back by titling his head, but it was gone. The ringing continued, louder, louder.

In his bedroom, the sun's morning light cut across the bed and shone in Jack's eyes. From beneath his closed eyelids, the sunlight glared yellow and orange. The telephone next to his bed stand was ringing. Disoriented, Jack answered it.

"Hello?" Jack answered in a deep groggy voice.

"I understand that you're selling a Stradivarius violin." A man with a mature voice said.

"Ah, yes," Jack said trying to wake up. "Who is this?"

"My name is Murland."

"How did you hear about the Stradivarius?"

"A friend told me."

"Who?" Jack asked sitting up in bed.

"Your father."

Jack was silent.

"I offered to buy it from him several times. Do you want to sell it?"

Still in his grog voice, Jack mumbled as he struggled to think clearly. "I was going to a broker in Manhattan later today."

"I understand," the calm deep voice responded. "Go to a broker, but bring the violin and come and see me first. If you don't like what I offer you, take it to a broker. I'll even recommend one. J.P. Stevens on 57th Street is one of the best. I will call him for you."

"What did you say your name is?"

"Murland."

Jack swings his legs over the edge of the bed, and gets up. He walks over to Peekaboo's cage and opens the door. Peekaboo climbs out on Jack's arm, as Jack talks to the stranger. "How did you know my father?" Jack asks scratching Peekaboo's head with his finger.

"We met many years ago when you were a little boy of three years old."

"Dad never mentioned you," Jack countered.

"I am sure there were many relationships that he had which you don't know about, just as you have relationships with people that he didn't know about."

Jack paused thinking about what Murland had just said.

"Jack, this is in your interest, Natalie's and your mother's. Your father would have wanted to sell the Stradivarius to me," Murland said calmly. "It is a rare instrument with an important family history, and I am a collector of rarities. I will give you far more than the current market value, and you are under no obligation to sell it to me. Just come by, let's talk and I will make you an offer that you won't believe."

Jack thought for a minute, and then placed Peekaboo back in the cage on his perch. "Okay," Jack said.

"Good. Let me give you the address," the old voice said.

Jack fumbled for a pen and paper.

"156 Stanton Street. It is in the Lower East Side. You know where it is?"

"I know the Lower East Side. What time?"

"Anytime, I'm always here. Just come by and bring the violin."

"Okay."

"Good-bye, Jacob. I shall see you soon."

"Good-bye."

Jack stood in his room looking out the window, thinking. Jack was keenly aware that his father knew so many people.

Jack did not tell his mother about taking the Stradivarius to Murland. She would never understand. She did not want to sell it. She would fight him, maybe even try to physically prevent him from leaving; besides, she was under far too much stress since Gage's death. So Jack left a note for his mother on the living room lamp table and departed before she awoke. The note read: *"Got a call this morning from a buyer interested in the Strad. Will be back soon. Love, Jack."*

CHAPTER 25

MURLAND

It was nearly ten o'clock in the morning and cloudy. Sitting in the backseat of a taxicab, Jack had a large suitcase laying on the seat next to him. His hand rested upon the suitcase. He was not about to be driven to an unknown location by a total stranger, locked in a backseat clutching a million dollar Stradivarius violin, so he cocooned the Stradivarius in an ordinary suitcase. In his other hand were the directions scribbled on a paper. He stared at the suitcase imagining the Stradivarius nestled inside. He saw his father cradling the violin, sweat running down his cheeks, as the master violinist closed his eyes and wrinkled his forehead playing before a spellbound crowd at Carnegie Hall, then Jack glanced out the taxi window. His eyes caught a New York Yankees banner hanging from a light pole. He stared at the banner as the cab passed by. His mind reached back to make any sense of what was currently unfolding.

Outside Yankee Stadium banners were flying everywhere. Jack looked up at the large blue letters *YANKEE STADIUM* above the entrance. He and his father walked with thousands of fans through the turnstiles. Vendors combed the crowds with flats stuffed with Yankee and Mets' pennants, ball caps, souvenir programs, baseballs, scorebooks, and little wooden bats engraved with the Yankee logo.

It was a cool brisk October day, game one in the 2000 Subway Series, the Yankees versus the Mets; it was a day with his father that Jack would never forget.

His Dad had gotten field boxes from a patron of the New York Philharmonic, first-base side, right behind the Yankee dugout, section 33. They were so close that Jack remarked to his father that he could see the players flex their fingers around the bat handle at home plate.

"I noticed that too. These are great seats, aren't they?" his Dad commented. "How about a hot dog?"

"I'll buy," Jack said.

"I got the dogs, you get the beer," Gage said.

Jack smiled and flagged down the beer vendor. Jack was never happier, watching the Yankees at the World Series eating a hot dog and drinking beer with his Dad. It was the bottom of the sixth when David Justice blasted a two-run double to give the Yankees the lead. Jack had never heard nor seen his father yell like this, so boisterous, so free. He loved it. His father plopped down in his seat and looked at Jack with a great broad smile on his face.

"When are you going to bring this girl Mary over, so we can meet her?"

"We're not seeing each other any more." Jack said.

"Why not?"

"She didn't like that I was married to my music."

"Isn't that just like a woman," Jack's father said "Wants you to be the best, but wants you to be home for dinner every night." Gage grinned and raised his beer and toasted Jack, it was a male bonding moment, a cliché. Both Jack and his father knew it, but they loved it anyway. Jack remembered every facial expression, every gesture, every word.

"Don't tell your mother that I said that," Gage said as he grinned and cocked his head, as if they were sealing a forever father-son secret. No matter how small it was, Jack didn't care, it was intimate.

It wasn't until the bottom of the 12th that the Yankees won the game with a dramatic two-run single off Mets pitcher Turk Wendell. The Yankees won 4-3 in the longest game ever played in World Series history, four hours and fifty-one minutes. It was one of the greatest times of Jack and his father's life.

As the taxi turned a corner in SoHo onto Stanton Street, Jack was still staring out the taxicab window. The taxi drove halfway down the street and stopped.

"Stanton Street. That'll be twelve forty-five," said the cabbie, as he turned around toward Jack.

Jack pulled a ten and a five-dollar bill from his pocket and handed it to the cabbie. He got out of the cab with the large suitcase, and the taxi drove off.

Jack scanned the city block. It was a mix of brownstones, shops and old office buildings. On the corner were a deli and a café. The entrance to 156 Stanton Street was down a flight of steps, seven steps to be exact. Jack counted every one, as he descended them lugging the suitcase. He stopped at the front door where chiseled gargoyles and coiled snakes scowled at any guest who would enter. Jack wondered if this was a good idea. After all, he did not know the stranger attached to the old voice in the phone. Here standing outside he was safe, holding onto a suitcase that cocooned a rare violin built centuries before in Old Europe by a master artisan whose trade had been forgotten a long time ago. Jack thought, what happens when I walk inside? He needed the money for Natalie, so he needed to sell the Stradivarius, but could he protect it once inside? What is beyond that door? Jack looked up at the three-story building. An ominous feeling came over him. He looked at the gargoyles with their gnashing teeth and the cornerstones decorated with sculpted granite serpents. It was an old building that conjured up feelings of classical history and magic.

Jack knocked twice on the heavy, dark wooden door. He waited. There was no response. Jack knocked again, only louder. Maybe, the man inside did not hear, or he was in the back somewhere. There still was no answer. Jack waited for nearly two minutes, and then knocked loudly for the last time. His knock was so loud that it echoed on Stanton Street. He looked up to the street to see if anyone was watching. He waited at the door. Still no answer.

Disheartened, Jack walked slowly up the stone steps carrying the suitcase. As he placed his weight upon each foot on each step, he felt the ancient past, and the deep earth flowing through the bottoms of his feet upward as it coursed up through his body. He did not understand what he was feeling, the electrical charge that surged through the muscles of his entire body. He was anxious. What was happening to him, he thought? He stared at the seven steps, which he just arduously climbed. The deep grey stones of granite that were chiseled and shaded were imprinted with the energy and wisdom of ancient worlds and the memories of times and people long past. Jack felt it in his being. It was alive in his muscles. Suddenly, he heard the front door lock click loudly. His muscles were still fluttering with high electrical charges. Frightened, he walked hurriedly down the steps with the Stradivarius in the suitcase, gripped the doorknob and opened it. The door opened quietly. Jack entered clutching the suitcase, cradling it, protecting it like a parent protecting an infant from unknown forces. As he closed the door, a shiny brass bell hanging on the top of the doorframe tinkled. The instant that it rang, every electrical surge that was overtaking Jack's body ceased. The sudden cessation of the vibrating energy at the exact moment of the tinkling bell startled him. He entered the strange room.

The shop ebbed with life from the past. Ancient artifacts hung from the walls. There were exotic masks and weapons from different tribes around the world. They were from Africa, Indonesia, South America, North America, the Far and Middle East, and Russia; some were masks made by the Eskimos. There were colorful costumes from strange cultures. Odd-shaped musical instruments lay on tables and hung from the ceiling.

On one wall hung numerous star charts of the galaxies and the universe. Early telescopes and sextants lay about on the tables, along with drawings by Leonardo da Vinci, and sea charts, which mapped the world. Old books were stacked up in the wood and glass bookcases. Ancient scrolls, rolled up and stained brown with age, were piled haphazardly atop a table. There were rare gems, trilobites and other fossils, and ancient tools of medicine and surgery. There were birds in cages—canaries, finches, a dodo bird, a blue-thighed lory, and a Haast eagle.

Jack knew from his readings in *Nature* magazine and a few lectures he had attended at Columbia University that the dodo, blue-thighed lory and Haast eagle were extinct. He was awed.

"Did you want to buy something?" The enthusiastic, childlike voice seemed to come out of the air from nowhere. Jack turned around looking for someone. An old man with white hair and a white beard stood before Jack. His eyes twinkled. He was dressed in a conservative three-piece suit. A watch fob dangled from his wrinkle-free vest pocket. It was the white-haired man, who had come to see Jack play in the EarthRock Café the night he was late to arrive at Carnegie Hall.

"You?" Jack blurted out in surprise.

"Who else?" The old man said exuberantly. "Welcome." He waved his hand around the room and smiled enthusiastically, like a boy showing off his exotic and valuable trading card collection.

"I thought you were an agent?"

"Me?" the old man chuckled, amused by Jack. "Hardly."

"What were you doing at the club?"

"Destiny." The man raised his eyebrows as if he knew something, which Jack did not know.

As a master musician, Jack knew how to interpret tone. Clearly, this would be no ordinary encounter. The Old Man took down an exotic parrot.

"See this bird?" The old man asked.

"Yes." Jack answered, eyeing the beautiful bird.

"Lorius tibialis. It is a blue-thighed Lory. They're extinct, you know!" The old man proclaimed exuberantly. "In fact, this is the last one! Like me!"

"How can you have an extinct bird?" Jack asked.

"With great care! Marvelous, isn't it? And extinct!" Murland chuckled with whimsy.

Jack was not amused. He looked around the strange room evaluating everything. "I think there's some mistake here."

"Living is never a mistake," replied the old man matter-of-factly.

Confused, Jack asked, "Did you call me?"

"Who did you come to see?" asked the old man playfully.

"Mr. Murland," replied Jack.

The old man raised his arms and smiled broadly. Jack's jaw dropped. He could not believe it.

"You sounded so different on the phone."

"You mean like this," Murland changed his voice to a deep formal tone. "My name is Murland." He sounded like a funeral parlor director, or a church usher.

"Just a ploy to get you in here!" Murland said in his whimsical manner.

Jack clutched the suitcase with the Stradivarius tightly, and took a step backwards.

"You don't think I am who I say I am. Wait, wait. I have a card, someplace."

Murland handed the Lory to Jack, who was taken aback by the old man's childlike friendliness. The bird climbed around on Jack's shoulder.

"He likes you! See?" Murland exclaimed, as he dug through the piles of scrolls, books, and ancient artifacts.

"Everything is someplace, isn't it? Therefore, it must be here. Yes." Finally, under a disheveled pile of papers, he found the card.

"Here it is!" Murland held up the card, pleased with himself. He handed the card to Jack.

Jack examined it checking both sides, but there was nothing on it.

"It's blank."

"Let me see." Murland said completely baffled. As Jack handed Murland the card, the Lory walked down Jack's arm to witness the exchange. Murland took the card, and looked at both sides.

"Yes, so it is!" Murland said chuckling to himself. "I told you that I was quite old. It's faded!"

Jack handed the Lory back to Murland and headed for the door clutching the Stradivarius. "That's it. I'm outta here." Jack said with finality in his voice.

"I want to purchase your Stradivarius!" Murland yelled out to Jack as he moved swiftly toward the front door.

Jack stopped and walked back toward Murland, who put the Lory back on Jack's shoulder.

"May I see the violin, please?"

Jack opened the suitcase cocooning the Stradivarius violin case. He carefully lifted the Stradivarius case out and opened it. Murland's eyes filled with wonder as stared down at the three hundred year old violin.

"What happened to the bridge?" he asked Jack, touching the charred Stradivarius' bridge.

"Lightning struck and killed my father, while he was holding the violin."

"I am sorry," Murland's voice was full of compassion.

Murland was respectful allowing Jack to make the first move. The etiquette impressed Jack and made him relax a little more with Murland. When he first opened the Stradivarius case and it lay exposed in the slightly shadowed light of this antiquity shop, Jack felt naked before this stranger Murland. Now he was more comfortable, as he gently lifted the Stradivarius out of its case and handed it to Murland, who handled it with reverence and awe. Murland turned the violin over in his hands, never taking his eyes off it. He ran his fingers gently along the strings; he felt the old deep-grained wood with his fingertips. Murland's eyes sparkled.

"Are you a musician?" Jack asked.

"Me? Oh, no!" Murland bounced back. "I just dabble!"

Without notice or warning, the Old Man's tone changed. He became serious, attentive only to the Stradivarius, as he raised it to his chin and played. As Murland played, tears welled up in Jack's eyes. Murland's playing was the sweetest music that Jack had heard since his father played on the mountain. After playing several minutes, Murland finished and handed Jack the violin.

"You play like my father," Jack's face was full of admiration for this odd man, and sadness for the hole in his life where his father used to be.

"Are you sure that you want to sell this?" Murland sounded a bit incredulous.

Jack took several seconds to think. "Yes," he answered resolutely.

Murland eyed the Stradivarius lovingly. "It is a magnificent instrument," he said, turning the violin over in his hands. As Murland became lost in the Stradivarius, Jack scanned the room. Hanging on the wall, he saw a large, bright oil-colored drawing on parchment. He stared at it. Etched at the bottom of the drawing was the name Juan de Santacruz Pachakuti Yamqui. The drawing was the dream, which Jack had the night before, but he could not remember the dream.

"Do you like that?" asked Murland.

"I feel like I've seen this before." Jack was baffled. He was having a déja vu experience and he did not understand it. This was something that he knew to be true and intimate to him, but he did not know how.

Murland studied Jack, who was engrossed in the drawing.

"Do you ever think that when you die," Murland speculated, "this life will become a dream, just like the dream you had last night or the night before?"

"No, I don't," Jack answered in an irritated tone. "Right now, all I am concerned about is this life."

"Me, too!" Murland answered playfully.

Jack turned to Murland. "What about the violin?"

"What about it?" Murland responded enthusiastically.

"Do you have enough money to buy it?"

"How much?"

"Three and a half million dollars," Jack said without hesitation.

"What kind of question is that?" answered Murland, like a child who could not understand why someone would even ask such a silly question. "Of course, I have it. It's only money!"

Murland reached into his pockets and pulled out wads of $1,000 bills. Jack's eyes bugged out, as hundreds of one thousand dollar bills fell to the floor. Murland dropped to the floor on his hands and knees and began scooping the bills up and stuffing them into his pockets.

"But I'm not going to give you money for the violin," Murland said matter-of-factly to Jack.

"You're not going to give me money?" Jack could not believe what he was hearing.

"No, that would be a waste—" Murland shook his head amused. "—for you."

"That's it. I'm outta here." Jack quickly stuffed the Stradivarius into the case, closed it, and tucked it beneath his arm. He grabbed the suitcase and walked swiftly to the front door.

Murland yelled, "Don't open the door!"

Jack opened the door. Outside was New York City, but it was miles below the shop! All around the open door floated white fluffy cumulus clouds. A wind swept through the shop and carried Jack out the door. Jack fell. He grabbed the doorknob and held on for his life. Dangling thousands of feet above New York City, he held onto the Stradivarius violin with his other hand.

"Oh, God!" Jack screamed for his life.

Papers, fossils, and artifacts flew out the open door in swirls of wind and plummeted toward the earth below. The exotic birds screeched and flew around; some flew out the open door disappearing into the blue sky. Gravity sucked everything out and down to New York City below. Jack dangled; he kicked his feet.

"Hang on! I'm coming!" Murland yelled to him over the sound of the roaring wind.

Holding onto the fastened down tables and chairs, Murland made his way slowly toward Jack. After fending off flying manuscripts, birds and ancient artifacts, Murland reached for Jack, who was gripping the doorknob for his life with one hand, and the Stradivarius with the other. Murland grabbed Jack's wrist tightly.

"Let go!" Murland yelled to Jack. With wide, white open eyes of fright, Jack looked at Murland. He was not about to let go of the doorknob.

"Let go!" Murland yelled again. Jack had to trust him. "You've got to let go!"

Finally, after several seconds that seemed like minutes, Jack let go of the doorknob. Murland held Jack's wrist tightly, as the young violinist swayed in the wind like a flag in a windstorm. With one yank, Murland jerked him back into the shop. The door slammed closed, and everything settled down. There was no wind, no sound, only silence. Jack gathered himself. He could hear his heart pounding in the silent room. Still clutching the Stradivarius, Jack pulled himself up off the floor.

Confused, Jack look quite shaken as he spoke in complete bewilderment to Murland, "What's going on here?"

"What do you want, Jack?" Murland took a step toward Jack and touched his forehead. Jack immediately calmed down. Murland patiently waited for Jack to catch his breath and compose himself.

"I want to get out of here!"

"No. What did you want when you came in here a few minutes ago?"

"I want to sell this violin." Jack said holding up the Stradivarius.

"No. That is your agenda. What is it that you want?"

Jack took time to think. "I want my sister to live."

"That is a most commendable goal. However, Natalie has her own destiny. If you are meant to change her life, it will happen."

Murland's words seeped deeply into Jack. "What do you want?" asked Murland one more time. "If you could accomplish one thing before you die, what would it be?"

Jack thought for a moment. "Quit trying to redirect my attention, like some magician doing a slight-of-hand trick. I came here to sell this violin."

"And sell it you will," Murland said with a calm reassuring voice.

Jack reflected. The room was silent. Murland saw the change in Jack's eyes. "I hear a different music in my head, music never heard before. It's rooted in the classical tradition, but is an organic and multi-ethnic fusion, a merging of cultures which have clashed for years over religion and politics. I see it so clearly as a great unifying force; it could bring nations together. The world needs it, needs what's behind it. That is what I want. I want to use my music to unify people at a critical point in human history. It is what I know, and what I can do."

"Good."

Murland walked around the table touching the music scrolls. He was pleased. "Jack, I can help you."

"Does that mean that you will buy the violin?" Jack asked anxiously.

"So to speak," replied Murland in a playful light manner.

"What do you mean?"

"I will purchase the violin with these." Murland said, as he produced three purple beans from his pocket. Each bean had a yellow corona around it. They glowed.

"Beans?" Jack blurted out. "What kind of beans are they?"

"Completely absurd, isn't it?" mused Murland. "These beans will give you what you need," Murland explained calmly, "and eventually what you desire."

"You want to give me beans for a three and a half million dollar Stradivarius violin that has been in my family for four generations!"

"Yes," responded Murland calmly, as if Jack was being offered the deal of a lifetime.

"You must think I'm crazy!"

"Crazy?" Murland had a mischievous look in his eyes. Jack saw it and it frightened him. "Now, crazy is a word that I love, but I don't have the faintest idea what it means," exclaimed Murland enthusiastically. "So, I wouldn't go around using that word in here!"

"Okay," Maybe this strange man really was crazy. The last thing that Jack wanted to do was piss him off.

"What about gold?" Murland egged Jack on. "Are you interested in gold?"

"You want to give me gold for the Stradivarius?" Jack said with a guarded tone.

"More gold than you could ever dream of!" Murland exclaimed waving his arms in a great arch, as if drawing in the air a gigantic world brimming with gold.

Jack stepped back. He scanned the room slowly taking in everything, the artifacts, the Leonardo da Vinci drawings, the Juan de Santacruz Pachakuti Yamqui
drawing on parchment, the ancient books and scrolls that laid about on the
tables, the gems, the exotic birds and fossils.

Murland waited for Jack. He knew Jack was trying to figure out if this eccentric old man was crazy or not.

Jack thought to himself. Who is this man? Is this a dream? Murland saw that
Jack was struggling to make a decision, so he removed the charred violin bridge
from the Stradivarius. He tossed it into the air right in front of Jack's eyes, where
it floated. Jack was stunned. He could not take his eyes off the hovering violin
bridge. As the bridge floated, it hummed in a beautiful harmony, reminiscent of
monks chanting. As the humming got louder, the violin bridge glowed with a
turquoise light that illuminated the room.

Murland raised his hands and addressed the floating violin bridge. His voice
echoed as if it was flowing through an ancient tunnel of time into the present of
the tiny magical room.

"Guide this one. Be his light. Be his music. By this instrument, the two songs
will become one."

The wooden bridge then slowly floated down to the table, and the turquoise
light faded. Murland matter-of-factly picked up the bridge from the Stradivarius
violin and handed it to Jack, who was speechless.

"The most profound truth is always unexpected," said Murland. "It usually
comes from the voice of a stranger. It has no country, no politics, and makes no
judgments. It is compassionate and wise. It lives in the whispers of every man's
heart."

He held the beans out for Jack to examine. Jack stared at the beans a long
time.

"Where these beans will take you is more than all the gold you could imagine." Murland urged Jack.

"I'm afraid," Jack said. "This is a three-and-a-half million dollar violin that has
been in my family for generations. Don't you think I should be nervous?"

"Yes. I would be—But I'm not because I'm me!" Murland exclaimed with
childlike whimsy.

Jack took a step backwards.

"Jack, listen and decide with your heart, not your head," Murland said calmly.

"What about Nat and my mother?"

"We fear what we don't know, especially after there has been so much tremendous loss." Murland said trying to reassure Jack. "So many people have lost so much, yet we must push through it with open hearts and courage."

"My father used to call me Jacob when he wanted my attention. Before he died, he said that he was afraid of how the world was changing, of losing my sister, of losing me to music that he detested."

"He loved you, Jack."

"I miss him. I wish he was here."

"We miss what we lose. It is a new world where we live. No one knows what's going to happen. It is frightening, but we face it with courage." Murland looked down at the beans in his hand.

Jack stared at the beans again. He was reluctant as he evaluated Murland's offer. How could he even consider such an irrational act?

"Jack, listen to your heart. Trust me, these beans will save Natalie, and do far more than you could ever imagine."

Jack could not take his eyes off the beans, yet they made him more nervous than he ever was at any performance in his entire life.

"Take them." Murland urged him again.

Jack was paralyzed. "Please, Jack, take them." Murland held the beans out. "This is the turning point of your life. Choose this path, or it will blow away in the wind."

"My father used those exact same words on the mountain that day." Jack was both shaken and stunned by Murland's choice of words. Murland did not respond, he merely stood there patiently, his hands motionless as they held the beans out before Jack's eyes.

Jack was still reluctant. Murland stared at Jack's pupils, black and hesitant.

"Your family has suffered great loss just as our world has. You are worried if Natalie will live or die; you are saddened that you and your father had not reconciled before his death; you worry about your mother; you worry about our world. If these things are to be healed, then you must take these beans and follow the path where they will lead you."

Murland extended the purple beans inches from Jack's eyes. Minutes passed as Jack considered the knowable consequences of his next move. It was so complicated, yet Murland made it seem so simple. Jack balked. His hands clutching the Stradivarius trembled.

"You want your music to be a force that brings diverse people and nations together, to be an umbilical cord nurturing man to his next evolutionary step. It will happen, but I will not lie to you. It will be the most difficult thing that you have done in your life, but it will be worth it. These beans are worth far more than you can ever imagine." Murland held the beans out.

Without saying a word, Jack gently picked the beans out of Murland's hand. Murland smiled and walked over to the wall. He peeled the Yamqui parchment drawing off the wall and waved his hand over it. The objects drawn on the flat piece of aged parchment lifted off the surface; they became three-dimensional and floated into the air. It was Jack's dream. A turquoise light radiated out from the drawing, and then the symbols flattened and returned to the paper. The turquoise light faded.

"You will need this," Murland handed the drawing to Jack, who was astonished.

"What for?"

"For the adventure of a millennium."

Murland took the Stradivarius violin from Jack's grasp and cradled it like a baby in his arms.

"Be sure," Murland said to Jack.

"Be sure of what?" Jack had no idea what Murland was talking about.

"Be sure," Murland said again, as he walked across the room. Slowly, he began to dissolve into the air. Jack yelled out.

"What should I be sure of?" Jack beckoned to Murland's ghost-like image.

There was nothing, but silence.

An ancient voice echoed through the room, "Be sure."

Just as Murland's voice faded, so did his image. He was gone, disappeared into the air. Stunned and unsure, Jack pocketed the beans, the diagram, and the violin bridge. Cautiously, he opened the door expecting anything, relieved that he was on the ground. The sky was dark and brooding. It was pouring, but Jack bolted outside into the pelting rain.

CHAPTER 26

PUSHED INTO A NEW WORLD

Waking up from his fall on the wet cavern floor, Jack began to stir. He sat up, held his aching head and looked around the cave. Slowly, he stood, taking in the cavern's beauty and its alluring danger. The cavern was an enormous tunnel, a passage of some kind over three hundred feet long and twenty-five feet wide. It was primitive. Fossils were imbedded in the wet, rocky walls. A layered white mist hung inches over the luminescent turquoise stream. A blue-green light glowed from beneath the water, but Jack could not make out the source of the iridescence. A ledge about eight inches wide and three feet above the water followed the stream, as it wound around the bend and disappeared from view. He looked at the ceiling hole from where he fell. A cone of light poured into the cave from the outside sky. Jack knew that he could not get out that way. After walking around and exploring his immediate surroundings, he stepped onto the ledge. He knew that he must follow the ledge; it was the only way out. The stream disappeared under hanging moss and jagged rocks at the tunnel's end. In the damp fossilized walls, he noticed hundreds of snake holes.

Jack slowly inched his way down the slippery ledge. In front of him, hundreds of matte-white bubbles broke the surface of the turquoise water. They reminded him of his high school chemistry class, when he made white bubbles by putting dry ice in a beaker of water. Jack stopped to watch the lusterless matte-white bubbles. Pop! Pop! Pop! He stooped down to get a closer look. Slowly, he saw hundreds of Trilobites surface and meet his gaze. The trilobites had bony furrowed backs, long antennae, and hundreds of sharp tiny teeth. Every tiny eye of every Trilobite stared at him.

"A welcoming committee. Nice." Jack said to himself and chuckled at his absurd, unknown fate.

Cautiously, Jack inched his way along the ledge, taking his eyes off the ledge every few steps to keep an eye on the Trilobites, who bobbed to the surface as they stalked him. Jack looked across the stream to the opposite wall, where ripples of light wavered across the cave wall. Something was moving there. He stopped. What was that? Jack wondered. Hundreds of pink-headed, snake-like creatures stuck their heads out of their holes to get a peek at Jack, who watched them, but he was more curious than afraid. They were Peekers and what they did was peek. The Peekers had long slender, bright pink necks; they looked almost like Flamingoes with red and yellow cat-like eyes. They watched every move that Jack made, as he inched his way along the slippery ledge. The cave pulsed with the popping of the Trilobites and the pigeon-like cooing made by the Peekers. It was a symphony of unusual sounds. Jack was fascinated. For a few brief moments, it transported him back to the sounds, which he and his band synthesized at the Earthrock Café. As he listened to the unique sounds and looked at the opposite wall, it occurred to him that there were probably just as many snake holes and Peekers on his side of the stream. Jack chuckled to himself more out of being in a predicament than being amused by these strange pink long-necked creatures. He looked down. Next to his leg was a bright pink Peeker staring up at him with its large oval, red and yellow cat eyes. It had a big grin across its long-beaked face. Motionless, the Peeker just stared.

"Do you talk?" Jack spoke to the Peeker, the same way that someone would talk to their dog or their cat, never expecting their pet to answer them back. Even Peekaboo, Jack's pet parrot, could only mimic. He suspected that this pink creature neither had the ability to talk back nor to understand him, but he thought why not. After all, there was nothing to lose, and he was all alone.

The Peeker just stared at Jack with a stupid smile on its face.

"I'm lost," Jack said. "You don't understand a word of what I am saying?"

Only the sounds of the popping bubbles and the Trilobites breaking the surface of the turquoise water filled the cave. The Peeker was silent. It simply stared and smiled.

"What am I doing?" Jack said, amusingly berating himself.

Carefully, Jack lifted his leg to step over the Peeker's neck. As Jack lifted his leg, the Peeker raised his long pink neck up between Jack's legs, just above his knees. With his beady red eyes opened wide, the Peeker never removed his stare from Jack's eyes. It was impossible for Jack to lift his leg over the Peeker's long and curvy pink neck. It was as if the Peeker was challenging him.

"Excuse me," Jack spoke now realizing that conversation was merely a futile exercise.

As expected, the Peeker said nothing and did nothing.

"I'd like to get by," Jack said, becoming irritated.

Suddenly, the Peeker sniggered. The Peeker opened its mouth revealing rows of razor sharp teeth. Jack screamed. Like a python, the Peeker wrapped its neck around Jack's ankle, stared directly into his terror-filled eyes and toppled him into the water. The Trilobites covered him. The Peeker chuckled as Jack was swept downstream. Swimming for his life, Jack bobbed up and down in the gurgling water under the weight of the Trilobites. He did everything he could to escape from them, chopped at them, tried to paddle past them, finally he dove under them through white-bubbled water and frog-legged his way through the turquoise water. From nowhere, dozens of curious bug-eyed fish called Curobites gathered all around Jack's head. They nibbled on his hair, at his fingers, and on the sparkly 24kt. gold amulet, dangling from his neck. Dozens of the Curobites gathered around the amulet fascinated by how it glittered in the light. The smaller Curobites were the most curious. Jack spotted a small door with a huge doorknob. He paddled down to it. He was running out of breath. There was a note attached to the door. Jack read it.

"Please ring bell and wait."

Jack pulled on the gold cord dangling next to the door. Nothing happened. He pulled the rope harder.

How long can I hold my breath! Panic clouded Jack's thoughts.

Frantic, Jack pounded on the door with his fist. He saw the Curobites getting closer. Even though he was convinced that he was on the verge of drowning, he thought that the Curobites were the most curious creatures he had ever seen. They knew that something was wrong. Jack was out of breath. The doorknob would not budge. The door would not open! Jack feared he would die like this. Instantly, the Curobites swarmed the fancy doorknob and nibbled at it. Click! The door opened, barely enough for Jack to squeeze through. Halfway through the door, Jack looked up. Light! He saw shimmering light at the surface. Frantically, Jack squeezed through the narrow opening, like a snake shedding its skin on the edge of a rock. Once free from the door, Jack kicked his feet wildly and swam to the surface.

A great green forest surrounded a small tranquil lagoon. The sounds of birds echoed in the air. This was Eden. Suddenly, in the middle of the still lagoon, the water rippled. Jack broke the surface and made a huge sound, as he gulped a great mouthful of air. He filled his lungs. Out of breath, he treaded water and tried to calm himself, as he took in his surroundings. He was enraptured with this new world. He heard exotic birds, saw a sky vibrant with color, tasted the freshness of sparkling deep turquoise water; the forest was lush and green. He spied the shore about one hundred yards away. Exhausted, Jack swam toward it. When he reached the beach, he crawled across the sand. The shiny black sand crystals were warm and tingly; the black grains tickled his hands. After pulling himself thirty feet across the black sand, he fell on his stomach where he laid on the beach trying to catch his breath. Above, a sun shined down on him. He had to squint. All around him, the black sand sparkled. Lying in the sand, Jack took a fist full of the black sand and sifted it through his fingers. As the black grains sparkled, little rainbows appeared in his open palm. Jack smiled.

"I'm in Oz," he said to himself.

Curious, he sat up, staring into the dense lush green forest that bordered the turquoise lagoon and the black sand beach. The jungle had an exotic air about it. It triggered images of ancient civilizations, which Jack had studied as a hobby. He was aware that this environment made him conscious of natural selection, the primal struggle to survive. Images of the dense tropical landscape similar to the jungle, which he and his father had traversed through when they traveled to Peru, flashed through mind. The images of Machu Picchu flickered in his head as he looked up and squinted at the bright sun. He looked down at the black sand, picked up a handful, and sifted the black grains repeatedly through his fingers as if unendingly overturning an hourglass. As he stared at the black sand trickling through his fingers, the rainbows arched across the palm of his hand. Behind the rainbows, the black grains sparkled all around with sunlight like stars shining against the deep blackness of the night sky. It reminded him of Machu Picchu at midnight when he and his father watched the millions of radiant stars of the Milky Way sparkling against the night sky. Jack became aware that this new unknown world aroused in his being a feeling of the ancients and the sacred.

CHAPTER 27

THE CAPTAIN AND THE
SCIENTIST

At McGuire Air Force Base, three U.S. Comanche military helicopters idled on the tarmac with their blades chopping the air. Fifteen Special Forces soldiers and Dr. Caitlin Bingham scrambled with all their gear into the choppers, five men into each chopper.

The number one helicopter sat on the tarmac with its blades cutting the air. The side of the chopper was painted with a striped Jaguar that had a tear falling from its threatening yellow eye. Underneath the proud cat was the inscription, "The Jaguar." Inside The Jaguar, the 1st Special Forces team waited in high-energy anticipation. Wearing a uniform with NASA insignia and a Special Forces helmet, Caitlin Bingham sat nervously next to Captain Riley Jordan. They had to yell over the sound of chopping helicopter blades.

"You know something about this?" shouted Captain Jordan.

"I don't know anything about this!" yelled Caitlin back above the din of the helicopter blades.

"I thought you were an astronomer who discovered a new planet and it's related to all of this," Captain Jordan responded with a confused tone.

"I study ancient civilizations and stars!" Caitlin yelled.

"Doctor, you know more than I do!" yelled Captain Jordan as he looked directly into Caitlin's eyes. "All I want is for you to let me know what's going on in your head, so I can make the right decisions and keep my men alive! Okay?" Caitlin thought carefully about his words. Captain Jordan wanted to be sure that she understood exactly what was expected of her. After several long seconds, Caitlin nodded. Captain Jordan relaxed and leaned back against the wall.

Captain William Tyler Jordan III was a graduate of West Point, a third generation lifer. Compared to his father and grandfather, he was the best, the smartest, the quickest, and the most apt military student and leader. He had graduated number one in his class, summa cum laude. Heading up this Special Forces team was his dream, and this was their first assignment. They had been training for an operation of this magnitude for years.

CHAPTER 28

ASSAULT IN THE SKY

High above Manhattan Island, three Comanche Helicopters climbed near the Giant Green Beanstalk. As each of the three helicopters neared the bottom of the cloud layer, the doors slid open. Inside, the Special Forces' soldiers sat lined up against the walls pumped and ready for action. In the first helicopter, *The Jaguar*, Caitlin's eyes were wide and her heart pounded, but her mind was sharp. Captain Jordan stood and adjusted his helmet and his headset. He looked at his men. Smiling, he studied each one, determined to protect each of the men under his command. Caitlin watched him. She was nervous; the palms of her hands were sweating.

A voice popped into Captain Jordan's headset, "Two minutes, Sir." It was the Comanche #1 pilot. The jump light in the helicopter changed from red to yellow.

"Thanks, Lieutenant." Captain Jordan answered. "Green Teams Two and Three, this is Green Team One. Get ready. Deployment is in two minutes," said Captain Jordan into his headset.

The two Sergeants commanding the other two choppers confirmed.

"Green Team Two, ready, sir!" answered Sergeant Hicks.

"Green Team Three, ready, sir!" answered Sergeant Stone.

Standing in the open door of "The Jaguar," Captain Jordon spoke into his headset. "Green Teams, hook-up, one minute to go." The soldiers in Captain Jordan's helicopter stood up and began preparing their rope belays. Caitlin stood up. Captain Jordan walked over and helped her tighten and adjust her ropes. In the headsets, Sergeant Hicks and Sergeant Stone gave commands to their men.

"One minute! Hook up!" Sergeant Hicks yelled to his men over the noise of the helicopter blades.

His men looked up at the jump indicator light in their chopper. It was yellow. In Comanche helicopter #3, Sergeant Stone alerted his men, "Hook up! One minute to jump!" All of his men adjusted their ropes and gear.

Beanstalk branches filled the deep blue sky. The three Comanche helicopters climbed and surrounded the Giant Beanstalk, like birds who spiraled upward around a tall tree to reach their nest. Inside each open helicopter door, the soldiers waited nervously.

The Jaguar hovered. Captain Jordan stood confident and ready in the open door. Caitlin stood behind him. She had never been this nervous in her entire life. Eighteen inches in front of her toes was the edge of the open chopper door. She looked down. Manhattan was two-and-a-half miles below; it looked like a toy-block city. A harpoon-like gun was fastened to the helicopter, its muzzle pointed out the door at the massive Beanstalk. Ropes were belayed to each anxious soldier. Everyone—Captain Jordan, Caitlin, and every Special Forces soldier waited and watched the yellow jump light.

The helicopter's voice crackled over the headsets, "Get ready!"

The jump light turned green. Captain Jordan yelled into his headset, "Go! Go! Go!"

The harpoon canons exploded, "Boom! Boom! Boom!" The harpoons rocketed into the Great Green Stalk. Green stalk fibers split and wrapped about the harpoons. The belayed ropes pulled taut. The soldiers swung out of the helicopters toward the Beanstalk. Captain Jordan looked at Caitlin, "Let's go!" he yelled above the roar of the helicopter blades. Caitlin had a rush of adrenalin. She pulled her rope taut and swung out the open helicopter door into the air above New York City. Swinging toward the massive Beanstalk, she grabbed one of the many offshoot branches. Once secure, she dropped a second rope down the Beanstalk. Hanging by the rope, Caitlin dangled above New York. She watched the other soldiers secure themselves.

Clinging to the Beanstalk, Caitlin and the fifteen Special Forces soldiers began their climb up the stalk like a mountain climbing team. The Comanche helicopters hovered, then peeled off and disappeared into the blue sky. Armed with high-tech lasers and weapons, the Special Forces soldiers climbed the Great Green Stalk. Caitlin carried no weapons. Three soldiers had video cameras mounted to their helmets. After nearly an hour of climbing, the team reached the swirling clouds. Captain Jordan spoke into his headset.

"This is Green Team One, we are stopped about ten feet beneath the cloud layer."

In a Washington D.C. Department of Defense conference room, generals, politicians, and the Vice-President gathered around a large conference table. On a large television screen, they monitored the assault by the Special Forces Team on the Beanstalk. Captain Jordan's words echoed through the large conference room.

"... We are entering the clouds. They are dense. Zero visibility. Stand-by."

Captain Jordan gave the go signal to Sergeant Hicks and Sergeant Stone. The politicians and generals who sat around the mahogany conference table were riveted to the large television monitor. They watched, as one-by-one, the Special Forces soldiers entered the swirling clouds. Caitlin was next to last. Captain Jordan would follow her. He watched her from below, as she pulled herself up by the ropes. Her head and torso disappeared in the cloud layer.

"There is a door here," she yelled back to Captain Jordan.

Suddenly, she was sucked into the clouds and disappeared from the television monitor in the Department of Defense conference room. All that was visible were turbulent clouds. Captain Jordan climbed into them and disappeared.

Caitlin was lying on the cavern floor, groaning from the fall into the cave. She looked around, but no one else was there. She was alone. Caitlin slowly pulled herself up from the hard wet cave floor. She stared at the enormous cavern with stalactites and stalagmites; the water glowed blue-green.

Caitlin called out, "Hello? Captain Jordan? Captain Jordan?"

Her voice echoed through the cavern. She waited. There was no answer. She was alone, and completely puzzled. She walked around the spot where she fell. She looked up at the hole, where a cone of light streamed into the cave.

"Is anyone there?" She yelled up at the cone of light.

"Dr. Bingham, where are you?" a voice came back. She recognized it. It was Captain Jordan's voice.

"I'm in a cavern of some kind," she answered. Her voice sounded anxious and confused. "Where are you?" she shouted back.

"I don't know. It's a white room like a cloud. Everyone else is here."

Inside a large white and misty room, Captain Jordan and all of his men were lost. They looked anxiously around with their weapons poised. The room had no ceiling, no walls, and no floor. The Special Forces Team was suspended in the white space.

"Somehow, I've been selected out." Caitlin's voice echoed in the white cloud room.

"Are you all right?" yelled Captain Jordan into the whiteness.

"I'm okay," Caitlin answered immediately. "How about you?"

Captain Jordan looked at his men. "We're all fine here. Is there a place to walk where you are?" His voice echoed through the strange cavern as if he was there.

Surrounded by cave stalagmites, Caitlin was standing twenty feet from the iridescent turquoise lagoon. She spied a ledge that wound around and followed the stream with the white mist.

"There's a ledge that I can follow. It looks like some kind of path." Caitlin yelled out into the cave.

"Okay," Captain Jordan's voice echoed back into the cave. "Follow that path and keep in voice communication, okay? Do you read me?"

"Loud and clear," Caitlin said as she began to walk over to the ledge.

"We'll reconnoiter this space," echoed Captain's Jordan's voice, "and we'll catch up with you. Be careful."

"I plan on it. See you soon," answered Caitlin. Resigned, she scanned the cavern and stepped gingerly onto the wet ledge. She looked into the glowing turquoise water with the white mist hanging over it.

Why did I agree to this? Caitlin thought as she inched her way onto the unstable narrow ledge and pieces of rock fell into the stream. The Trilobites followed her making popping sounds, as they opened and closed their mouths exposing rows of tiny sharp teeth.

CHAPTER 29

POTTER SIMS

The underbrush and foliage in the Great Forest was dense. There were no paths or clearings, so Jack walked warily as he explored his surroundings. Everywhere were oddly-shaped, leafy green fronds, exotic flowers like wild pink anthophores and tiger-striped posies, great green ferns that were translucent in streams of sunlight and enormous coniferous trees dangling with thin light green vines that trailed down to the forest floor. The Great Forest resonated with a symphony of birds chirping, trilling, cawing, chattering and warbling. Jack plodded deeper into this unknown, but enchanting territory. As a musician, he was captivated by every chirp and trill. Every twenty feet he would stop and look up into the gigantic trees and wispy vines to see birds with brilliantly colored plumage perched on leafy branches or soaring through the canopy of the Great Forest. He saw hundreds of birds, each different. Though he was rapt with the forest's beauty, he had to go forward, but where was forward? His eyes scanned the beautiful dense forest. Though he was infatuated in this magical land, Jack was still lost. He could not return the way he arrived, and there were no trails to follow.

Suddenly, there was a loud twittering above Jack's head. Out of the corner of his eye, Jack spotted a colorful shape swooping down near his head. A strange voice screamed, "Watch out!" Barely missing Jack's head, a large colorful insect swooped down on him.

The insect crashed into the bushes. Uncoordinated, he flopped around chirping loudly. His veined, transparent wings entangled around his spastic body. Utterly flabbergasted, the insect pulled himself up from the dirt.

"I hate dirt!" the insect said, as he flicked specks of dirt from his black waiter's jacket. Jack could not believe what he was seeing. The insect was a mosquito, but far from an ordinary one. Five-feet tall and dapper, his face had near human features. He wore shiny-red, high-top boots, a starched white shirt with shiny gold cuff links, a red bow tie, a black waiter's tuxedo vest with tails, and white gloves. His eyes were bright, and his proboscis-like nose was long.

"I hate dirt!" The strange creature exclaimed as again he brushed more dirt off of his black jacket with the backs of his white gloves.

"A talking mosquito?" Jack exclaimed aloud, while he laughed in disbelief.

"I am not a mosquito! I am Potter Sims." The dapper five-foot tall mosquito extended his white-gloved hand to Jack, who was very amused. Guarded, Jack shook Potter Sims' hand.

"What kind of name is that?" asked Jack.

"It happens to be a very respectable name," Potter Sims proudly responded. "What is your name?"

"Jacob Tott," Jack answered. "My family and friends call me Jack."

"Tott! Jacob Tott!" exclaimed Potter Sims. "I don't think you have any room to criticize my name!"

"I wasn't criticizing your name, it's just unusual, that's all," Jack defended himself.

"Do I look ordinary to you?"

"Hardly," Jack said staring at his outrageous outfit.

In the deep turquoise lagoon, Caitlin swam toward the shore. She walked onto the black sand beach and scanned the dense green forest surrounding her. The sun created tiny rainbows that arched across the sparkling black sand. Fascinated, Caitlin scooped grains of the black sand into her palm. Sifting them through her fingers, she watched the rainbows arch across her palm onto the beach. After a few minutes of this fascination, Caitlin called out into the Great Forest.

"Hello! Is anybody there?"

The only sounds that she heard were those of the Great Forest. Birds were calling and insects were chirping.

"Can you hear me?" she called out again.

"Captain Jordan?" Caitlin yelled back toward the center of the lagoon, where she surfaced. She waited. There was nothing but silence in the lagoon. "Captain Jordan, can you hear me?" No response.

On the twilight horizon, Caitlin saw stars shining. As an astronomer, her curiosity was aroused by the patterns the stars made in the sky above the Great Forest. One star shined brightly, but it was foreign to her. She studied it for a few moments, and then walked into the Great Forest.

Deeper in the Great Forest, Jack and Potter Sims were surrounded by the giant ferns and trees.

"What is this place?" Jack asked.

"It's called Edonas. Just what are you doing here anyway?"

"I wish I knew."

"You mean you came here and you don't know why?" Potter Sims asked incredulous.

"I came here for my sister."

"Well, she is not here! I would know."

"I know that," Jack said getting perturbed at this creature's persnickety manner. "I was told that there is a lot of gold here. Is there?"

"More gold than you can imagine or cart away, but you won't." Potter Sims said as he stopped on the path and stared at Jack.

"Why's that?"

"Because it belongs to Ens, that's why."

"Who is Ens?" Jack asked.

"He is the charming fellow who owns this place," said Potter Sims with a whimsical tone in his voice.

Suddenly, a loud voice penetrated the thick forest. "Captain Jordan, are you there? Can you hear me?"

Disturbed by the noise, Potter Sims commented, "What is that?"

"Why are you looking at me?" Jack complained. "How should I know who it is?"

"What is this? Some kind of invasion?" Potter Sims said, most perturbed by all the invading of his privacy.

"Is anybody there?" Caitlin's voice was closer.

"Do you think we are deaf!" Potter Sims yelled into the woods.

"Where are you?" The voice in the wild asked.

"We're over here!" Jack cupped his hands over his mouth and called blindly out into the thick forest.

"I heartily dislike screaming! It is impolite. It is rude. But mostly, it hurts my ears!" exclaimed Potter Sims impatiently.

Just in front of Jack and Potter, the ferns parted. Caitlin stood looking at Potter Sims, who was nearer to her. She stood motionless and silent, unable to take her eyes off this five-foot tall, flamboyant mosquito.

"What is your problem?" Potter Sims demanded of Caitlin.

"Wow! What are you?" Caitlin exclaimed, shocked by Potter Sims' appearance.

"What?" exclaimed Potter Sims. "What?" he repeated. He was sure that Caitlin had insulted him. "I am not a 'what'!"

"His name is Potter Sims," Jack answered calmly.

Caitlin gave Potter Sims a careful going-over, studying his clothes, his face and eyes, his proboscis, his long transparent wings and tinder-like black spiny legs.

"I don't believe it," Caitlin exclaimed.

"What is it that is so hard to believe?" countered Potter Sims defending himself. "You two are the ones who are hard to believe! This is my home! You came here! You are strange to my eyes!"

Potter Sims was becoming increasingly impatient. He was very sensitive about his appearance and manner. He felt that these intruders had attacked both, laughing at his color and his style.

"Who are you?" Potter Sims demanded.

"Yes, who are you?" echoed Jack.

Potter Sims could not believe that Jack was questioning this person's identity; Afterall, this Jack creature was also uninvited.

"I am Caitlin Bingham," Caitlin answered. "I am an archeoastronomer. I do research and teach at a Colgate University in New York. I also work for NASA. Where is Captain Jordan?"

"Who is Captain Jordan?" Potter Sims asked.

"I came up here with him," said Caitlin.

"Do you mean that there are more of you?" Potter Sims asked.

"I came up here with a Special Forces team, fifteen in all," Caitlin explained. "They didn't get through."

"Up? There is no up here!" Potter Sims was getting impatient.

"We climbed up," countered Caitlin.

"Me, too, but when I came up, I fell down. Everything was upside down," Jack explained.

"To you maybe, but not to us," defended Potter Sims. "It's all perfectly normal, it is you who are turned around."

"Why are you so difficult?" asked Caitlin.

"I could say that about you. After all, it is you who came here uninvited!" Potter Sims was irritated that an invader would have the gall to question him.

At this, Jack spoke up, "Where are the soldiers?"

"I don't know," Caitlin answered. "When I fell into the cave, they weren't with me, but I could hear them."

"What a pity they couldn't all join us!" exclaimed Potter Sims. "Maybe the trilobites had them for dinner!"

"So, you've been to the cave?" Jack asked Potter Sims most curious.

"I've never been, but I know of it."

"We have to go back and find them." Caitlin insisted.

"Oh, you can't go back!" Potter Sims exclaimed.

"Why not?" Caitlin exclaimed.

"Because there is no way to get back." Potter Sims answered. "Are you here to find his sister?" Potter Sims points at Jack.

"Find his sister? I don't think so. I am here to find him," she pointed to Jack. "You are Jacob Tott, aren't you?"

"Yes."

"Are you famous?" Potter Sims asked Jack.

"Yes, he is," Caitlin interjected. "For the moment anyway," responded Caitlin. "That's the way things are where we're from. One minute you're famous, the next nobody cares."

"So, are you looking for gold, too?" Potter Sims said to Caitlin.

"No," answered Caitlin, "I have no interest in gold. I am only here to find him and find out why everything is happening."

"What do you mean 'everything is happening'?"

"Oh, nothing much," Caitlin explained. "Just the disappearance of a planet, a giant Beanstalk sprouting in New York, chaos across the planet, this place—minor things like that."

"Disappearance of a planet?" Jack's interest was aroused.

"Two days ago, a new planet in our solar system called Pachakutek disappeared right out of the sky," Caitlin said as she pointed to the sky above the Great Forest. "I discovered it, and now it is gone."

"How is that possible?" Jack asked.

"I don't know."

"So are you famous?" Potter Sims asked Caitlin.

"No. I spend my life looking through a telescope and sitting in front of a computer, not a very glamorous life. The media like glamour, things that do something, things that you can see. According to the recent polls, most people glance up at the stars only about five times per year because stars don't do anything. They just hang there."

Jack liked Caitlin. He liked her humor. She had a funny tongue-in-her cheek way about her.

"I don't have any idea what you are talking about!" responded Potter Sims. "But I am certainly glad that we have all found one another!"

"Since we can't go back, then you won't mind being our guide," Jack touched Potter Sims' arm, "and take us forward."

"Me? A guide!" responded Potter Sims indignantly. "Why would I commit myself to such a pedestrian task as being your guide?"

"Because you like all this attention," Jack answered sharply.

"Humph!" Potter Sims raised his head in arrogance.

"Good, then it's settled," Jack said and smiled. He began walking into the Great Forest, but Caitlin did not budge. She stood motionless in a patch of giant ferns.

"The soldiers could help!" Caitlin attempted to persuade Potter Sims and Jack to return to the Lagoon. "We should make an effort to find them."

"Are you deaf? Or I am speaking in a language that you don't understand!" exclaimed Potter Sims quite perturbed. "There is no way back!"

"How is it that you speak English, our language?" Jack asked curiously.

"How should I know?" Potter Sims exclaimed. "Perhaps it is you who speak my language!"

"It is an upside down world, isn't it?" Jack said calmly. "I'm afraid that the soldiers are on their own, just as we are." Jack turned his back on Caitlin and walked into the thick jungle.

Caitlin was angry, and Jack was stubborn. He knew that under no circumstances would he go back to search for people, who for some reason were sent to find him. Caitlin was stewing, furious. Potter Sims flapped his transparent wings and bounced clumsily along next to Jack, like a bug on a pogo stick. With every bounce, Potter Sims talked to himself, but he made sure that Jack could hear him clearly. "A guide!" Potter shook his head in disgust. "I never thought that I would lower myself to be someone's guide!"

"Do you always talk this much?" Jack cut him off.

"Usually more, especially when I've been alone for awhile."

"I'm sorry, but I can't take it." Jack said annoyed with Potter Sims' constant chattering. "I am going alone, if there is going to be all this constant jabbering."

"You don't have to be rude about it!" Potter Sims defended himself. "I can be quiet. I will hate it! But I can be quiet!"

They walked through the Great Forest. Behind them, Caitlin was deliberately lingering. Jack stopped and turned around. He could no longer see her. All he could see were the huge fronds, gigantic trees, and exotic vines twisting their way along the Great Forest floor. Caitlin certainly must have been lost. He stopped, turned around and screamed into the Great Forest.

"Are you coming?"

The Great Forest soaked up Jack's words, like a sponge. After nearly a minute, a muffled voice answered.

"Don't wait for me!"

Jack smiled, turned, and he and Potter Sims walked into a dense path overgrown with ferns and flowers. It wound around through the Great Forest. As Jack traipsed down the path, he was awestruck by the forest's primeval beauty. Caitlin stayed behind hoping that the soldiers would show up.

After nearly an hour, Jack and Potter Sims were exhausted. They were sitting on the ground in a small clearing. Jack was sweaty and dirty. Disgusted, Potter Sims flicked tiny specks of dirt from his black waiter's jacket with his white glove, while Jack scanned the dense jungle behind them.

"I wonder where she is?" Jack asked with concern in his voice.

"Who cares?" countered Potter Sims.

"She could be in trouble."

"We're all in trouble most of the time," Potter Sims answered in a voice that suggested he had been through some trying times.

"Sounds like you come from where we live."

"Trouble is a universal condition, especially here," Potter Sims added.

"Until you've seen where I come from, you haven't seen trouble," Jack said to Potter Sims trying to one-up him.

"I really would like to hear about it, but right now, I am concerned about this!" Potter Sims pointed to the scratches and mud caked on his shiny red boots. "This is trouble! More trouble than I can handle!" Potter Sims tried to polish the scratches and mud from his boots.

"I hate dirt!" he exclaimed. "Look at this! I absolutely loathe dirt!"

"Well, I absolutely loathe hunger," Jack said matter-of-factly, while watching Potter Sims as he cleaned and rubbed his bright red boots. Just then, just beyond their small clearing, the lush ferns parted and Caitlin appeared, flustered and perturbed.

Looking up from his shiny red boots, Potter Sims said, "He was worried about you."

"Not that worried," Jack countered.

"I'm quite capable of taking care of myself."

"I'm sure you are." Jack turned to Potter Sims. "I'm hungry. You're our guide, what is there to eat?"

"What do you eat?"

"Hamburgers, but I don't think there's a Burger Joint up here." Jack answered.

"I don't eat hamburgers. I'm a vegetarian," Caitlin said.

"What are hamburgers?" What little eyebrows Potter Sims had lifted up suspiciously.

"Well, where we are from, they breed cows for steak and hamburgers and roast beef sandwiches." Jack explained.

"Cows? Hum. What do they look like?" Potter Sims asked.

"They're big. They have ears about this big." Jack demonstrated. "And noses at the tip of a rectangular face with big round bulging eyes, and hooves." As Jack described a cow, he pointed to different parts of his own body. Caitlin watched him, amused by his animated rendering of a cow. Potter Sims was most curious.

"They come in many colors," Jack continued. "Some are brown, some black, some in patchy black and white. People design ice cream stores after the black and white ones, and mugs, sides of buses and milk trucks, greeting cards, computers, lunch boxes, wrapping paper, everything."

"I don't understand how these cows, as you call them, are sources of food?" Potter Sims was most curious.

Caitlin pointed to Jack, as if he had the magic answer. "Go on," she urged Jack on in a voice reeking with sarcasm.

"We get milk from the patchy white and black ones. They are like mothers, women, female, mother earth. The brown and black ones are important too, but they don't have milk. We use them as a source of protein," Jack explained.

"We slaughter them," Caitlin said with a matter-of-fact tone. "Thousands and thousands of them every day."

"Meat is protein," Jack defended himself. "Besides, it is quick and they don't feel anything."

Potter Sims' eyes were beginning to open wide.

"After," Jack continued, "we grind them up, wrap them in plastic, and lay them out in a supermarket display case. You pick out the freshest one and take it home."

Potter Sims' eyes opened wider.

Colorfully, Jack used his hands to describe the entire process in detail. "We put them in a cooler or in a refrigerator, so they don't go bad. We make round patties out of them, and cook them on a barbecue grill or in a skillet and when they are nice and juicy, you put them between two pieces of bread, add a little mustard, a little ketchup, maybe some pickles, onions, a tomato, slice of cheese and then we eat them." Jack shrugged his shoulders and smiled.

"Disgusting!" Potter Sims exclaimed.

"It's food, protein." Jack defended himself.

Potter Sims was thoroughly shocked. He could hardly control himself.

"Well, what do you eat? Don't you suck blood?" Jack asked.

"Suck blood!" Potter Sims shouted loudly. "That is the most revolting thing I've ever heard!"

"I agree. He's got more sense than you do," Caitlin said to Jack.

"I would like to see the place you two come from!" Potter Sims exclaimed in wild mockery.

"It's called Earth," said Jack.

"You mean like dirt?" Potter Sims could not believe what he was hearing. "I hate dirt!"

"Earth is a class M, earth-based planet," Caitlin's tone was scholarly, as if she was back delivering an astronomy lecture. "It has a mass of 5.97×10^{24th} kilograms with an oxygen and nitrogen atmosphere, a sidereal rotation of 23.93 hours, an elliptical orbit of 365.25 days, plate tectonics, a temperature range from 0 to 40 degrees Celsius and one natural satellite, the moon."

"Look, we're impressed, but I am starving," Jack interrupted. "What do you eat here?"

"You say 'I won't like your place', well you probably won't like what I eat," Potter Sims said as he flapped his wings, lifting himself over the giant ferns to hover around the strange vines that encircled the giant trees. Odd shaped, brightly-colored fruit and vegetables hung from the vines high above the forest floor. Highest up on the tree, white and black donut shaped vegetables hung parallel to the ground measuring two to three inches in diameter. Like donuts, they had holes, but the holes were plugged up with a thin sparkling translucent gold membrane. Dangling in the tree's mid section were phosphorescent blue, flat pancake fruits that varied in diameter between five and eight inches. Thousands of bright red and yellow corkscrew fruits dangled at the bottom of the tree, their tips pointing at the ground. Twelve inches long, they twisted slightly in the wind. They looked like ornaments suspended on a Christmas tree.

Jack and Caitlin watched, as Potter Sims buzzed up and down the vines pulling off handfuls of fruits and odd vegetables. After a few minutes, Potter Sims hovered above Jack and Caitlin with his arms weighed down with the colorful fruit. Potter Sims screamed as he tilted off-balance and sideways, like a helicopter steered by an inept pilot. He flapped his transparent wings so rapidly, that the buzzing of his wings drowned out every other sound in the Great Forest.

"Watch out!" Potter Sims screamed, as he crashed down next to Caitlin spilling the fruit and vegetables all over the forest ground.

"Are you all right?" Caitlin asked.

"I hate flying!" Potter Sims shouted angrily, a jumbled heap lying on the forest floor. Jack extended his hand; Potter Sims reluctantly took it and stood. His thin spiny legs wobbled. As he straightened his disheveled wings, he reiterated his predicament, "I hate flying!"

Jack and Caitlin were amused and did their best, however unsuccessfully, to hide the hilarity of the moment.

"This is not funny!" Potter protested.

"We're not laughing," Jack said.

"Maybe you should try to walk more until you get a little better at it." Caitlin advised.

"Then what would you eat?" Potter Sims snapped back as he flecked tiny specks of dirt off his jacket. Jack and Caitlin merely shrugged their shoulders. They did not want any more confrontation. All they wanted to do was eat.

After Potter Sims flicked the specks of dirt off his waiter's tuxedo jacket, the three gathered up the exotic fruits and vegetables, which lay all over the ground.

"What is this?" Caitlin asked holding up one of the white and black donut vegetables.

"It is called a Cirgusto. Some consider it the tastiest of all foods."

"And these?" Caitlin picked up a couple of the bright blue, flat pancake fruits. "Pannikin."

Caitlin took a bite. "It tastes like a cheese mango."

"What about these big ones?" Jack held up two of the bright red and yellow corkscrew-shaped fruits, one in each hand.

"They are fruits called Torcs," Potter Sims answered.

Jack bit into the bright red one. It was juicy. The juice ran down the side of his mouth; he wiped it with the back of his hand.

"What's it taste like?" Caitlin asked.

"Like peanut butter and bananas. These are actually very good. Thank you." Jack complimented Potter Sims, who was busy wiping off his red shiny boots.

"If we're stuck here, we might as well like the food," said Caitlin as she chewed on a Cirgusto.

The three travelers sat on the Great Forest floor eating for an hour. After they finished, Caitlin pointed to the necklace dangling from Jack's neck. It was the twenty-four karat, sun-shaped amulet, which his mother had given him.

"Can I see your necklace?" she asked.

Jack removed the necklace. As he handed it to Caitlin, the amulet, which dangled from the end of the gold Inca chain, sparkled.

"This is Inca," Caitlin said.

"Inca? I didn't know," Jack said.

"Where did you get it?" Potter Sims asked.

"It's been in my father's family for generations. My father gave it to my mother, and she gave it to me just before I came up here," Jack said.

Caitlin pointed to the symbols etched into the gold amulet.

"These are Inca star and sun symbols. This dates back to the late 15th Century," Caitlin explained.

"I had no idea," Jack was amazed.

"The Inca are here," Potter Sims commented.

"That is impossible," Caitlin exclaimed adamantly, but with a tone of bewilderment in her voice.

"What purpose would I have in lying to you?"

"Where we are from, Earth—"Caitlin said.

"—Dirt." Potter Sims abruptly interrupted her humorously.

"No, I meant what I said—Earth," countered Caitlin. "Over 500 years ago, the Incas were the most powerful and the wealthiest people on the planet. Their reign covered all of South America."

"Did they have gold?" Potter Sims asked.

"Mountains full of it, until the Spaniards conquered the Incas and stole it," said Jack. Caitlin was surprised at Jack's knowledge of Inca history.

"But the Spaniards wanted gold because they could trade it," Caitlin added. "The Incas didn't care about that. To the Incas, gold was important because it harnessed the light and purity of the sun. It held intrinsic power. The sun gave them life."

"How could the Incas possibly be here?" Jack asked bothered, mystified.

"Why do you doubt what I tell you?" asked Potter Sims. "Is it because of the way I look?" Potter Sims waved his white-gloved hand down his body.

Jack and Caitlin just looked at each other.

"The Incas are here," continued Potter Sims. "Ens has the gold, and the Incas are with Ens. You want gold, you find Ens."

"Who's Ens?" asked Caitlin.

"Is Ens like the king or something?" Jack asked.

"Not something, Ens is everything," Potter Sims corrected Jack. "He rules."

CHAPTER 30

THE MYTH UNFOLDS

At CNN Headquarters in Atlanta, Georgia, news anchor Wolf Leitzer spoke to the worldwide television audience. Behind him, there was a world map and a large monitor showing the Beanstalk that rose from the hole in the ground that was once the World Trade Center Plaza. Other monitors at CNN broadcast headquarters showed Red Square, the Eiffel Tower, the Vatican, London, Peking, Pakistan, Rio de Janeiro, Istanbul and other cities.

"Today in New York, religious and political leaders, and scientists are meeting to discuss the significance of this event and why it has happened," commented Wolf Leitzer. "In a video-taped message, some Islamic fundamentalist leaders from the Middle East have claimed that it is a sign from Allah, which will bring the West to justice. I understand we are going to Nobel Prize winning author Dr. Rudd Fleming, who is giving a press conference in lower Manhattan near the giant Beanstalk."

It was 8:30 a.m. as Dr. Rudd Fleming walked to the podium. Dozens of television and radio microphones from news organizations around the globe were mounted on the podium. Hundreds of camera shutters clicked and news cameras rolled. Dressed in a brown tweed suit, blue dress shirt and conservative tie, Dr. Fleming was a slight man in his early 60's. Though a world-renowned author of books about important contemporary political and sociological periods of history, he was a humble man. He preferred the quiet to the limelight. However, today was different; today the world awaited his wisdom. In front of the Great

Beanstalk, which towered over the skyscraper city, Dr. Fleming spoke to the world press.

"Good morning," Dr. Fleming addressed the crowd and the television cameras. "The world is asking how could this happen? Can we explain this event? The answer is we cannot. If we look through ancient and historical texts, there are many strange, even impossible events, which have happened over millennia. Some we can explain scientifically, some we cannot. The Old Testament tells a story about the Battle of Jericho, where Joshua held up his hands and the sun stopped in the sky."

While Dr. Fleming spoke, the sun shined hot in the sky over Tel Aviv, Israel. It was 3:30 p.m. and hot in the streets, as many Israelis gathered around a television monitor that lay on a table at an outdoor café. They were watching and listening to Dr. Rudd Fleming's speech in New York. The Great Beanstalk loomed behind Dr. Fleming on the small television image.

In Tokyo, Japan, it was temperate and comfortable at 10:31 p.m. People sat in silence before an enormous video screen in a seafood restaurant watching and listening to Dr. Rudd Fleming.

In Santiago, Chile, it was 9:31 a.m. At a dock eatery, a dozen Chilean fishermen gathered around a portable television as they listened to the commentary by Dr. Fleming. Their fishing nets, buoys and lines lay on the dock.

In lower Manhattan, Dr. Fleming spoke, "Natural law tells us that if the sun stopped in the sky, then the earth would fly out of its orbit. However, thousands of years of oral and written tradition are not wrong. The interpretation of this particular event is not literal, but something did happen that day. Today, scientists are certain that a giant meteor striking the Earth in the Yucatán Peninsula in Chicxulub, Mexico caused the extinction of the dinosaurs. Records of a flood exist in every major culture and religion throughout the world. Was there a Noah's ark? Was there sweeping loss of life across our planet caused by the flood? Something did happen. Thousands of years of oral tradition and recorded history found in nearly every culture of our planet cannot be wrong. So, what do we know? These historical stories are embedded in myth. In essence, myth is about our origins, our lives, and our death. Maybe in two thousand, five thousand, or ten thousand years from this day, if we are still here and our planet survives, this event and this day will be re-told as another great turning point myth."

In Moscow, Russia, it was 4:32 p.m. A Russian family sat around their television set watching the interview.

In Darling Harbor, Sydney, Australia it was 11:32 p.m. Dr. Fleming's voice echoed from hundreds of televisions and radios that played inside docked boats.

His voice echoed over the sounds of the waves lapping up against the boats' hulls and the docks.

In Egypt, the sun was high and hot at 3:33 p.m. In Giza, thousands of tourists walked around the Great Pyramid and the Sphinx. Near the Great Pyramid, an Egyptian cashier watched a television in his souvenir shop. Tourists stopped shopping to watch the broadcast from Manhattan.

It was overcast and 2:34 p.m. at the base of the Eiffel Tower in Paris, France. A businessman watched his Blackberry which was tuned to the V-cast of Professor Fleming's speech.

In New York, where nearly ten thousand people gathered in front of the Giant Beanstalk, Dr. Rudd Fleming continued, "What we think is that this manifestation may be a warning or statement for our planet. For what, we do not know. Only the future will tell. May we have the wisdom to hear what we are supposed to hear, and see what we are supposed to see. May God help us and bless us all. Thank you." As Dr. Fleming finished his last words, journalists yelled out questions to him. He stepped away from the microphone, as cameras flashed and press photographers followed him clicking off hundreds of photographs. Dr. Fleming did not answer a single question. As he walked away, he merely looked out at the throng of people shadowed by the Great Beanstalk.

CHAPTER 31

***

GANDOR

With the border of the Great Forest just behind them, Jack, Caitlin and Potter Sims stood in awe before Devastation Plain.

Devastation Plain was a barren wasteland. The trees were lone dead stalks. They looked like scorched white toothpicks sticking upright out of a timeless horizon. Red, gray and brown cinders covered the ground. In the background were fortress-like mountains. There was no life here.

"Devastation Plain," Potter Sims pointed to the barren wasteland before them.

"We have to cross this?" asked Jack.

"I told you this wasn't going to be easy."

Suddenly, there was a loud swooshing and flapping of the air above them followed by a booming voice.

"Remove yourselves!" The deep voice bellowed.

"I was afraid of that," Potter Sims said as he shook his head, and a look of disgust passed across his face.

"Of what?" Jack asked, as they looked up to the sky.

"Remove yourselves, I say!" The deep voice above them boomed again.

"Who is he?" Caitlin asked, while shading her eyes from the sun, as she tried to get a good look at the creature that was swooping just above her.

"His name is Gandor," answered Potter Sims. "He is an arrogant, self-righteous busy-body. I heartily dislike him!"

"He lives here?" Jack asked.

"Now that his family has gone," replied Potter Sims.

"Where did they go?" Caitlin asked.

"Ens killed them."

Gandor swooped down twenty feet over their heads. His wings had a twelve-foot wingspan and his body resembled an Andean Condor. However, his head looked like a Dodo bird's. His webbed duck-like feet were bright turquoise blue, like the Galapagos' blue-footed booby, and his face looked disturbingly almost human. He landed his plumpness on a branch of a dead tree. From his vest pocket, he removed a gold watch fob, which dangled on a gold chain. He checked the time, then closed the gold engraved watch cover and slipped it neatly back into his vest pocket.

Potter Sims turned to Jack and Caitlin. "He is always checking his watch as if it's going to make a difference!"

"Come closer!" Gandor said to Jack, Caitlin and Potter Sims. "Explain yourself! Who are you?" boomed Gandor, as he stood perched solemn and stiff on a dead tree branch.

"I am Jack, this is Caitlin," Jack answered and stepped forward.

"I can speak for myself." Caitlin hurled a discontented look at Jack.

"Good for you, young lady. I am Gandor, the last of my line."

"What melodrama!" Potter Sims exclaimed as he threw up his arms.

Gandor took a Sherlock Holmes pipe out of his vest, lit it, took a puff and blew a huge blue smoke ring into the air. Then, he checked his gold watch fob.

"Are you the last one, too?" Caitlin asked Potter Sims.

"Poppycock!" blurted out Gandor. "Sims is a commoner, there are thousands like him. He is a vagabond. His people wander aimlessly about the land!" Gandor blew another smoke ring.

"Commoner?" Potter Sims protested.

Paying no attention to Potter Sims, Gandor directed his conversation to Jack and Caitlin, who had now taken an interest in Gandor's plight. Gandor explained, "On the other hand, my people are, excuse me, they *were* ... territorial. The Great Forest was their home."

"What bald-faced rubbish!" Potter Sims exclaimed.

With the pipe in his mouth, and red angry cheeks, Gandor swooped down off the dead branch landing only feet in front of Potter Sims. He stretched his elegant wings into the air, ruffled the feathers into order, and then pulled them down about his sides.

"Silence, Sims!" Gandor yelled. "Or I will have you banished!"

"Nonsense! By whom?" Potter Sims asked. "By Ens?"

"That's exactly who!" boomed Gandor.

"Ha! He terrifies you!" exclaimed Potter Sims right in Gandor's face.

"Ens controls all of this?" Jack asked.

"Everything," Gandor waved his arms indicating everything that they could see. "Ens is pure evil. He eradicated my entire family."

"Couldn't happen to a nicer bunch," Potter Sims commented.

"That is a tasteless comment, Sims, even for you," Gandor said indignant.

As Gandor spoke, the ground rumbled and shook. An enormous wind, like a great tornado, cut a path across Devastation Plain. As the wind roared, clouds of red, brown, and grey cinders flew through the air stinging the foursome. The cinders hissed as they struck against one another. Jack, Caitlin, Potter Sims and Gandor saw dark bat-like wings inside the impenetrable whirling cloud of dust. They beat with great power. The tips of the bat wings stuck outside the edge of the tornado, and then disappeared back into the swirling dust cloud. The ground trembled.

After several minutes, several of the creatures with bat-like wings emerged from the dark swirling clouds. They were primal. They were called The Corps, a mix of man and animal. Their human-like faces were grotesquely hard and their bodies were muscular and raw, contoured with wiry hair. Each of the Corps stood seven feet tall. Power rose magnificently from their shoulders in their enormous black wings that extended twenty feet from tip to tip. Just beneath the dark leathery skin covering their wings, Jack and Caitlin saw their bones. Each wing looked like a fossil from a primitive species unearthed by a civilization after millions of years.

Stepping calmly and elegantly out from behind The Corps was Ens. He raised his arms and the wind stopped. The red, brown, and grey cinders abruptly fell to the ground. The tornado stopped swirling and disappeared. Within seconds, the air became pure and clear. Gandor squawked, while trying to fly away. Instantly, The Corps surrounded him and kept him from leaving along with Jack, Caitlin, and Potter Sims.

"Welcome," Ens addressed Jack. "I've been expecting you."

"The park restroom, the storm," The image of Ens standing in the doorway of the dark wet restroom during the great storm filled Jack's mind.

"Glad to know that I made an impression," Ens said amusedly.

Ens stood over ten feet tall. Even though he was muscular, there was a feminine elegance and charm about him. He looked like a pure balance of male and female. He wore a long white gown. His hands were huge. His fingers were large and long. His eyes were a slightly speckled golden yellow with a rich brown corona around them. Ens' gaze penetrated.

"It was a nasty night, wasn't it?" Ens prodded. "Don't get me wrong, I kind of liked it, but I don't think many people did."

"So, you're Ens?" Jack asked.

"In the flesh. You're on my turf now," Ens smiled.

"You two have met?"

"The night of the storm, the night the Beanstalk grew," Jack answered Caitlin. Jack and Caitlin noticed that Gandor was trembling uncontrollably. Ens walked over to him.

"Come on, Gandor, get a grip," Ens poked Gandor lightly with his huge finger trying to taunt him.

Ens turned to Caitlin, "Did you find your planet yet?"

"How do you know about that?"

"I know everything," Ens replied. "Pachakutek. Herald of the great change. I like the name. It'll turn up."

"If you know that, then maybe you could tell me how a planet could disappear from its orbit?" Caitlin decided to test Ens no matter how intimidating he was.

With a cold amused tone in his voice, he answered, "Anything is possible."

"Even changing the physical laws of nature?" Caitlin challenged.

"Anything," Ens prided himself on being menacing. It worked on everyone except Potter Sims.

"That's a laugh!" exclaimed Potter Sims.

"You're pushing it, Sims," Ens' voice was full of peril. "If I were you, I would be a bit more respectful. Just ask Gandor."

Still guarded by The Corps, Gandor was still shaking uncontrollably. Ens put his enormous hand upon Gandor's quivering shoulder.

"My dear Gandor, get a hold of yourself or your heart will stop," Ens played. "Be a pity, wouldn't it? To lose such a fine species."

Gandor was terrified. He could not speak. He hyperventilated and struggled to breathe. Ens stared into Gandor's eyes. He saw the fear and terror.

"Would you like to leave?" Ens asked Gandor.

Jack, Caitlin and Potter Sims waited for Gandor to answer, but there was no response. Only silence.

"Answer me," Ens demanded.

Gandor shook uncontrollably. He could not even look at Ens. "Yes," he said.

"It will cost you," responded Ens as he pointed to the area in front of them. "The mating dance. Do it." Gandor balked, he did not want to do this. It would be too painful of a recollection.

"You either do the dance," Ens added. "Or you end up like Alba, and that would truly be 'the end,' wouldn't it?"

"Who is Alba?" Caitlin asked.

Potter Sims spoke up, "His mate, Ens killed her."

Ens waited. There was a long silence, as Ens, The Corps, Jack, Caitlin, and Potter Sims waited for Gandor to respond. Jack and Caitlin felt helpless, as they watched nervously.

"So, what's it going to be, my dear Gandor?"

Shaking, Gandor briefly looked up at Ens and said in a deep, thoughtful voice, "I shall do the dance."

Gandor nervously waddled into the center of the group. He calmed himself down into a squat-like posture. He took a deep breath and began the dance. Lifting his bright blue webbed feet alternately, he rocked from side-to-side, rotating as he swayed. Except for his total attention to the sacred movements of this mating ritual, Gandor appeared clownish. The dance was an unfolding paradox. Jack and Caitlin were riveted by each move Gandor made. Even Ens and his grotesque Corps were totally absorbed in the dance ritual. As Gandor danced, he forgot where he was. He lost himself in the thousands of years of behavior and ritual gifted to him by his ancestors. Gandor was not just beautiful to watch, he was a marvel. He stopped. He raised his beak, pointed toward the sky, and clacked his beak rapidly together over-and-over creating a beat, making music with each clack. The clacks echoed. Jack had never heard or seen anything like this. He was overwhelmed.

After the clacking, Gandor snapped his head abruptly down and stopped the beak clacking. He waited. A natural silence hovered over them all. Something special was happening. Jack and Caitlin felt it. Slowly the transparent image of his life partner Alba faded into view. She stood directly across from Gandor. They stared into each other's eyes. In perfect sync, they danced in split-second time with each other. It was as if time, distance and tragic events had never separated the couple.

Together, the couple faced each other. Each waddled in circles around the other alternately lifting his or her right blue-foot high in the air, followed by the left blue-foot. Everyone felt the magic of the moment. Caitlin thought that here she was witnessing the pure ritual of survival, a mating dance passed down over millions of years. As a musician, Jack knew that this ritual dance with its perfectly timed clacking and stomping was the music of creation, rhythms of the universe, rhythms of their ancestors. It was pure organic music which life had encoded into their genes.

Gandor leaned his bill forward until it touched Alba's bill halfway down the tip. Then, as if drawing a half-circle around Gandor's bill, Alba slid her bill on top of his. They walked around each other repeating the bill touching over-and-over creating a wooden clacking noise. Suddenly, Gandor stopped. He abruptly stepped back and stood bolt upright like a statue. Motionless, he stared at Alba. His eyebrows became conspicuously raised and prominent. After a few seconds, Alba imitated her mate and took a step backwards. Together in perfect synchronization, they dipped their long necks alternately from side-to-side nearly touching the ground between their blue-webbed feet. Gandor bowed his head and neck to the right; Alba bowed her head and neck to the right. As they faced each other, they bowed down toward the ground in opposite directions. They did this numerous times over many minutes until Gandor stopped, threw his head back, and pointed his beak skyward. He let out a long high-pitched whoo-o-o-o-o. In unison, they resumed bowing from side-to-side until they both clicked their heads toward the sky with their bills slightly open. Like Spanish dancers with castanets, Gandor and Alba clicked their beaks open in rapid succession, rat-tat-tat. Rat-tat-tat. Rat-tat-tat. Rat-tat-tat. Then, they stopped at the same exact split-second. They skypointed with their necks stretched vertical, like two sharpened pieces of wood pointing up to the heavens. After repeated loud clacks of their beaks, they lowered their heads and waddled in a circle around each other, lifting their bright-blue feet high into the air as if they were strutting clowns in a circus sideshow.

It was the dance of life. When it ended, standing opposite, Alba and Gandor stared into each other's eyes. Then, in the silence of the loneliness of Devastation Plain, Alba's image faded into nothingness. Gandor let out a long high-pitched whoo-o-o-o! His face was drawn and wrinkled with sadness.

"Why did you kill her?" Jack asked Ens.

"They killed themselves." Ens replied.

While Gandor hung his head, Jack, Caitlin and Potter Sims stood in the silence of Devastation Plain waiting to hear an explanation from Ens. Minutes passed.

"As a species, Gandor and his clan had an opportunity to choose. They made the wrong choice," explained Ens.

"What did they choose?" asked Caitlin.

"Fear."

Ens turned to Gandor, who was sad and silent.

"You may go, Gandor." Ens said.

Without saying a word, Gandor flapped his great wings and lifted his bright-blue webbed feet off the ground. In one subdued, yet powerful sweep of his wings, Gandor lifted twenty feet off the ground. Ens nodded to Hranknor, who was the leader of The Corps. In a lightning move, Hranknor snatched Gandor right out of the air and dropped him harshly onto the ground surrounded by The Corps.

Hranknor was Ens' right hand lieutenant. Hranknor stood over seven feet tall. His posture was erect and authoritative, unlike the rest of The Corps, who shuffled and walked slightly hunched over. Hranknor's body was grotesquely muscular with wiry brown hair that covered his legs, his back and his arms. His black bat-like wings projected great power. Darker than the other Corps, Hranknor's wings spanned twenty-five feet from tip-to-tip. They were threatening. Even though he projected a primitive appearance, his eyes revealed incisive intelligence, far above those whom he commanded.

The Corps encircled Gandor. They were seven feet tall. Gandor was a mere three feet. The Corps' leaned down and poked and pecked at Gandor. He squawked in terror. Some of Gandor's feathers flew out of his skin.

"Stop it!" Jack screamed.

Gandor screeched louder. Ens raised his hand, and The Corps stopped taunting the beaten bird.

"Gandor will be fine," said Ens. "We're just exercising our sense of humor."

"Oh, this is real funny!" Potter Sims exclaimed.

"Be careful, Sims, we wouldn't want to lose you too," Ens wagged his finger toward Potter Sims.

Ens pointed to the sky and The Corps flew off. Feathers frayed and beaten, Gandor waddled over to Jack, Caitlin, and Potter Sims. Caitlin stroked Gandor's head, trying to comfort him.

"Survival and compassion are strange bedfellows, don't you think?" Ens asked. Ens stared at Jack and held his hand out, "Let me see the diagram."

"How did you know about that?" Jack asked.

"Come on, let me see it," Ens was becoming impatient with their underestimation of his knowledge and power.

Jack removed the Yamqui drawing from his back pocket.

"You still don't know who you are dealing with, do you?" said Ens as he examined the map.

"Fine work," Ens commented as his eyes scoured the paper. "I like the ideas in here." Ens turned to Caitlin, "Do you like them?"

"I haven't seen it," Caitlin said with surprise in her voice.

"You should take a look, I think that you'll be interested," Ens added. He turned to Jack, "Do you see the gold?" Ens pointed enthusiastically to the large gold oval in the center of the Yamqui drawing. Jack was quiet. Ens dropped a brilliant gold nugget into Jack's hand.

"How is your sister Natalie?" Ens asked.

"What about my sister?"

"If you want to save her, you better do whatever you have to do to find me. Don't make the mistake Gandor did." Ens said as he handed Jack the Yamqui drawing.

Gandor's entire posture was hunched over in shame and sorrow, his eyes lowered to the ground.

"Be sure." Ens said looking at Jack.

"Be sure of what?" blurted out Potter Sims.

"He knows," Ens replied.

Ens pointed to the ground. There was a great rumble and a flash. A blue lightning bolt connected the land with the sky. Ens disappeared into the bolt. The air crackled all around. Ens was gone. There was nothing left but Jack, Caitlin, Potter Sims and Gandor and the barren wasteland of Devastation Plain.

CHAPTER 32

THE DRAWING OF JUAN DE SANTACRUZ PACHACUTI YAMQUI

Several minutes had passed until Gandor calmed down.

"Can I see the drawing?" asked Caitlin, as she held her hand out to Jack. He handed her the Juan de Santacruz Pachacuti Yamqui drawing. She had spent years scrolling through manuscripts and deciphering ancient drawings. Now, she carefully scrutinized every detail of the Yamqui drawing.

"Where did you get this?" she asked Jack.

"A man named Murland gave it to me."

"Who is he?" Gandor asked.

"I'm not sure, but he was more like a magician than anything," Jack answered uncertainly.

"How did he get this?" Caitlin asked completely puzzled, Jack saw it in her bewildered expression.

"I don't know. Why?" Jack asked.

Caitlin stared long at the Juan de Santacruz Pachacuti Yamqui drawing with anxiety and questions wrinkling her brow.

"So what's the problem?" Potter Sims asked.

"Do you know what this is?" Caitlin said as she held the drawing up in the air for everyone to see.

"It looks like a bunch of gibberish!" Potter Sims blurted.

"Hardly." Caitlin said glaring at Potter Sims. "This is a famous Inca drawing. And this is the original manuscript!"

"What does that mean?" Potter Sims asked.

"It means, Sims, that it is not a copy, it is the actual paper drawn by the artist," Gandor explained as he blew smoke into the air.

"I'm not that—" Before Potter Sims finished, Caitlin cut him off.

"It means that this document," Caitlin held up the Yamqui drawing, "is four hundred years old, and somehow this man Murland got it and gave it to you." Caitlin looked at Jack.

"How is that possible?" Jack questioned.

"It's not," Caitlin said flatly.

"Well, obviously it is because you are holding it!" Potter Sims said curtly, as he shook his head.

"Perhaps this Murland person somehow knew that he was going to need it," Gandor said as he puffed on his pipe and proudly blew smoke symbols into the air in the shapes of the rainbow and lightning images on the Yamqui drawing.

"Of course he knew that he was going to need it, you pompous windbag! Why else would he have given it to him?" Potter Sims yelled at Gandor.

"Who asked you, Sims!" Gandor yelled back.

"That's enough!" Jack exclaimed, as he waved his arms in front of Gandor and Potter Sims trying to end their bickering.

"May I say something?" Caitlin interjected with a calm, confident voice.

They all stopped and looked at Caitlin.

"I am an archeoastronomer," Caitlin explained.

"You already told us that!" Potter Sims interrupted.

Caitlin glared at Potter Sims, while she continued to speak. "I study ancient cultures and stars. This is a blueprint of the Inca world. It shows how the Incas perceived their world as it related to the universe that surrounded them."

Jack, Potter Sims and Gandor stepped forward to examine the Yamqui drawing closely. Caitlin held it out for them to see. As she stared at the Yamqui drawing, her eyes glassed over and her mind slipped into the past.

A frayed piece of paper, discolored from age, lay on the large mahogany desk in a den. Great books filled the bookcases that were ten feet high and lined the two long walls of the stately library. There were volumes about international politics, annual reports of the U.S. State Department, books on Andean cultures, National Geographic and the Royal Geographic travel books, histories of the Revolutionary War to World War II, books on native American Indians, and volumes about the Jewish holocaust.

Four year-old Caitlin Rose Bingham stood alone in her grandfather's library staring down at the old frayed parchment. Her blondish light brown hair hung loosely just above her shoulders. Her hazel eyes reflected her clarity and an insatiable intelligent mind. When strangers met her, they were instantly struck by her penetrating stare and her adult manner, especially if they took the time to converse with her. Caitlin gently picked up the parchment knowing that this old yellowed piece of paper was important. She held it in her fingers. It was the cosmological diagram of Juan de Santacruz Pachacuti Yamqui. Suddenly, the door opened and in walked her grandfather, Hiram Bingham IV. He smiled at her as he walked up next to her and put his fingers next to hers on the diagram.

"Do you like that?" he asked.

"Yes, it is interesting. I like the pictures on it," she answered.

"It is interesting," said the 83 year-old, white-haired grandfather. "But do you know what?"

"What?" Caitlin said.

"I find you interesting, too."

Caitlin smiled as her grandfather pulled her to his side giving her a big hug.

Hiram Bingham IV was a gentile classy man. At eighty-three years old, his white hair was trimmed and combed meticulously back. He wore wire-rimmed glasses that revealed his kind eyes and rested comfortably on his high rounded cheekbones. He had the most caring smile, which endeared him to everyone who met him.

Greatness had passed down through generations in the Bingham family. Harry's father was Hiram Bingham III, the famous explorer and discoverer of Machu Picchu in the year 1911. Risk was a common denominator in the Bingham line. Hiram III spent years trudging through the jungles of South America and climbing the rocky peaks of the Andes in search of the Inca lost city. His son Hiram the IV, known as Harry, risked his career and life by defying the policy and directives of President Roosevelt's administration and the cautious policies of the U.S. government. While serving as American vice-consul in Marseilles, France, Hiram IV saved thousands of Jewish refugees. Though he had never climbed the peaks of the Andes or explored the jungles of the Amazon, Harry had studied his father's work, read the thousand of pages of his father's diary, and seen every photograph from every expedition, especially the discovery of the hidden Inca settlement of Machu Picchu.

By the time she was six years old, Caitlin had spent countless hours with her grandfather, Hiram Bingham IV in his home in Salem, Connecticut where she listened to his stories that his own father had told him. In her mind, she could still see the photos showing the Incas living on the mountainsides of the Andes. In her head, she could still hear her grandfather's voice recounting the rainy days when his explorer father cut his way through the thick vertical jungles on Peruvian expeditions looking for the lost city of Machu Picchu.

Caitlin remembered sitting in the big red leather chair lined with brass tacks that she touched with her fingertips. She remembered how her grandfather recounted that day in 1911 when his father, with the help of a young Inca boy from a local village, first saw Machu Picchu. It was nestled into the jungle on the side of a mountain, hidden from view by overgrown vines and trees. Caitlin Bingham's imagination was branded with the story-told images that would drive her more than twenty years later to the greatest search of her life.

In the clearing, Caitlin was still holding onto the Yamqui drawing, as Jack pointed to a rainbow over a lake on the left side of the drawing.

"Look at the rainbow," Jack said, while Caitlin drew her attention back to the drawing. "When I was on the black beach near the lagoon, there were little rainbows in the grains of black sand."

"I saw them," Caitlin said.

"And the lightning," Jack denoted the lightning on the Yamqui drawing. Before Jack could finish his thoughts, his mind flashed to the image of the lighting bolt striking his father at the base of the Great Oak tree in the Catskill Mountains. He became lost in the image of blue lightning impaling his father; the Stradivarius violin flying through the air—the smoking, charred violin bridge lying in the green grass.

"So, what does all of this mean?" Potter Sims blurted out.

"It means that for some reason the four of us were drawn to this place at this point in time. And this diagram has something to do with it."

"I don't believe in stuff like that," Caitlin said. "People see what they want to see."

"I heartily agree," said Gandor as he puffed solemnly on his pipe and exhaled the bluish, mathematical smoke symbols Alpha, omega, infinity, and pi into the air.

"I agree—people see what they want to see." Potter Sims said, impatient with this mysterious talk. "We see what we see! And that's that!"

"Sims, you're as simple as those stupid red boots!" Gandor puffed on his Sherlock Holmes pipe.

"Oh, you have all the answers to everything, right? If you and your kin are so smart, then why are you the last of them? Huh?"

Gandor saw red. Like a bull, he charged Potter Sims, who buzzed his wings and lifted straight up off the ground. With his wings outstretched, Gandor ran just beneath Potter Sims trying to gore the pesky insect with his beak.

"Stop it, you two!" yelled Caitlin.

Jack reached up in the air and grabbed Potter Sims by his nose. Buzzing his wings and kicking his red boots wildly, Potter Sims spun around like a tether ball around the pole. He landed with a thud to the ground. He screamed, "Arumph! Harumph! Harumph!" No one understood a word that Potter Sims said because Jack was squeezing his nose. It sounded like he had a mouth full of stones.

"You both know the territory," Jack said to both Gandor and Potter Sims. "You two are going to guide us to Ens and the Incas."

Jack released Potter Sims, who plopped firmly on the ground. Potter Sims shook his head and grabbed his bruised nose. He hyperventilated as he struggled to catch his breath.

"Why didn't you grab *him*?" Potter Sims asked as he huffed and panted pointing to Gandor.

"Because you were closer," Jack explained.

"Are you going to take us to Ens?" Jack asked both Potter Sims and Gandor.

"Does he have to go?" Potter Sims protested.

"Sims, it is I who must endure the humiliation of traveling with cultural counterfeit as yourself," Gandor said.

"Cultural counterfeit!" responded Potter Sims in a fit.

"That's it! We are leaving!" Caitlin roared aloud as she walked toward Devastation Plain alone leaving Jack, Potter Sims and Gandor behind.

Gandor yelled at Caitlin, "I will do it for you, my new friends!" Caitlin was so disgusted that she didn't even turn around, even though she heard every word.

"Thank you," Jack replied politely to Gandor.

"I have never been so insulted!" exclaimed Potter Sims.

"Get used to it," Jack grumpily spouted off as he walked off following Caitlin onto Devastation Plain. "Let's go!" he yelled back to Potter Sims and Gandor.

Reluctantly, Gandor followed several steps behind Jack.

Gandor yelled over his shoulder. "Don't get too close, Sims! Keep your distance!"

"Don't worry! If you were the last creature in the world, I wouldn't get near you!" Potter Sims yelled back. Gandor was by now twenty feet ahead of Potter Sims, as they traipsed off into desolation.

CHAPTER 33

THE VISIT

The New York night was temperate and clear. Spotlights arranged in a circle around the base of the Giant Beanstalk threw beams of light across the night sky illuminating the Beanstalk. It glowed in the night like a lighthouse guiding sailors toward a port. From as far as twenty-five miles away, people could see it, whether they were in Manhattan, Brooklyn, Queens, Staten Island, Jersey City, Union City, or Hoboken standing on a street corner, sitting on their porch steps or gathering in parks as they talked and stared in awe at the Giant Green Beanstalk that towered over the city.

Two blocks away from the World Trade Center site and the Beanstalk, thousands of people had gathered for a candlelight vigil. Each person held a white candle attached to a small disposable aluminum plate. The candlelight illuminated each person's face with a soft glow. A priest, a minister and a rabbi led them in prayer and songs.

From the very top of the Beanstalk, where it disappeared into the clouds, a slow wind blew down the shaft spreading through the branches and rustling its giant leaves. The sounds of the leaves fluttering in the warm wind echoed for city blocks around the World Trade Center Plaza site. It was incessant like the sound of a million cicadas. The buzzing reverberated for miles away from the Beanstalk. The wind spread from the base of the Beanstalk down every Manhattan street; it whistled through the Bronx, across the Brooklyn Bridge, through the Lincoln and Holland Tunnels, and across the Hudson River to New Jersey. It was a slow warm wind, gentle at first, but it picked up strength as a harbinger of something greater to come.

Elsewhere in Manhattan, Mattie and Natalie had moved into a friend's simple two-bedroom apartment in Chelsea. Dressed in jeans and sweatshirt and wearing a Yankees baseball cap, Natalie stood at the living room window staring out at the Giant Beanstalk that glowed bright green in the Manhattan night sky. Her mother Mattie sat on the couch fretting. The HDTV television droned with the evening news, but she stared blankly at it; her mind was elsewhere.

"Jack is all right, mother. He is with friends." Natalie said as she looked away from the Beanstalk at her mother.

Mattie stared at her daughter with a puzzled look. "How would you know that?"

"Because we know things about each other." Natalie's tone was upbeat. "We have always known things about each other as long as I can remember. No matter how far apart we were. When Jack was traveling with Dad performing in Europe and I was getting chemo treatments, he knew that I was down and having a rough time. He would call me just when I needed him to."

"So you know each other's thoughts?" Mattie asked, curiously.

"And more," Natalie explained. Her voice was matter-of-fact, as she had long before accepted this ability as a private, natural understanding between her and her brother. "I haven't told anyone about it, not even Dad, until now."

Just then, the ground began to rumble. The apartment shook. Manhattan trembled for thirty seconds as if it was having a 5.0 earthquake. Vases and framed photos fell off the shelves shattering on the hardwood floor of the Chelsea apartment. Mattie stood by Natalie near the window and they stared at the Giant Beanstalk.

At the top of Beanstalk where it disappeared into the swirling clouds, the huge branches shook. Inside the clouds, there was an explosion of red, orange and yellow light, like a brilliant sunset radiating outward and parting the clouds with a circular hole. Out of the blinding light, The Corps streamed into the night sky above Manhattan. Hranknor led hundreds of them like geese flying in v-formation diving down the Beanstalk toward the city. People saw the burst of light at the top of the Beanstalk, then the indistinct, shadowy images of the Harpy-like creatures as they darted in and out of the distinct beams of light created by the spotlights. The Corps cut the air like knives; their wings flapped loudly creating a sound like a thousand whips cracking in the dark all round the Giant Beanstalk.

People on the ground scattered. They ran for cover into buildings and the subways.

The rumbling had stopped at their Chelsea apartment. Standing side-by-side at the window, Natalie and Mattie saw black specks in the distance flitting in-and-out of the huge searchlights at the World Trade Center site. Like the rest of the city, they watched in terror and awe not knowing what was to come.

Just then, there was a knock at the door. Nervously, Mattie walked to the door and looked out the peephole. Standing in the hallway was Murland. He was dressed in a conservative dark three-piece suit and wore a bright multi-colored tie embroidered with stars, the planets, the moon and sun.

"Mrs. Tott?" Through the closed door, Murland spoke at the peephole.

"Yes?" Mattie answered apprehensively from behind the closed door.

"I am Murland, a close friend of Jacob's … Jack. I need to speak with you." There was a long silence, while Mattie thought. "Please, Mrs. Tott, it is about Jack and Natalie!"

Mattie looked at Natalie, who walked over to the door and spied out the peephole at Murland. She looked at his white beard and clothes; she particularly liked his tie. She smiled at her mother, then removed the latch from the door, unbolted the deadbolt and opened the door. Murland stood in the threshold.

"Hello!" he said with a big smile. "May I come in?"

"You gave Jack the beans?" Mattie asked.

"Yes."

Mattie's mouth dropped in disbelief. She was confused. While Mattie searched Murland's turquoise eyes, Natalie opened the door wider.

"Please come in," she said.

"Why thank you, Natalie." Murland said gratefully as he stepped into the room and shut the door behind him.

"How do you know her?" Mattie asked suspiciously.

"From Jack, but I already knew about you." Murland felt Mattie's suspicions and paranoia. "Don't get me all wrong, I'm not a spy or anything like that! Heaven forbid! You do believe in heaven, don't you? I do! No, that's not right. I don't *believe* in heaven because you can't believe in something that you know is fact! That would be like believing in gravity!" Murland laughed. Natalie liked Murland.

By this time, Murland noticed that Mattie was wide-eyed with bewilderment.

"I'm sorry for being so, what's the word … loquacious. That's a good word, isn't it? But I can't do anything about being that way, like the spots on a leopard!" Murland let silence settle the room, and then he spoke quietly. "I just know about things and people, that's all. It's my job."

"What do you want?" Mattie asked.

"I want to help." Murland looked at Natalie. "I see you're up and about?"

"I'm having a good day today."

"Good. Maybe we can sit down?" Murland pointed to the couch.

"I suppose," Mattie said with some reluctance. Murland waited for her to move toward the couch. Natalie sat next to her mother, and then Murland sat next to them. To Mattie, the moment felt strangely like home. Instinctively, it felt like they were family. Though her heart felt it, she could not understand.

"I am a long-time collector of ancient artifacts. One day, Jack wandered into my shop. Before too long, we discovered that we shared common passions. One thing led to another, and here I am!"

Mattie was not convinced. Murland reached over and took her hand.

"Mattie, you must know that things are going to be all right." Murland's voice was assuring and calm.

Just then, there was a loud cacophonous flapping outside the window.

"What's that?" Mattie cried out.

From the couch, they looked out the living room's sliding glass door, beyond the balcony to where Hranknor and The Corps were flying like pigeons circling the loft. It was dark. Their quick indistinct forms darted in and out the shadows and the street light. Murland walked across the living room toward the balcony, his eyes were bright, filled with wonder. Fearlessly, Natalie followed close behind him.

"Natalie, don't!" Mattie cried out.

"It's all right, mother."

Murland slid the sliding glass door open. Instantly the sound of The Corps' beating wings cracking the air echoed through the apartment. The sound was unearthly, like something from a demonic netherworld. It frightened Mattie. It fascinated Natalie. It exhilarated Murland.

Then, like Dracula or Batman, Hranknor extended his enormous wings skyward, fanned the air, and floated gently to the apartment's balcony railing. His thick, black scaly toes wrapped around the railing, and his talons scratched the metal. With a powerful, but gentle lift of his wings, Hranknor lifted himself vertically and, like a ballerina, stepped gracefully to the porch. Seven-foot wings spanned twenty-five feet across the ends of the balcony. Hranknor took two steps across the red tiled balcony deck toward the sliding glass door, where only the screen separated Hranknor from Murland, Natalie, and Mattie. Behind Hranknor, The Corps circled the building, flapping their giant wings. On the couch, Mattie was terrified. Though she was standing arm-to-arm with Murland, Natalie, too, was frightened. She gripped the arm of Murland's suit jacket with her thumb and index finger. Murland patted her hand gently, which calmed her fears. Murland and Hranknor stared directly into each other's eyes for several minutes. While the anxious silence hung in the balcony air, Murland picked up images and thoughts from Hranknor about Jack's welfare. He saw Jack with friends—Caitlin, Gandor and Potter Sims—on Devastation Plain. He saw images of the Great Forest, where they all met and ate remarkable fruits and vegetables together. Murland's face got sad as he saw the suffering that Gandor endured from Ens, Hranknor and The Corps. He saw Jack handing the Juan de Santacruz Pachacuti drawing to Ens, then Caitlin examining it. A faint smile passed across Murland's lips, as he turned slightly to Mattie.

"It's all right. He is a messenger. Jack is fine." Murland reassured Mattie, who immediately sighed and broke down, partly out of the hopeful belief that her son was safe and partly out of releasing her fear of this hideous creature.

Hranknor looked at Natalie, who stared back. It was as if they were exchanging greetings. Then, with no warning, Hranknor lifted his great wings vertically above his head and swept the air. In one quick motion, he was thirty feet above the balcony. His muscular body spun effortlessly in the air and with The Corps following him, they flew off as black specks streaking across the Manhattan night skyline. Mattie joined her daughter and Murland on the balcony, as they watched The Corps flying toward the Beanstalk in the distance.

At the base of the Giant Beanstalk, people gathered as The Corps rumbled, their wings cracking the air as they rose like a squadron of jet fighters straight up the Beanstalk until they disappeared into the clouds.

CHAPTER 34

DEVASTATION PLAIN

Together, but separated, Caitlin, Jack, Gandor and Potter Sims walked in a line behind one another across the barren and unknown horizon of Devastation Plain.

It was twilight. The setting sun painted rich red, yellow and orange ochre, deep burgundy and cool violets across the barren wasteland and on the purple majestic mountains beyond Devastation Plain. Jack, Caitlin, Potter Sims and Gandor stood in the middle of Devastation Plain staring in awe at the palette of colors before them. After several minutes of silence and reflection, the four pushed on toward the mountains, which they had to reach before nightfall. It would get cold soon, too cold to survive on the plains. Though the sun lit Devastation Plain with fire reds and oranges, the temperature would soon drop fifty degrees. At the base of the mountains were small trees and scrub brush growing between the jagged rocks.

"How much daylight do we have?" Jack was concerned. One weekend three years ago, he and a friend went on a day backpacking trip into the Adirondack Mountains. While high in the mountains, a sudden snowstorm blew in and they got trapped at night on the mountain top. They would have frozen to death had it not been for a determined rescue effort sent to find them. Jack knew the hazards of the cold.

"Only about two hours," answered Gandor.

"Then we better pick up our pace," Caitlin added.

"You don't have to stay with us," Potter Sims prodded Gandor. "You can fly there five times faster than we can walk."

"I stay with my friends, Sims, contrary to what you would do, that is, if you could fly," countered Gandor.

"Humph!"

"Let's keep walking," Jack said as he and Caitlin kept a steady pace toward the mountains that were dead ahead of them. Gandor and Potter Sims followed closely behind.

After nearly two hours, Jack, Caitlin, Potter Sims, and Gandor arrived at the base of the Great Mountain Range, which bordered Devastation Plain. Exhausted, the four trekkers crumpled to the black jagged rocks, but there was no time to rest. They had to build a fire. The temperature had dropped to -8° Centigrade, and it was still dropping rapidly. Potter Sims shook uncontrollably. The breath of each of the four adventurers crystallized in the brittle air. Gandor's thick plumage insulated him from the biting cold, but he still helped Jack and Caitlin gather up sticks, pieces of scrub brush, and dead leaves. Though he was shivering, Potter Sims scavenged the ground for anything that would burn. As he picked up the dead wood, he made strange noises with his proboscis, like a toothless old man who chewed on his gums making annoying smacking and sucking noises. They arranged the sticks and brush in a teepee shape. Caitlin placed handfuls of dried leaves and twigs inside the wood pyramid. Jack motioned to Gandor, who waddled over to the three-foot high wooden teepee.

"You light it, Gandor," Jack said, his lips blue with cold.

Everyone waited anxiously. Gandor leaned over the wooden teepee, struck one of his purple and green triangular matches and lit the kindling. The wood sucked the fire from the triangular match as a magnet pulls a piece of metal to its center. Immediately, the flames spurted out of the wooden teepee.

"I hate the cold!" Potter Sims blurted out, as he warmed his white-gloved hands by the fire. "I thought I was going to freeze!"

"At least that would have shut you up for awhile, Sims." Gandor joked.

"I am not going to say a word," replied Potter Sims. "I am going to be civil since you lit the fire," Potter Sims said to everyone's surprise. Jack and Caitlin looked at each other in amazement, but they knew that it would take far more than freezing to death to cement a peace between Potter Sims and Gandor.

It was late at night. Millions of stars filled the sky, and the fire was still burning strong. Under the bright stars, Jack, Caitlin, Potter Sims, and Gandor rested their backs uncomfortably against the jagged black lava rock. In the distance, just beyond another ridge of jagged rocks was a great volcano. Red and orange plumes of fire spurted high into the air above the great cone crater. A huge column of black smoke spiraled out of enormous fingers of fire that lit up the night sky. The volcano spewed lava hundreds of feet into the night sky, as ribbons of lava snaked down the mountainside. It was a gigantic spectacle of nature.

"The rocks are warm," Jack said as he felt a black rock with his palm.

"Too bad we didn't know earlier," said Potter Sims.

"This whole area is exothermically active," Caitlin instructed them.

"What does that mean?" Potter Sims blurted.

"It means hot because of the changes deep under the ground. Don't you know anything, Sims?" Gandor proudly puffed on his pipe and bellowed smoke into the air.

"I know arrogance when I see it!" Potter Sims stared at Gandor.

"Enough, you two!" Jack yelled.

"Do you all see the mountain ridges over there?" Caitlin pointed to a distant ridge, highlighted by starlight. "Those are volcanic cones along that ridge. Most of them are probably active."

"It has been this way for many, many years," explained Gandor. "At least for as long as I can remember."

"What happened?" asked Potter Sims.

"Geologic transformation," Caitlin said. "It's a cycle. A region of vegetation and settlement are entirely destroyed by volcanic activity, then grow back sometimes even more abundant than before because of the rich nutrients in the soil."

"Devastation Plain was once part of the Great Forest," Gandor said.

"Then, it will grow back," Potter Sims said.

"Under the proper conditions, a forest can evolve after thousands sometimes even hundreds of years from a region like this," Caitlin explained. "Look at the Highlands in the Galapagos Islands, the Hawaiian Islands, Canary Islands, they all evolved out of a volcanic base."

"It is so primeval," exclaimed Jack, as he stared at the erupting volcano.

"It's how it all started," Caitlin said. "I've hiked into volcanoes, but I've never seen an active one."

"I hate fire," Potter Sims said.

"How could you hate that?" Caitlin said, pointing to the magnificent fireworks display over the erupting volcano. She was irritated by Potter Sims' remark, and increasingly impatient with his impulsive behavior.

"It is fire, that's how," Potter Sims said.

"Is there anything you don't hate?" Caitlin asked.

"Music, good music," Potter Sims answered.

"Now, there is something that you and I have in common, Potter." Jack smiled at Potter Sims.

"Hopefully," Gandor said puffing confidently on his pipe, "that is the only thing that you and he have in common."

"Who asked you?" Potter Sims shouted.

"It is amazing how a world can perish so quickly. There can be so much abundance, and then in the next moment, everything is gone," Jack said.

The four stared out at the lava flow, and the glowing red molten rock spraying high into the night sky. Gandor stared longer than anyone; it was as if he knew something that the others didn't. Something he was unwilling to tell.

"Anything wrong, Gandor?" Jack asked.

"No." Gandor answered abruptly and turned away to puff on his pipe.

As they watched the lava flow and the molten rock, they drifted off to sleep. The morning light swept gently across Devastation Plain as the sun warmed away the night chill. In the distance, the volcano was still spouting its dramatic red lava against the cerulean blue sky. The shadows and light rolled across the Devastation Plain. Earthy colors came to life. The day was on. Slowly, Jack, Caitlin, Potter Sims, and Gandor awakened. After reorganizing themselves, they headed off through a mountain pass.

After hours of treading softly across the sharp black igneous rock in the mountain pass, they finally arrived on top of the Great Mountain, where they stopped to rest. Far away, the volcano's blistered skin hurled its molten entrails into the sky. As they turned to look out over the boundless, bare plains, they saw great etchings carved into the raw plains they had just crossed. They stood in silence looking at the etchings chiseled into Devastation Plain for as far as they could see. There were ground etchings of a condor, a hummingbird, a long, winding serpent eating its tail, and a jaguar. There were imprints of the sun, of the crescent moon, and of star-like clusters.

"Gandor, have you seen these before?" Jack asked.

"Never." Gandor chewed on the tip of his pipe.

"How could you not see these? You fly over them, don't you?" accused Potter Sims.

"Devastation Plain is immense." Gandor defended himself.

"You should know. This is your territory!"

"It doesn't matter! What matters is that they are here!" Caitlin exclaimed.

"How old are these?" Jack asked.

"I can't be sure, but those symbols over there," Caitlin pointed to the right where there were a series of thirteen star-like circles. "They are the Pleiades. The Incas called them Nuchu Verano, Stars of Summer, and there's Orion's belt."

"What is that?" Potter Sims pointed to the ground etching of an animal with feline characteristics.

"It looks like a cat," Jack answered.

"It is a jaguar," Caitlin corrected him emphatically.

"Maybe that's me? That bird over there?" Gandor pointed with his pipe.

"I don't think so!" Potter Sims spouted back.

"Who asked you, Sims?"

"Most likely, it is a condor or an eagle," Caitlin offered.

"See." Potter Sims said proud of himself, but more because Gandor's ego had been temporarily put in place.

"They look like the Nazca lines," Jack said to Caitlin.

"You know about those?" Caitlin was impressed.

"I've been there, five years ago."

"These are exactly like the Nazca lines, except …" Caitlin trailed off. "Let me see that drawing," Caitlin held her hand out waiting for Jack to hand her the Yamqui drawing. Jack pulled the Yamqui drawing from his pocket and placed it in Caitlin's palm.

"See here," Caitlin said, as she pointed to it. "The Pleiades, Nuchu Verano, are here, and the sun and the moon."

"Maybe the people who carved out those etchings also made that map?" Potter Sims mused.

"I don't think so, besides it's not a map," said Caitlin. "It is an Inca concept drawing, and I have no idea how these lines got here and who made them."

"Maybe that's part of why we are here," Jack was still trying to figure out the mysterious events that brought them all together.

"Maybe."

"Whatever, we must get going," Jack said.

"I agree," Gandor nodded his head.

"Well, what are we waiting for!" exclaimed Potter Sims.

As the four walked to the other side of the mountain, Caitlin stopped by a gigantic obsidian rock. It was shiny and black. Large chunks were missing, fractured out of the corners. Caitlin stooped down to examine the obsidian.

"What is it?" asked Jack.

"It's obsidian, but it's not from here. It's been brought here from somewhere else." Caitlin noticed a rocky ridge about fifty meters away from where they stood. "It's as if they were—" Completely focused, she stopped abruptly and walked toward the ridge. Jack, Potter Sims, and Gandor watched her as she walked over and examined the jagged rock formation. The three walked over to the ridge where Caitlin was stooping down. Below in the distance, worn by erosion and time, and buried under rocks, were what appeared to be the battered remains of an elaborate ancient city covered by cinder and ash.

"What is this, Gandor?" Caitlin asked.

"I don't know. I have never heard of it. We had no record of it." Gandor was quite perplexed as he puffed on his pipe.

"Obviously, it is a city!" exclaimed Potter Sims.

"We know that, Sims! But what is it doing here?"

"What do you mean 'what is it doing here?'" Potter Sims exclaimed. "They were living here! And now, they are gone! Why does everyone make such a big deal out of the obvious!"

"Because maybe it's not so obvious to some of us," Jack tried to explain calmly.

"This was a highly advanced civilization. The stone that they used to build their city was not from anywhere remotely near this region. It is geologically different from the other igneous rock here," Caitlin explained.

Caitlin left the group, and walked back to look at the giant obsidian block. Again, Jack, Potter Sims, and Gandor followed her. Caitlin stood over the chipped obsidian block. Jutting out from one edge of the shiny black stone was a narrow and chiseled piece of granite about twenty feet long.

Caitlin touched the granite with her fingertips. "The obsidian, this black rock, was used as an accent or artistic frame," she said.

"For what?" Jack asked.

"I don't know. I've never seen anything like it."

Caitlin dusted the black and gray cinders off the granite slab with the palm of her hand. The granite was a polished stone, mottled and light gray. Eroded by time and weather was a message etched into the granite slab. Jack read the inscription aloud. "Look upon my works, ye mighty, and despair."

There was nothing left but the inscription in the granite around the decay of the colossal cracked hulk of the obsidian and the boundless and bare city beneath it.

"This was a giant gateway to that city," explained Caitlin.

"And now it's gone," Gandor held his Sherlock Holmes pipe, and had the glazed look as if he was remembering an event or some other place. Caitlin noticed his detachment.

"Do you know something about these ruins?" Caitlin asked.

Gandor took a long puff on his pipe and exhaled a large, expanding blue smoke ring into the air, where it rose over the ruins. "Nothing that would change anything," he said. Gandor knew something, they knew it by his tone, but they also knew that he was staunchly unwilling to reveal it. Even Potter Sims did not press him.

"This was a civilization," Potter Sims said. "See where ego gets you!"

"Do you think the people who did this, also made the etchings and lines in Devastation Plain?" Jack asked.

"I don't know."

"I am not trying to break this up," interrupted Gandor, "but if we don't get off this mountain before the light is gone, we will become part of this city."

"Gandor is right." Potter Sims said.

Together, Jack, Caitlin, Potter Sims, and Gandor left the mountaintop and walked down the other side where, after nearly an hour of walking, they saw an enormous field of thorns covering the distant plains below them that stretched to the horizon and beyond. They were awestruck.

CHAPTER 35

THE THORN MAZE

The Thorn Maze was fifty feet high and disappeared beyond the horizon in every direction, except where it had its back to the Great Mountains. There, between the mountains and the maze, was a twenty-foot perimeter of sand spotted with mounds of black jagged rock. Inside the Great Maze, there were thousands of vines, and millions of thorns. Like a giant curved tusk of a great elephant, each thorn was three to six feet long and grew on a wooden vine. Even though they varied in thickness, the vines averaged about eighteen inches in diameter. Twisting and turning in every possible direction, the vines strangled and twisted about themselves in a struggle for territorial survival. The thorns and the vines were made of mahogany. They were finely polished with a beautiful deep black grain. Thousands of contorted wooden growths, like polished mahogany bulbs with eerie knots, clung to the twisted vines. Three-foot wide paths meandered through the Great Thorn Maze leaving little room for safe navigation. Many of the great thorns protruded into the meandering paths. When the setting sun shone on the Great Maze, it was a spectacle beyond comparison. The deep mahogany of the Great Maze glistened in the light of the dying sun. It was as if the red lips of the sun sucked the red of the Maze's wood to its surface. The Thorn Maze was fatally beautiful. The complexity and the simplicity of the Great Thorn Maze was a paradox, a testament to the mathematics of death. There was no architecture like this anywhere.

Jack, Caitlin, Potter Sims, and Gandor walked down the side of the mountain and they stood in the small sand perimeter before the Great Thorn Maze. No one spoke, silenced by the immensity and dark beauty of this spectacle.

CHAPTER 36

THE CLOUD ROOM

Somewhere far off in another space without walls or a ceiling and neither a beginning nor end, Captain Jordan and his Special Forces soldiers waited. This was the Cloud Room. The soldiers were lost. From nowhere, like an omnipotent force, Ens materialized out of the boundless white into the Cloud Room. Alarmed, the soldiers raised their weapons. Ens approached Captain Jordan, who was struck by Ens' elegance and grace.

"Captain Jordan."

"How do you know my name?" Captain Jordan asked. He raised his 45 Springfield semi-automatic pistol and pointed it at Ens.

"There is little that I don't know."

"Who are you?"

"I am Ens. I am. I am."

"Is Dr. Bingham with you?"

"She is. Don't worry, she is safe."

"Where are we?" Captain Jordan asked.

"Where you are is not important. It is where you are going that matters."

Without a blink of his eye or hint of fear in his voice, Captain Jordan asked, "Where is that?"

"Choose two men," Ens replied. "The three of you will accompany me."

"Where are we going?" asked Captain Jordan.

"To teach," Ens said. "Your other men should know that you will not return."

"Are we going to die?" Captain Jordan asked.

"Do you know how a caterpillar metamorphoses into a beautiful butterfly?" Ens answered.

"Captain?" Billy, a young nervous soldier spoke up.

"It's all right, Billy," Captain Jordan said to Billy, trying to dispel his fears.

"Hold your positions!" Captain Jordan commanded. Sergeant Hicks and Sergeant Stone kept their assault rifles aimed directly at Ens.

"Nobody's going anywhere," Captain Jordan stood firm.

Ens was calm. "Captain, I understand that this must be difficult for you." Captain Jordan did not move his weapon an inch, nor did his soldiers move theirs. Their eyes were fixed upon the ten-foot tall intruder.

"In times of crisis," Ens explained calmly, "people in military service are called upon, not just to protect, but to sacrifice, and when they do, they become models of selflessness for others to emulate. They put their jobs and their convictions above their personal attachments. This is one of those times, Captain. This is an opportunity for you to complete what you have committed your life to."

Ens pointed to Captain Jordan's raised 45 Springfield semi-automatic pistol. "There is no need for that." Ens voice was disarmingly soothing.

Just as Captain Jordan was weighing Ens' words, three of The Corps descended into the Cloud Room. Terrified, some of the soldiers fired their automatic weapons at The Corps. As the bullets burst from each rifle barrel, they slowed to a near stop and hung in the air of the Cloud Room. With a pop, each bullet exploded like a champagne cork and became a soft patch of root-like fibers about three inches round. Thousands of the fibrous patches floated like brown feathers from pillows in the white space above the soldiers' heads. Watching the floating patches, Captain Jordan lowered his 45 caliber pistol.

"Hold your fire," Captain Jordan commanded his soldiers.

The soldiers stopped firing. Captain Jordan realized the futility of force. He knew that he had no power. It was time to surrender.

"The only choice you have is how you come with me," said Ens. "You can be taken away delirious with fear, or you can surrender with calm and strength."

"They're frightened," said Captain Jordan.

Ens was silent.

"Will my men be safe?" Captain Jordan asked in a compassionate voice.

There was a long silence, and then Ens responded. "They will live or die, but as soldiers. I can do no more and no less than that."

Resolute, Captain Jordan ordered his men. "Lower your weapons." The soldiers lowered their rifles. Calmly, Ens pointed to the soldier Billy and the other private. The Corps grabbed them along with Captain Jordan. With a few rapid sweeps of their wings, The Corps lifted the three soldiers swiftly and vertically from the Cloud Room. The other soldiers watched their weapons dropped behind and they faded out of sight. Just as he had entered, Ens faded away into the room's whiteness. Surrounded by thousands of fibrous patches that floated in the Cloud Room, all that the soldiers could do was watch in a state of mounting terror.

CHAPTER 37

THE SACRIFICE

At the Great Thorn Maze, it was late afternoon and hot, when Jack, Caitlin, Potter Sims, and Gandor arrived at its edge. With the mountains at their backs, they stood in the narrow sand perimeter twelve feet from the wall of thorns. Stunned by the volume and power of the Great Thorn Maze, they stood in silence staring at its grand beauty. *This must be on the map,* Jack thought. He took the Yamqui drawing from his back pocket and slowly unfolded it. Potter Sims and Gandor gathered around to see.

"I remembered seeing this. Look," Jack pointed to the cross-hatchings at the bottom of the Yamqui drawing.

"Doesn't it say right there, 'Land of Agriculture: Maze of Life?'" Gandor asked as he pointed his wing tip at the crossed-hatched lines on the bottom of the Yamqui drawing.

"It could be the Thorn Maze," Jack conjectured.

"There is nothing on that piece of paper that even suggests a Thorn Maze." Potter Sims said to everyone's surprise.

"Then, where is it, Sims? Everything that has happened has been on this map. So where is it?" Gandor pressed.

"This is not a map. You are seeing what you want to see," Caitlin said. "I agree with Potter Sims. Nowhere on this paper, does it say 'Maze of Thorns' or 'Great Thorn Maze!'"

"But it does say 'Maze,'" said Jack. "And we've come across many things that are on this drawing—a rainbow, the lagoon, mountains, the Pleiades—lightning."

"What's the use?" Caitlin surrendered. "How can I convince you that this drawing was never designed as a map?"

"Perhaps it was never designed as a map, but it has become one." Jack suggested.

"That is an interesting idea," Gandor said as he puffed on his pipe.

Potter Sims takes the Yamqui drawing in his hand and holds it up. "The purpose of a map is to guide. A map shows you where you have been, and where you are going. Most maps are precise. This one is not. However, it serves a purpose. It reinforces destinations where we have been or where we are going. So far, they have been on this drawing. I believe this is both, a concept drawing and a map. In both cases, it gives us information, and that is essential for our survival."

"Well said, Sims!" Gandor said.

"I guess it's both, if Potter says so. He is our guide," Jack said.

"I do not have the energy to debate it," Caitlin said.

As the four stood in front of the enormous wall of the Thorns, they saw Captain Jordan, Private William "Billy" Ketchum, and another soldier materialize out of the purple shadows made by the black jagged rocks in the white sand. The four were astounded, speechless. Caitlin was so close to Captain Jordan that she could see his blue eyes. Everything happened in a flash. One second, Caitlin was standing with Jack and Potter Sims and Gandor, the next she found herself walking hurriedly toward Captain Jordan. Jack was caught off guard.

"Captain!" Caitlin yelled.

Captain Jordan turned, he saw Caitlin. As he did, Ens materialized out of the purple and black shadows. Captain Jordan stopped. Caitlin stopped. Jack ran to catch her.

"Who is that?" Jack asked.

"It's Captain Jordan and two of the soldiers I came up here with."

Potter Sims and Gandor had reached Caitlin and Jack.

"Why are they here?" Potter Sims asked.

"I don't know," Caitlin responded uneasily.

After feeling his evil in Central Park, and seeing what Ens did to Gandor, Jack knew that the Captain and his men were in danger. Ens' sudden appearance with the soldiers, the Great Thorn Maze, the look on Caitlin's face, it all fit and disturbed Jack greatly.

The ten-foot tall Ens stared at Caitlin, Jack, Potter Sims, and Gandor.

"Who are they?" Captain Jordan asked.

"Jacob Tott, and two creatures we met here."

"Creatures?" Potter Sims exclaimed.

"Hum." Gandor pondered Caitlin's choice of words.

"Why are they here?" Captain Jordan asked.

"Because they are part of what is going to happen," Ens smiled.

"Just what *is* going to happen?" Caitlin asked.

Ens did not answer. Silence filled the white sand perimeter, as everyone felt that something horrible was about to happen. The Great Thorn Maze seemed to feed off of their fear. It delighted Ens.

Beneath everyone's feet, deep in the bowels of the ground, a rumbling intensified as seconds seemed like minutes. Slowly, Ens shifted into a giant black Jaguar. Captain Jordan and the two soldiers were horrified. The Jaguar's eyes burned with desire and death as it stared at Captain Jordan, who could feel and hear the pounding of his own heart. He took small careful steps backwards, never taking his eyes off the Jaguar's piercing yellow eyes. The soldiers followed their Captain. The Great Jaguar snarled, displaying enormous white teeth that stood out against his bright pink gums that were speckled with black dots. It watched the three soldiers patiently, playing with them, stalking them.

Jack, Caitlin, Potter Sims, and Gandor stood like stones watching everything unfold. Nearly one hundred feet separated Captain Jordan and the soldiers from the Great Jaguar. It was time. It all unfolded in a matter of seconds. The giant Jaguar charged toward the Captain and his men, kicking up the perimeter's white sand into the air. The soldiers fled into the Great Thorn Maze. Caitlin raced after them.

"Don't go in there!" Potter Sims screamed.

Ignoring Potter Sims, Caitlin raced faster toward the Great Thorn Maze, where Captain Jordan and his men were running.

"Stop her!" screamed Potter Sims.

Jack bolted after Caitlin. From behind, Potter Sims and Gandor watched. At the same moment, Captain Jordan and the soldiers disappeared into the Great Thorn Maze. Jack grabbed Caitlin's arm; she struggled ferociously to break his hold, but Jack dug his fingers deeper into her arm. They tumbled to the white sand. On all fours, down in the sand, Jack and Caitlin peered into the dense, intertwined mahogany stems and thorns of the Great Thorn Maze, but they could see nothing. The soldiers and Jaguar had disappeared. Animal squeals and human cries ripped through the serenity of the twilight.

"I'm going in there," Caitlin insisted.

"If you do, young lady, it will be your end!" Gandor said.

"You can't help them!" Potter Sims insisted.

"Is it the thorns?" Jack asked.

"Yes," Gandor said puffing rapidly on his pipe.

"But it's more than just getting stuck!" Potter Sims warned.

"What do I have to do to be safe?" Caitlin asked.

"It's simple. Don't go in there!" Potter Sims pleaded.

Gandor took a puff on his pipe and exhaled the smoke in a large ring. Then, he spoke calmly, "Under no conditions, go near a thorn or touch one."

"If we don't touch a thorn, then we will be all right?" Jack pressed Gandor and Potter Sims. Caitlin was shocked that Jack, who had no connection to Captain Jordan and his men, was willing to risk himself to enter the Great Thorn Maze.

"Why would you go in there?" she asked.

"You don't think I'm going to let you go in there by yourself, do you?"

"I don't understand why either of you are going in there." Potter Sims said.

"Look, those men are in there partly because of me," explained Caitlin.

"That doesn't mean that you have to die for them," Potter Sims argued.

There was a brief silence as Caitlin considered Potter Sims' words.

"Am I the other part? Am I the reason that they're up here?" Jack asked.

Caitlin ignored Jack's question, she did not even look at him. "If they are in trouble, I'm going to help them."

An understanding passed between Jack and Caitlin as they looked at each other. Together, they walked past Potter Sims and Gandor toward the Great Thorn Maze.

"Whatever you do, don't touch the thorns!" Potter Sims yelled out.

Jack and Caitlin disappeared into a narrow path that opened into the Great Thorn Maze. Potter Sims looked at Gandor with a look that Gandor understood all too well.

"Sims, you really don't think that I am going in there, do you?" Gandor took several backward steps away from the Maze.

"Not in a million years," Potter Sims answered with a sardonic tone. Potter Sims walked right up to the wall of Thorns, which towered over him. The thorns were pressing, ominous. He looked down the narrow path that disappeared into the Great Thorn Maze, where Captain Jordan and his men ran when chased by the Giant Jaguar. It was the spot where Jack and Caitlin had entered sixty seconds ago. Potter Sims took three small, cautious steps forward.

"Why do I do these things?" he said to himself as he entered the Great Thorn Maze.

There were steep walls of thorns. It felt like a prison of death. The sharp points of the beautiful mahogany thorns were everywhere; they protruded into the winding paths. Jack and Caitlin cautiously navigated through the Maze in fear and awe. At a very tight juncture, where the path forked, they stopped to look. Neither of them spoke, for they both thought the same thing, the paradox, what an incredibly beautiful design for death.

Caitlin viewed the twisted, intertwined mahogany stems and thorns as ruled by an invisible mathematic. She wondered what kind of culture produces such an architecture? As an astronomer, she mused whether the Thorn Maze was based upon any stellar movements.

As an artist, Jack thought, though complex the Great Thorn Maze was simple. Great art is a set of simple rules. Jack knew that great symphonies were but simple patterns of notes, arranged and rearranged mathematically to manipulate a repeating pattern. And, there is a pattern here, Jack thought as he combed the dense Thorn Maze with his eyes.

Groans from deep within the Great Thorn Maze interrupted Jack and Caitlin's thoughts.

"We better get going," Jack said.

They followed the groaning. Through the dense tangle of stems and thorns, Jack and Caitlin spotted Captain Jordan. He was impaled by an enormous thorn, which ran straight through his back with the thorn tip sticking out of the center of his chest, just missing his heart. On each side of Captain Jordan hung Private William "Billie" Ketchum and the other private; each was skewered, paralyzed by a thorn, which completely supported their weight. Their feet dangled twelve inches off the ground. Warily, Jack and Caitlin followed the narrow path that led to the Captain and his two men. Jack and Caitlin looked around; the Giant Jaguar was nowhere in sight. Caitlin walked up and stood three feet from Captain Jordan. His body hung on the massive mahogany thorn, so that his feet dangled a foot off the ground.

"I am sorry," Caitlin said with tears welling up in her eyes.

Captain Jordan looked down and recognized Caitlin. She saw it in his eyes. He could not move any part of his body, only his eyes and even those only slightly.

Hidden from view, behind a dense thicket of the thorns some distance away, was Ens, no longer a Jaguar. He watched everything.

Just then, Potter Sims arrived. When he saw Jack and Caitlin, he was relieved, until he saw Captain Jordan and the other two soldiers. Out of reverence for the Captain and his two men, Potter Sims whispered to Jack and Caitlin.

"I was worried about you two."

Jack and Caitlin acknowledged Potter Sims, but said nothing. All they could think about was Captain Jordan and his men. Jack leaned forward. Extending his arm under the massive thorn, which protruded from the Captain's chest, Jack carefully grasped each side of Captain's Jordan's rib cage. Jack tried to pry Captain Jordan off the thorn. Potter Sims rushed quickly next to Jack and spoke in an urgent whisper in Jack's ear.

"Don't do that. There is nothing that anyone can do for him now."

Captain Jordan heard Potter Sims.

"We can at least give him some comfort," Jack said supporting the Captain.

"You don't understand," whispered Potter Sims, "there is more to come. You cannot be touching him."

Jack looked directly into Potter Sims' eyes, and then looked into Captain Jordan's eyes. In a fraction of a second, the Captain was certain of two things, Jack's first instinct was for his own survival, second, there was a mixture of sadness with guilt in Jack's eyes. Jack lowered his eyes from Captain Jordan's, gently released his grip on the hanging soldier and took a couple of steps backwards. Despair and fear instantly colored the Captain's face. The highly-trained, tough and determined commander knew that the remainder of his life was a matter of seconds, but what bothered him the most was that although he knew that he was about to die, he had no idea how. Thoughts raced through his mind. What is going to happen to me? Maggie, my love. Tyler. My little Cathy Ann. Will they be all right without me? I miss them. I am sorry. Oh, God, how long will this take? Will it hurt? How much? End it! Please! Though so many thoughts and emotions coursed with frantic life through Captain's Jordan's mind, his body was paralyzed.

Jack, Caitlin and Potter Sims stood helpless in front of him. Stone silence filled the Great Thorn arena. They glanced at each of Captain Jordan's men, who also hung helplessly impaled by the thorns. The quiet of the Great Thorn Maze was like the silence deep in the womb of the Great Forest, except that here, there was no tranquility, only the silence which magnified the fear of the unknown and anticipated death. After several minutes, the Captain's labored breaths echoed throughout the Maze, like a fevered gasp for life. Mingled with the sounds of the forced breathing was a deep raspy voice.

"Fee Fi Fo Fum," the guttural chant vibrated through the Great Thorn Maze. The color left Jack's face. Caitlin's eyes opened wide in fear. Potter Sims was speechless, frozen. Nobody responded with more terror than Captain Jordan whose eyes filled with astonishment. He and Caitlin exchanged glances. The

Captain and Jack exchanged glances. He could not turn away out of respect for the Captain, but he also did not want to watch. He heard his own heart beating; it felt like it was going to pop out of his chest.

Captain Jordan's eyes opened wider, he was trying to drink in the whole world. He looked at Caitlin, then as fast as a blink of an eye Captain Jordan's eyes glazed over lifeless, like an animal put to sleep. Caitlin cried out aloud, but the sounds of creaking and twisting wood silenced her. Nailed by the huge thorns to the rigid wooden mahogany stems, the bodies of all three soldiers twisted and contorted. Slowly, they were being changed and fused into the mahogany architecture of the Great Thorn Maze. Captain Jordan's arms and legs tightened. The wrinkles of his skin and his fingerprints became swirled patterns of a beautiful tight, mahogany wood grain. His forearm muscles and biceps twisted. His thighs and calves creaked, as they contorted. His torso, his hips, his arms and legs, every finger, every toe, bent and twisted inward in a counter-clockwise direction, every part of his body spiraled around his heart, as if it was the center of a powerful tornado. Everything was sucked inward with enormous centripetal force. It twisted and screwed every muscle, bone and sinew in the Captain's body, until his face spiraled inward counter-clockwise; his expression became an unhuman dead gaze. As his eyes rotated, they became dark black knots of wood in the mahogany grain. The metamorphosed bodies of Captain Jordan, Private Billy Ketchum and the other private had become part of the life of the Great Thorn Maze.

Caitlin crossed her arms and clutched her sides tightly, crying. Jack could not take his eyes off the bump in the wood, which was once Captain Jordan. Potter Sims' white eyes were open wide and white, full of panic.

"We must get out of here, now!" screamed Potter Sims.

Jack and Caitlin followed Potter Sims with great care retracing their steps out of the Great Thorn Maze. As they wound their way out of the Great Thorn Maze, taking measured, cautious steps, they saw dozens of twisted wooden bumps, like growths, spiraled tightly into the mahogany branches. No one spoke, but everyone knew that these were once living beings.

At the perimeter of the Great Thorn Maze, Gandor puffed on his pipe, staring into the dense thicket of thorns. The sun was beginning to set; the sky was bright orange and red. Suddenly, Jack, Caitlin, and Potter Sims exited the Thorn Maze at the exact spot they had entered.

"I'm surprised you are still here," Potter Sims said.

"I did not expect to see you, either. I thought you might become part of the décor."

"That would please you to no end, wouldn't it?" Potter Sims replied.

"Believe it or not, no, it wouldn't," Gandor answered.

"Humph!" Potter Sims said wide-eyed, as he turned to Jack and Caitlin. "There is a way to get through," Potter Sims told them, "but we must wait until morning."

"Why can't we go around it?" Jack asked.

"Because there is no way around." Potter Sims said as he pointed. "This extends as far as you can see."

"I didn't come up here to die in there like that," Caitlin said.

"But you can't return the way you came and you can't go around. If you stay here, you will certainly die," Gandor said.

"We have a good chance of getting through, I promise you," Potter Sims said, "but we can't go until the morning. I will explain it to you, then." Potter Sims was firm and confident. It made them more secure. For the first time, Caitlin and Jack had a respect for Potter Sims.

CHAPTER 38

⊰❧⊱

THE NIGHT BEFORE

It was twilight and the sun was setting fast. The purples, reds and oranges of twilight seeped into the deep mahogany of the Thorn Maze making it exquisitely beautiful. All four of the travelers stood silently in the twelve-foot perimeter awestruck by the beauty of the Great Thorn Maze, which became increasingly dramatic as the sun set.

Later that night, after the sun had disappeared and the red sky had turned to black, Jack, Caitlin, Potter Sims, and Gandor huddled together in the perimeter of the Great Thorn Maze to keep warm. The moon was bright, white and full. Suddenly, Jack tilted his head toward the Great Thorn Maze. He thought that he had heard something. He listened. Caitlin noticed that something had caught Jack's attention.

"What is it?" she asked.

"Shhh," he raised his open hand. "There's singing coming from the Maze," Jack said, baffled.

"I can't hear anything." Caitlin said.

"I have great ears," he said.

"It is the Thorns," Potter Sims explained.

"You mean those giant thorns are making music?" Caitlin asked.

"No," responded Gandor, "Ens has an army of workers called The Thorns."

"What do they do?" Jack asked.

"They build and polish the Great Thorn Maze."

As Potter Sims explained in colorful detail about the Thorns, they could see hundreds of torches, which looked like points of light, moving through the Great Thorn Maze's dense tangle of mahogany briars. Jack, Caitlin, Potter Sims, and Gandor heard the chanting. It was a drone. It crept into the still of the night.

"It's a chant," Jack mused.

All four were silent, listening to the chanting which rose from the Great Thorn Maze. Like the deep and croaky chant of Buddhist monks cloistered in a small chapel, the chant had a sacred beauty, but it also sounded like a death knell. Jack walked closer to the edge of the Great Thorn Maze. Through the tangle of briars, he saw The Thorns, thousands of them. They were squat, hump-backed workers, who carried ladders, hammers, and ropes. Each Thorn worker had several of the sharp giant mahogany thorns strapped to his back by means of ropes. Hundreds of pimples covered the exposed parts of their faces, necks, arms and hands. Each pimple had a tiny pinprick hole in the center. Confined in the tight spaces of the Great Thorn Maze, The Thorns were pricked all over their bodies by the giant mahogany thorns, as they worked. The Thorns' walk was a side-to-side waddle, caused by trying to balance the weight of the ladders and thorns upon their hard squat backs. They looked like disfigured Gnomes. As the Thorns chanted, they swarmed over the maze, like worker bees in a hive.

In one section, Jack, Caitlin, Potter Sims, and Gandor could see The Thorns as they climbed on ladders, hammering and gluing the giant thorns to the mahogany stems, and polishing the deep mahogany thorns to a deadly sheen. Then, meticulously, so as not to be pricked, the Thorns painted the sharp thorn tips with a bright red gelatin.

"Looks like your boots, Sims!" Gandor joked.

"You think so, huh?" Potter Sims flared back.

"What is that red liquid?" Caitlin asked.

"It's called glop. It's what changed the Captain and the others and made them part of the Great Thorn Maze." Potter Sims said.

"A paralyzing venom?" Jack asked.

"Exacting I would say," Gandor said, as he blew great blue smoke rings that rose and looked like that they might encircle the moon.

Everyone stared at The Thorns humping their gnome-like bodies through the Thorn Maze. Using long black thick-bristled brushes, they coated the thorn tips with the red viscous glop.

"The Thorns come here twice a year, when the day and the night are the same." Potter Sims said.

"The equinox," Caitlin said.

"What is that?" Gandor asked.

"On our planet," explained Caitlin, "there are only two days during the entire year when the light of the day and the dark of the night are equal. They are called the equinoxes. One is the vernal equinox; it comes in the Spring. The other is the autumnal equinox; it comes in the Fall."

"Maybe our worlds are not so different," observed Gandor.

Jack's mind was elsewhere. Aesthetic observations about music and art had always sculpted his philosophical perspective of the world. Here was an extreme, but prime, example, the equinox, where light and dark are balanced, life and death.

Jack replayed the way Captain Jordan died, the look of astonishment on his face at the instant of his death. In a flash, he saw the lightning bolt impaling his father on the mountaintop beneath the Great Oak Tree. These deaths were connected, Jack thought. He needed a symbol, a metaphor from nature, something that might explain and put the senseless deaths into a perspective—his father, Captain Jordan, the fallen city on top of the Great Mountain at the edge of Devastation Plain, the Great Thorn Maze, all of it.

As Caitlin stared at the Great Thorn Maze, she thought about the architectural wonders that she had seen on Earth, the great civilizations, who had designed astonishing structures: the Pyramids and Sphinx at Giza, Stonehenge, the Mayan ruins, Machu Picchu. Was this one of the great architectural wonders of this world? Usually lucid in her thinking, the Thorn Maze and Captain Jordan's death churned up conflicts of thought and emotion. They had clouded her.

"The Thorns will be gone at dawn," Potter Sims said. "We need to get an early start to make it through the maze."

"Who put you in charge?" Gandor asked.

"Who else is going to get us out of here? You?" Potter Sims replied.

"You're right, Potter. We need to get some sleep." Jack said.

Caitlin was lost in thought. The images of Captain Jordan dying haunted her. His eyes and mouth open wide in terror. Edvard Munch's 'Scream.' Needing time to sort her thoughts, Caitlin walked away from the group along the white sand perimeter of the Great Thorn Maze. Jack waited a few moments, and then quietly followed her.

"Where are you two going?" Potter Sims yelled.

"Don't bother them, Sims." Gandor said softly.

Potter Sims and Gandor exchanged glances. They knew that their new friends needed time to themselves. Gandor stood before the Great Thorn Maze puffing on his pipe as he watched The Thorns with their torches and ladders climb around inside the Thorn Maze. Potter Sims sat on the ground, a few feet away from Gandor, digging his fingers into the sand, letting it sift through his white-gloved fingers over-and-over, as he replayed the events of the last few hours in his mind.

Farther down the perimeter, Caitlin was sitting on the sand staring into the Thorn Maze, her knees pulled up to her chest, her arms wrapped around her knees. As Jack approached her, he could see that her face was flushed and tears were running down her cheeks. He sat down quietly next to her.

"I'm sorry," he said.

Caitlin did not speak. She just stared into the maze.

After a few moments, Jack tore off a piece of his shirt, folded it neatly so that a clean spot was on top, and leaned over to wipe the tears away from her face. Caitlin put her hand up as if to block him, and moved her head a few inches away from his reach. Jack pulled his hand slowly back still clutching the piece of cloth.

"I'm sorry, I'll leave you alone," he said. He stood up and began to walk away, when she touched his pants leg.

"No, please stay," she said.

He sat down next to her in the sand.

"I'll take that cloth," she said.

Jack reached into his pocket and took out the piece of cloth that he had ripped from his shirt. He handed it to her, but she did not take it, instead she turned her face toward him. Gently, he put his fingers inside the soft cotton cloth and wiped her face. She closed her eyes. When he was finished, he slipped the cloth back into his pocket.

"I am so sorry," he said.

"I liked him," Caitlin said. "He was a good man."

They both sat in the sand staring into the Thorn Maze at the thousands of swollen wooden bumps that covered the stems. The torches carried by The Thorns highlighted the maze's mahogany finish and created deep red reflections of the thousands of flames. The Thorns' chanting echoed with bass vibrations through the wood.

"Why did you come up here?" Jack asked.

"Pachakutek. The planet I discovered disappeared. A committee of senators and NASA officials thought that it might be connected to the Beanstalk. They really don't know anything, but they thought that I knew more than anyone else. So here I am."

"What about you?" she asked.

"I planted the Beanstalk, so to speak."

Caitlin was dumbstruck. It had never occurred to her. The drone of The Thorns working in the Great Thorn Maze made her more confused and edgy.

"My father was a great concert violist. He toured in just about every country around the world."

"Wait. Your last name is Tott?"

"Yeah."

"As in Gage Tott?"

"Yes. He is—was my father."

Caitlin was shocked for she had heard Gage Tott play a Felix Mendelssohn piece with the New York Philharmonic at Carnegie Hall three years before she took on her appointment at Colgate University.

"We played a lot of violin concerts worldwide as a father and son duet team, but I was becoming more interested in a new experimental music which he hated. It was a very stormy time for us. We argued a lot. On a picnic, after we had a huge argument, a lightning bolt struck my father. He had just finished playing an excerpt from Beethoven's *Pastoral*. He was holding his Stradivarius violin, the violin that he was bequeathing to me. It flew twenty feet away from him, and was burned in places."

As Jack spoke, his bottom lip quivered. Caitlin noticed. Jack reached into his back pocket and pulled out the charred Stradivarius bridge. He held it up. "This is the bridge from the violin. I traded the violin to the man whom I told you about, Murland. He also gave me the Yamqui drawing, and—" Jack paused partly out of embarrassment, partly out of guilt, "—and three beans, three beans for my father's Stradivarius violin."

"I'm sorry about your father."

"The look on my father's face when he was struck by lightning was the same look that Captain Jordan had on his face, seconds before he died. Astonishment."

"Why did you come up here?" Caitlin asked.

"My sister Natalie has leukemia. Murland told me that if she is to live, I had to take the beans and follow wherever they took me."

"That's serious baggage to lay on someone, don't you think?" Caitlin asked.

"I love her. I would do anything for her, and he knew it."

"So it's okay to threaten you with your sister's life?"

"Murland is not like that. It wasn't a threat. I was afraid to sell the Stradivarius. I had the distinct feeling that it was his way of convincing me to commit to a journey that I did not want, even though it might somehow be the most important thing in my life."

"Whatever you call it, it is blackmail."

"Perhaps, but he knew things about me, my father and Natalie. Every violinist worth his salt has a personal way of playing, a penmanship. When he played the Stradivarius in his shop, if I had closed my eyes, I would have sworn that it was my father playing."

Caitlin listened attentively to every word Jack said and watched his every facial inflection as he spoke. She was puzzled, just as Jack was.

"So where will this take us?" Caitlin pointed to the Thorn Maze.

"If we make it through, it will lead to Ens. From there, I have no idea."

Caitlin stared for several minutes at the Great Thorn Maze. "I'm really scared, and I don't frighten easily," she said.

"Me, too."

Jack edged closer to Caitlin and put his arm around her. She liked being held close by him. Even though she was independent and strong-willed, being-held tightly by Jack made her feel inexplicably secure.

He liked holding her. She made him feel complete. It was a new feeling for him.

Together, they watched as the Thorns worked steadily in the Great Thorn Maze, until the early hours of the morning. The Thorns smeared the thorns with the red glop, while their droning chant echoed eerily through the maze, eventually putting Jack and Caitlin to sleep.

CHAPTER 39

━━━━━ ❦ ━━━━━

A TRUFFLE IN THE GROUND

It was a red sunrise on the white sand and rock perimeter of the Great Thorn Maze. The sun bathed the deep mahogany of the stems and giant thorns of the Maze with red light making it exquisitely beautiful. The four travelers slowly awoke. The Thorns were gone. It was quiet. The Thorn Maze looked almost peaceful. Even as they stared at the Maze with its palette of rich color, each one knew there was no way to avoid the journey, and inside was possible death.

"Have you ever read William Blake's '*The Tiger?*'" Jack asked.

"No," Caitlin said.

"Who was that?" Potter Sims wanted to know.

"He was a poet. One of his poems "*The Tiger*" asked what creator would create incredible beauty and horrendous death," Jack said as he recited a line from the poem. 'What immortal hand or eye dare frame thy fearful symmetry?'"

"It is survival of the fittest, nature's warning, the blue iridescent rings of the blue-ringed octopus, or the beautiful intricate web of the deadly orb weaver spider," said Caitlin.

"I simply don't understand you all," Gandor said, groggy and barely awake, as he pulled his pipe from his vest pocket. "There is nothing beautiful about that." He pointed to the Great Thorn Maze with the tip of his pipe. "It is death. It is misguided to romanticize it, no matter what color it is!"

"You're right, Gandor," said Caitlin "but where we come there are people who worship power and death, and would subconsciously like nothing better than to see a giant mushroom cloud."

"What is a mushroom cloud?" Potter Sims asked.

"It's a great cloud of death and destruction created out of physics, mathematics and war. It is worse than a thousand Thorn Mazes," Jack said.

"A thousand mazes? Can't imagine!" Potter Sims said.

"I can," Gandor said. "I know about death. I know the fear of dying, the fear of being the last living creature of your species. Not a day goes by that I do not think, Will I say the wrong thing to Ens? Will I be in the wrong place at the wrong time? Will it be my fault that my clan becomes extinct?"

"It doesn't have to be that way, you know." Potter Sims responded.

"Oh, no?" Gandor said, "Just how would you fix it?"

"When we're growing up, my clan had rites of passage that you must pass to be considered an adult. It was more than a trial, it was a game played in a large arena with enormous obstacles and threats. Males used one arena; females used another. Both were equally difficult. It tested your strength, your wit and intelligence, your endurance, your ability to fly—" Potter Sims said when Gandor interrupted him.

"You? Skill at flying? I think you failed!"

"What do you know, Gandor? When I was younger, I was the all-time champion of these rites." Potter Sims said.

Gandor blew a series of perfect concentric smoke rings into the air to demonstrate his prowess. Potter Sims ignored it.

"If you faced the trial with fear, then you failed, and you were not permitted to participate in the clan's planning, nor teach its children, nor make its laws, nor care for its sick and elderly. If you failed, you were given two more opportunities to redeem yourself and pass. You had to tackle each ordeal in the arena with an open heart, a passion for truth, and courage. If you approached any part of the trial with fear, you failed. You asked me, Gandor, how I would fix it? Rid yourself of fear. Seek out the truth. Be open and courageous."

"If you're such a champion, then why are you out here alone? Where is the rest of your clan?" Gandor said.

"I left them to take a journey."

"What kind of journey?" Jack asked.

"I'm not discussing it."

"Why not?" Caitlin asked.

"I've already told you too much!"

"What are you hiding, Sims?" Gandor asked.

Potter Sims confronted Gandor. "Are you going with us?"

"Not me," Gandor said as he puffed on his pipe and blew smoke into the tangle of briars in the Great Thorn Maze. "My wings will take me to the other side where I will meet you."

"What a surprise!" Potter Sims said.

"Why should I go through the Maze when I can fly over? I cannot risk the extinction of my species. It is far more important than my personal survival." Gandor said.

"What's on the other side?" asked Jack.

"The Salt Flats," Gandor answered.

"How wide are they?" Caitlin asked.

"I do not know, I have never been there," Gandor answered.

Potter Sims walked away from the threesome to a black patch of dirt in the middle of the sand perimeter. He got down on his knees, unfastened his cufflinks, and rolled up the sleeves of his white shirt. Jack, Caitlin, and Gandor walked over and surrounded him.

"What are you doing?" Jack asked.

Ignoring Jack's question, Potter Sims removed his white gloves, mumbling, "I hate dirt! I hate dirt!" He dug his bare fingers into the strange black humus and mold.

"What are you doing?" Caitlin asked.

Potter Sims dug his fingers deeper into the black humus until the dirt was up to his elbows. "I hate dirt!"

"You are running out of time, Sims!" Gandor said, as he snapped shut the glass cover of his watch fob.

"Would you please shut up?" Potter Sims yelled.

"Just what is it that we are looking for?" Jack wanted an answer.

Potter Sims rooted deeper in the black humus. His delicate fingers touched something small. He pulled it up, and held it in the air for Jack, Caitlin, and Gandor to see. It was a velvety black mushroom bulb without a stem, which looked like a small truffle mushroom.

"This," he answered.

"You eat them?" Caitlin asked.

"We do, or we die," said Potter Sims.

"I don't require them," said Gandor confidently, puffing on his pipe.

"One day, you're going to look out for your own neck once too often," Potter Sims said.

"I have no choice. I must survive. And I am not sorry!"

"Gandor, let me tell you something," Potter Sims stepped closer to him. "Times are changing, no person, no clan, no nation survives alone."

Potter Sims looked at Jack and Caitlin. "You need to dig," he said. "In the black soil, about this far down," Potter Sims spread his arms apart. "You'll feel the dirt is wetter where the black mushroom bulbs root."

Jack and Caitlin got down on their knees next to Potter Sims and began to dig in the black humus. Gandor watched, while puffing on his pipe and blowing thorns of smoke that dissipated when they hit in the Great Thorn Maze.

Jack found a black mushroom bulb and held it up.

"What do these do?" he asked.

"It will make your vision sharp, so you know exactly by a finger's breadth how near you are to a thorn. Without it, you will not make it. With it, you have a chance," Potter Sims said.

Potter Sims raised his proboscis, so he could open his mouth and he popped in his black mushroom. He began chewing. Jack and Caitlin popped a black mushroom bulb into their mouths. While they sat on the white sand peering into the Great Thorn Maze, they chewed on the black mushroom bulbs.

"How long does it take?" Jack asked.

"By the time we get inside the maze, it'll be working," Potter Sims said as he stood and walked toward the Thorn Maze. Jack and Caitlin followed him.

Gandor yelled out, "See you on the other side, my friends!"

"You use that word too loosely," Potter Sims yelled back.

"Sims, don't stick yourself, be a shame to lose you!" Gandor yelled before he spread his enormous graceful wings and lifted into the air. Jack, Caitlin, and Potter Sims watched Gandor as he soared over the Thorn Maze. They stood at the threshold of the Thorn Maze, at its extensive web of tangled mahogany thorns and stems. The black bulbs were working. For each of them, the colors and details of the Thorn Maze were magnified. It was as if each had acquired a sixth sense, a surreal ability to perceive the supra natural. Each saw the Thorn Maze clearly, for what it was. They knew, at the brink of their journey, that the Great Thorn Maze was thick and perilous. There was no beauty here.

Potter Sims led the way into the Thorn Maze. As Jack entered, in his peripheral vision, he saw the silhouette of someone watching him. He whipped around, but the silhouette was gone. Caitlin saw the startled look on his face.

"What is it?" she asked.

"I don't know. I thought somebody was watching us."

Caitlin was worried. As they wound and twisted their way through the path of the Great Thorn Maze, Jack and Caitlin continually looked around for anyone or anything, who might be spying on them.

"We must keep moving," Potter Sims said without losing a step.

The black bulbs gave them the eyes of an eagle. They avoided every thorn. Potter Sims became their expert guide, for he knew every inch of the Great Thorn Maze.

"How is it that you know so much about this Maze?" Caitlin asked.

"You learn what is worth listening to and what is not."

The path through the Great Thorn Maze narrowed. A dense tunnel of thorns was only twenty feet in front of them. Inside the low tunnel, they squatted to pass.

"Keep low!" Potter Sims yelled behind him.

The tunnel was dark. Once inside the tunnel, all that they could see were the giant mahogany thorns everywhere, but they appeared nearly black. The tangle of thorns was so thick that it blocked out the light. Thorns were all around them, to their left, to their right and above. They were entombed in a catacomb of huge thorns.

CHAPTER 40

THE WHITE WAIT

Faraway, in the Cloud Room, the remaining twelve Special Forces soldiers waited, lost in the white boundless void, as thousands of feathery fibrous patches floated above their heads. The patches began floating downward toward the men. Some soldiers touched the floating patches with their fingers and muzzles of their rifles, while others evaded them. The patches floated freely everywhere. They drifted in a slow attack towards the soldiers, who ducked, twisted and ran. The faster the men moved, the faster the patches chased them. Panicked, the soldiers fired their weapons at the patches, but each bullet that exploded in the white void became a new feathery patch that joined in chasing the soldiers. The soldiers ran, but there was nowhere to go. Some men screamed in panic, as they swung their rifles wildly at the attacking feathery patches. The patches stuck to their rifles, clung to the soldiers' fingers, to their hands, to their faces. The brown feathery fibers burrowed in the soldiers' eyes, snaked up their noses, dug into their ears, and entered their open, screaming mouths. In the White Cloud room, the men's screams were choked and muffled by the brown floating fibrous patches that covered every inch of their bodies and weapons, completely wrapping them in cocoons.

CHAPTER 41

TWO BECOME ONE

In the Great Thorn Maze, Jack, Caitlin and Potter Sims approached the end of the tunnel where they saw rays of light. The thorns were not as dense, and the tunnel began to open. Single-file, Caitlin and Jack followed Potter Sims. As Potter Sims exited the tunnel, he followed the path forking to the right. Caitlin cleared the tunnel, but still crouched down, unsure whether she was away from the giant thorns. With caution, Jack approached the end of the tunnel when he saw a large dark form moving just inside the wall of thorns. The silhouette moved. Jack turned to see. He whipped around, the weight of the 24-karat amulet swung the gold necklace around, where it lassoed a giant thorn. Twisting off balance and falling backwards, Jack thrust his hand out to break his fall. A two-foot long thorn skewered his left palm like an ice pick, the thorn protruding four inches out of the top of his hand.

"Augh!" Jack screamed a cry that echoed through the Great Thorn Maze.

Behind a thicket of giant thorns, Ens watched Jack screaming, clutching his bleeding hand. Hearing the scream, Caitlin and Potter Sims turned. Potter Sims' eyes opened white with horror. Blood poured from the wound in Jack's left hand. His screams were primal, yet muffled by the dense tangle of mahogany stems and thorns. Buried beneath his screams was a barely audible low-pitch hum. To everyone's surprise, it sounded remarkably similar to The Thorns' droning chant; it was coming from Jack's skewered hand.

"Get it out! You must get it out!" Potter Sims yelled.

Caitlin pulled on Jack's arm. The wound stopped bleeding. The remaining blood around the wound changed from a bright red to a reddish-brown mahogany. As the humming got louder, Jack's flesh slowly turned brown and coarse around the center of his palm. Radiating out from the center of Jack's hand, the wrinkles and lines in his palm began transforming into wood.

"We've got to get him loose!" Potter Sims yelled.

They struggled to free Jack's hand. With all their might and will, Caitlin and Potter Sims pulled on Jack's arm, but his flesh was metamorphosing too fast into solid wood causing the tissue in his hand to swell and press tightly against the thorn, binding Jack's flesh to the giant thorn. As the droning from Jack's skewered hand got louder, another faint hum rang in the air. Jack's fingers were turning to wood. Knotholes swirled from deep inside the pulp of his thumb and fingers grew and tightened, where his fingerprints used to be. Potter Sims and Caitlin tugged furiously on Jack's arm with all of their strength. Under normal conditions, the torque placed upon his arm would have broken the bone in two, skewering his muscles and jutting out the top of his arm, but his flesh was fast becoming mahogany. The suppleness was gone. Excruciating seconds seemed like minutes. Finally, they yanked Jack's hand free from the thorn's grip. Jack's veins, forearm muscles and arm hairs were turning into wood. Jack was terrified. He began to hyperventilate. He knew that he had less than sixty seconds to live. He would die an agonizing death. *This is how Captain Jordan died.* The second hum got louder, as the reddish-brown mahogany traveled up his arm from his wrist to his forearm. The hum merged with the drone coming from his hardening flesh.

"Listen!" Jack yelled as loud as he could.

Caitlin and Potter Sims froze. Nothing could be heard, except the sound of Jack's arm creaking as wood does when it expands and bends, and a beautiful harmony created by the two hums merging, a bass and a tenor. It was magical. One song was coming from somewhere on Jack. They listened. The hum originated from Jack's back pocket.

"Quick! My back pocket!" Jack yelled to Caitlin. "The violin bridge! Take it out!"

Caitlin reached into Jack's back pocket and pulled out the charred Stradivarius bridge. It was radiating a brilliant turquoise light that lit up the surrounding Thorn Maze, like a phosphorescent glow stick. The violin bridge hum was a different tone than the hum coming from Jack's palm. Each was in a different octave, but they created the purest, most beautiful harmonic. It was if the hum coming from the Stradivarius bridge was binding the hum of the Thorn Maze to itself to form a new harmony. Like a wave of flesh-eating gangrene, the mahogany hardened and deadness traveled steadily up Jack's forearm toward his elbow.

"What is that?" Potter Sims asked quickly.

"Murland said, 'Where two songs become one!'" Jack exclaimed. He stared at Caitlin with wild eyes. "Jam it into my elbow! Now!" Caitlin looked at him disbelievingly, while still holding the bridge in her hand. "Now!" Jack yelled. The thorn's poison was working rapidly, cell by cell of Jack's flesh was quickly turning to mahogany wood. Caitlin saw it. She gripped the Stradivarius bridge tightly and thrust it into the soft pulp of Jack's elbow. The hum from the Stradivarius violin bridge got louder, as did the drone coming from Jack's wooden palm. A reverberating crescendo filled the space of the Great Thorn Maze like the finale of great musical performance. The two songs had merged. The shape of the Stradivarius bridge melded into the indentation of Jack's elbow, just as the wood of the bridge merged with Jack's wooden flesh. *Two became one*, Jack thought. Gradually, the humming faded. The Great Thorn Maze was silent. Jack's arm had stopped hardening. Jack's left arm from his elbow to his fingertips was beautiful mahogany wood with knots and grain. All three stood in total silence staring down at Jack's transformed flesh.

"It stopped," Potter Sims said.

"How did you know?" Caitlin asked.

Jack could not speak. Slowly, he slumped to the ground in shock and despair. His head down, his right hand limp on his lap, he was afraid to touch his new wooden arm. He was terrified, numb. All he could do was to stare at his wooden arm. A deep sadness grew from deep inside his being, as Caitlin and Potter Sims sat down on the ground on each side of him. Caitlin gently touched his shoulder with her fingers. She did not know what to say.

After many tense seconds of quiet, Potter Sims spoke up. "I'm sorry, but we must get out of here." Potter Sims looked at Jack. "Can you go on?"

Jack could barely speak. His voice quivered from a deep sadness and terror. "It was from my father's violin. Murland gave it to me when he gave me the beans and map. When he gave me the bridge, he said 'By this instrument the two songs will become one.'"

Caitlin's eyes were full of compassion, but Potter Sims, even though he cared, knew that they had to leave the Thorn Maze immediately before the effects of the mushrooms wore off. "We must go," Potter Sims said as he stood up and held his hand out for Jack to take. Jack looked at him and took his gloved hand. Potter Sims helped him up. Caitlin followed.

"I'm ready," Jack said, clutching his wooden arm with his good arm.

Potter Sims led them through the final dark of the maze. After they broke their single file, Caitlin took Jack's good hand in hers, and they never looked back at the Thorn Maze.

CHAPTER 42

BAD DAY, GOOD MEDICINE

In the Chelsea apartment where Mattie and Natalie were staying, Natalie lay motionless in her home hospital bed staring at her bed covers, tears running down her cheeks. Her mother Mattie sat next to her in a wicker chair holding her hand. Natalie's eyes were red and puffy, her lips swollen, her cheeks flushed. She was extremely depressed; she had never before been this depressed. The depression came on so suddenly that Mattie had no idea what had brought it on or what to do about it. For hours, she tried to speak with her daughter, but Natalie would not answer her, nor even give her the slightest eye contact; she just stared down at the bed covers. Suddenly, the front door buzzer broke the tension. Mattie immediately stood up. She kissed Natalie on her wet cheek, walked out of the room and briskly down the hallway to the intercom. She noticed a chip in the round black intercom button. She pressed it.

"Yes?"

"It's Doctor Winter, Mrs. Tott." A voice came back over the intercom.

"Please come up. It's number 927." Mattie pushed the button on the intercom. Through the intercom speaker, she heard the buzzer opening the front door lock. After several minutes, Doctor Winter appeared at the open front door where Mattie was waiting.

Doctor Winter extended his hand, "Mrs. Tott, I got here as soon as I could."

Mattie shook his hand, but the gesture was so automatic and clouded by her worry over Natalie's condition that she could not remember greeting him. Mattie escorted him into the living room and closed the door.

When Doctor Winter walked into the living room, he walked with a noticeable limp. He had worn a prosthetic right leg since he was eighteen years old, when he was in an automobile accident, after a high school graduation party. He was tall and handsome in his early thirties. His eyes were brown, hair black, his cheekbones were high and strong, and his nose pronounced and slightly squared. Except for his limp, he had the physique and upright stature of a marathon runner.

"The work that Natalie does with her website helps so many kids. I learned so much about her, and yet we have never met. I want you to know, Mrs. Tott, that I will do everything I can to help her," Doctor Winter said.

Tears filled Mattie's eyes. "She is so depressed. I've never seen her like this. And there's something wrong with her left arm."

"Why don't I take a look at her?"

Mattie turned and walked toward Natalie's bedroom. Doctor Winter followed.

When they walked into the room, Natalie was turned on her side in the bed with her head buried in the pillow. She did not budge when they entered. The doctor immediately sat on the edge of the bed.

"Hi, Natalie, I'm Doctor Winter. We've spoken many times over the last two years."

Natalie did not respond. She did not turn her head, move her arms, her legs; she did not even acknowledge him. With her head deep in the pillow, she kept staring out the window, her face flushed, her eyes red and swollen.

Doctor Winter took her left hand in his hand and noticed something odd. It did not feel like flesh; it felt rubbery; it felt dead.

"Natalie, do you have any feeling in your arm?" he asked.

Natalie did not answer; she just stared out the window. Mattie stood anxiously by the bed and watched. Doctor Winter held her left wrist and checked for a pulse. A baffled look crossed his face. Then he lifted her right wrist and took her pulse. He felt the muscles in her left forearm. He tickled her forearm with the tips of his fingers, but got no response. Puzzled and frustrated, he pinched Natalie's arm leaving a fingernail indentation.

"Do you feel that?"

She did not respond. He gently placed Natalie's left arm down on the bed and covered it gently with the comforter. She never looked at him.

"Can I talk to you outside, please?" he spoke in a low voice to Mattie.

Mattie and Doctor Winter walked into the living room.

"I don't know what's wrong with her. She is very depressed, but I am concerned about her arm. I have never seen anything like it. Her left arm has lost all of its feeling. It has no suppleness, there's no—" Dr. Winter searched for the right words. "—it is as if her left arm is not even flesh. She has no pulse in her left arm. There is no color to her skin, no warmth."

"What caused this?" Mattie asked, fighting back tears.

"I don't know."

"The depression came on so suddenly. One minute she was reading, the next when I brought her lunch, she was like this. Is her arm causing the depression?"

"I don't know," Doctor Winter said. "Do you have a way to get to Mount Sinai Hospital this afternoon?"

"Yes."

"Good."

Doctor Winter took out his cell phone and pressed the speed dial. When the voice answered, he spoke in a familiar tone. "Margie, I am sending a woman named Mattie Tott and her daughter Natalie to see you. I want you to run a complete blood series on the daughter Natalie, then do an MRI on her left arm, a muscle stress analyzer on her left arm, an EKG and an EEG."

Mattie could hear a voice over the speaker on his cell phone, but she could not make out what the voice was saying.

"Check her into a private room in the hospital." Doctor Winter spoke into his cell phone.

The voice said something back, but Mattie could not make it out.

"No, I want these tests done tomorrow ... I don't care if there is no room on the MRI schedule, make room."

Doctor Winter spoke for a few more minutes to Margie, then closed his cell phone and clipped it to his pants.

"You need to check Natalie into Mount Sinai by six o'clock tonight."

"All right."

"If you need anything, you call me. Here is my card with my office number, my cell phone, and my home phone number."

"Thank you."

"I will stop by her room early tomorrow morning to see her."

Doctor Winter opened the front door and walked into the hallway. Mattie could tell that he was in a hurry to get back to his office, so she did not ask any more questions. Besides, she thought, he already said that he did not know what was wrong with her, so she thanked him. He smiled and walked into the elevator. The doors closed. He was gone. Mattie stared at the elevator doors. She stepped inside the apartment and closed the door. She was alone. She walked down the hallway into Natalie's room and circled the bed, so she could see Natalie's face. She had stopped crying, and her eyes were closed. To Mattie, she looked more peaceful than she had for two days. Mattie stood motionless next to the bed watching her daughter. The room was still. Suddenly, the buzzer to the front door rang breaking the quiet. Mattie stared at Natalie's head buried deep into her pillow, hoping that the loud buzzing did not wake her from a much-needed rest. Natalie did not stir, so Mattie briskly left the room to get to the intercom before it could buzz again.

Mattie pushed the black intercom button and spoke with a worried, curious voice into the tiny speaker, "Yes?"

"Mrs. Tott?"

"Yes?"

"It is Murland."

"Oh," she sighed, "Please come up."

Mattie stood at the door waiting for Murland. He stepped out of the elevator with a broad smile on his face. "How are you?" he said as he gently touched her shoulder.

"Natalie's very sick."

"I know," Murland said with a calming voice.

He stepped inside, and closed the door. They walked into the living room and sat on the couch.

"I have to take her to the hospital later this afternoon." Mattie said.

"Please let me take a look at her."

"She's asleep. I don't want to disturb her."

"Of course not, but I think she's awake."

Murland was certain that Natalie was awake. Mattie saw the sureness deep in his turquoise eyes. Without saying another word, she stood up, walked down the hallway, quietly opened Natalie's door and saw Natalie sitting up in bed, awake. Mattie stepped into the room.

"You didn't sleep long, honey," Mattie said, but Natalie did not answer her.

Just then, Murland appeared in the doorway, smiling. Mattie turned and looked at him with a slight scowl, which she instantly tried to hide. She did not know whether to trust this man or not. He was a stranger who had mysteriously intruded into their lives, not just into their privacy, but was becoming privy to their intimate family matters.

"May I, please?" At the door of Natalie's room, Murland spoke respectfully to Mattie and gestured for permission to enter the room.

"It would be better for Natalie if you waited in the living room," Mattie said.

"I'd like him to come in, mother," Natalie said.

With shock, Mattie turned to Natalie who was looking at her. The look that passed between the daughter and the mother revealed more in two seconds than could be communicated in an entire conversation. Natalie needed to speak with Murland more than anyone, even her own mother. Mattie knew it. She also knew that during Murland's last visit, when The Corps appeared at the apartment, Natalie and Murland had connected in a way that Mattie and her daughter could never connect. She knew it then, but she had denied it. She chose to shove it to the back of her mind. It bothered Mattie greatly, but there was nothing that she could do about it. As a mother, she knew and trusted her daughter's instincts.

Murland stood patiently at the doorway waiting for Mattie's permission to enter the room. Mattie nodded to Murland, who stepped into the room with a broad smile on his face. He walked over and sat on the edge of the bed.

"How are you doing, young lady?" Murland said, taking her hand in his.

"Not very well," Natalie said sadly, as she looked into Murland's blue eyes.

Mattie stood in the background watching uneasy, envious.

"Do you remember any dreams that you had last night or the night before?"

"Yes, last night." Natalie spoke while staring down at her bedcovers.

"Can you tell me?"

"Yes."

A hypnotic gaze passed across Natalie's face, as if she was looking at something far away. Mattie took a couple of steps forward.

"I was walking through this field of flowers, there were thousands of them," Natalie recounted, "parting them with my hands to make a path. There were poppies and roses, daisies and sunflowers, lilies, and their colors were brilliant royal purple, and a deep indigo, blue and green, yellow and orange and red. Then a wind came up, slow at first. The flowers swayed back and forth, like they were dancing. Then I heard laughing behind me. I turned around and saw it was coming from the red and orange poppies. They had these little faces outlined by their petals. Their tiny mouths were opened wide and their petals shook as they laughed. They were so loud. At first, it was funny, so I started to giggle, but then I heard this crying. First one voice, then another, and another, until there were hundreds of these voices, crying. They were sad and sobbing. It got louder and louder, until it nearly drowned out the laughing. I tried to see where it was coming from, but I couldn't see, so I ran through the flowers to get away, but the sobbing chased me. I tripped and fell down in a patch of bright green lilies. Next to them were roses that were a beautiful silvery violet. The lilies and roses were all sobbing, it was so sad. The green heads of the lilies dropped down low nearly touching the ground; they shook every time they cried. I stood up and saw the violet roses raising their heads up to the sky. They were crying, too. Tears fell from their violet petals and soaked into this black dirt. I got so sad that I ran, and I saw this gigantic forest with tall green trees, so tall I couldn't see the tops of the trees. So I ran inside and it got quiet. It was totally silent. I walked a little way through all these ferns and plants and came upon a brown wooden cottage with a thatched roof and two square windows that had hanging curtains pulled back on each side. There was a path made of cobblestones that were clean and neatly aligned. The path led up to the front door that was in the center of the house. There were square windows on each side of the door. As I walked slowly up the path, through the window, I saw something moving inside in the shadows. It could have been an animal or a person, maybe, I wasn't sure. I stepped down off the cobblestones and looked inside through the square window. There was a shaft of sunlight that cut across a long wooden kitchen table with empty wooden chairs. Little black birds with thick, bright blue beaks and tiny yellow feet with red tips were walking all over the table, running in and out of the sunlight. I could hear their tiny feet skittering across the table. Suddenly, the ground and the house shook. The shaking got stronger and stronger. I got scared. The glass in the window made sharp creaking and scratching noises like it was going to break, then small cracks, like thin spider webs traveled slowly everywhere through the glass until the whole window was one big web. It was beautiful, but I thought it was going to shatter; then, the shaking stopped. The spider web cracks in the glass glowed purple and yellow in the sunlight. I just stood there looking at the window with the sunlight glowing purple and yellow out from the cracks. It was beautiful. And then I woke up."

"It's a good dream," Murland said.

"What does it mean?" Natalie asked.

"It means there are some very important changes taking place."

"For me?"

"Yes. But first your mother and I will talk about it. All right?"

Natalie nodded and looked at her mother. Murland smiled and walked out of the room. Mattie pulled the bedcovers up around Natalie, kissed her cheek, and left the room.

In the living room, Murland sat on the couch waiting for Mattie. She sat down across from him looking apprehensively into his bright blue eyes, impatient, wanting to know what he knew.

"She doesn't need tests. The problem is not with her," he said.

"How do you know that?"

"Her dream. It's about Jack. He is going through a very difficult time right now, and subconsciously Natalie knows it. They are unusually close."

Mattie could not believe what she was hearing. She had only recently learned from Natalie how close she and Jack had been since they were toddlers, how they felt each other's feelings, how they knew each other's experiences. How could this stranger know these things?

"You know all this from her dream?"

"The dream only confirmed what I already knew."

Mattie reached up to her heart to touch the 24-karat amulet, but it was gone. In an instant, she remembered that Jack had it. Murland saw the look of loss in her eyes.

"I know things about people. Your son and daughter are very special people."

"What does Natalie's dream mean?" Mattie shifted forward and balanced herself on the edge of the chair.

"Jack is experiencing enormous change right now. He's lost the use of his left arm. It is a test."

"Doctor Winter said that something is wrong with Natalie's arm."

"Yes." Murland's manner and voice were calm.

"What's happened to Jack?"

"I don't know, but he's safe now. I can't lie to you, he's very depressed and sad. That's why Natalie is depressed."

At that moment, Mattie felt like she had lost control over everything that mattered to her. She began to cry.

"You did this." Mattie spoke lowly to Murland through her tears. "You called Jack, you gave him the beans, you took the violin. This is your fault."

"At the present moment, it seems like it, Mattie. I am sorry for what you are feeling. All I can tell you is that Jack is with new friends, who love him."

"My family is falling apart. I've lost my husband. Jack is gone, and I don't know if I will ever see him again. Natalie doesn't want my help; she won't even talk to me."

"This will pass. What she doesn't need right now is to be poked with needles and pasted all over with electrodes."

"You can't stop me," Mattie said.

"No, I can't." Murland's voice was not just calm, it challenged Mattie, put the onus of making a deeply honest decision clearly into her hands. Silence fell between them as Mattie considered what Murland had said to her.

"Deep inside, you know that taking her to a hospital is not what Natalie needs right now. I know that you know that."

Mattie was desperate. "What are we going to do?" she asked.

"Let me help."

Tears welled-up in Mattie's eyes again. She became confused. Murland had a way of calming people down by his presence. All he had to do was to feel calm, be calm and want to give it to those around him and it flowed out of his body to them, like a scent. He stayed with Mattie until she was quiet, then he left her sitting on the couch and walked back to Natalie's room.

Murland entered Natalie's room and found her sitting upright in bed looking out the window. Eyes wide, she turned immediately toward Murland when he walked into the room.

"It's Jack, isn't it?" she said.

"Yes."

"You know, I think he'll be all right," she said.

Murland smiled broadly, as he walked closer to the bed.

"Just as you will," he said.

Murland sat on the edge of the bed.

"Do you know what the greatest power is?" Murland asked.

"No."

"It is light."

"Light? Light is what killed my father."

"Yes. Lightning did kill your father. But there are many people who have been struck by lightning who survived and they just became transformed."

"What do you mean?"

"They were made aware of powers which they had and never used, or by the lightning strike, they were chosen and given special powers."

"What kind of powers?"

"The power to heal. Light has the power to heal."

"Why wasn't my father transformed?"

"Because it wasn't his destiny." Though Murland's words were direct, his tone was compassionate. Natalie needed time to consider his words, take them in, and Murland let her. She had never considered the idea that each person had his or her own destiny, and that her father's was not to be with her. For a fourteen year-old girl, who saw her father in heroic terms, it was a tough lesson to learn. The lesson on light and its power to kill or heal had a profound impact on her.

"Light is mentioned over and over again in every religion and in every sacred religious text on the planet. Light surrounds and goes through everything that exists. It even goes through you, is all around you." Murland traced around Natalie's body with his finger. "It connects you to other people, to animals, to plants and trees, even rocks. Everyone has a light energy field that that surrounds them like an egg shell."

"Can you see it?"

"Some people can. Do you know what a holy card is?"

"Isn't it like trading card, only instead of a picture of a baseball player, it has one of a holy person?"

"That's right," Murland chuckled. "They're called saints."

"Did you notice anything on the card when you saw it?"

"The saint had a gold ring around his head, up here." Natalie drew a circle in the air above her head.

"It's called a halo. It is the light radiating out of the saint's body, his crown." Murland pointed to just above Natalie's head. "Everyone has an aura, some people's auras shine more than others."

"So is that the light you were talking about?" Natalie asked.

"Yes, some people use light to heal."

"Are you going to heal me with light?"

"If you want."

"I do."

"Close your eyes and let any light and color that you see come in. Don't stop it. I am going to move my hands through your aura and around your light energy field to help you, okay?"

"Okay," Natalie said as she closed her eyes.

Murland spread his hands out six inches above her head with his fingers opened wide and palms cupped. Slowly he traced the outline of her body with his hands. A peaceful smile settled on her face. She breathed deeply and relaxed. A serenity filled her.

CHAPTER 43

THE SALT FLATS

It was twilight. The Great Thorn Maze receded far behind Jack, Caitlin, and Potter Sims, where it became a barely visible dot on the horizon as the dying light bled out of the sky. After trekking their last weary mile, they arrived at the edge of the Salt Flats, where they stood in silence staring at what lay before them. The Salt Flats was a barren and lifeless white desert that extended to the horizon as far as they could see. *Endless.* The word echoed repeatedly through Jack's mind. The orange and red light of the setting sun scattered across the white salt surface as if a raging fire was burning there, a subliminal warning to anyone who dared even think about crossing.

"We have to cross this?" Jack asked.

"We could go back to the Thorn Maze," Potter Sims said with a satirical tone in his voice. Though he did not show it, the sight of the Salt Flats startled him. Over the years, he had heard what he considered tall tales about despair and death on the Salt Flats, but now after seeing the Salt Flats, he was not so sure that they were tall tales.

"How far does it extend?" Caitlin asked.

"I've never been here before." Potter Sims answered.

"But you must know somebody who has." Jack said.

"I've heard stories, but everyone exaggerates."

"What did they say?" Caitlin asked.

"Dozens have tried to cross, but only three made it, and it took them two days. They almost died."

Nobody said anything. They just stared at the endless landscape painted crimson and purple by the waning sun.

Out of nowhere, a sound, like a wind parting the air, broke the silence above their heads. It was Gandor. He glided out of the indigo sky right in front of them. He spread his enormous wings wide and lifted them high above his head. Skidding his bright blue webbed feet into the ground, like an airplane coming in on its belly for a crash landing, his great wings flapped rapidly and whipped the air like helicopter blades causing a great swoosh-chopping sound.

"Nice landing! We were wondering where you were! In fact, we were just saying how much we missed you!" Potter Sims said.

"I am sure you were." Gandor said as he tucked his wings snugly into his sides. He pulled his pipe from beneath his vest and noticed Jack's arm. "What happened?"

"I fell on a thorn," Jack held his arm out for Gandor to see.

"Don't misunderstand me," Gandor said as he lit his pipe, taking three rapid puffs. Three blue smoke rings rose into the crimson sky. "Why aren't you dead?"

"You weren't there, so it's none of your business!" Potter Sims barked.

"I disagree with you. Gandor is here, as he promised. So it is his business." Caitlin said.

"Sims, why would I endanger myself and my species by coming here? I could have just flown off and never come back!" Gandor said.

"Because you needed us," Potter Sims said.

"Perhaps so. Perhaps so." Gandor said as he blew another blue smoke ring into the air.

For the first time, Potter Sims was at a loss for something to say. "Hum" was all that he could think of and all that came out of his mouth.

"We're glad to see you, Gandor." Jack said.

"Thank you," Gandor answered. "How did you survive?"

"By the strange gift from a friend and a stranger prophecy."

Gandor stared at the point on Jack's arm where the wood stopped at his elbow and his flesh began. "You were lucky," he said.

"We need to figure out how to cross this." Caitlin said as she pointed to the Salt Flats.

"I can help," Gandor said.

"How are you going to help?" Potter Sims said.

"While you were crossing the Thorn Maze, I knew that you must cross the Salt Flats, so I flew over them in every direction from exactly this point where we are standing."

"Why didn't you say so earlier?" Potter Sims asked.

"Because I just got here, Sims."

"That's great, Gandor. What did you find?" Caitlin asked.

"It will take nearly two days to cross the Salt Flats."

"Saving news! I told you the same thing before he even got here!" Potter Sims said.

Caitlin and Jack looked at each other with immediate concern. The feud between Gandor and Potter Sims was insignificant when compared to their current predicament. It was survival. They had hoped that Gandor would know more.

"Is there anything else you can tell us?" Caitlin asked.

"No matter which direction you go, it will take you two days from this spot." Gandor added.

"That's not true. If we are three degrees off, we will end up walking in a circle and never get out. We need a way to orient ourselves out there every minute," Jack said.

"We have one," Caitlin said.

They turned expectantly toward her.

"The sun."

"Exactly," Gandor said. "How did you know?"

"It was a guess," Caitlin said.

Gandor took a long deep puff on his pipe and carefully blew a great blue ring into the night air. He watched it as it floated skyward toward the stars. "I discovered as I was flying," he said, "that the sun traveled in a relatively straight line as it crossed the Salt Flats. When we leave, if we keep our shadows in the same position relative to our bodies, then we will travel in a straight line."

"That's brilliant, Gandor!" Potter Sims said.

"Why thank you, Sims. Sometimes even you surprise me." Gandor puffed out his chest slightly and boosted his head high.

"There's something else that might help us." Jack said as he removed the Yamqui drawing from his back pocket.

"Just what would that be?" Potter Sims asked

"Look." Everyone gathered curiously around the Yamqui drawing which Jack unfolded. "A lot of images on this map," Jack gave Caitlin a deferential nod, "excuse me, on this drawing represent places or events that triggered turning points on our journey," Jack pointed to the illustrations on the Yamqui drawing as he spoke. "—the lightning, rainbows, a river, the black cat, a maze."

"So you think maybe something out there on the Salt Flats is on this map?" Gandor said.

"Yes." Jack said.

"It's possible. I've been thinking about it, too." Caitlin said as she took the Yamqui drawing from Jack. She held the drawing out so everyone could see it clearly. Jack, Potter Sims and Gandor gathered around her, as she pointed to a group of stars. "You see the Pleiades, Nuchu Verano, right here just above the rainbow. Just below the cluster of stars, there is a star." She pointed to a lone star far outside of the Pleiades. "I don't think that's a star at all. I think it is a planet. I think it is my planet."

"Pachakutek?" Jack asked.

"I'm sure of it."

"How could it be? This drawing was made over 500 hundred years ago, but you only recently discovered Pachakutek." Jack asked.

"How could Murland possibly know that you would need the Stradivarius bridge and this drawing before there was even a Beanstalk?" Caitlin said.

Touché. Jack smiled.

"Big deal. This Yamqui draws a picture over 500 hundred years ago, and it suddenly becomes a big mystery. How's that going to help us?" Potter Sims asked.

"Sims, sometimes you're so simple!" Gandor said.

"Do you know the answer?" Potter Sims said.

"I do. Follow me," Caitlin interrupted and began walking toward the Salt Flats with Jack, Potter Sims and Gandor following close behind. She went about forty yards and stopped.

The sun had long since set, the deep crimsons and indigos on the horizon blended into night, as if a gentle hand had airbrushed them into the black sky above, and peeking out all around were stars, millions of them.

Caitlin pointed to a tight grouping of stars a fingernail above the horizon. "Do you see that cluster of stars?"

They all looked in the direction where she was pointing. "Those are the Nuchu Verano, the Pleiades. If we wait awhile, Pachakutek will appear."

"How do you know that?" Potter Sims asked.

"Call it an educated guess," she said.

"You mean an intuition or a feeling?" Jack asked her with a slight tone of derision in his voice.

"Maybe."

"Not very scientific," Jack said.

"No, it isn't," Caitlin smiled, not hiding anything. "Why don't we wait and see?"

"What's so important about this planet?" Potter Sims asked.

"Anytime a new planet is discovered, it's a major astronomical event. It gives us more information about our universe, in this case our solar system," Caitlin said.

"It's like a new neighbor," Jack said.

"That's the most ridiculous thing I ever heard!" Potter Sims said. "Look at that!" He pointed to the stars near the horizon. "Do they look like neighbors to you?"

"It's a metaphor, Sims. It means the planet is closer." Gandor said.

"Doesn't look closer to me!"

"You gotta squint, Potter." Jack said.

"Humph!" Potter Sims said folding his arms and squinting his big eyes at the dim starlight.

"Planets are different from stars," Caitlin spoke to Potter Sims. "Not only are they smaller, but they usually orbit around a star, like our planet Earth orbits around the sun."

"Why did you name it Pachakutek?" Gandor asked.

"In Quechua, there is a word, Pachakuti. It means the overturning of space and time, as we know it. It is about change, about the end of one cycle and the beginning of the next," Caitlin said. "It became an Inca belief after the ninth ruler of the Incas, Pachakutek, who was a great wise ruler, made visionary changes for the Inca people."

"So you named the planet after him?" Jack asked.

"Yes," Caitlin answered, "but that's not the only reason." She wanted Potter Sims and Gandor to comprehend not just why she chose the name of *Pachakutek*, but the significance of its appearance and subsequent disappearance. "Our planet is on the brink of total destruction. Ironically, we are on the horizon of our greatest technological and medical discoveries; so the choices to destroy or create are inexorably linked together. We are at the end of one cycle of mankind's evolution, and the beginning of the next. Hence, Pachakutek."

"Where is Pachakutek?" Potter Sims asked, looking up into the sky.

"It's not up yet," Caitlin answered. "Be patient. It will come up right over there," Caitlin pointed to the horizon where the Nuchu Verano, the Pleiades, were rising.

"Can we use Pachakutek as a navigational point like Polaris or the Star of Bethlehem? That way, we can travel across the Salt Flats at night before it gets too hot." Jack said.

"Brilliant," Gandor said choking on a blue smoke ring as he spoke.

"Good idea!" Potter Sims exclaimed.

"If it appears, it'll work. Pachakutek will travel along the ecliptic, right there," Caitlin traced her finger in a slight curve across the sky." Jack, Potter Sims and Gandor followed it.

"When the sun comes up, we'll be halfway across the Salt Flats," Jack said.

Side-by-side, they sat down on the Salt Flats in a near semi-circle staring at the Pleiades, which slowly rose through the dying crimson and deep purple glow of the horizon. The stars came to life. Gandor drew in a long deep breath on his pipe and blew smoke symbols into the tranquil night sky. As they rose, they expanded and formed the mathematical symbols for pi, alpha, and omega, fitting props on the infinite night stage of the Milky Way and the Salt Flats.

"Why mathematical symbols?" Jack asked.

"Numbers have no end," Gandor explained.

"Did you ever think that maybe that's why you're nearly extinct?" Potter Sims said.

"Because of mathematics?" Gandor said, irritated by Potter Sims' question.

"No, because of that disgusting pipe!" countered Potter Sims.

Jack and Caitlin chuckled, as they watched the Pleiades rising higher above the horizon, but there was still no sign of Pachakutek.

"Gandor, Ens said that your ancestors made the wrong choice. What was the choice?" Caitlin asked.

Gandor hung his head. The shadow of regret and blush of embarrassment powdered his complexion. His body was still, immobile. Nobody spoke, not even Potter Sims. They felt sad as they watched Gandor withdraw into a bubble of remorse, a demeanor so unlike his proud and often arrogant personality. He had become attached to these strangers, whom he now called his friends. When Gandor was not with them, he thought about them. When he was with them, he felt like he belonged. Vulnerability was not something that Gandor, the proud and self-righteous survivor of his species, had permitted himself to feel for as long as he could remember. It was a matter of survival. However, he had unwittingly made Jack, Caitlin and Potter Sims his family; even they were unaware of the commitment he had made to them. Potter Sims, who detested Gandor at times, knew that something had changed, for he had voluntarily scouted the Salt Flats for them and was humble about it. Yet, it was not the scouting of the Salt Flats that impressed Potter Sims, but it was that Gandor expected and hoped to see Jack, Caitlin, and Potter Sims safely exiting the Thorn Maze, and he looked forward to that.

"What good would it do to speak of my people's demise? Will it change anything?" Gandor said as he lifted his head.

"You can't hide from it!" Potter Sims said.

"I hide from nothing!" Gandor puffed his chest out.

Potter Sims stepped toward him and pointed a disagreeing finger, but Jack shook his head abruptly at him. Potter Sims was silent.

"It's your history, Gandor. History is important." Caitlin said.

"Unbearable is a more accurate word," Gandor said.

"I study ancient civilizations. Many cultures have disappeared," Caitlin said. "Please. You could teach me something."

"You could teach us all something, except maybe for Potter," Jack said.

"That's funny!" Potter Sims said.

"Well in that case," Gandor said as he settled down comfortably on the ground.

"Is the planet up yet?" Potter Sims asked.

Caitlin looked up to the night sky to see if Pachakutek had appeared in the wake of the Pleiades, but it was nowhere in sight.

"Not yet," she said.

"You sure it will be there?" Potter Sims asked.

"I'd bet your life on it," Caitlin said.

"Humph!" Potter Sims shrugged.

They all relaxed around Gandor to listen, as they waited for the arrival of Pachakutek.

CHAPTER 44

COLLAPSE OF A CLAN

"My home was Rafus Island. You won't find it on any maps or drawings, it is as if it never existed. It took generations for our people to die off, for the collapse." Gandor said as he puffed reflectively on his pipe. "Ens said that we 'killed ourselves,' but what he did not say was that we did it unknowingly."

As Gandor, the only survivor of his species *Raphus gryphus*, spoke about the decline of his ancestors and their eventual extinction, billions of stars came out and shined radiantly in the night sky. Jack, Caitlin, and Potter Sims listened so attentively that they could hear the silence of the Salt Flats between Gandor's words. For a creature as arrogant and fearful as Gandor was, they knew that this was a rare and revealing moment.

"For centuries we had a love-hate relationship with our neighboring tribes. We traded with them, but still plotted secretly against them as they did to us. We had wars with them. We thought that we were better than they were; we were smarter, more educated and civilized. We were wealthier than they were; we were more advanced. As we became more self sufficient, we cut off trade with most of the surrounding nations. We isolated ourselves. At the peak of wealth and influence, twin brothers were born to the royal family of Rafus Island. Their father King Artuj died in a battle, and at twelve years-old they took over as the rulers of Rafus. One was named Inac, the other was Ebal. For over a decade, they tried to outdo each other by constructing enormous statues and monuments of gold and a rare blue mineral called Ubunite. Hundreds of thousands of Rafulite people were indentured to build the great monuments. During the 12th year, a civil war broke out between the two brothers, and it divided our nation into two camps, those loyal to Inac and those loyal to Ebal. During the Truce for Peace that Inac called in the Sacred Heart of the Great Forest, Ebal was poisoned by his brother and his loyalists were executed. It took five years for the nation to recover, but we did. King Inac restructured every part of our kingdom, the tax system, education, land ownership, technical and medical research, and the military. It was a very unstable period. He decided that the Great Forest was too large and provided too much cover for our enemies. It made us vulnerable. Therefore, by order of King Inac, our engineers designed a plan that would eliminate our vulnerability. We would burn down every tree of the Great Forest five miles out from the perimeter of our nation. That way our military could monitor every invader and protect us."

Endless rolls of black clouds billowed into the air obliterating the sun and turning the bright blue sky to charcoal. For two years, the horizon around Rafus Island was blazing red and orange. Exotic birds and four-legged animals, snakes and lizards of every color and kind, scrambled and slithered onto the charred wasteland to escape the raging flames that devoured the Great Forest. The ground was black. The sky was black. The only green left on the horizon in any direction was Rafus Island. It became an oasis. It was a lush, circular green patch of the Great Forest, ten miles in diameter, surrounded by a barren charred wilderness. The people of Rufus Island felt safe.

"For a decade after the fires had stopped and the sky had returned to blue, our nation prospered," Gandor spoke as he puffed on his pipe, spellbinding Jack, Caitlin and Potter Sims with the vivid details of the collapse of his species *Raphus gryphus*. "We learned to use the abundant resources within our boundaries to build, plant, and irrigate. Then one morning, a huge violent trembling shook the ground of Rufus Island. Everyone fled their homes, their places of work, and collected in groups, terrified. In the distance, we could see the sky glowing red and orange, and an enormous plume of black smoke rising. A volcano thirty miles away had erupted. It spewed out lava, ash and black smoke for an entire year. It covered every inch of the land, as far as we could see. What we did not obliterate when we burned down the Great Forest, the volcano did only a thousand times worse. It left not a tree, nor a bush standing. The ground hardened over with black lava. Miraculously, or so we thought, the lava only covered about two miles of Rufus Island, so we were spared."

"But what about the nuclear winter?" Caitlin asked.

"What is that?" Gandor asked.

"It's the black soot and ash that go into the atmosphere and blot out the sunlight," she said.

Gandor took a deep draw on his pipe and blew a huge puff of bluish-black smoke into the night air. Everyone watched it float upward.

"That is what killed us," Gandor said. "A great darkness covered the land for three years. All of our crops died, our water dried up. There was nothing to eat, no water to drink. Disease spread everywhere. Alba, my wife, was one of the last to die. You remember her from the dance."

"How did Ens kill her?" Jack asked.

"He didn't kill her. He could have saved her life, but he didn't," Gandor answered. "Ens showed up when little was left of Rufus Island; everybody was sick and dying. He could have intervened, opened the clouds and let the sun shine in upon us, stopped the disease, but he refused to help."

"Why should he? You brought it upon yourselves," Potter Sims said.

"Those were his exact words," Gandor said. He was surprised not only by Potter Sims' directness, but also because he echoed Ens' words and judgment. However, Potter Sims did not gloat. He was more horrified to hear the choices that Gandor's clan had made. At one time, he detested Gandor for his arrogant and proud manner, now Potter Sims pitied him. Gandor hung his head, as he continued to speak. "Ens told the remaining survivors that we had made the wrong choice. After a year, everyone died, but me. Why I remained as the last survivor of our species, I do not know. I am lonely. I am lost. Rafus Island became Devastation Plain. This journey with you is the first time I have left. It has always been my home."

Gandor was silent; he dropped his head in surrender. Caitlin touched his drooping shoulder. "Thank you for telling us. I am truly sorry for you and your species."

Jack and Potter Sims did not know what to say. Their silence heightened the awe and humility they felt for being witnesses to Gandor's story and his deeply painful honesty.

Caitlin looked up to the wide night sky that shimmered above the Salt Flats, peppered by billions of stars. On the ecliptic, she saw the Incas' Nuchu Verano, which modern man labeled as the Pleiades. Behind them, just rising over the horizon, was Pachakutek. She smiled.

"Pachakutek," she said as she pointed to the distant rising planet.

"So that is our way out?" Potter Sims asked.

"All we need to do is follow Pachakutek," Caitlin said.

"It is our way out in many, many ways," Jack said. "If we are to survive, we must follow it. Let's go," Jack said as he stood up and held his good hand out for Caitlin to take. Gandor and Potter Sims stood together. All four walked onto the Salt Flats following Pachakutek as it rose in the endless night sky.

CHAPTER 45

PROPHECIES REVEALED

Jack, Caitlin, Potter Sims and Gandor walked side-by-side across the Salt Flats. A waxing crescent moon hung high in the night sky, where surrounded by millions of radiant stars, it cast a cool reflective light upon the plain's white surface. There was no wind, no rustling of tree leaves or plants of any kind, no sound of a bird or an animal, no sounds of insects, no rumblings from the distant mountains, and no trickle of running water. It was still. The only sound breaking the quiet was the crunching and scraping footsteps of the four friends as they walked across the Salt bed. Caitlin looked up at The Pleiades and her planet Pachakutek, as they walked along.

"Beautiful, aren't they?" she said.

"It's a magical night," Gandor said.

"Are you sure we are walking in the right direction?" Potter Sims asked.

"As long as we follow Pachakutek." Jack said.

"Do you know what the heliacal rise is?" Caitlin asked.

"No." Jack said.

Potter Sims and Gandor both shook their heads and answered no.

"Look at the horizon in front of you," Caitlin pointed. "Just before dawn, when the sky gets light, some stars appear as they rise just above the horizon, then less than two minutes later, they fade. That's the heliacal rise."

"So what?" Potter Sims said.

"You're so impolite, Sims," Gandor said.

"It's his way of saying that he wants to know more," Jack said.

"That's exactly right," Potter Sims said.

"See, Potter, I am getting to know how you tick," Jack said.

"During the winter solstice on a clear summer night, the Stars of the Summer, the Pleiades, will rise there 35 minutes before the sun actually rises," Caitlin said.

"And what is the significance?" Gandor said.

"You and Potter Sims talked about the Incas," Caitlin said. "The Incas based their planting and harvesting upon the heliacal rise of the Nuchu Verano. Everything the Incas did, planting their crops, designing a radial architecture for their cities, constructing the buildings of gold that captured the light of the rising sun, their entire culture was designed around the movements of the stars and planets, particularly the sun."

"I don't care about the Incas! We've got to get across this!" Potter Sims pointed impatiently to the Salt Flats.

"Stop. Everybody, stop," Caitlin said. She, Jack and Gandor stopped, but Potter Sims kept walking. "Potter!" Caitlin screamed so loud at Potter Sims that her voice pierced the still of the night. It shocked Jack and pleased Gandor, who grinned and puffed calmly on his pipe. Potter Sims stopped abruptly. When he turned, his eyes were white and wide with surprise.

"This is Inca prophecy! It is far bigger than four people crossing this desert!" Caitlin said.

"These are Salt Flats," Potter Sims said in a dry monotone.

Caitlin glared at Potter Sims, but before she could say anything Jack spoke up.

"What kind of prophecy?"

"On June 19, 650 C.E. the night of the winter solstice in the Andes, the Nuchu Verano, or the Pleiades, did not rise."

"How's that possible?" Potter Sims challenged.

"I don't know, but it is Inca legend." Caitlin said.

"What does it mean?" Gandor asked.

"Inca elders and some scholars think that it foretells a great shift or change, a new beginning or an end to our world."

"Pachakuti?" Jack asked.

"Yes," Caitlin said.

"Do you believe it? That the stars actually stopped turning in the sky?" Jack asked.

"I don't know. Most archeoastronomers believed that it was a myth for a great upheaval, but—" Caitlin stopped herself to look up into the night sky, where Pachakutek was shining brightly, "—before Pachakutek disappeared, in a million years I wouldn't believe that it could possibly happen. Now, I honestly don't know."

"What do you know about the Hopi?" Jack asked.

"Who are they?" Gandor asked.

"The Hopi are a Native American Indian tribe on our planet; they are a deeply religious people. They believe in humility, community, respect for all of creation, and being caretakers of planet Earth. Like the Incas, their ceremonies were based upon the phases of the moon and solstices of the sun." Jack said.

"Did they make a prophecy, too?" Potter Sims asked.

"Several," Jack said. "Did you know that the Hopi considered themselves to be direct descendants of the Pleiades?" asked Jack.

"Yes, besides astronomy, I specialized in ethnic cultures," Caitlin said. She was amazed at Jack's knowledge of the Hopi. As a researcher and teacher, she was familiar with the lore of indigenous and ancient cultures; it was her specialty, but it was not Jack's field, so it surprised her. She was not quite sure what to make of it.

"The Hopi called the Pleiades constellation, *Chuhukon*. In Hopi, it means 'those who cling together.'" Jack said. "They believed that when they died their spirit would return south to the Pleiades."

"When you die, you think that you're going to somehow fly from here all the way up there?" Potter Sims pointed to the Pleiades. "That's the most ridiculous thing I ever heard!"

"It's a spiritual belief, Potter. There are many unusual strange spiritual beliefs," Jack said.

"I can certainly believe that!" Potter Sims said.

"What did they predict?" Gandor asked.

"The Hopi prophesied World War I and II, which were major wars that occurred on Earth. They said that World War III will be started by the peoples of the earth who first received the light; that could mean intelligence and a spiritual light—India, China, Africa, Egypt, and Pakistan. The prophecies say that the people and land of the United States, where Caitlin and I are from, will be destroyed by atomic bombs and radioactivity. This will happen when the Great House in the sky is completed. Many scholars think that the Great House in the Sky is the International Space Station."

"When is it supposed to be finished?" Gandor puffed on his pipe.

"Somewhere around 2010," Caitlin said. "I love the Hopi philosophy and their way of life, but did you ever consider that the Hopi had every reason to say that the United States will perish from atomic bombs and radiation, after what we did to them?"

"What did you do to them?" Potter Sims asked.

"We took their lands, drove them from their homes, hunted their animals to near extinction and waged wars against them. Then, we gave them small parcels of land as reparation, to satisfy our guilt for what we did to them," Jack said.

"You're not so different from us." Gandor said.

"No, we're not." Caitlin said.

"The Hopi were a very special people. Their name means 'People of peace.' Let me show you something," Jack said as he stooped down to ground of the Salt Flats. With his wooden finger, he drew a replica of a sacred Hopi petroglyph in the salt bed.

Besides being a professional musician, Jack was an avid reader. He read fast and remembered everything. His musical training endowed him with a remarkable memory for detail, especially anything visual.

"I read everything that I can," Jack said, "mostly non-fiction books and periodicals, *Nature* magazine, *National Geographic,* and *Archaeology.* I went through my 'Hopi period' about two years ago. I read everything that I could find about the Hopi.

As he drew with his wooden finger in the salt bed, each line glistened with silvery sparkles in the moonlight. He drew two parallel horizontal lines; then, he drew three vertical lines that intersected at a perpendicular to the parallel lines. He drew three stick people wearing hats that were standing on the top line; their heads were separated from their bodies, as if they were beheaded.

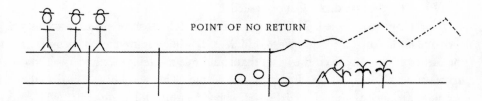

"What's the matter with their heads?" Potter Sims asked.

"Looks like they lost them, Sims, just like you do," Gandor said.

"I think that's enough, Gandor," Jack said.

"I agree," Potter Sims said.

Gandor turned his head away and puffed on his pipe blowing blue smoke rings into the air.

"What you noticed about the heads is correct. The Hopi drew the stick men as beheaded to show that they had lost their minds. Their minds became detached from their true selves, and they subsequently lost their faith and spiritual path," Jack said.

"For the Hopi, the two parallel lines represent two paths or choices that humankind, a nation or an individual person can make," Jack said. "The top line is a life chosen out of greed, selfishness, lack of respect for nature and the Earth, and weakness; the bottom line represents the love of others, respect for the Earth, balance, and strength. As we live our life, we explore the world and ourselves by crossing from one kind of life to another; we can move freely back and forth testing these two different paths, but the third line is the point of no return where the top line breaks up and zigzags. Once you are there, at the third intersecting point, it is too late to return to the other path."

Caitlin, Potter Sims and Gandor were riveted by Jack's explanation of the Hopi. They stared at the diagram etched into the bed of the Salt Flats. The lines glistened with little tiny sparkles that shone brightly against the moonlit white salt bed.

"Just as the Inca speak of Pachakuti," Jack said, "the Hopi speak of three 'Great Shakings of the Earth.' The first was World War I; the second was World War II; and the third shaking will be determined by which path humanity chooses. It's the point of no return, the third vertical line on the diagram. The Hopi call it our 'Choice Point.'"

"Pretty impressive for a musician," Caitlin said.

"What does that mean?" Jack said.

"It means that you are very unusual. The musicians I know aren't really interested in anything but their own music."

"You don't know many musicians, do you?"

Caitlin did not answer Jack; she just turned to the stars.

"I gave a lecture at Columbia University on astronomy, music and architecture in the rise and fall of ancient civilizations," Caitlin spoke still staring at the stars. "A jazz musician attended the lecture, and convinced me to go to a wine and cheese bar afterwards. His name was John. We dated for nearly three years. I was in love with him. Then, when I was on a trip to the Keck Observatory in Mauna Kea, I came back early and caught him red-handed with an old girlfriend. I had compromised my time and work, and I swore that I would never do that again."

"So you swore off musicians?" Jack said.

"Something like that."

Potter Sims deliberately broke the silence, "The drawing is too simple!"

"You would think that, Sims." Gandor chimed in as he exhaled a double-ringed blue smoke ring, which rose slowly just above the Hopi etching into the night sky.

"The Hopi were a simple people," Jack said.

"Humph!" Potter Sims merely crossed his arms.

Caitlin looked up at Pachakutek. "We should get going," she said.

"You're right," Jack said as he and Caitlin led the way across the Salt Flats following Pachakutek. As they walked across the Salt bed, the stars flickered brightly above them, and Pachakutek rose on the ecliptic across the night sky, where following the Pleiades and the constellations, it guided them to their unknown destiny.

CHAPTER 46

MATHEMATICAL PROPHECY FROM THE PAST

Though the stars glistened radiantly against the black sky and the Salt Flats glimmered bluish-white under the cool moonlight, the four travelers knew that the night would be short; soon the sun would rise up over the distant mountains and scorch the flat plains. They had little time. Every step taken was a race for survival against each tick of the clock.

In front, Jack and Caitlin led the way keeping a brisk pace. Behind them, Potter Sims and Gandor followed, Potter Sims flapping his transparent wings and bouncing clumsily along next to Gandor, who waddled with a steady rocking back and forth motion with each step.

"What do you know about the Mayan calendar?" Caitlin asked.

"I know their calendar ends on the solstice in 2012."

"I did my doctoral dissertation on the Mayans," Caitlin said as she gazed into Jack's rich, green eyes. "The Mayan calendar is based upon thirteen cycles called baktuns, or Heavens. A baktun is a period of a 400 tuns. Each tun equals 360-days …"

"Baktuns!" Potter Sims interrupts yelling from behind. "Are you kidding?"

Caitlin turns, "No, I am not. You should pay attention, you might learn something!"

Potter Sims and Gandor quicken their pace to catch up with Jack and Caitlin.

"Our calendar on earth has 365 days in a year; the Mayan calendar has 360 days. Therefore, each of the thirteen baktuns, or Heavens, is 400 tuns times the number of days, which is 360. That equals 394 solar years. That means that the Mayans predicted political and social events, conflicts and wars, the conquests of entire nations and civilizations, and the prospering of nations according to these thirteen baktuns of 394 years."

"What nations?" Gandor asked as he chugged along trying to keep up.

"Our planet has always had a struggle between the East and the West. During the baktuns or Heavens with odd numbers, there was expansion and conquest movement toward the east and the west midline, which passes through Central Europe and Central Africa. Heaven or Baktun Number 9 saw the expansion of the Roman Empire during the time of Christ. It was roughly around 40 CE. Three hundred and ninety-four years later, according to the Mayan calendar, mankind entered Heaven 10, an even number baktun. That was around 434 CE and it marked the invasion of the Huns under Attila. It was the collapse of the Roman Empire."

"Tuns! Baktuns! Heavens!" Potter Sims exclaimed. "What does it mean?"

"It means," explained Caitlin calmly, "that the end of the thirteen Heavens, or Baktuns is the year 2012, that is the end of the Mayan Calendar. The Mayans predicted that the year 2012 would end one era and signal a new era of great change."

"Like the Great Shift in Inca prophecy." Jack said.

"And the Hopi," Caitlin said as the two kept pace with each other.

"All of these indigenous peoples, separated by continents and hundreds of years, having no contact with one another, all have similar prophecies," Jack mused while he looked up at the sparkling stars.

"Remarkable isn't it." Caitlin said in a monotone that underscored a tone of detached, academic reflection.

"Do you know who Dr. Eliyahu Rips is?" Jack asked.

"No."

"He is a famous Israeli mathematician. He used a super computer and discovered a series of embedded codes in the Torah."

"What kind of codes?" Caitlin asked.

"Can you slow down?" Potter Sims yelled from behind them, as he bounced along buzzing his wings in spurts and Gandor waddled in his hurried back and forth cadence like a penguin.

"Keep up!" Jack yelled back.

"Easy for you to say!" Potter Sims shouted back.

Jack looked to Caitlin and grinned. Using his hands, he became animated while he walked, as if he was drawing words in the night air. "Dr. Rips removed all of the spaces, all the capitalizations and punctuation from the Torah, and fed the text into the computer. The computer found patterns of words and phrases that prophesied events that had not yet happened when the Torah was written. Some of these events have already happened, some have not."

"What kinds of events are you talking about?" Caitlin asked with skepticism in her voice.

"World War II, the assassination of John Kennedy, of Yitzhak Rabin in 1995, and 9-11," Jack said.

Caitlin listened silently, captivated by Jack's wealth of information, but she was guarded. What he said sent up red flags; it had the earmarks of information that her academic discipline disparaged, like the fodder printed in the *National Enquirer*, ideas embraced by soothsayers and mystics.

"The year," Jack continued, "that stands out is '2012,' the end of the Mayan calendar. Other words in the Torah's text spell out, 'Earth annihilated.'"

"Look, I don't believe in things like that. I never have. I am a scientist."

"What about the disappearance of Pachakutek?"

"I am sure there is a scientific explanation for it. We just haven't found it yet," Caitlin answered confidently. "Can I be frank?"

"Sure."

"Obviously, you are bright and well read, but frankly, I am surprised that you believe in things like that."

"By things like that, do you mean religion?" Jack's voice had an edge in it. Religion was a powerful word that raised an eyebrow in many intellectual circles, and he knew it.

"What people call religion. Spirituality. Mysteries. Unexplained phenomena." Caitlin answered.

"Look up there," Jack said pointing up to the millions of stars sparkling in the crisp black night sky.

Caitlin looked up at the vastness of the universe hanging above the Salt Flats, as if looking up at the stars was something novel to this famous astronomer, who had a zealous fascination for stargazing since she was six years old. Nevertheless, she humored him.

"You think mankind is going to know everything about all of that?" Jack said.

"Eventually."

"Don't you think that is arrogant?"

"I am not arrogant," Caitlin defended herself.

"Perhaps arrogant is not the right word. Pride. The Greeks called it hubris. It is the idea that man's discoveries and technical advances will allow him to eventually know and manipulate anything."

"You make it sound criminal."

"Not criminal, dangerous. You see, I think that there are things that we will never understand because there are forces far, far greater than us that we must surrender to," Jack said.

Caitlin did not respond.

"I think that I am finally beginning to understand," Jack said. "Arrogance and pride will be the downfall of our planet, and your planet Pachakutek is the omen. It's a warning of doomsday or the herald of a new and visionary world."

Nobody said anything as their steps crunched on the Salt Flats. It became an unnerving crunching noise, a constant sound pushing each traveler to reflect. In the distance, the gentle fingers of pink painted the indigo sky. The sun was coming.

"Are we still going the right way?" Potter Sims broke the silence.

Caitlin turned slightly around while she kept walking. "Pachakutek is still there," she said as she pointed to the planet surrendering its light to the purples and pinks of the air brushed dawn. "We are following it, so we are not lost."

"Good!" Potter Sims said.

"Sims, you are such a phrenetic!" Gandor said as he rapped his pipe hard against his side, dropping shreds of burnt tobacco on the white salt bed.

"You can fly out of here! We can't!"

"How many times have I told you that I am not going to leave my friends!" Gandor said.

"That a way, Gandor." Jack said.

"Humph!" Potter Sims grumbled to himself.

Jack looked at Caitlin and they both forced a smile. As the temperature rose with the sun, so did their anxieties for they had a long way to go.

CHAPTER 47

IN THE HEAT OF THE MOMENT

Slowly, they heard the salt crackling as the sun peeked its scorching white face over the mountains and heated up the Salt Flats. Waves of heat rippled over the horizon.

"I hate the heat." Potter Sims complained as he plodded slowly along.

"You think any of us like it?" Gandor said.

"Shut up and save your energy, you're going to need it," Jack said.

Hours passed as the four friends trudged steadily on, but with great difficulty. The sun rose higher and higher, baking the Salt Flats and everything on them. Jack and Caitlin's lips were dry and cracked, their faces blistered, along with their exposed hands and arms. Caitlin was fading. Jack could tell, so he took her hand in his and pulled her slightly with each step, giving her a strength that she did not know that she had; he pushed her beyond the limits that she had pushed herself before. Together, they walked and walked. As Caitlin pushed herself each sweltering step, she felt herself bonding more to Jack, depending upon him.

Behind them, Gandor and Potter Sims hardly noticed. Gandor's rotund belly dragged slowly only inches above the salt bed, collecting the heat that reflected off the blazing white surface. He did not sweat, but it was clear that the heat was draining him. While his feathers kept the sun from burning his skin, they trapped in the heat. Gandor's footsteps and gait grew increasingly sluggish. He was roasting, but determined not to leave his friends, no matter what. Potter Sims was the only one not as affected by the heat. The heat bothered him, but he was physically more resilient to the heat than his friends were; however, being parched was not a condition that his body easily tolerated.

"I hate being thirsty!" Potter Sims said, but nobody paid attention.

Jack had unusual stamina and endurance, which he inherited from his father's side of the family. His physique and endurance were a match to a survivalist environment. His grandfather, Edward Jacob Tott, a fourth generation farmer, farmed tirelessly from 5 a.m. to 8 p.m. every day of his life in the blistering summer heat, in the biting winter, never taking a vacation, never sleeping late, working through sickness, and through the death of family and friends.

Four generations of Tott farmers had given Jacob George Tott, "Jack", the genes that he needed to survive in this harsh, unforgiving landscape. Every hour spent by a surviving ancestor plowing in the fields of Alta Vista, Kansas worked now to drive Jack relentlessly across the blistering Salt Flats.

Before Jack, Caitlin, Potter Sims and Gandor was the dried skeleton and decayed flesh of a large animal sprawled upon the sizzling white plains. Without saying a word, Gandor strayed from the others over to the sun-dried animal. With his beak, he ripped into the carrion, eating its dead tissue. As he chewed the baked flesh, he looked up at his three companions, who stopped to watch him. Gandor was embarrassed.

"That is disgusting!" exclaimed Potter Sims.

"Right now, anything looks good, even to a vegetarian." Caitlin said.

"Don't die, Potter," Jack chuckled, "see what will happen to you." Jack walked on, and the others followed. Gandor remained behind to finish his meal.

They plodded on as if there was no end. Gandor had joined them. They had walked over fifteen miles over the blistering salt for nearly six hours. The Salt Flats were endless. Suddenly, in the distance through the waves of heat rippling off the salt bed, they spotted dozens of wavy, translucent black specks on the horizon. They looked like black mirages.

"I am truly sorry," Gandor said as he flapped his wings violently and flew off.

"I told you he would leave!" Potter Sims yelled.

A loud flapping echoed over the Salt Flats, as dozens of flying creatures closed in and circled Jack, Caitlin and Potter Sims. The three stared up into the sky. They had to squint. The sun was blinding. Suddenly, Potter Sims recognized the invaders.

"It is The Corps!" he exclaimed shielding his eyes.

"I don't like this," Caitlin moved closer to Jack. With wings sweeping, stirring up the fine salt crystals into the air, The Corps landed on the salt bed thirty feet from Jack, Caitlin and Potter Sims. Hranknor, the leader of The Corps, walked toward the three exhausted travelers. He stood over seven feet tall. His dark muscular wings extended twenty-five feet from tip-to-tip. He stepped closer to the three wary travelers. Intimidated by the powerful being, Jack and Caitlin stepped backward. Potter Sims stood his ground firmly.

"Grundig nräng ut kandu udrang!" Hranknor looked deeply into Jack's eyes. His voice was deep and guttural, as if each word came from his bowels.

Potter Sims was the only one not frightened. "Whatever it is," he said, "you tell Ens, we want nothing to do with it!"

Hranknor stared at Potter Sims. He pointed sharply at Caitlin. "Grundig nräng ut kandu udrang!"

"What does he want?" Caitlin asked fearfully.

"He wants you," Potter Sims answered.

Hranknor watched Caitlin and Jack carefully, evaluating them.

"Ut Grundig nräng it tatzui kandu udrang, ut zut!"

"You can't have her," Jack stepped between Caitlin and Hranknor.

"That's telling him!" Potter Sims egged Jack on.

Hranknor stood silently riveted on Caitlin. He ignored Potter Sims, which irked Potter Sims beyond words. It made him feel lowly, even more insignificant than the way Gandor usually made him feel. At least Gandor argued with him.

"What about me?" Potter Sims asked.

Hranknor ignored Potter Sims.

"I'm scared," Caitlin said.

"You're not going anywhere," Jack said.

"Just how do you intend to stop them?" asked Caitlin. "I mean, look at them."

Jack quickly tried to figure out what to do while Hranknor was staring him down. Slowly, he began moving in a circle around Hranknor, pointing his wooden arm in front of him like a spear. With his other arm, he kept Caitlin behind him. Hranknor stared at Jack's wooden arm, as he circled. As Jack turned, Hranknor began laughing. His large gruff shoulders and great wings shook. The Corps joined in the laughter, as if this was a game.

"What are you doing?" Potter Sims yelled to Jack, as he circled Hranknor.

"Buying time," Jack said.

"For what?" Potter Sims asked.

"To think!"

Jack did not know what else to do. Though he was amused, Hranknor was becoming impatient. Finally, Jack stopped. Caitlin stopped. Hranknor stopped. All three stared at one another.

"Ut Grundig! Nräng kandu udrang!" Hranknor said.

With one sweep of his enormous black wings, Hranknor grabbed Jack and pitched him twenty feet through the air. He dropped to the Salt Flats with a thump. Hranknor grabbed Caitlin and with one whip of his wings lifted her twenty-five feet into the air. She screamed. In three seconds, Caitlin was over two hundred feet above the Salt Flats held tightly by Hranknor's hairy arms. The Corps followed. As Hranknor and The Corps flew off, Caitlin's screams faded into the distant rippling whiteness. Caitlin and The Corps were now black specks in the bright blue sky, until they disappeared into the harsh white nothingness of the horizon.

"Dammit!" Jack yelled into the empty white space of the Salt Flats.

"What are we going to do now?" Potter Sims asked.

Desperate, Jack scanned the empty white horizon. He feared for her safety, but could do nothing to help her. The fingers of his good hand trembled.

"We've got to find her."

"Just how are we supposed to do that?" Potter Sims asked.

"We have to cross this." Jack's voice was stern and resolute, as he trudged off across the Salt Flats leaving Potter Sims to scurry after him, his wings buzzing frantically in the scorching heat.

"Wait! Wait!" Potter Sims yelled, but Jack would not slow down. "I hate the heat!" Potter Sims said as he stomped on the salt bed with his red-boots.

CHAPTER 48

THE TREE OF LIFE

Jack and Potter Sims walked for hours under the scorching sun. Inside Potter Sims' shiny red boots, his feet were baking. The heat scorched the soles of Jack's feet through his tennis shoes. His lips were dry and cracked. The short once tacky black hairs on Potter Sims' arms and legs were dry and bleached white from the salt. Over the last hour, their pace had slowed down to one-quarter of what it had been.

"I don't know if I can go much farther," Potter Sims said. His words trickled out with the knell of surrender. He stopped, his body slumped over, his white-gloved hands resting on his tired knees, so that his proboscis was only three inches from the salt bed.

"Look at me." Jack waited, but Potter Sims did not move. "Potter, look at me."

Slowly, Potter Sims raised his head and stared at Jack.

"You don't have a choice," Jack said with an inflectionless voice, like a giant immovable rock. "I am not leaving you and I cannot carry you. Therefore, you must keep moving." Jack turned and walked into the boundless and bare Salt Flats.

"You don't have to get so snippy about it!" Potter Sims said as he snapped his head up. Using all of his energy, Potter Sims beat his wings frantically to catch up.

For three hours, they walked on the glaring white Salt Flats. It felt like an eternity, as if hell itself had reached up through the Salt Flats to suck every drop of water out of their already dried, parched bodies. Potter Sims would have given up long ago, if it were not for Jack with his great will to save his sister, his physical stamina, and his drive to find Caitlin.

Ahead, when they thought that they could take not one more step, Jack spotted a blurry object in the distance. It was a mirage, Jack thought. It was just a mirage. Had to be. As he shuffled across the sweltering salt bed, he squinted to see the distant, massive object more clearly, but his eyes burned and were teary from the arid salty air. He was sure that it must be fifty feet high! Jack wiped the salty tears away from his eyes. The more he squinted, the more his eyes watered. Twenty-feet behind him, Potter Sims dragged his red boots slowly across the blistering salt desert. Hunched over, Potter Sims' head was down. He did not see the blurred object, all that he could see was the white glare of the Salt Flats.

The distant object was a Great Green Tree in the middle of the barren Salt Flats. Its lowest leafy branches were about eighteen feet above the parched salt desert. Its round symmetrical form was a stark contrast against the deep azure sky.

As Jack neared the tree, he wiped his eyes. "Potter, do you see that?"

Potter Sims did not respond, but shuffled robotically across the desert floor.

"Potter, look!" Jack took Potter Sims by the chin and raised his head, so Potter Sims' proboscis was pointed directly at the Great Tree isolated in the barren white wasteland. Jack pulled the Yamqui map out of his pocket, and opened it.

"It's on the map!" Jack pointed to the tree on the bottom right corner of the Yamqui drawing. "It is a tree. We are where we are supposed to be!" Jack said.

"That just makes me so happy," Potter Sims said matter-of-factly.

"Come on, let's go, survival is in that tree."

Jack hurried him. Supporting each other, Jack and Potter Sims walked across the Salt Flats toward the giant tree. Nearly an hour passed before they arrived at the base of the Great Tree. The tree towered over them by sixty feet. Jack smelled the air; a scent of pine with a hint of mint filled the air all around the Great Tree.

"What's that smell?" Potter Sims asked.

"It's coming from the tree."

"At least, it smells better than salt! I hate salt!" Potter Sims said.

Somehow, Jack knew instinctively that every part of the tree embodied the Golden Mean. He had read about the Golden Ratio extensively, it was a ratio of 1.618, which existed in music, biology, astronomy, art and architecture, in daVinci's works, in the Fibonacci number sequence. He could hardly believe that he was a short distance away from a tree that contained the five Platonic solids.

Jack and Potter Sims stood in the rim of the tree's shadow looking at the heart-shaped jade leaves and the thousands of fruits dangling from its thick branches. On every branch hung hundreds of brightly colored, palm-sized pieces of fruit in perfect geometric shapes. The tree looked like the most magnificent Christmas tree ever decorated. The colored fruits were of five distinct shapes: tetrahedron, cube, octahedron, dodecahedron, and icosahedron. Their brilliant red, yellow, blue, orange, and purple colors caused them to stand out against the tree's vivid jade leaves. Inside some of the fruits just below their skins, pinpoints of light sparkled like little stars, gathering and concentrating the bright light from the hot desert sun. Each fruit was different, but they all shared the same characteristics of intense color, perfect geometric form, and radiant light. They were perfect scientific and artistic structures, equilateral pyramids, tetras, and cubes. Their shapes were pleasing to look at because they were similar to the double helix DNA, a crystal molecule, or a Nautilus shell. The fruits embodied the Golden Mean. It was the Tree of Life. The smell of the Great Tree gave Jack and Potter Sims strength.

"You need to fly up there and get us some fruit," said Jack.

"I hate flying, and I don't have the energy."

"Well I hate dying. We must eat, and you have to go up there."

Potter Sims said nothing, he knew that Jack was not just right, he was adamant. Exhausted, dirty and disgusted, Potter Sims looked up at the tall tree. Using his last ounce of strength, he buzzed his wings. As he lifted off the ground, Jack heard him muttering, "I hate flying." Potter Sims hovered around the lower branches of the tree looking at the brightly colored fruit. Standing anxiously just beyond the tree's circle of shade, Jack watched Potter Sims as he floated around the tree's sprawling limbs. In the silence of the Salt Flats, Potter Sims' wings buzzed loudly. Potter Sims grabbed a bright yellow cube fruit. He pulled it off the tree branch and dropped it down to Jack. As soon as the fruit hit Jack's hands, a musical tone vibrated from inside the fruit. It was one long pure note, an E. Jack did not believe what he was hearing. He turned the bright yellow fruit over in his hand. As it vibrated, pinpoints of gold light sparkled just beneath the surface of the fruit's skin. Jack watched it, until Potter Sims broke his concentration.

"Do you want to eat or not!" yelled Potter Sims impatiently as he hovered thirty feet above Jack. Potter Sims held three more pieces of fruit in his arms.

Jack set the yellow cube of fruit down at his feet, and held his hands up to catch the next that Potter Sims was about to drop. Jack was curious, like a kid on

Christmas Eve. Potter Sims dropped another fruit, a red tetrahedron. It was a perfect pyramid, and it fit into the palm of his hand. As soon as it hit Jack's palm, it sang out a cord of three notes, C major. Jack's dry cracked lips smiled. *Is Potter Sims hearing these?* Jack wondered. Jack set the red tetrahedron down next to the yellow cube. Their notes merged. Smiling, Jack looked up to Potter Sims, who dropped several different kinds of fruits, one-at-a time into Jack's hands. The first was indigo blue and in the shape of an icosahedron, twenty sides, each side an equilateral triangle. It hummed in the key of A major. Spellbound by the fruit, he set the icosahedron fruit down in the pile and waited for Potter Sims to drop him the last. Clutching the remaining fruits, Potter Sims' wings flapped rapidly to keep him above the Salt bed.

"You ready?" Potter Sims yelled to Jack, forty feet below in the shadow of the Great Tree.

"Drop it!" Jack yelled with his arms outstretched.

Potter Sims let it go, a brilliant turquoise blue octahedron. Even with his wooden arm, Jack thought, I'm Brooks Robinson at third base! Effortless. The moment it hit Jack's cupped hands it sang out a note in G major. Jack smiled.

"Last one!" Potter Sims yelled down.

"Let it rip!" Jack said as he set the blue octahedron quickly down with the other fruit.

Potter Sims let the purple dodecahedron fruit, a twelve-faced equilateral, fall. It fell as if in slow motion, like time itself had stopped. When it impacted Jack's hands, sparkles of prickly golden light dotted the dodecahedron's surface, but this one did not sing. It was silent. Jack held the purple fruit up to his ear. He shook it. No sound emerged. Puzzled, Jack set it down next to the other fruits. Potter Sims had picked dozens of the colorful palm-sized fruits of five different geometric forms. In the pile beneath the Great Tree, all of them sang, except for the twelve-side dodecahedron.

Finished, Potter Sims swooped around the tree and crashed hard onto the dry Salt Flats. Jack helped Potter Sims to his feet.

"I hate flying!" Potter Sims grumbled, as he brushed himself off. "And I hate dirt!" he added.

By now, the fruits had stopped singing, as they quietly rested on the Salt bed in the shade of the Tree of Life.

"Did you hear them?" asked Jack.

"Did I hear them? I could hear nothing else! They nearly made me deaf!"

"I've never seen anything like this!" Jack exclaimed.

Jack walked over to the pile of colorful geometric-shaped fruits under the shade of the Great Tree. He sat down on the salt bed. Potter Sims sat next to him. Jack picked up the red tetrahedron shaped fruit. It vibrated immediately in the key of C, a single powerful note in Jack's palm. Potter Sims picked up, what appeared to be in angle and form, the most basic of all the fruits, the yellow cube. When his white gloved fingers touched the yellow cube, it wobbled like Jello.

"Look at that!" Potter Sims yelled with an irritated tone.

Jack laughed. A song in the key of E major rang out from each of the six sides of the cube creating an incredible harmony.

"I almost hate to eat them," Jack said.

"Not me," said Potter Sims as he bit into a singing yellow cube. As soon as he bit into the fruit, the key changed. Jack laughed, not believing it.

"It changed from an E major to an E minor!" Jack exclaimed. "Potter, when you took a bite, the fruit changed its musical key!"

"Key! Who cares about key! It's hot!" Potter Sims said as he wiped his mouth on his sleeve, making spitting noises out his proboscis and his mouth.

"Let me see," Jack took the fruit from Potter Sims and nibbled off a taste.

"Chili peppers! It tastes like chili peppers, Potter!" Jack grinned.

"Hot! I call it hot!" Potter Sims said.

Jack laughed. He stared at the red tetrahedron fruit closely. It had deep swirling pools of red and mauve inside. In his palm, it sang out an endless simple C note. Like a kid eating a new kind of lollipop, Jack licked the fruit. It sang louder, as if it liked being touched and tickled. Jack roared. Potter Sims was surprised by Jack's childlike response.

"This is great!" Jack exclaimed, as Potter Sims watched him.

Slowly Jack sank his teeth into the red tetrahedron. His eyes were wide open. Red juice dripped down the side of Jack's mouth; it coated his blistered, parched lips like a moist, rich red salve.

"Pomegranate!" Jack exclaimed as the deep red juice melted in his mouth. The fruit's song dropped from a C major to an A major. Jack laughed with his mouth open and full of rich red fruit, an absolute failure in even the most cavalier book of food etiquette. Fruit juice dribbled down a corner of his mouth. When Jack set the red tetrahedron fruit down on the salt bed, it stopped singing. Next, he picked up a turquoise blue octahedron, an eight-sided shaped fruit, each face being an equilateral triangle. The fruit had tiny, luminescent silver and violet dots of light, which streaked through it and sparkled like the neon lines on a comb jelly. Jack was awed. His eyes twinkled. The turquoise blue octahedron vibrated in the key of G, but the tone was a G cord. Jack put his ear to the fruit, his eyes opened wide and he smiled ecstatically. Each side of the octahedron vibrated with a note of a G major cord. He took a bite and immediately began licking his parched lips repeatedly with his tongue.

"Salt water. It tastes and smells like the ocean!" Jack said.

"Haven't we had enough salt!"

Jack and Potter Sims sat down under the shade of the Great Tree. Jack grabbed a large icosahedron shaped fruit. It was deep indigo in color. Where his fingers touched the fruit, the color changed from indigo to violet with shades of gold around the tips of his fingers. He handed the fruit to Potter Sims.

"Go on," he said.

"Is this a trick?" Potter Sims asked.

"No, Potter, maybe it will enlighten you."

"What does that mean?" Potter Sims said.

"It means that it will probably taste good. Not hot."

Potter Sims took the fruit from Jack's hands and slowly bit into it. Instantly, the fruit hummed in A Major. Then, sparkles fizzled out of the icosahedron like tiny fireworks hitting Potter Sims in the face. He blinked his eyes quickly over-and-over as if his eyeballs were being showered by thousands of painless pin-pricks. Jack smelled the air.

"Ginger ale! It smells like ginger ale. I love ginger ale!" Jack exclaimed.

"It tickles!" Potter Sims said as he kept his face close to the icosahedron. The fizzles kept popping in his face, until he smiled.

After Jack and Potter Sims had fully satisfied themselves on all but one of the colored geometric fruits, Jack picked up the one remaining fruit, the purple dodecahedron. It was the only dodecahedron and it made no sound.

"What's wrong with it?" asked Potter Sims.

"Maybe nothing," Jack said calmly.

"It doesn't do anything!" complained Potter Sims.

Jack held the purple dodecahedron in his fingers and examined it. The scorching sun was setting. Its light spread out over the evening sky laying its red and violet colors gently down over the white mantle of the Salt Flats.

"Listen," Jack exclaimed as he held the purple dodecahedron up, each face was a perfect pentagon. As Jack held it in the air and rolled it around in his good hand to look at it, and serenity rolled across the Salt Flats like a sacred silence.

"Listen to what?" Potter Sims blurted out, breaking the silence.

"Shhh!" Jack gripped Potter Sims' proboscis firmly with his fingers and gently held it. Potter Sims could not believe that this Jacob Tott person had the audacity to infringe upon his person so. How could he be so forward! Nevertheless, he followed Jack's command and was silent.

Both of them sat beneath the Great Tree with its greenness and fresh scent of cut pine and mint, and listened to the silence. As Jack held the purple dodecahedron up, the air felt sacred, like the hallowed empty space of a monastery.

When the time was right, Jack pressed the purple dodecahedron along its center edges. Potter Sims watched him without saying a word. Gradually, Jack put more pressure upon the dodecahedron. Suddenly, the purple dodecahedron broke in two. Spilling out onto the salt ground were thirteen golden seeds that vibrated a tone in the key of A major. Jack's mouth dropped open. A smell of honey filled the air.

"What are they?" Potter Sims blurted out as he scrambled on his knees to get away from the golden seeds, which bounced up and down on the hard salt bed like thirteen golden tiny jumping beans. The golden seeds created a perfect chant in the key of A, thirteen tiny seeds, thirteen harmonics in the key of A, chanting "Ahh" like a chorus of Buddhist monks. The two pieces of the purple dodecahedron lay in Jack's open palms. As the thirteen golden seeds chanted in the key of A, the purple fruit glowed with a golden halo.

"Isn't this great?" Jack was ecstatic. He stood up and danced around. The golden seeds chanted louder, feeding off Jack's energy. Baffled, Potter Sims watched Jack dance around excitedly under the tree.

"It's not that unusual." Potter Sims said, trying to deny what he knew was an outright lie.

Suddenly, all of the fruits on the Tree of Life joined in and began to vibrate musical tones, a symphony of harmony, the purest music Jack had ever heard. It had a pulse and rhythm, which originated from the very stillness of the Salt desert, from the stars, from life itself.

"So, this is not unusual, huh?" Jack challenged Potter Sims.

"Not *that* unusual, I said." Potter Sims countered.

Jack smiled and took Potter Sims by the hand. Jack danced to the music beneath the Tree of Life in the middle of the barren Salt Flats. He prodded Potter Sims to join him, but Potter Sims was at first reluctant and embarrassed. After several minutes of Jack's unabashed persistence, Potter Sims relented. He started to dance. Shortly thereafter, Jack and Potter Sims lost themselves in the music. They danced.

The desert sun had just set and all around the desert sky glowed with reds, oranges, yellows, deep indigo blues, purples and even a touch of green. On the horizon opposite the setting sun, the Pleiades, Nuchu Verano, were rising. It was the helical rise. As the colorful geometric fruits on the Tree sang, Jacob Tott and Potter Sims, once on the brink of death, danced under the Great Tree of Life surrounded by the Great Salt Desert into the wee-hours of the star-studded night.

CHAPTER 49

WALK IN THE PARK

Early spring rain brought a vibrant green to New York's Central Park, where The Mall was an arch of trees, which formed a walkway through an idyllic pastoral. It lifted people temporarily away from their problems. The sunlight shone through the leaves creating a beautiful green luminescence, where Mattie and Natalie strolled freely to escape the worries about medications and intravenous feedings. Natalie was dressed comfortably, a Yankee ball cap, gray sweatshirt and a pair of jeans. Her mother Mattie wore her usual colorful flowing blouse and skirt.

"You can feel Jack? You know how he's doing?" Mattie asked.

"Usually."

"How do you do it?" Mattie asked.

"I just let it happen. If I try too hard, it doesn't work."

"How is he doing right now?"

Natalie looked at her mother, and then looked at the archway of trees, where light was streaming. She was quiet for several minutes; Mattie waited patiently not pressing her. It was silent as the wind whistled through the leaves that rustled against one another. Natalie listened.

"Today was the best day of his life," Natalie spoke softly.

Mattie signed with relief and took Natalie's hand. Tears began forming in her eyes. They walked on through the path of trees to Bethesda Terrace, where hundreds of people were rollerblading or skating or just walking around the circular fountain, throwing coins in it. In the background, beyond the trees and the tall expensive real estate that lined Central Park, the Giant Beanstalk loomed over the city, disappearing miles up into the endless blue sky. Mattie and Natalie looked at the Beanstalk, but neither remarked about it. Natalie stared at the sculpture of the Winged Angel of the Waters in the center of the fountain, as they walked around it. Just then, a man touched Mattie upon the shoulder.

"Mattie?" the man said.

Mattie turned. It was Loren Fazcel, conductor of the New York Philharmonic.

"Loren, hi!" Mattie gave him a hug. "Have you met my daughter, Natalie?"

"No, but Gage told me a lot about her."

Mattie's complexion changed suddenly.

"I'm sorry, that was thoughtless of me," the conductor said.

"No, no it wasn't. Sometimes, it just creeps up on me."

"Give it some time." Loren Fazcel said as he patted Mattie's hand. He turned to Natalie and held out his hand. She took it. "I am very pleased to meet you."

"Me, too," Natalie said. "Dad talked about you, too."

Loren Fazcel was noticeably quiet wondering what Gage Tott had said about him. Natalie was playing with the conductor, but he did not know her well enough to appreciate her humor. After a few seconds, Natalie spoke.

"It was always good," Natalie said.

The conductor smiled widely. He turned, opened his arms and gave Mattie a hug.

"If you need anything, you call me. Okay?" he said.

"I will," Mattie replied.

Loren Fazcel began to walk away, when Natalie called out.

"Mr. Fazcel?"

The conductor stopped and walked back.

"Yes, Natalie?" he said.

"Jack had the best musical experience of his life today," Natalie said.

The conductor stared at Natalie with a completely baffled expression. He did not know what to say. A confused silence hung in the air between them for many long seconds, until Mattie tried to smooth over the moment.

"She had a sense that Jack is all right," Mattie said.

Loren Fazcel's eyes glanced at the giant Beanstalk looming in the distance, and then looked back into Mattie's eyes.

"That's good," he said.

He nodded, turned and walked away. Mattie and Natalie watched him.

CHAPTER 50

FROZEN IN TIME AND SPACE

It was early in the morning just before dawn, when the sky was slate gray and the salt bed was cool from the night's chill. Energized by the fruit, Jack and Potter Sims awoke where they had slept beneath the Great Tree and headed off to cross the Salt Flats. They kept a brisk pace and followed the direction which Caitlin had aligned using the path of Pachakutek.

After four hours of walking, as the sun was beginning to rise higher in the blue sky, Jack and Potter Sims saw tall blades of green grass that sprinkled the barren salt landscape. Encouraged, Jack and Potter Sims walked faster; they knew that the thin green stalks of grass meant that their journey through the salty arid desert was nearly over. They had survived. Many times during the last twenty-four hours Jack, the extreme optimist that he was, had wondered if they would ever escape the blistering heat of the salty wasteland. Potter Sims was convinced that they would never make it out.

Less than an hour after spotting the first green grass shoot, they were tramping through a meadow of tall, soft lemon grass. Blown by the wind, each blade brushed against the blade next to it creating a soft peaceful hissing sound, which swept like a hush across the meadow. Jack and Potter Sims walked through the waist-high grass with their palms opened to feel the tickle of the soft blades. The invigorating smell of fresh lemon filled the air; new life was being blown and touched into the two weary travelers.

"Just before we entered the Thorn Maze, you said that you were on a journey," Jack said.

"Yes." Potter Sims answered.

"What journey?"

Potter Sims took his time to answer, as they walked through the meadow grass. He had not spoken about his journey to anyone, except for the slip he had made at the Thorn Maze telling Jack, Caitlin and Gandor briefly about his past athletic ability and his journey. Letting his tongue be so loose bothered him greatly, but Potter Sims knew that he needed someone to share it with, a friend.

"In my tribe, I am a mapmaker. I take journeys into uncharted regions to map them for our people."

"That's why you knew about the Cave, the Thorn Maze and the Salt Flats." Jack said.

"Yes."

Potter Sims brushed the soft tips of the lemon grass with his open gloveless palm as if to gather information from the new land he was experiencing.

"Years ago," he continued, "I was chosen for a distinctive honor. The sacred council of our tribe asked me to be Tribe Storyteller. Our tribe has only one storyteller. If you accept it, it is a lifetime appointment. Every past storyteller pledges himself to a code of integrity and years of journey. With my colorful imagination," Potter Sims chuckled, "the Tribe Storyteller position fit the tribe perfectly."

"What about you?"

"It is always about service," Potter Sims said, "how you can help the tribe."

"So this journey is a map quest for your tribe?" Jack asked.

"No. It is a pilgrimage for me," Potter Sims said.

Just beyond the green grassland meadow were distant mountains. The rocky-toothed peaks created spectacular formations and silhouettes against the deep blue sky. Jack wanted to get through the great open space of lemon grass to arrive at the mountains, but what Potter Sims was about to tell him was far more important than hurrying, so they took their time and talked.

"I have a sis—had a sister," Potter Sims slipped. "Had a sister, she was my best friend. She was a teacher, the most caring and intelligent person I have ever met. We shared everything."

"What happened to her?" Jack asked apprehensively.

"She died of a rare disease that one in a million gets. I could not eat. I could not sleep, or work. I became critical. Negative. After three months, the elders ordered me to take a pilgrimage to an unknown land where I had never been, of my own choosing, where I would heal, and where I would slowly be open to my sister's spirit. They said that if I opened myself to her that she would lead me into a land that would reawaken my imagination and my desire to tell stories."

"What was her name?" Jack asked quietly.

"Cordula."

"A beautiful name," Jack said.

"Yes, it is. Thank you." Potter Sims said.

Jack was quiet. His thoughts went back to Natalie; he could see her face. Potter Sims saw Jack's blank stare, as if he was somewhere else.

"What is it?" Potter Sims asked.

"I have a sister. Her name is Natalie, and she too is my best friend. She is dying of leukemia."

"I'm sorry," Potter Sims said. His voice was full of compassion.

"I, too, Potter, am on a pilgrimage just as you are. A man named Murland told me that if Natalie is to live that I must take the beans, which he gave me and follow the path where they take me. Therefore, I did. And I am."

"Guess we are in the right place then," Potter Sims said

"I think so," Jack said as he focused on the purple snow-capped mountains in the distance that were alluring and vibrant under the bright midday sun.

"As your guide, I should remind you that we both have a path and we need to get a move on," Potter Sims said as he started walking toward the mountains. Jack said nothing; he merely grinned slightly and followed Potter Sims through the final green acres of lemon grass.

"Do you think we were destined to meet?" Potter Sims asked.

"Yes." Jack said. "It's just the beginning, Potter, just the beginning."

Potter Sims smiled as they walked.

"I hate talking. I don't talk. Not about me, anyway! But I liked this! I definitely liked this, but you have to make me a promise." Potter Sims said.

"What is it?"

"What I told you about my sister and me is private, between you and me, no one else! Not even Caitlin! Okay?" Potter Sims asked.

"Okay." Jack said.

They heard a loud flapping directly above their heads. Seconds later, with his enormous wings spread, Gandor swooped down with a loud swoosh only six feet above their heads.

"Git! Git away from here!" Potter Sims yelled skyward.

Gandor extended his great wings, stopping himself mid-air like a floating bal-lerina tiptoeing his blue-webbed feet down in the meadow. Drawing his wings tightly to his body and ruffling his feathers in place, he turned to Potter Sims.

"Do you own this land?" bellowed Gandor.

"You haven't earned the right to be here!" Potter Sims barked back.

"Earned! You tell me that I have not earned the right!" Gandor was furious, but Jack cut him off abruptly.

"You two, stop this bickering! I mean it!"

"Isn't he supposed to be a guide, too?" Potter Sims questioned, "He deserted us!"

"He is trying to survive, just like we are." Jack said adamantly.

"You do understand," Gandor relaxed.

"We are going to get along," Jack wagged his finger at both Potter Sims and Gandor. "We are going to get along. We are going to get to Ens. And we are going to find Caitlin. Now, let's go,"

Jack pointed in the direction of the mountains, waiting for Gandor and Potter Sims to lead the way. Potter Sims and Gandor grumpily shuffled forward, while Jack traipsed through the grasses behind them, watching every move and listen-ing to every possible complaint. But nobody spoke.

After two hours of walking through the grasslands, they arrived at the shores of Lake Saquasohuh, an enormous turquoise lake surrounded on three sides by the snow-capped mountains.

Lake Saquasohuh's shores were bordered by tall olive green reeds called Totoro with clusters of small, nutlike seeds at the top. Cut and dried, the Totoro reeds turned golden brown and retained their strength and pliability, which made them ideal for weaving into useful structures: a hut, a fence, an animal pen, or taut navigable boat. Navigating through the paths cut in the Totoro reeds, Jack, Potter Sims, and Gandor walked some distance along the shoreline that was pep-pered with wild flowers, and reeds and exotic plants. The mud close to the lake was made of a rich black earth, nutrients essential to the sturdy growth of the Totoro reeds. Close to the shore of Lake Saquasohuh, the lake's water was dotted with clumps of the green Totoro clusters.

As they rambled along the shoreline in a thicket of Totoro, Potter Sims spot-ted a boat made from the reeds.

"Hey, look at this!"

Potter Sims spread the Totoro reeds with his white-gloved hands.

"Good," said Jack, "we can paddle across the lake."

"I hate water," Potter Sims' eyes were wide with fright.

"You are going to be on it, Sims, not in it!" added Gandor.

"Then, you go in the boat!" Potter Sims yelled at Gandor.

"Why would I ride in a boat, when I can fly above it?"

"Just like you did on the Salt Flats!"

"I am here, aren't I?" Gandor ruffled his feathers.

"You are going to get in the boat, Potter. And Gandor, you fly above us," said Jack.

"A perfectly acceptable idea," said Gandor.

"It's unfair!" countered Potter.

"That's the way it is, now help me here," Jack indicated for Potter Sims and Gandor to help him with the wedged-in Totoro boat that was stuck in the reeds.

Potter Sims and Gandor each grabbed a side of the reed boat and pulled it through the dense cluster of Totoro reeds into Lake Saquasohuh.

"Potter, you first," Jack steadied the boat.

Puffing on his pipe, Gandor watched as Potter Sims clumsily put one foot in the boat. The boat wobbled. Potter Sims teetered back-and-forth trying to keep his balance.

"I hate boats!" Potter Sims said, unwilling to lift his other foot out of the black mud and put it into the Totoro boat. The thick black mud held his foot in place with enormous suction. Getting into any boat and floating on the water was the last thing that he wanted to do. He was not going to step into this flimsy boat and float out on some lake.

"Potter, please get in the boat." Jack insisted.

"I hate boats!"

"Get into the boat!" Jack yelled feeling badly that he had to raise his voice.

"You don't have to yell!" Potter Sims lashed back.

With great trepidation and struggle, Potter Sims tugged on his foot. As it pulled free from the thick black mud, it made a huge sucking noise. Shaking, he succeeded in stepping into the Totoro reed boat with regret, angst. As he stood up in the boat, he looked down at his red boots that were covered with the viscous black mud.

"Look at my boots!" he exclaimed.

"Sit down, Potter!" Jack yelled. "The boat's wobbling!" Like a rickety canoe, the Totoro reed boat rocked unsteadily back-and-forth.

"Look at my boots!"

"Sit down!" Jack yelled. The Totoro boat nearly tipped.

Finally, Potter Sims sat down in the boat, but he never took his eyes off his red boots, coated thick with the black lake mud. Jack shoved the Totoro boat out onto the Lake and jumped in. He handed Potter Sims a wooden paddle lying on the seat.

"Paddle," Jack said.

Potter Sims was completely flabbergasted. While he belligerently dipped the paddle into the blue water, Jack grabbed the other paddle for himself. On shore, Gandor promptly raised his enormous wings and lifted off the Lake Saquasohuh shoreline to fly above them. In the bow of the boat, Potter Sims struggled with the paddle, as he kept looking down at his red boots covered with the thick black mud. Besides paying meticulous attention to his red high top boots, Potter Sims was laughably uncoordinated. No more could he paddle a rickety handmade boat on the choppy waters of a lake, than he could fly through the great forest without crashing into trees. He was unable to maneuver the Totoro boat at all. Behind him, Jack watched, shaking his head in disbelief.

"Smooth, Potter, smooth. Dip the paddle in, pull it back, and then feather." Jack said trying to keep his voice calm, so as not to rile up his friend any more than he already was.

"Maybe for you! I hate water!" Potter Sims said struggling with the paddle.

"Try it again, dip, pull, feather. Di-i-i-p, pu-u-ll, fea-ea-ea-thur-ur-ur." Jack elongated his words slowly to coincide with his paddling hoping that Potter Sims would get the idea, but all Potter Sims could do was fumble with his paddle. Above them, Gandor circled and watched.

"I don't like this! My boots are ruined!"

"Why am I not surprised that you hate this," said Jack as he smiled.

Jack watched Potter Sims for several minutes. Potter Sims amused him greatly. From the stern, Jack raised his paddle and slashed the water with the paddle's thin wooden edge propelling thousands of water droplets upon Potter Sims' back.

"Stop it! Stop it!" Potter Sims fought the water off by striking at the air.

Jack laughed and continued paddling. "Lighten up, Potter." Jack said, while Potter Sims swatted the water droplets off his clothes. "I hate water!"

They paddled a half mile onto Lake Saquasohuh, while Gandor circled above. About three hundred yards away just to the starboard side of the bow, Jack saw a strange blue-white cloud moving only ten feet above the water.

"Do you see that?"

"I don't see anything!" Potter Sims grumbled.

"Potter, stop paddling and look."

Potter Sims pulled the paddle into the reed boat and looked at the odd blue-white cloud. "It's a blue cloud, that's all," he dismissed.

"Clouds aren't blue." Jack mused.

Jack put his paddle down and removed the Yamqui diagram from his pocket, and examined it. Blue clouds were drawn above the lake.

"There's a blue cloud on the map, just above the lake!"

Jack folded the map up and jammed it into his pocket. He picked up his paddle and began paddling faster.

"I am so happy!" Potter Sims said satirically annoyed by their predicament.

"We gotta paddle faster, Potter. We've gotta get to that cloud!"

"I am going as fast as I can!" Potter Sims awkwardly dug the paddle back into the lake, only deeper. He pulled harder. The Totoro reed boat picked up speed. Above them, Gandor watched curiously.

As Jack and Potter Sims drew nearer to the cloud, they saw that it had indistinct bluish-white particles within it that were constantly moving.

"What kind of cloud is that?" Potter Sims was now interested, but baffled. It distracted him from his fear of the boat and the water.

"It's not a cloud," Jack said.

As they paddled closer toward the cloud, they heard a flitting in the air. They paddled faster. Twenty feet away, they saw the blue cloud fluttering, blue and white colors flickering inside. Every inch of the cloud was in constant motion from the outer edge to the core. Above, Gandor circled and watched.

"They are Karner Blue butterflies!" Jack said in shock.

"What?"

"Karner Blue butterflies, Potter. They are on the verge of extinction!"

"Do they look extinct to you?" said Potter Sims as he laid the paddle across his lap to watch the butterflies. Jack stopped paddling also, as their Totoro boat drifted to the edge of the fluttering blue mass, where thousands of tiny blue wings fluttered and flicked the air, five feet above the surface of the water. This was the same species of blue butterfly, which Gage, Mattie, Natalie, and Jack had seen in the Catskills.

"There must be 10,000 of them!" Jack blurted out.

"There's too many!" Potter Sims grumbled and worried.

Why would they be here? Jack thought.

"Natalie. They are connected to Natalie," Jack said totally mystified and confused.

"Your sister?"

"Yes."

"Why?"

"I don't know." Jack's voice had a low and quizzical tone in it.

As they drifted near the edge of the cloud, three Karner Blues flew toward Potter Sims. Two flitted around his head; one landed on Potter Sims' wrist just above his white gloves.

"Git! Git away!" Potter Sims shook his hand back-and-forth in rapid jerks to knock the butterfly off of his white shirt sleeve.

"Potter, listen. Do you hear the wind?" Jack asked looking around, but Potter Sims was too absorbed with the meddling butterflies.

"Get off! Get off of me!" Potter Sims yelled and swatted.

While Potter Sims swatted at the butterflies, a great wind roared through the grassland meadow, over the mountains, and across the Lake. It was on them. It all happened in seconds. The sound of cracking ice reverberated in the air. Overwhelmed, Jack could not believe what was happening. He could not absorb it all—fluttering butterfly wings, roaring wind, and the cracking water and air. At the same time, Potter Sims was rocking the boat as he swatted wildly at the Karner Blue butterflies.

"You're going to flip the boat! Potter! Stop it!"

"I hate bugs! I hate bugs!" Potter Sims exclaimed.

Nervously, Gandor flew above them, watching and feeling the air as it cracked around him. He yelled down to Jack and Potter Sims, but they could not hear him. Suddenly, the air crystallized around Gandor. It encased him completely in ice.

A line of ice swept across the grasslands, over the great purple snow-capped mountains, and across the lake. As the water changed to ice, it crackled. The Totoro reed boat glided out of the cloud of Karner Blue butterflies. Jack looked up. Just as he did, he saw the sky as it crystallized around Gandor.

"Gandor!" Jack yelled.

Hearing the cracking as it got louder, Jack looked toward the shore. He stood up, but not completely for fear of tipping the boat. He saw the line of ice sweeping across the lake toward the Totoro reed boat. Potter Sims turned sharply.

"What is happening?" Potter Sims yelled, and then he stood straight up in the boat to see the freeze line sweeping across the Lake.

"Potter, sit down!" Jack yelled fearfully.

Potter Sims began to lose his balance. He extended his arms. His spiny legs wobbled, as the boat rocked to-and-fro wildly.

"Sit down! You're going to flip the boat!"

Jack held onto the gunwales of the Totoro boat as it rocked in the churning turquoise water. The Totoro boat had drifted twenty-five feet away from the Karner Blue butterflies. As Jack watched Potter Sims struggling to sit down and trying to balance himself, he saw the butterfly cloud rising off the surface of the water, as if the entire cloud was climbing toward the crystallized sky of ice. Suddenly, the Totoro boat flipped spilling Potter Sims and Jack into the frigid Lake. Potter Sims could not swim. He swallowed huge gulps of water. He was choking and gagging. Jack saw him drowning; he swam as fast as he could toward Potter Sims. As he did, the freezing and cracking of the lake became deafening. The freeze line was nearly upon them. As Jack reached for Potter Sims' arm, he saw the ice line approaching. Drowning, Potter Sims sank below the surface. Jack did a surface deep down to reach Potter Sims in the clear icy blue lake.

All around them, the water crackled. Underwater, the cracking sounds hurt their ears. Jack saw the white terror in Potter Sims' eyes, as he reached for Potter Sims' hand. In an instant, when the tip of Jack's index finger barely touched the tip of Potter Sims' gloved index finger, the water froze, encasing them in the frozen world of Lake Saquasohuh. Frozen in the moment of time, Jack's life was recorded, reaching to save Potter Sims' life. Eyes open, they were looking at each other. The frozen sculpture of Jack and Potter Sims nearly touching each other's fingers looked like a three-dimensional re-enactment of Michaelangelo's "*The Creation of Man.*" Jack's eyes were wide in awe, his mouth slightly open in astonishment, while his Inca amulet glistened in the bright sunlight that cut through the crystal turquoise water. Cocooned in ice.

In the sky just above them, Gandor was frozen alone in the crystallized air. Cocooned in air. The lake, grasslands, the mountains, the shore, the air—everything was frozen still. There was not one sound, not even wind.

CHAPTER 51

CONNECTION

New York City was cold and unusually quiet. An eerie silence rolled through the city like a thick fog. Even though the night sky was clear and stars shone brightly, baseball-sized hail began to fall like missiles upon Manhattan. The temperature plummeted. Hail pummeled the city, shattering windows, denting cars. The ground trembled. It was deep and guttural. It terrified the thousands of people, who screamed and ran for cover.

Inside their Chelsea apartment, Natalie lay in bed, delirious in fever and ice cold, as Mattie wrapped her tightly with two more blankets. Natalie's lips quivered purple and her teeth chattered. Sitting on the bed, Mattie was terrified for her daughter, who had suddenly become deathly cold. She touched her daughter's face with her palm; her skin was freezing, nearly frostbitten. Tears formed in Mattie's eyes, as she frantically rubbed Natalie's cold hand. Suddenly, there was a loud knock at the front door, then another quick knock, only louder and more persistent. Mattie slid Natalie's hand under the blanket, and walked quickly to the living room; she answered the door. It was Murland. He stepped quickly, but gracefully inside.

"She's freezing. She's like a block of ice!" Mattie exclaimed to Murland.

"Let me see her."

Murland closed the door, and together they walked toward Natalie's bedroom. Murland took one look at Natalie and turned to Mattie. Everything about him was calm, his voice gentle.

"How long has she been like this?" Murland asked.

"About five hours. It was so sudden. She was listening to music, and she just collapsed. I ran to her and she was ice cold. I put her in bed, and then the hail started falling," Mattie said with her voice cracking.

"I'll do everything I can to help her."

"What's happening?" Mattie asked.

"It is a time of great change, Mattie."

"Why is it affecting my baby?" Mattie asked with tears welling up in her eyes.

"She is acutely sensitive to the world."

Mattie was confused, but she had grown to trust Murland, so she sat down in the white wicker chair near Natalie's bed. Murland sat on the edge of Natalie's bed and gently took her hand in his. He felt her arm, her cheek. Mattie watched sitting on the edge of the wicker chair. Murland opened his hand, palm open facing Natalie and his fingers outspread about three inches above Natalie's forehead, when her eyes opened.

"Close your eyes and dream, my dear." Murland's voice was gentle and compassionate.

Murland placed his hands on her face, and Natalie closed her eyes. Murland moved his hands over her forehead, then her throat, and heart, over her sternum, and lastly her navel. He read the health of her chakras, and the life balance of her luminous energy field, which radiated out like an aura and surrounded her body. From the chair, Mattie watched every move Murland made, and more importantly looked for any response from her daughter, but there was none. Now she slept.

"There is nothing we can do," he said.

"What's wrong with her?"

"Nothing is wrong with her. It is Jack."

"What?" Mattie's voice cracked with trepidation.

"Jack's journey and her path have merged, and there is nothing that we or anyone else can do about it."

Wailing noises bleated out uncontrollably between Mattie's trembling lips, her legs quivered as her eyes filled with tears.

"You know! I want you to tell me what is wrong with Jack!" Mattie demanded almost hysterical.

"He is in a deep hibernation."

"What?" Mattie could hardly believe what she was hearing. She began to sob.

"Mattie, you must believe in your son. Trust that there is a greater design at work here."

"I'm terrified."

"I know. However, this will pass, I promise you. There is a far, far greater world that lies ahead, which outweighs the temporary discomforts right now." Murland took her hand.

Her sobbing continued as her hand went limp in his hands.

"Close your eyes, Mattie."

Mattie gave her will to Murland and closed her eyes, as he put his hands on her back, just behind her heart, and gently rubbed it in circles. Within seconds, Mattie calmed down. A peaceful look passed over her face, and she fell into a deep sleep. Murland stood up and walked to the window. With Natalie and Mattie resting in the room, Murland looked up to the sky and closed his eyes in a fervent meditation.

Chapter 52

The Extraction

At Lake Saquasohuh, a blue-gray sky painted a drab mood. A loud cracking broke the frozen stillness, as The Corps appeared. Hranknor led them. Like icebreakers, they violently split the white ice with their powerful black wings. Swooping down on the frozen turquoise Lake, they pierced the frozen water with their enormous black wings carving out a huge turquoise block of ice, which entombed Jack and Potter Sims together. The block of ice bobbed like a large cork in the deep blue water. Thousands of other fractured ice chunks floated and bobbed up and down. Led by Hranknor, The Corps lifted the giant frozen block of ice that encased Jack and Potter Sims and flew off. Gandor remained frozen in the air. Two Corps flew around him. Like icebreakers in the North Atlantic, The Corps cut through the crystallized air. They chiseled the frozen Gandor out of the frozen sky, and flew him away until they disappeared on the blue-gray horizon.

CHAPTER 53

THE UNDISCOVERED COUNTRY

A full moon shone over the village of Machu Picchu. Huayna Picchu, a mountain on the northwestern edge of the village, overlooked the great Inca city. The steep descent down the side of Huayna Picchu made it a spectacular backdrop for the village. Carrying the block of ice that cocooned Jack and Potter Sims and the frozen crystallized Gandor, The Corps descended over the peak of Huayna Picchu and over the Sacred Rock, a twenty-five foot long rock sitting upon its own pedestal. Two *wayronas*, large three-sided stone huts with a thatched A-frame roof flanked the Sacred Rock on either side. The shape of the Sacred Rock deliberately mimicked Mount Yanantin in the background. The Corps buzzed low over the Sacred Rock and headed toward a long grassy area about the size of a football field in the center of the Machu Picchu village. Interlocking block walls twelve feet high surrounded the main plaza. The Corps swooped toward the Principle Temple, where they set the great block of ice and the frozen Gandor down in the center on the granite floor. Hranknor and The Corps stood next to the block of ice and Gandor, soldiers standing guard waiting for their next command.

The Principle Temple was the sacred gathering place of worship. Designed in the shape of a rectangle with only three sides of finely carved interlocking stones, it was a perfect site for worship, an open cathedral, where the views of the Andes and the stars were unimpeded.

On the backside of the Principle Temple was a small room of exceptional masonry. It had five striking and uniformly designed Inca trapezoidal windows, each one about five feet above the solid granite floor. The Sacristy was a quiet room, where the Shaman high priest could hear a whisper. Standing in the Sacristy with his eyes closed in meditation was not a Shaman, but Ens. Caitlin was with him, quiet and motionless, unaware of what was lying only feet away on the other side of the magnificently crafted wall in the Principle Temple.

"Follow me," he said.

Ens walked around the great wall. Without questioning, Caitlin followed him. When they rounded the corner and entered the Principle Temple, Caitlin gasped and came to an abrupt halt. Ten feet in front of her was the enormous block of ice that cocooned Jack and Potter Sims. Caitlin's eyes were riveted to the ice. Hranknor and The Corps stood on either side of the block, like guards at the tomb of the Unknown Soldier. Caitlin walked slowly to the block of ice, and stood so close that she could feel the wall of cold against her thigh. She leaned down and stared into the ice. Her stare froze on the bodies of Jack and Potter Sims suspended in a crystal-clear frigid world. The ice was so clear that she could see Jack's eyelashes and the hairs on Potter Sims' arms. Tears welled up in her eyes and flowed down her cheeks. She tried to be a scientist, study Jack and Potter Sims, their suspension in time and space, but it was impossible. Ens watched her with great interest. Caitlin's mind needed an explanation, a rationale to explain how this could be possible. She put her hand on the ice, only eighteen inches away from Jack's face, as if she was trying to touch his yet rosy cheek. His lips are so red, and his rosy cheeks, Caitlin thought. She struggled for clarity, but all she could do was to stare down blankly into the clear block of ice at Jack, who had a live, yet suspended expression.

"They are not dead?" she asked.

"They are dreaming."

Caitlin then turned to Gandor. She studied his frozen crystallized form. Gandor looked like a preserved specimen of an extinct species displayed in a glass case tucked away in some corner of a Natural History Museum. As she stared at Gandor, she wondered if humankind had devised a perfectly detailed record of an extinct species, and if that rationale had unconsciously made extinction less heinous.

"People learn to accept the life that they choose to live," Ens said.

"I believe we choose the life we are willing to live."

"It always comes down to choice, doesn't it?" Ens said.

It suddenly occurred to Caitlin that Ens was reading her mind, and speaking to her through telepathy.

"You know what I am thinking?" Caitlin asked.

"And more," Ens said.

This time, he did open his mouth. "Your species always figures a way to rationalize your decisions and behavior, just as Gandor and his people of Rafus Island did. You are visual beings. You create on a grand scale and you destroy on a grand scale. You have a need to memorialize your mistakes with monuments and yearly tributes to the fallen. Take this for what is worth. One day, if you are not extremely vigilant, there will be no one left in your world to memorialize it. Just as Gandor is frozen in state, you call it 'lying in state', you are paralyzed, and that will inevitably lead to your extinction. Therefore, grieve not just for Gandor."

Caitlin was struck hard by Ens' words. She stared at Gandor, frozen and paralyzed. "Is Gandor dead?"

"No, actually he is quite alive, merely suspended in time and space in the infinitely unfolding present, as well as the past, and the infinitely changing future. He has no memories, no origins, no future, just the now."

"Why?"

"Always the scientist, you will have to wait for the answer."

Ens walked toward the door, but Caitlin would not follow. Ever since she was a young child, as far back as she could remember, Caitlin had a will, some called it an attitude.

"How can we possibly be in Machu Picchu?" Her tone was questioning.

"You are in Machu Picchu, but years before you were born, before your grandfather's grandfather was a tiny speck in the ether," Ens said.

"Have we ascended into the past?"

"You are in the past to see the future," Ens said.

"I don't understand."

"You will," Ens said. He walked, knowing that Caitlin would follow him. She did.

Together, they walked around the north side of the Principle Temple toward a huge hill. They walked up the steps to the highest point of Machu Picchu, Intihuatana, which was located atop of a small mountain that was shaped like a pyramid.

Caitlin knew Intihuatana well. It was a holy shrine hewn out of one enormous piece of stone, shaped like a triangle. Since it was used as a stellar observatory by the Incas, she had stood there dozens of times over the years for her research. She liked the colloquial name, which was coined for the massive shrine, 'the hitching post of the sun.' Though not very scientific, it was clever. Caitlin had great respect not for the spirituality of Intihuatana, but for its remarkable design, architecture and purpose; it was situated higher than the Royal Residence, higher than the Principle Temple, even higher than the Temple of the Sun. It was, in fact, the highest in design, mind, and geography of the entire village.

Standing at the vertex of Intihuatana was Sebastian Yamqui, shaman of the Inca village. He was dressed in ceremonial Inca gold and alpaca woolen garments. His ceremonial hat made from the finest alpaca wool, beads, and leather displayed every color of the rainbow. Above him, the stars were spectacular. Sebastian and Jack were about the same age. Sebastian watched the stars above the Andes for several minutes inhaling the brisk night mountain air before Ens and Caitlin arrived.

"Inca Shaman Sebastian Yamqui stands before you," Ens said. "Caitlin Bingham stands here."

It was an odd way for Ens to introduce Caitlin to Shaman Sebastian Yamqui, in fact, she was not even sure if it was an introduction. Nevertheless, she greeted the holy man.

She knew this was a great Inca shaman, a legendary healer and visionary. "I am honored. I have read much about you. You are a legend," Caitlin said awkwardly, immediately bothered by what she felt was an adulatory greeting. Sebastian Yamqui did not speak to Caitlin; he merely nodded then turned his attention back to the stars. Ens pointed to the spectacular night sky.

"What do you see?"

Caitlin studied the dense Milky Way, the positions of the stars and the constellations. The night air was crisp and clear, so the stars shined radiantly.

"What do you want? Obviously, you are looking for something." She said with an irritated tone.

Ens chuckled. "Always that edge. The date. Give us your best guess."

Caitlin stared at the millions of stars that filled the sky. "It looks like the night of the Winter Solstice or the day before or after. Without taking measurements, I cannot be sure. The Pleiades should rise right there." Caitlin pointed to a mountain peak on the horizon.

"Like this?" Ens swept his arm in a great arch across the night sky. Time sped up and the Milky Way rotated rapidly across the sky. As the sky lightened before Dawn, the Milky Way faded.

"There they are," Ens pointed across the horizon and the Pleiades rose in the pre-dawn sky, twinkling brightly.

"How did you do that?" Caitlin was stupefied.

"This is always how it is. I only gave it a nudge," said Ens.

"How? It was an illusion. That is just not possible," Caitlin argued strongly.

"What's the matter? This is the moment you wished for all of your life, to see the Andean sky as the Incas did. Now, you have seen it."

Ens snapped his fingers. The predawn sky turned to night, and the rising Pleiades disappeared from the lip of the horizon, where they had shared the sun's light. Now, the sun was gone as rapidly as it rose. It was as dark as it was when they had first walked outside.

Sebastian Yamqui turned to Ens, "It is time."

Ens nodded. Sebastian looked at Caitlin and pointed the way down the seven steps leading from Intihuatana not far from the Principle Temple. Caitlin descended the steps; Sebastian and Ens followed. The three walked to the Principle Temple, where Jack and Potter Sims were encased in the block of ice, and where Gandor was crystallized in a frozen state of time. Hranknor and The Corps still stood guard on either side of the enormous block of ice and Gandor.

Ens spoke to Hranknor. "Zuit nräng ut Grundig tanzui ut kanduit udran."

Hranknor nodded slightly, and then he and The Corps lifted the huge block of ice and Gandor. Sebastian Yamqui led Caitlin in a procession as they followed Ens, Hranknor, The Corps, Jack and Potter Sims and Gandor through the village in the pre-dawn. After they walked in procession through the sacred plaza, they took the stairs that passed between the main living quarters of the village and the Royal residence. Other Inca villagers, elders, families with men, women, and children swaddled in bright woolen pachas and carried on their mothers' backs, joined in the procession. Many of the Inca villagers played panpipes, drums, rattles, and reed flutes, as they walked toward the Temple. Together, the entire village walked through a series of narrow corridors and trapezoidal doorways to the Temple of the Sun.

Ens entered the Temple of the Sun first, followed by Hranknor and The Corps, who shouldered the block of ice that encased Jack and Potter Sims. The Corps set the block down in the middle of the Temple of the Sun. Gandor, who was crystallized and frozen in time, was set down next to the ice block, as if he was a gargoyle protecting Jack and Potter Sims. Sebastian and Caitlin followed them to the inner sanctum of the Temple. Hranknor and The Corps left the Temple of the Sun; only Ens, Sebastian and Caitlin remained in the inner sanctum. On the outside of the Temple of the Sun the villagers played their instruments, waiting patiently, for they knew that something remarkable was about to happen. The music from the panpipes and flutes filled Machu Picchu; it prepared and sanctified the village as it echoed off the walls and mountains.

The Temple of the Sun was a semi-circular architecture with some of the finest stone masonry in Machu Picchu. The Incas designed it after the Coricancha in Cuzco, Peru, also called the Temple of the Sun, but they had conceived and constructed the Temple in Cuzco to catch the sun and hold it at the epicenter, the very heart of the great Inca culture and capital. In Machu Picchu, the curved stone walls of the Temple of the Sun were lined with 24-karat gold plates. Each plate was two-and-a-half feet long and about two feet wide. This sacred golden enclosure captured the radiance of the sun when it rose in the east on the Winter Solstice. The walls lined with 24-karat gold scattered the particles of sunlight as they ricocheted like golden bullets in the sacred enclosure, creating a brilliant spectacle of gold and light.

In the center of the Temple of the Sun, cocooned in the block of ice, Jack and Potter Sims waited for the sun to peek over the mountain ridge into the golden enclosure, when they would be awakened from deep sleep. To the side, Gandor waited crystallized in the ever-changing present, frozen from his past and future.

Stars filled the indigo sky, as dawn approached. Sebastian raised his arms to the stars. Caitlin looked to the waning night sky for the Nuchu Verano, Pleiades, but she was bewildered as her eyes scanned the predawn horizon. The music from the villagers, standing outside the Temple of the Sun, rose in the air as the indigo in the sky changed to blue-grey, then bled mauve to pink with a tint of orange. The stars were fading. Just below the horizon, the sun was coming. Caitlin frantically searched the horizon.

"Where are the Nuchu Verano, the Pleiades?" she asked Ens.

"They are gone."

"That can't be! It's impossible," Caitlin responded as she scanned the surrendering blue-grey horizon.

"Is that so hard to believe?" asked Ens. "You've read about this. It is the Winter Solstice, June 19, 650 C.E. As an astronomer and archaeologist, Dr. Bingham, you studied this event."

"By every physical law, the Pleiades should have risen right there." Caitlin pointed to the western horizon directly opposite the sun, "but they didn't."

"You studied it, but you never really believed it," Ens made his point.

"No, I guess I didn't," Caitlin's voice dropped.

"When the new planet *Pachakutek* disappeared, you knew it was true because you saw it. Yet, you doubted this. Why?"

"I don't know."

"I know," said Ens.

Caitlin stared at Ens waiting for him to finish, needing him to finish. What was it that Ens knew? The Andean music rose in the early morning air, but Caitlin could not hear it, all she heard were Ens' echoing words, while she watched the empty pre-dawn sky. Time itself had stopped for her.

"In your heart, you do not yet believe that anything is possible."

Caitlin was struck by Ens' words. Her mind worked rapidly, he was right, and she knew it as soon as he had spoken.

"Is it so hard to believe in things that you cannot see?" Ens asked her.

As they stood in the Temple of the Sun, the sun rose over the eastern Andes. Slowly, one-by-one the stars rapidly disappeared from the sky. Sunlight streamed in through the Inca trapezoidal window into the Temple of the Sun. Captured by the Temple's 24-karat gold walls, the brilliant golden sun shined upon the huge block of ice encasing Jack and Potter Sims. As Shaman Sebastian Yamqui raised his arms to the sun in prayer, the ice began to melt.

"Today," Ens said to Caitlin, "just as the Incas will awaken to a new era, so will you and your friends. Tomorrow, so will your planet."

Deep inside the ice, Jack's Inca amulet sparkled in the brilliant sunlight. His finger tips touched Potter Sims. With his arms raised to the rising sun, Sebastian began to chant in unison with the Inca villagers' music outside the Temple walls. The sunlight reflected off the semicircular gold walls; it was so brilliant that Caitlin shaded her eyes. Ens stood motionless before the block of melting ice, his eyes wide open watching the sun. Gandor remained unmoved, fixed in his crystallized state. The interior air of the enclosure radiated enormous warmth and blinding golden light.

For the first time, Sebastian spoke to Caitlin. "This is Jack's choice point."

"I don't understand," she answered.

"During the next two minutes," Sebastian explained, "he will experience the greatest pain in his life. He will have two choices, and he will know each choice with total clarity. He must make the choice with his heart, not his head. Avoid the pain and go back to sleep, or stay alert and endure it. If he chooses the courage to bear it, he must meditate on it, use his heart to take strength from the pain, and then commit to change. He knows that his sister Natalie's life depends upon it."

"What can I do?" Caitlin asked with desperation in her voice.

Sebastian put his crossed hands over her heart, "You must open your heart," the warmth from his hands filled her, opened her spirit.

"Open your heart," he said.

His hands transmitted enormous warmth and energy into her. He looked around her body at the glowing and expanding aura of her luminous energy field.

Slowly, like little fingers, the sunlight smoothed the ice away. The droplets from the ice dripped onto the Temple's granite floor, where it turned into a crystal stream flowing through the sacred golden enclosure. For several minutes, the sun appeared to stop, held tightly in the trapezoidal window. The ice melted away inch-by-inch exposing more of Jack and Potter Sims' bodies. Suddenly, Jack's eyes fluttered and opened. He moaned. His face was clean and fresh, as if he had been cleansed. As the ice melted rapidly away from his body, thorn-like pimples began to appear on his wooden arm; they got larger. The looked like thorns from the Thorn Maze. Jack could barely move, yet a deep guttural sound of pain rumbled out of his chest. He was paralyzed, crippled by pain, struggling to breathe.

"See Natalie's face, Jack. See her face." Caitlin said.

Jack's breathing became uneven and strained; he struggled with the pain. Even though he was locked in a block of ice, excruciating pain pulsed through every nerve in his body. White hard tips of puss formed on the bumps embedded in his wooden arm, as Jack closed his eyes.

In Manhattan, Natalie lay in bed nearly unconscious, whimpering from a pain over which she had no control.

"What's the matter with her?" Mattie yelled, jumping out of her wicker chair to stand next to Natalie's bed.

"It is Jack. He is at the choice point." Murland's voice was calm, but Mattie's was desperate.

"What choice point?"

"Choosing between life and death." Murland explained.

Mattie began crying, as Natalie's skin broke out everywhere in sharp red bumps with white tips, like the thorns on a rose. She rolled in a delirium and cried in anguish.

"Look at her skin!" Mattie yelled.

"Do you want to help her?" Murland asked in loud voice.

"Yes!"

"Rid yourself of emotion, Mattie," Murland said calmly.

"How can I?" Mattie screamed.

"To help her, you <u>must</u> rid yourself of all emotion."

Mattie struggled to calm herself, as she sat on the edge of the bed. Murland waited thirty seconds. His hands were gently gripping Natalie's arm that was covered with red thorny-like bumps.

"Close your eyes. Hold her hand, and see Jack's face."

With Natalie still moaning from the pain, Mattie closed her eyes.

"See his face. Give him strength, Mattie," Murland said again.

Mattie kept her eyes closed and saw Jack playing the violin with Gage. She saw him smiling. She filtered out Natalie's moans.

In the Temple of the Sun, where the sunlight streamed in upon the block of ice, Jack rotated his head an inch to see Caitlin, who was standing next to him. With tears in her eyes, she leaned down to the ice, her lips inches away from his cheek. He saw the tears running down her face, dripping over her partially open lips. She whispered, as her tears flowed.

"I did not want to fall in love with you. I loved a musician once, and he broke my heart, so I lost myself in my work. My head told me to stay away from you, but my heart could not. Damn musicians! I am in love with you. I love you. Please don't die. Please."

Jack was still struggling with the pain, and then in a matter of seconds, it was gone. He had released it, conquered it. The sharp red thorny pimples with puss-filled tips slowly shrank into the grain of his wooden arm; the wood became mahogany. It shined with a high gloss. It was beautiful to behold. Jack exhaled long and deep, and Caitlin knew that it was over. Even though Jack's head and body were rigid, he could move his eyes. He looked at her, and his eyes filled up with tears. Caitlin saw them and they pleased her. It was his vow of love to her. It was his vow to his sister, Natalie. He had passed. He managed to crack a smile, and then he closed his eyes. Potter Sims still had not moved. His fingertips were still touching Jack's fingertips.

Ens watched it all, as the music played. Sebastian held up his arms to the life-giving light of the golden sun and prayed.

Chapter 54

--- ❧❧❧ ---

Linked by the Fathers

Inside the home of Sebastian Juan de Santacruz Pachacuti Yamqui, Jack and Potter Sims lay in a thatched straw bed, side-by-side. In another part of the room, Sebastian's wife, Paola Rosa, cut vegetables for a pot of soup that boiled in the hearth. Their three year-old son Enrique played with colored beads and white strings made from Alpaca wool, as he sprawled across the hut's stone floor.

With a simply crafted cup filled with tea made from herbs, Sebastian walked over and sat down on the bed's edge next to Jack. Sebastian handed him the cup of tea. Slowly, Jack sipped it.

"What about me?" yelled Potter Sims, "Don't I get some?"

Without saying a word, Sebastian smiled at Potter Sims, as Jack handed Potter Sims the cup. After Potter Sims finished drinking, Sebastian took the cup away and walked over to the hearth, where he grabbed a tightly-wrapped bundle of incense and stuck it into the fire until the tip caught and glowed red. Lifting the fiery bundle into the air, he blew the fire abruptly out and blue smoke began wafting throughout the room. Potter Sims' eyes got bigger.

"I hate smoke." Potter Sims said loudly.

Sebastian ignored him. He chanted, as he walked toward Jack and Potter Sims' bed and waved the incense in circles over their bodies.

"Excuse me?" Potter Sims said. "The smoke makes my eyes water."

"I think he's blessing us," Jack said.

Sebastian waved the bundle of incense around more.

Potter Sims waited as long as he could, as long as he could possibly stand it, and then spoke up. "I'm most grateful for your hospitality ..." Potter Sims leaned forward as close as he could get to the fervent Shaman, as if he was trying to convey to this holy gracious host his gratitude. "... but you see, I hate smoke!"

Sebastian ignored Potter Sims. Jack smiled, amused.

After Sebastian finished incensing Jack and Potter Sims, he went to a nearby table, where his simple red, yellow and green cloth mesa lay. He opened it revealing thirteen stones, khuyas. He took the shiny reddish-clay earthy stone with black inclusions, the khuya that his father Yamqui had given him when Sebastian was struck by lightning. He walked over to Jack, who watched silently knowing that a sacred moment was unfolding. Sebastian held out the red earthy stone for Jack to see. Potter Sims was silent and respectful, at least for the moment.

"This khuya is from the spot where I was struck by lightning. Within it holds the spirit power of apu Machu Picchu. It was a gift from my father."

Sebastian placed the khuya into Jack's hand, who held it loosely in his hands, and then he closed his fingers around the sacred stone. He could feel the heat from the stone against his palm and radiating out into his fingers. He opened it up and looked at it long.

"Keep this khuya while you heal, then return it to me," Sebastian said.

"Don't I get one?" Potter Sims said.

"No," Sebastian answered. "You do not need one."

"Humph!" Potter Sims exclaimed.

Many nights later, Jack and Shaman Sebastian stood on the Terrace of the Ceremonial Rock overlooking Machu Picchu, which rested majestic and serene in the blue quiet of the moonlight.

The Terrace of the Ceremonial Rock was located at an optimal position from where to view Machu Picchu. The moon shone brightly. Thousands of silvery mica particles embedded in the village's white granite stones sparkled. The clear sky glittered with stars. Jack and Sebastian looked down upon the village, as they spoke.

"My father was a great shaman," said Sebastian. His voice was tranquil. "He taught me about the stars, and the ways of life, of vision."

"My father was a great musician, a world famous violinist, who taught me how to love music," said Jack.

"Do you still play?" asked Sebastian.

"Not anymore."

Jack raised his wooden arm. Sebastian smiled.

"The Thorns," Sebastian said. "How did you stop the wood from overtaking you?"

"Here," Jack pointed to the Stradivarius bridge imbedded in his arm. "It is a violin bridge. It was from my father's Stradivarius violin."

Sebastian stared long at the Stradivarius bridge buried in Jack's left arm, then at the amulet hanging from Jack's neck. "Like a violin," he said, "you have become the instrument of your own music."

Sebastian's observation was a profound revelation for Jack. Sebastian pointed to the amulet, "You are Inca, as I am."

The shaman was silent allowing time for Jack to comprehend the profound truth, which bound them together for centuries and generations. When he saw the light of revelation in Jack's eyes, he knew that he understood. "I, too, have been given a gift," the Great Shaman spoke humbly, as he rolled up his left sleeve. His entire wrist, forearm and elbow were disfigured with burn scars.

"When I was eighteen years old, a bolt of lightning struck me. You became one with your music," Sebastian pointed to the violin bridge imbedded in Jack's arm, "I became one with the light. For a moment, I became light. Just as, for a moment, your body vibrated the harmony of music."

"Light and music." Jack said.

"It is that way, it will always be that way," Sebastian said.

"My father was killed by lightning. His name was Gage. What was your father's name?" Jack asked.

"Juan Pachakuti Yamqui."

"Yamqui?" Jack was stunned.

Jack took the Yamqui drawing from his pocket, and showed it to Sebastian.

"It is my father's drawing," said Sebastian Yamqui.

"This is what brought me here." Jack held up the drawing.

"Let me show you something." Sebastian took the Yamqui drawing from Jack and traced the drawing with his fingers.

"Do you see Orion and Southern Cross here?"

"Yes."

"Look," Sebastian pointed to Orion and the Southern Cross in the sky. Then, he noted the Yamqui drawing.

"This oval is the sacred Temple of the Incas. It is marked by Orion and the Southern Cross."

Jack traced his finger along the bright yellow oval in the drawing. "Is this oval Inca gold?"

"Yes, it is the gold you came to find for your sister."

Jack flushed red with embarrassment.

"You have no reason to be uncomfortable or self-conscious here with me. Greed lives nowhere in you. You came here because you love your sister, and you wanted to save her life. I know that," Sebastian said.

"I am glad that you know that," Jack answered humbly.

Sebastian said nothing, only smiled slightly.

Together, they looked up to the river of stars in the Milky Way. While looking up at the stars, Jack reached into his pocket and took out the red earthy khuya that Sebastian had given to him.

"Thank you," Jack said as he handed the khuya to Sebastian.

"Did it help?"

"Yes," Jack answered. "I never remember dreaming so much."

"It has great and powerful energy."

Sebastian carefully put the red earthy khuya into a small pouch that hung by his side.

There was a silence, once again. After several minutes passed, Jack broke it.

"Who is Ens?" he asked.

Sebastian did not answer Jack. It was a comfortable and accepting silence; nevertheless, it nagged at Jack. To be willing to wipe out Gandor's entire lineage was inconceivable, but to hide Ens' identity? What was the reason? Jack wondered. Though he did not understand it, Jack accepted the Shaman's reasons in his heart.

Side-by-side, they stood on the Terrace of the Ceremonial Rock looking down upon Machu Picchu, as they gazed up at the Pleiades. While they stood there in the chilled Andean silence, thousands of tiny lights descended out of the night sky. The lights materialized out of the Pleiades star cluster. They were called The Fires, and they traveled toward the Andean mountaintop chanting, like a boys' choir. To the naked eye, these floating points of light were but specks of twinkling particles, but upon closer examination, each Fire looked like a tiny butterfly with a human-like face, transparent wings and sparkling eyes, some were green and some were blue. Their singing was divine, of the gods.

The irony was that neither Jack nor Sebastian could see or hear them.

CHAPTER 55

BREAKING THROUGH

It was just before dawn in Machu Picchu. In the eastern sky just above the Andes, the crimson horizon bled upward into the periwinkle sky, where one-by-one the stars faded to sleep into the day.

On the southern slope of Huayna Picchu, Ens led a procession up the steep face of the mother mountain, following him were Sebastian, Jack, Caitlin and Potter Sims. The perilous trail of dirt was laden with slippery granite and boulders. Cautiously, they climbed the magnificent mountain. Just behind Potter Sims, Hranknor led The Corps, who bore the crystallized Gandor on a simple gold litter. Behind The Corps, hundreds of villagers from Machu Picchu followed, adept and conditioned to climbing the steep ascent of the cloud mountain.

Huayna Picchu was striking. It rose magnificently 2,000 feet above the village of Machu Picchu. On the side opposite the village, it was steep and rocky, a treacherous 5,500 foot drop down to the Urumbamba River and Valley.

After an hour of climbing, the procession reached the summit of Huayna Picchu. The sun had risen and shone brightly upon the gold litter, which held the frozen crystallized Gandor. The Corps set the litter with Gandor down in the center of everyone: Ens, Sebastian, Jack, Caitlin, Potter Sims, Hranknor, The Corps, and the Machu Picchu villagers. Ens stepped forward.

"Sacrifice is essential for the survival of any village," Ens said.

"Is this the part where we all become enlightened?" blurted out Potter Sims.

"Can't resist that nit picky tongue of yours, can you, Sims?" Ens stared hard at Potter Sims.

"Humph!" Potter Sims folded his arms.

"Unfortunately, only some of us will become enlightened." Ens turned to Potter Sims. He grabbed Potter Sims' arm. With Potter Sims' red boots dragging on the ground, Ens hauled him over to the edge of Huayna Picchu. It was a straight drop, thousands of feet to the gorge.

"Augh! Augh! Augh!" Potter Sims yelled.

Potter Sims' wings flapped spasmodically causing him to spin like a tether wildly around Ens, while his red boots kicked as he dangled over the precipice. Hranknor and The Corps laughed. Jack and Caitlin were stunned. Sebastian quietly watched with no reaction.

"Get your filthy hands off of me!" screamed Potter Sims, as he flailed in the air. "Get off me! Let me go, or I will—!" Potter Sims' words trailed off.

"What are you doing?" Jack screamed.

"Let him go!" Caitlin was horrified.

"Or you will what, Sims"? asked Ens as he held Potter Sims firmly over the precipice. Potter Sims screamed and kicked until Ens brought him in. Potter Sims straightened the wrinkles in his vest, pulled his white gloves tight around his fingers, and flicked the dirt from his jacket with the back of his hand.

"I hate jokes!" Potter Sims blurted at Ens indignantly.

"This is no joke," Ens said.

"If I was bigger, I'd show you," Potter Sims said.

"It always comes down to size and ego, doesn't it?" Ens mused.

Ens nodded. Hranknor and another Corps took the paralyzed Gandor off the gold litter and carried him to the edge. Chanting in a low whisper and shaking a rattle attached to a three-foot long black Great Condor feather, Sebastian walked around Gandor blessing him, inscribing circles and geometric figures in the air just above Gandor's head, his heart, and his plump torso. Jack and Caitlin watched every move the Shaman Sebastian made, as the Inca villagers prayed.

"You can't do this, he's the sole survivor of his species!' said Caitlin.

"Do you want to join him?"

"There's nothing we can do," Jack whispered to Caitlin.

"Hopefully, he doesn't know what's happening to him," Caitlin said.

"He knows exactly what's happening to him," Potter Sims said. He knew because he had also been frozen and paralyzed like Gandor.

"Are you showing compassion for Gandor, Sims?" Ens said. "I guess there's hope for everyone."

As everyone watched Gandor, Sebastian chanted and shook the rattle inches away from Gandor, who moved his eyes back-and-forth in their sockets. He heard everything; he understood everything, and everyone near him saw the awareness in his eyes. The villagers' chants echoed off the surrounding mountains.

"What could possibly be gained by doing this?" Jack pleaded.

"Watch."

At Ens' command, Sebastian picked Gandor up gripping him at his neck and rump. Sebastian walked to the edge of Huayna Picchu's 5,000-foot precipice. Gandor's eyes opened wide in terror, but his body remained like a marble statue. With certainty, Sebastian hurled Gandor over the edge. Caitlin screamed.

"No-o-o-o-o-o!"

Gandor fell. Caitlin's screams echoed off the surrounding mountains in the distance. Gandor plummeted toward his death, his body barely missed the protruding rocks.

The reflected living world flashed by in Gandor's eyes. While Gandor fell like a rock toward the Urumbamba valley, images of his mate Alba, his parents, his family, his friends and community, Raphus Island, Devastation Plain, Jack, Caitlin, and even Potter Sims fleeted by as rapid reflections in his eyes. 5,000 feet—4,000 feet—3,000 feet—2,000 feet—1,000 feet—

From the edge of Huayna Picchu, where Ens, Sebastian, Jack, Caitlin, Potter Sims, Hranknor, The Corps, and Inca villagers watched, the plunge seemed endless, as Gandor's body became smaller and smaller. At the last minute, Gandor jerked his enormous wings open, powerful and graceful, and he soared silently slicing through the air, up and around, and around and around the Andes.

"Yeah!" Jack screamed. "Yeah!"

"I knew he was going to make it!" exclaimed Potter Sims. "I knew it!"

"Sims, you slay me," Ens said.

Caitlin did not speak. Tears ran down her cheeks.

The villagers reverently watched in silence.

"Do you know how much pain he had to endure to break free?" Ens asked.

"I know," Jack answered.

"So this was a test?" Caitlin asked.

"Fee-Fi-Fo-Fum. Isn't that how it goes?" Ens asked.

"What's that supposed to mean?" Potter Sims said, perturbed by Ens' levity.

"It means we all must break through, in one way or another. If Gandor's clan had shown this much courage and vision for their own survival, they would be here today."

"For once, I agree with you!" Potter Sims said nodding his head in rapid agreement with Ens.

"This has made my day, Sims, that you have agreed with me! How could I possibly go on without your approval."

"Humph!" Potter Sims grunted, crossed his arms and turned away from Ens.

Within moments, Ens, Sebastian, Jack, Caitlin, and Potter Sims left the steep slope of Huayna Picchu and hiked down the backside of the mountain. The Inca villagers hiked down the opposite side and returned to their homes. Hranknor and The Corps flew off. After a one-hour long descent, Ens and Sebastian guided the others into a small grotto, a cave of gold chiseled into the side of Huayna Picchu. While they stood at the entrance of the grotto, they saw Gandor soaring gracefully between the adjacent mountains. He swooped down toward them. In one motion, he stretched his enormous wings, set his big blue feet down nimbly on the sparkling white granite, and then tucked his wings snugly to his sides.

"You waited long enough to open your wings!" said Potter Sims.

"Maybe you could've done better!" Gandor yelled back.

Jack and Caitlin were pleased to see Gandor. They walked over to him. They wanted to hug him, but Gandor was not very huggable, so they had to be satisfied with merely a pat or the head or a feathery pat on the back. Even though Gandor was not too keen on people touching him, he nevertheless tolerated it. Something in Gandor had changed; he felt like part of a community. It had been many years since he felt this way. He acknowledged this new change and acceptance by letting Jack and Caitlin freely touch him.

"We were worried. You did well," Jack said.

"I didn't have much choice, did I?" Gandor said.

"You did, you just made the right one, as Jack did." Caitlin said as she slipped her arm under Jack's.

They arrived inside the cave of gold behind Ens and Sebastian. The grotto was a gold mine, 100 feet long, 80 feet wide, and 60 feet high. It was shaped like a cathedral with arched walls that curved up to a point on the roof and sanctuary. Every inch of the walls glistened with gold. The grotto ledge was small and the opening to the mountain was narrow, yet the sunlight scattered off the gold walls. Inside, it was radiant, as if the stars of heaven were born there. The shape of the cave was similar to the oval drawn on the Yamqui map. Jack removed the Yamqui map from his pocket.

"This is on the map," Jack observed.

"There's a lot more on that diagram than gold," Ens said.

"Oh! The whole world's on that little piece of paper!" Potter Sims exclaimed.

"More than you can imagine, Sims." Ens walked towards Potter Sims pushing him backwards. It was the first time Potter Sims had feared Ens. "Aside from that, you are getting a bit too pushy!" Then, Ens turned and walked calmly toward Jack, and pointed to the gold in the grotto.

"So the story goes, you came for gold."

"No. I came to help my sister."

"Gold will not help?" Ens said.

"Of course, gold will help. Money and gold always help. But what I endured the other day with Potter was far more important to my sister, than gold." Jack answered.

"How do you know that you helped your sister?" Sebastian asked.

"I knew it. I felt it. Just as Gandor knew and felt that he must choose survival and endure whatever he must endure. His choice was pure and it will reap a future," Jack answered.

Sebastian smiled widely, his eyes glowed radiantly as he and Jack exchanged looks.

Ens walked over to a ledge deep inside the grotto. The ledge was solid gold. He opened his cape revealing two enormous black wings. Jack and Caitlin were shocked by the appearance of his giant wings. Ens opened one wing and extended it eight feet into the air. Like a reaper with a sickle, Ens swept his giant wing through the air ripping into the gold ledge with a loud chink! Sparks flew everywhere. With a heavy thud, a baseball size chunk of gold dropped to the grotto floor. Sebastian picked it up and handed it to Jack. It sparkled.

"To the Incas," Sebastian explained, "gold harnesses the sun. It contains the very essence of life. The symbol on your necklace."

"So, you search for gold, and you find kinship," Ens spoke to Jack, then he turned to Caitlin. "What about you, Dr. Bingham? What are you searching for?"

Caitlin reflected for a moment. "I am looking for a connection with the past."

"You both are," Sebastian acknowledged.

"My great-grandfather was the explorer Hiram Bingham. In 1911, he discovered Machu Picchu," Caitlin revealed.

"So we were drawn here?" Jack asked, suspecting it all along.

"Yes," Caitlin said.

Sebastian took the Yamqui map, his father Juan Pachakuti Yamqui's drawing. He pointed to the man and woman on the map on the bottom of the drawing.

"The Inca world is one of balance, man and woman. Everything on the left side of the drawing is male, everything on the on the right is female." He spoke directly to Jack and Caitlin. "You are real people, with careers, ambition, love, but you also represent the male and female, art and science, musician and astron-omer. One who lives by intuition, the other by facts. Balance."

Potter Sims moved closer. He strained his neck to see.

"Where am I?" Potter Sims interrupted looking down at the Yamqui drawing.

"You're not even a speck on that paper, Sims!" Gandor blurted out.

"I don't see you on there!" Potter Sims replied indignantly.

"Why the Beanstalk? You have a plan. What is it?" Jack asked Ens.

Ens took a long time to answer.

"You are here to learn something of great consequence," Ens said. "If you don't learn it, then your world will cease to exist."

Silence filled the great gold grotto, as Ens took the gold chunk from Jack. Ens closed his giant hand around the gold chunk. There was a deep crushing sound. Then, he opened his palm. Nothing but black dust remained. It was like a black hole, where no light escaped.

"Like one possible future for Gandor, your light will burn out of existence."

"Not good," Potter Sims commented.

Slowly, Ens poured the black dust into Jack's polished wooden hand.

CHAPTER 56

BIRTH

All of the Incas were gathered on the Main Plaza of Machu Picchu for a ritual celebration. Torches rimmed the entire plaza. Millions of stars shined in the night sky. In the center of the plaza, Incas played panpipes, drums, rattles, and flutes, while dancing around a giant bonfire. The music echoed off the surrounding mountains; the drumming and the rattling pulsed like a throbbing heart. Wearing an ornate gold headdress and costume made of black and white feathers from the Great Andean Condor, Sebastian danced around the bonfire. He flapped his huge wings in flight as he danced.

Jack, Caitlin, and Potter Sims stood to the side watching the spectacle. Upon a gold litter near the bonfire, Gandor was seated, regal and pompous, head raised high. He liked this idolatrous attention. Incas danced around him, while Sebastian blessed him.

"He doesn't need this, his ego is big enough!" Potter Sims complained.

"Besides the condor being the sacred bird of the Incas," Caitlin explained, "Gandor is the last surviving creature of his entire species. Don't you think that deserves a tribute?"

"Humph!" Potter Sims responded with his arms folded.

As the music in the center of the Main Plaza swelled, Gandor extended his enormous wings and lifted into the air. He circled above the fire and the Incas, while they danced and played their instruments.

The white smoke rose from the bonfire on Machu Picchu. It wafted up and around the Andes, spiraled up to the stars, winding through the constellations, and finding its way, it descended into the Cloud Room. Suspended in the Cloud Room were twelve cocoons made of dense fibrous roots. Slowly the white wisps of smoke from the fire seeped into each cocoon, penetrating them like a morning fog. Into the Cloud Room, The Corps descended.

At Machu Picchu, the Inca ritual was in full swing. The music and dancing were reaching a crescendo. As Sebastian raised his arms to the luminous Milky Way, The Corps descended, each one holding a cocoon. Shock and awe passed through the ritual arena by the unreal sight of the bizarre cocoons. Jack, Caitlin, and Potter Sims were stunned. By now, Gandor had joined them.

"What is this?" Jack asked.

"Cocoons! They look like cocoons!" Potter Sims said.

"This is not Inca ritual," Caitlin said.

The Corps released the cocoons, which floated upright three feet above the ground defying gravity. Each cocoon looked like a large egg made of dense brown intertwined fibers. Arranged in three columns of four, they looked like a platoon.

"The soldiers." Caitlin's said, her voice low and barely discernible as she could hardly believe what she was seeing.

"What soldiers?" Potter Sims asked.

"Remember Captain Jordan?"

"Yes," Gandor answered, clutching his watch.

"I came up here with fifteen soldiers," Caitlin explained. "Captain Jordan and two of the soldiers went into the Thorn Maze. That leaves twelve. There are twelve cocoons."

Jack stared at the cocoons, oblivious to anything else. Gandor noted Jack's silence and focus upon the egg-like cocoons.

"What do you know about this?" Gandor asked.

There was a long silence before Jack spoke. He was completely absorbed with the cocoons. He could not take his eyes off them.

"I know what it's like to be inside," Jack said.

"They are changing, and they know it," Potter Sims added.

"I agree, Sims." Gandor said. For the first time, Gandor's voice was free of antagonism and criticism of Potter Sims. Caitlin was shocked by his tone, quite aware that his experience had transformed Gandor in a deep way. There was, though still submerged and afraid to surface except for a random moment here and there, a newfound harmony between these two adversaries.

"It was painful," Jack recollected, "but after the pain was gone, and I woke up, it was the most invigorating moment of my life. I never felt more alive."

The villagers celebrated around the cocoons, and The Fires traveled down from the Pleiades where they converged around the cocoons. Like lightning bugs, they flitted around the cocoons producing a multi-octave hum, which blended with the music. The music rose to the stars of the Milky Way, where the fox chased the llama. The Fires grouped into a swarm and swirled like a tornado of light. Everyone was awed.

The Fires' music changed pitch. A finger stuck out of a cocoon and into the swirling Fires. Then a hand. Another hand. Arms and legs. They stuck out of the brown fibers into the tornado of The Fires.

His eyes open in wild disbelief, Jack asked. "What's happening?"

"I've never seen anything like it," Caitlin answered. In all of her travels and research, she had never encountered such a phenomenon.

Suddenly, a bare buttocks stuck out of one cocoon. Like eggs breaking, the cocoons cracked open spilling full-sized, human adults onto the ground. Lighted by the orange and red flames of the bonfire, each body writhed on the cold stone ground. They had no hair. They were bald and pinkish, like newborn babies.

"This is the most disgusting thing I've ever seen!" Potter Sims yelled.

"My God, they're like grown infants," Caitlin said.

"This is almost demonic. What is this?" Jack asked.

Ens stood behind Jack, Caitlin, Potter Sims, and Gandor.

"It is not demonic," Ens said. "It is birth."

"New life, how would you make it happen?" Shaman Sebastian asked looking at each member of the group. "Life emerges all around us, but we never consider how life changes…. So, <u>how</u> does it?" Sebastian waits for the answer, but it is quiet. "Because the greatest secret of life is so simple. In order to grow and change, everything in existence is cocooned in one form or another, an embryo in a womb, caterpillar in a silk sack, chick in a egg, flower in a seed. So are we all cocooned in one way or another, in flesh, in fibers of dirt, in ice. The question is will we let nature take its course so we can evolve the way nature intended us to, or will we fight it?"

As the twelve soldiers came alive on the cold stone ground of the Main Plaza, The Fires scattered into the night sky toward the Milky Way, back toward the Pleiades star cluster in the constellation of Taurus. The Incas played music, while others wiped the soldiers down with cloths made of llama wool, and anointed their naked bodies with incense and oil.

Later that evening, everyone shared in a communal feast. The bonfire roared. The flute and panpipe music echoed off the walls of Machu Picchu's temples and the surrounding mountains. Families interacted. Inca children played a game like kickball with a ball made from llama wool, grasses, and bark. Though clumsy and uncoordinated, Potter Sims played with them enjoying himself wildly. The bald and smooth-faced soldiers wore black ponchos made from the finest alpaca wool and sat on a knee-high wall next to Jack and Caitlin, who were holding hands. Sebastian and his wife Paola Rosa sat on the stone, watching their son Enrique as he played kickball with the other Inca children.

"What I need are two more feet!" Potter Sims yelled over to Jack, who was enjoying the spectacle of Potter Sims kicking the ball with the Inca children. It caused great humor and uproar.

"What you need, Sims, is a new body!" Gandor yelled in good fun.

"I don't see you out here!" Potter Sims yelled as he shuffled after the ball.

Everyone was amused. It was joyous. It was a community. There was a remarkable unity, and everyone felt it. Sebastian turned to Sergeant Jerome Hicks.

"Sergeant Hicks, how do you feel?"

"Good, sir. I don't think I have ever felt more alive," answered Sergeant Hicks.

"Do you have children?" Sebastian asked.

"I have four kids." He pointed to the kickball game. "They play a game just like that in the street right in front of our house."

"In New York?" Caitlin asked.

"Brooklyn."

"A small world. We come all this way, and talk about Brooklyn." Jack said.

"Do you have kids?" Sergeant Hicks asked Jack.

"Me? No. I have a younger sister, Natalie, and there is my mother."

Sergeant Hicks turned to Caitlin, who shook her head.

"I've spent my entire life looking through a telescope." Caitlin answered.

For a few moments, silence settled in, as they watched the children play. It was a peaceful at-home feeling, the way things should have been. Like a protective father, Sergeant Hicks watched the soldiers in his platoon interact with the Incas. The Inca panpipe and flute music rose into the pristine air to the shining stars. Ens walked over to the group. He stood before them, as they all sat on the Inca wall of stone in the Main Plaza.

"It is time to go," his voice was calm and sure.

Everyone was puzzled.

"Go where?" Jack asked.

Ens nodded to Sergeant Hicks, "You are a soldier, a protector, father and husband."

"You are a musician," he said to Jack, "guardian of your sister, surviving son, and you are of Inca ancestry."

"Caitlin Bingham," Ens said, "You are a scientist, discoverer of a new planet, searcher of your great grandfather's past, observer of history, and descendant of an Inca discoverer."

"Potter Sims, you are a map maker, you live by integrity, you are a most loyal friend, you are a traveler and guide; your life is about service."

"And you, Gandor," Ens finished, "You fly above earth, alone. You know the skies; you fear the bowels of the earth beneath you. You are the only survivor of your species. You have great will and determination."

Ens stopped and apprehension filled the air. Everyone knew Ens' power and knew they were trapped. Something was going to happen.

"Gandor, your species was arrogant, short-sighted and proud," Ens stared directly into Gandor's eyes as if to scold, not him, but his ancestors. "Your leaders with giant egos and small eyes polarized and isolated your entire society. They thought that they could do anything to their surrounding neighboring tribes, and the environment, and they did not see the effects of their aggression because they did not want to see. Gandor, where are they now?"

Shaman Sebastian spoke quietly and soberly to everyone in the group. "You are about to see a great civilization, one of the greatest on the planet, collapse. It is my people, the Inca, but in the future. They fall as the result of pride and arrogance. Like the war on Rafus," Sebastian looked at Gandor, "between two brothers who both wanted to control the kingdom alone." Then Sebastian returned his focus to everyone, "My people, the great Inca nation, will fall because of the civil war for greed and power, which polarized an entire continent. Our leaders created such a climate, one of conflict over compromise, retribution over compassion, right over truth. Everyday people, bright, hard-working men and women with families, as we speak right here and now, are becoming caught up in the nation's petty squabbles for territory, riches, and their rigid ideologies. Those became the ingredients for the collapse of the great Inca Empire."

"We send you there to witness, to understand, to be part of history," Ens spoke. "All of you walk on the same ground beneath the same stars. This moment is a blink in time, last night's forgotten dream. Learn from it." Ens smiled.

There was an eerie feel in the air. Fear of the unknown. No one spoke. Ens snapped his fingers. At light speed, everyone in Machu Picchu dissolved and faded into the past. Gone.

CHAPTER 57

A GREAT CIVILIZATION FALLS

Cajamarca was a quaint town of approximately two thousand Inca residents. Located in the rolling hills of Northern Peru, it was about one hundred miles inland from Peru's coast. The valley of Cajamarca was green, fertile and flat. It was prime topography for farming and planting, unusual in a country traversed by the Andes Mountains.

Nestled between the Andes Mountains on the pastoral hillsides just outside the town of Cajamarca were nearly 10,000 campfires. Nearly 80,000 Inca soldiers camped out waiting to meet Fernando Pizarro and the Spanish Conquistadores the next morning. Like brilliant stars of the Milky Way, the Inca campfires dotted the dark Cajamarca Valley landscape.

Several tents were arranged in a circle around each campfire, where Inca warriors sat drinking and smoking, singing and conversing. The hills of Cajamarca were dotted with thousands of these tent complexes.

Inside one of the complexes, Jack and Potter Sims materialized out of the air into the cluster of Inca warriors. No one seemed to notice; it was as if Jack and Potter Sims had been there all along.

"Where are we? What happened!" Potter Sims exclaimed.

"How should I know!" Jack answered.

"Look at your clothes!" Potter Sims exclaimed.

Jack looked down at his clothes. They were made of the finest weave and gold trim. Part of his tunic was made of deep blue, fine llama wool. On one hip hung a battle-axe; on the other hip hung a flute. The Inca amulet, which his mother Mattie had given him, still hung about his neck. Stunned, Jack rubbed the gold trim of his tunic between his fingers, lifted the battle-axe out of its scabbard and ran his thumb against the blade. *Sharp.*

Jack and Potter Sims stood next to the Inca warriors, who were warming themselves by the huge campfire.

"I hate things like this! I hate fire!" Potter Sims said backing away from the blazing campfire. As Potter Sims rambled on, an Inca warrior approached Jack.

"Sir, would you like more to eat?"

Jack recognized him; in fact, Jack sat near him at the Machu Picchu feast. The Inca warrior was one of the cocooned soldiers from Captain Jordan's platoon.

"We just ate! Doesn't he remember?" Potter Sims said loudly, so the warrior could hear, but the Inca warrior ignored him.

"No, thank you," Jack said.

The warrior bowed his head slightly to acknowledge Jack's disinterest in eating. "Then, Atahualpa would like to see you," the Inca warrior requested.

"I will be there shortly," Jack answered politely, then he turned to Potter Sims. "I am very afraid. I do not know where we are, but from what Ens and Sebastian said we are somehow going to witness the downfall of the Incas. My knowledge of Inca history is sketchy."

"What happened?" Potter Sims pressed Jack.

"I am trying to remember! Everything is happening too fast! What I do know is that the Spaniards conquered them, and the way it happened was stunning." Jack was very nervous, and that did not calm Potter Sims.

Several of the Inca warriors sat around the campfire watching Jack speak to the air. To them Potter Sims was invisible; they could only see Jack speaking and gesturing wildly to the air. It made them most uneasy and insecure that one of their leaders was crazy and disoriented. Jack, though he did not realize it yet, was one of the prestigious chosen leaders of the Inca Empire, but he did notice them staring at him as he spoke to Potter Sims.

As an Inca warrior was walking away from them, Jack spoke to Potter Sims. "Quick, ask him where Atahualpa's tent is. Hurry."

"Why?" Potter Sims asked Jack.

"Hurry up, go on." Jack said as he nodded at the Inca warrior who was walking away. Potter Sims scrambled after the Inca warrior and stepped just to the front side of him in the warrior's line of sight. Jack watched.

"Excuse me," Potter Sims blurted out, "where is Atahualpa's tent?"

Potter Sims tapped the Inca's shoulder. "Please! I am talking to you! Will you please answer me!" Potter Sims persisted.

Potter Sims was incensed. Jack watched everything, as Potter Sims stepped in front of the Inca warrior, but the man never broke stride.

"I hate arrogance. I hate rude people!" yelled Potter Sims over to Jack. He yelled loud enough to be sure that every Inca gathered around the campfire heard him, but nobody turned a head.

"They can't hear or see you, Potter!" Jack yelled across the clearing.

Several of the Incas sitting around the campfire stared at Jack, who spoke to the air. They furrowed their brows, shook their heads, and then returned to their conversations.

Potter Sims stomped his way back to where Jack watched the entire exchange. Jack whispered in his ear, "They cannot hear you, but they do hear and see me."

"You knew this was going to happen, didn't you?"

"I suspected it," Jack was amused. He knew that it would perturb Potter Sims to no end that nobody could hear him, see his rants and his atypical colorful clothing.

"You used me!"

"Potter, I am sorry, but I had to see," Jack said.

"I hate being ignored!" protested Potter Sims.

"They are **not** ignoring you. They do not see you. You are dressed as you always are, but look at me." Jack pointed to his beautiful fine clothing. "I am Inca, down to the gold braid."

"So now what?" Potter Sims asked.

"I'm going to see Atahualpa. You wait here until I return."

"Why? They can't see me!"

Jack walked through the Incas, who sat around the campfire. He stopped at one of the Incas, whom he recognized as one of the swat team members at the Machu Picchu celebration.

"Where is Atahualpa's tent?"

The Inca immediately stood up, bowed toward Jack, and gave him a perplexed look since he did not understand why Jack did not know how to recognize Atahualpa's tent, since he had been in it hundreds of times. Nevertheless, he humored Jack and pointed to a huge tent embroidered with gold stars, brightly colored fish, and animals.

"There," the soldier said.

"Thank you," Jack nodded to the soldier and walked away. The Inca soldier shook his head, made a funny comment about too much drink, and sat back down to warm himself in front of the campfire.

Jack walked gracefully toward the huge embroidered tent. Armed with spears and swords, stout Inca warriors guarded the tent entrance. They parted for Jack as he approached, and one guard opened the tent flap. Jack nodded a thank you and entered with Potter Sims following right behind him.

"This could actually be fun!" Potter Sims yelled aloud as they entered the tent. Jack gave him a sideways glance.

Inside Atahualpa's tent were three large Inca soldiers guarding the Inca king, who sat on an elevated gold stool saddled with a colorful llama cushion. Servants and holy Inca women constantly tended to Atahualpa. Chosen for their beauty, these Inca women were considered the privileged select of the Inca Emperor. A handful of Inca nobles also occupied the tent.

Atahualpa's clothes were made of brilliant gold and silver weave. Around his neck was a collar fashioned out of 24-karat gold and embedded with stunning emeralds. On his head, he wore a golden crown of precious jewels, which glistened in the torchlight. As Jack and Potter Sims approached, Atahualpa beckoned to Jack. As Jack walked forward, Potter Sims walked invisibly beside him. The Inca nobles bowed and stepped aside. As Jack approached, his gold Inca amulet glistened in the warm glow of the torchlight.

"I like this." Potter Sims said.

When Jack approached, Atahualpa stepped down from his elevated gold stool to greet Jack. "I know of no other king," Atahualpa said, "who has as great a friend, who is both a distinguished musician and a fierce warrior."

"You are too kind to me, lord," Jack replied hoping that he had said the right thing.

"Why do you always call me lord? I am your friend," mused Atahualpa.

"Ask him if I'm his friend, too?" blurted out Potter Sims.

Jack gave Potter Sims a glance. Atahualpa noticed Jack turning his attention to the side and staring at the air.

"Is there something bothering you?" asked the great Inca Emperor.

"No," answered Jack, "I was merely distracted for a moment, I thought that I heard some words of substance from over there, but it was nothing, just prattle in the wind."

"Prattle? Prattle! Humph!" Potter Sims stomped the dirt.

"Musicians have ears tuned to the things of the world that others of us can neither hear nor appreciate," Atahualpa explained.

"See? He appreciates me!" yelled out Potter Sims. Jack ignored Potter Sims and kept his eyes focused upon his Inca Emperor.

"Thank you," Jack answered Atahualpa.

"Would you play a peaceful melody to put us to sleep, so we may dream before we meet the Spaniards tomorrow?"

Jack nodded and removed the flute from its gold and silver case. He played. The music flowed like a warm tropical wind through the Inca encampment. The attentions of the nobles, of the servants, and especially of Atahualpa focused upon Jack.

Outside the tent, the Inca warriors sitting around the campfire listened to the flute music, while they talked in low voices. The music echoed across the hills of Cajamarca to the Square below and rose to the river of stars in the Milky Way.

Cajamarca Square was the center of the town of Cajamarca. The square of Cajamarca was shaped in a great-elongated U. On each side of the U was a one-story building about two hundred yards long. Inside two of the buildings, one hundred and fifty Spanish Conquistadors waited cramped and scared; their saddled horses were with them. The mood was somber. The flute aroused their emotions. It caused them to reflect about their distant homeland, their families, their friends, and what they were about to lose forever. Some of the Conquistadors cried quietly with tears running slowly down into the thick beards of their cheeks. Others prayed because they believed that tonight was their last night. It was their last supper, the night before they die.

In 1532, Francisco Pizarro left Panama on his third expedition to Peru. On a previous expedition, Spanish ships encountered a large boat, built of balsa wood and sturdy, tightly seamed, cotton sails, a vessel crafted for ocean voyages. On the vessel were huge containers of gold crowns, silver jewelry, belts and bracelets, exquisitely crafted breastplates for battle, silver and gold cups, clothes of vibrant colors with elaborate embroidered fish, birds, and llamas, and bags of emeralds, rubies and fine crystals. These were the products of a great civilization, the Incas. The boundaries of the Inca Empire under the venerated Inca ruler Huayna-Capac stretched for 3,000 miles along the Andes from the southern border of Columbia to Chile.

Two years after Huayna-Capac died from an epidemic, a civil war broke out between his two sons, Huascar and Atahualpa, who were vying for total control of the Inca Empire. Huayna-Capac wanted the Inca kingdom divided in two between his sons. Atahualpa would rule from Quito; and Huascar would rule from Cuzco. In his ruthless quest for ruling the Inca Empire, Atahualpa had his brother killed by an escort in the mountains just south of Cajamarca. Atahualpa's journey to be sole emperor of the Inca dynasty knew no boundaries. He would do anything to secure the kingdom, even if it involved waging war against his brother or anyone who supported his brother.

Years before, one of Huascar's generals, a man named Atoc, imprisoned Atahualpa just before the civil war broke out. After Atahualpa's eventual release, he vowed revenge against his brother and General Atoc. During the first major battle of the Inca civil war in Amato, Atahualpa conquered the Incas and another tribe called the Canari, who were loyal to his brother. Atahualpa butchered thousands of men and boys, even though they openly surrendered and asked for mercy. Atahualpa then beheaded Atoc, and kept his head as a personal reminder of the civil war and forces conspiring against him. After the flesh and tissues of Atoc's head had tanned with age, Atahualpa had a golden bowl attached to the top of Atoc's head, where it rested on the skull's wiry dried hair. He had a silver spout clamped tightly between Atoc's closed teeth. When it suited his fancy, Atahualpa would have the gold bowl filled with chicha and he would drink from the spout staring directly into the holes that once were General Atoc's eyes.

It was 2 a.m. on November 16, 1532. Francisco Pizarro, citizen of Panama, long-time adventurer, soldier and conqueror for Spain, now in his mid-fifties, waited in a building of Cajamarca Square with one hundred and fifty of his soldiers and their saddled horses. In a few hours, he would come face-to-face with the most powerful and ruthless leader of the Inca Empire, Atahualpa. Francisco Pizarro had been preparing for this opportunity for years, but now he and his men were not just scared, they were terrified. He finally realized the seriousness of his situation. His Spanish cohort was only one hundred and fifty strong, surrounded by a skilled Inca army of nearly 80,000, who had not only survived the bloodiest civil war in South American history, but had done so under extremely adverse conditions using sophisticated military strategy. In his march to reach Cajamarca, Pizarro had led three expeditions, all of which had conditioned his military and governing instincts up to this point in time. After leading a contingent of men who were wiped out by hunger and disease, Pizarro led an arduous expedition down the coast of Ecuador and Peru where he had killed a chief of a village to instill fear into the villagers and gained control of the territory.

Atahualpa was about to meet his match.

Inside the Governor's quarters of the Cajamarca Square complex, Pizarro and his Conquistadors sat on benches with their backs against the wall, as they anxiously waited for the night to pass. Every hour, a designated Spanish officer looked out to the hillside from one of the twenty large openings in the Cajamarca square buildings. The 10,000 small campfires dotted the Cajamarca night landscape, neither random nor arranged haphazardly, but in aligned geometric formations suggesting a total adherence to military order and discipline. This was a professional army. Even as small a detail as a campfire contributed to the Spaniards' growing fears. Throughout the night, Pizarro's officers spied on the hillside swarming with Incas to get any information that might give them a strategic upper hand.

Into a cluster of huddled Conquistadors, nine soldiers from Captain Jordan's platoon materialized out of the cold night air into the Spanish cohort. Not one of Governor Pizarro's soldiers saw them incarnate out of the air. Dressed as Spanish Conquistadors, the soldiers were confused. They had hair. Some had long beards. They wore Spanish armored breastplates and helmets. They carried Spanish swords. Sergeant Hicks, who by his uniform appeared to be a ranking Conquistador, looked around the room for the other men in his squad, then at the Spanish soldiers. He maintained his composure trying not to draw attention to himself or his men.

"Sir, what happened?" one of his young soldiers whispered in his ear as he leaned toward his Sergeant.

"You know as much as I do," Sergeant Hicks answered quietly.

Sergeant Stone, one of Captain Jordan's soldiers cocooned in the Cloud Room, walked over to Sergeant Hicks, after assessing the situation.

"This isn't going to turn out well," Sergeant Stone whispered to Sergeant Hicks.

"Why do you say that?" asked Sergeant Hicks.

"Look at these men," Sergeant Stone nodded indicating the Spanish Conquistadors. "They're terrified. They look like they are about to be executed."

Sergeant Hicks surveyed Pizarro's men, who sat brooding somberly in the confines of the Governor's quarters. He knew that Sergeant Stone was correct in his assessment. His silence and his eyes gave him away. During the same time, the music from Jack's flute flowed through the quarters; it was peaceful dew in the early morning. The cocooned soldiers of Captain Jordan's platoon remained together, but in masse trying to blend in with the other Conquistadors.

In the center of the Cajamarca Square courtyard, Ens and Caitlin suddenly materialized out of the clear night sky. Being only three days past the full moon, Ens and Caitlin cast shadows upon the large dirt quadrangle. The Spanish Conquistadors could not see them; they were invisible to everyone. Caitlin was astonished.

"Where are we?" Caitlin asked.

"Cajamarca."

"Peru?" Caitlin was incredulous.

"Yes."

Jack's flute music filled the hills of Cajamarca; it bounced off the walls of the Square. The bright blue moonlight shined softy upon them. It was a moment of magic. Caitlin knew so well that this was a significant time and place in history. As a scientist, Caitlin had many questions about her leap through time and space, but she withheld them.

"Do you hear that?" Caitlin asked.

"Yes." Ens answered, amused by Caitlin's absorption in the music.

"The music is beautiful," she mused as she listened entranced by the notes that flowed so freely through entire square and countryside. Her body swayed slightly in the faint breeze to the music, and then she stopped. Her face changed.

"It's Jack."

"It is." Ens answered.

Caitlin gasped. She listened intently, and then she whirled slowly around scanning the hillsides above the square to discover where the music originated. Her gaze fixed upon the star-studied Cajamarca hillside lighted by the ten thousand campfires. She knew that Jack was somewhere up there. But where?

"Let's take a walk," Ens beckoned Caitlin.

Ens walked toward the Governor's quarter of Cajamarca Square. Puzzled and confused, Caitlin followed him. Leaving the soft blue moonlight, they entered the building. Inside, they saw dozens of Spanish soldiers huddled in fear into the corners of the night. Some Conquistadors were crying; others clinched rosary beads between their fingers, as they mouthed repeated Hail Marys. Caitlin spotted Sergeant Hicks and Sergeant Stone, and soldiers from their squad, soldiers whom she had sat next to just thirty minutes ago at the celebration at Machu Picchu. However, they could not see nor hear him or Ens.

"There's Sergeant Hicks and Stone!"

"Yes. It is."

Caitlin thought, Jack is playing music on the hillsides of Cajamarca. Then he is Inca. Sergeants Hicks and Stone sit here anxiously waiting. They are Spanish Conquistadors. Why? Then, it hit her.

"This is Cajamarca. It is 1532," Caitlin said, her eyes were wide, full of foreboding and astonishment as she spoke to Ens. "Jack is on the hills outside of Cajamarca. He is Inca. Hicks and Stone and are Pizarro's Conquistadors. Good God."

"That is correct," Ens said. "A great lesson in arrogance and pride will not just be learned, but lived in a matter of hours."

"The Incas were slaughtered," Caitlin's voice quivered with terror. "You can't do this!"

"My Dear Dr. Bingham, this is the past, it has already happened."

Ens smiled, then before Caitlin could say anything, Ens snapped his fingers and they both disappeared into the air.

It was the middle of the night on the hillsides just outside of Cajamarca. Inside Atahualpa's tent, the Inca emperor watched Jack as he played the flute. Jack's music flowed out the Inca encampment and down through the Cajamarca Valley. With a gentle flourish and finale, Jack finished the flute solo and placed the flute on his belt. Potter Sims was still invisible and impatient.

"I was beginning to wonder if I was going to have to listen to that noise all night!" said Potter Sims.

Jack glared at Potter Sims, just as Atahualpa spoke.

"That was magnificent. I am a warrior, a conqueror, an Inca king. But you, you are a musician. The harmony of life plays inside you."

"You honor me too much," Jack lowered his eyes.

"I speak the truth," said Atahualpa. "I know who I am. I know what I am. When all of this fighting and killing is finished, it is music that will last. Music is the paste that binds friends to foes, nations to nations."

"Oh, brother!" exclaimed Potter Sims. "What balderdash!"

Without saying a word, Jack humbly nodded to Atahualpa. He ignored Potter Sims.

Dawn. The sun rose in the eastern sky over the Cajamarca hillside. It painted the crystal sky with reds and oranges; the frosted green grass was bathed in the tint of blood. In the Inca encampment, horses whinnied and neighed as they awakened to the warm sunlight rising upon their bare backs. In each Inca tent site, soldiers rose in the brisk morning air to dust the early morning frost off their tents and weapons. Eighty thousand Inca warriors, sprawled across the Cajamarca landscape, prepared for the march down into Cajamarca Valley. The Inca warriors saddled their horses; they adjusted their ceremonial dress. Gold and silver adornments sparkled with blinding points of light in the warm morning sun. By mid-morning, the tents were struck, horses were mounted, and six thousand soldiers and noblemen loyal to Atahualpa walked slowly down the green Peruvian hillside toward the Cajamarca Square.

The six thousand Incas were unarmed, except for small battle-axes, slings and pouches of stone, which they carried at their sides. The front platoons of Incas wore wide tunics of checkered design, red and gold with black trim. Some were silver and yellow with blue trim. These soldiers paved the way by sweeping the ground and removing all sticks, straw and stones in the path of the approaching Inca Emperor. Other Incas were dressed in full ceremonial garb with headdresses of gold and silver discs like crowns upon their heads.

The sun rose high and bright in the blue sky, while eighty Inca noblemen wearing uniforms of a deep rich ceremonial blue carried Atahualpa upon their shoulders on an ornate litter. The litter was lined with parrot feathers of dazzling turquoise, red, green, orange and yellow and with plates of gold and silver that reflected in the noon sun. Atahualpa was richly and colorfully dressed. Around his neck hung an ornate gold collar embedded with huge perfect emeralds, and on his head he wore a magnificent gold crown. Near the litter, some Incas rode in ceremonial dress on horseback. Jack rode a white horse lavishly decorated in gold, silver and turquoise. Trying to keep up, Potter Sims flew alongside of Jack leaping sporadically into the air, while buzzing his transparent wings, as if he was trying to balance himself on a pogo stick.

"Why can't I ride?" Potter Sims asked as he bounced up and down while buzzing his wings in spastic spurts.

"Because there is no room up here, that's why!" Jack pointed to the Atahualpa's litter bearers. "Besides, they are walking." Several of the Incas turned and looked at Jack who was speaking to the air

"I am not a litter bearer! I hate walking! I hate flying!" yelled Potter Sims.

"It is not that far, Potter," Jack indicated the square of Cajamarca a short distance from them.

"It is a matter of principle!" Potter Sims said as he gave his wings another spurt. "This is obviously a parade of some kind! Not long ago, the Incas celebrated us! Remember? So, why can't I ride?"

"Because they cannot see you, Potter, that's why! I don't even know what I am doing up here!" Jack was getting perturbed with Potter Sims as he spurted alongside buzzing and flapping his wings, lifting his bright red boots sporadically off the ground all the while non-stop complaining. Some of the Incas turned and looked again at Jack. In whispered conversations, the soldiers discussed how strange the musician was, but they did not make an issue of it. He was a close friend of Atahualpa.

Jack and Potter Sims had no idea where they were going or why. They merely followed the crowd, who followed Atahualpa. Anxious and nervous, Jack absorbed everything as they approached Cajamarca Square. Then, it hit him. He spoke lowly under his breath, so no one could hear, but maybe Potter Sims, who bounced along closer to the horse that Jack rode.

"This is Cajamarca. The Incas were slaughtered there, and then conquered."

"But you are Inca," Potter Sims said with grave concern in his voice.

"I know," Jack responded in an anxious whisper.

"What are you going to do?" asked Potter Sims.

"I am going to try and stop it."

Cajamarca Square was desolate, stone quiet. Nobody was there, except for Ens and Caitlin who had faded into the Square out of the thin air. They stood near the center of the square waiting, but they were transparent, invisible. They watched as Incas dressed in ceremonial garb paraded through the high gate into the Cajamarca courtyard. In their checkered uniforms, the advanced platoon of Incas paved the way by sweeping a dirt path for Atahualpa's arrival. The second Inca cohort, wearing gold and silver disc headdresses, marched in formation to the center of Cajamarca Square, where they parted and waited for the nobles and litter-bearers carrying Atahualpa. Inside the buildings of Cajamarca Square, Sergeant Hicks and Sergeant Stone waited in hiding along with their men and Pizarro with his Conquistadores. Some of the Spanish Conquistadors were so terrified that they urinated on themselves without even knowing it.

Suddenly, an elegant bird like the great Andean condor flew above Cajamarca Square, circling it. It swooped down to get a better view of the pomp and ceremony in the courtyard below. The bird was Gandor. With his enormous wings spread, he glided above watching the events unfold. Jack and Potter Sims saw him, but said nothing.

After hours of ceremonial procession through the gates of Cajamarca, after six thousand Incas filled up the courtyard, after they fell in perfect rank and file to honor the arrival of their Inca king, Jack entered through the gate on his decorated white horse with Potter Sims by his side. Just behind him was Atahualpa and the rest of his colorful cortege.

"There's Jack! And Potter Sims!" Caitlin scanned the crowd of ceremoniously dressed Incas. "Three of Captain Jordan's soldiers." Caitlin was frightened. "This is history. It is the conquest of the Incas. They don't know what's going to happen to them."

"Jack does. They don't." Ens said calmly.

"Why?"

"Because this is about the future." Ens said.

"From my world, the 21st Century, this is the past," countered Caitlin.

"Is it?" Ens stared directly at Caitlin. It made her uncomfortable. Ens pointed to the great Inca emperor Atahualpa and his army standing in ceremonial splendor in Cajamarca Square. "Pride and arrogance repeat themselves in every great, and even in the smallest, nations. And the consequences are always the same."

"The Incas were the most powerful Empire on the Earth. They owned almost all of the world's wealth in gold," said Ens. "They had visionary architecture, revolutionary design in urban planning, unparalleled tapestry, advanced concepts of astronomy, great armies and weaponry, profound spiritual philosophy, and a great grasp of the South American world. They saw themselves not as conquerors, but as spreaders of the truths and success of their culture. But their nation was destroyed from the inside by greed, rival egos and a need to conquer."

As Ens spoke, Atahualpa arrived in the center of Cajamarca Square, but he did not see anyone there except Incas. Atahualpa wondered where the Conquistadores were? Perhaps, he could not see them. The king Atahualpa stood up on his litter to get a better view. Slowly, he scanned the courtyard. Quickly, Jack dismounted his horse and walked over to Inca king. Potter Sims followed closely. Jack looked at Atahualpa standing upon his litter, which made him even taller because the litter was raised off the ground. Jack had to shade his eyes from the sun, since he was staring straight into the sun to speak to the Inca king.

"This is a trap," Jack warned. Jack spoke in Quechua. The Inca warriors and litter-carriers nearby were perplexed not only by Jack's announcement to their king, but because of his brazen approach.

"What do you speak?" Atahualpa asked staring down at Jack with the sun burning down over his shoulder.

"This is the hour of Inca downfall," Jack said. Atahualpa's face contorted and began to turn crimson. The surrounding warriors and litter-carriers were shocked by Jack's announcement.

"What are you saying? You are my friend!" Atahualpa's tone was harsh, filled with pride and confusion. "Why would you say such a thing?"

"Because it is true," Jack said humbly. "We must leave this square immediately to protect you and the entire nation!"

"Enough!" Atahualpa pointed his finger down at Jack, as the surrounding warriors and litter-carriers trembled. They had never seen their King so furious. "You will speak no more! The Inca nation is the greatest nation! No nation or people can bring us to the earth!" As Atahualpa spoke, the sun burned down hot from the blue sky just over his massive shoulder decorated with gold and gems.

"I beg you, my king and my friend, please let us leave here!" Jack pleaded.

"Are you aware of the punishment for such traitorous speech?" Atahualpa spoke, his words were searing and angry at Jack.

"I don't know, my king."

"It is death!" Atahualpa yelled. The surrounding warriors and litter-carriers could not believe what they were hearing and watching because Atahualpa and Jack were the closest of friends. It made them most uneasy.

"I was telling you this as your friend because I have great respect and love for you," Jack spoke humbly, but the Inca King cut him off. His face was stern and red.

"You are my friend no more. You will be silent, or I will have you executed right here and now on this very spot," Atahualpa's words were final. He nodded at two warriors who approached Jack with large hand axes, ready to sever Jack's head from his body with the slightest nod from Atahualpa. Jack stared at Atahualpa. In Jack's eyes was the look of compassion. Potter Sims grabbed Jack by his arm, for he knew that nobody could see him.

"There is nothing that anyone can do," Potter Sims said to Jack tugging on his arm trying to pull him away from the proud Inca King Atahualpa. "You must let it go, you have done your best."

Jack turned his eyes away from Atahualpa and looked at Potter Sims. Jack walked back to his horse and mounted it, where he waited in silence in the burning heat of the noon-day sun.

It was silent as the Incas stood in the dead air of Cajamarca Square. Suddenly, two men appeared in the doorway of the Governor's quarters and walked toward the Atahualpa. The two men were Friar Vicente de Valverde, a Spanish priest in the Dominican order and a young interpreter named Martin. He was Inca, captured aboard a balsa wood Inca trading ship, then trained as a translator by the Spanish. One day, the Spaniards knew that they would need Martin's knowledge of Quechua to conquer the Inca empire.

In one hand, Friar Vicente de Valverde carried a large gold cross and in the other, a bible. The interpreter Martin walked by his side. The Inca warriors wearing gold and silver disc headdresses and the Inca nobles wearing rich blue uniforms parted to make way for the Spanish priest and his young interpreter.

From inside the Governor's Quarters of Cajamarca Square, Pizarro watched and listened, undetected. The Conquistadors huddled in the buildings also watched, particularly Sergeant Hicks and Sergeant Stone with their men. The desperate crying and praying had stopped. The moment was at hand.

Friar Vicente de Valverde and the interpreter Martin arrived at Atahualpa's litter. They stared at the great Inca Emperor. Atahualpa, a quick study of people, attempted to read Valverde's face. Friar Vicente de Valverde was religious, uncompromising and stern. What the Inca emperor saw in the Spanish Dominican's face was an unwillingness to compromise. Atahualpa also was proud; he would not step down from his litter. The great emperor thought, this person must come to me. This is my Inca nation. This is my Inca army. These Spaniards are surrounded. I could kill them all.

Friar Vicente de Valverde felt Atahualpa's pride. He was a smart soldier. He knew that this Inca would not budge. The priest cautiously walked forward to Atahualpa's litter. He had a cross and bible clutched tightly in each hand. He stopped at the litter. Atahualpa looked down upon the Spanish priest and his young interpreter. From inside the Governor's Quarters, Pizarro watched everything. About forty feet away from the litter, Ens and Caitlin watched invisible to everyone. Jack and Potter Sims stood ten feet from Atahualpa; they could see Atahualpa's and Valverde's eyes. Jack watched every flinch and squint, every move and every gesture. Caitlin looked up and saw Gandor encircling above the crowded silent square. Caitlin turned to Ens.

"Where is Sebastian?" asked Caitlin.

"This is November 16, 1532. We left Sebastian at Machu Picchu in 1527. From your world, it is over 474 years ago, but for Sebastian the Incas will not fall in Cajamarca for five years." Ens answered.

"Sebastian knows?" asked Caitlin.

"Yes. He can track into the future. He has already seen it."

Caitlin and Ens turned their attentions to Atahualpa and Friar Vicente de Valverde. Atahualpa held out his hand to Friar Vicente de Valverde. Atahualpa wanted to examine the large red book, which the Spanish priest gripped tightly in his fingers. Friar Vicente de Valverde handed Atahualpa the book never letting his eyes, which were colored with religious judgment, drift away from the Inca king. After all, Friar Vicente de Valverde knew that this Inca like all Incas was a barbarian, and not yet saved.

Atahualpa took the closed bible and without opening it, turned it over in his giant hands. Touching the gold embossed letters "The Bible" with his fingertips, Atahualpa studied the red book. He tried to open it, but he had difficulty. He turned the book over in his hands struggling with it. Friar Vicente de Valverde reached across to open the bible for the Inca king, but Atahualpa angrily cracked the priest's arm sharply. He would open the book himself! Friar Valverde was shocked by Atahualpa's belligerence, by his invasive act. Valverde curled his lips ever-so-slightly in disgust as he considered the arrogance and primitive stupidity of this pagan! Yet, the Dominican remained poker-faced, as he watched the Inca king struggle with the holy book. Finally, Atahualpa succeeded in opening the bible. Like a child, he slowly leafed through the pages. He ran his fingertips over the print, as if by doing so would cause the black marks to rub off. The proud

Inca king looked at his fingers. With a stiffened index finger, Friar Valverde pointed to the holy bible. His tone was arrogant.

"Those words are God's holy words! God speaks to us!"

Martin translated the priest's words. Atahualpa held the bible up to his ear. He listened, but silence was the only sound in Cajamarca Square. Atahualpa's eyes opened wide with growing disbelief.

"If you submit to the Holy Catholic Church and to the King of Spain," said Friar Vicente de Valverde, "no harm will come to you and your people!"

Nervously, the young interpreter Martin translated the message into Quechua for the Inca king. After a few moments, Atahualpa's face flushed red with anger. He hurled the holy bible to the ground and yelled to his Inca warriors to prepare themselves. Young Martin scrambled to pick the bible out of the Cajamarca Square dirt and returned it graciously to Friar Valverde.

Tension in Cajamarca Square was thick. It hung like a wet fog in the air. From inside the Governor's quarters, Pizarro watched. His Spanish conquistadores waited shaking in their armor, clutching their unsheathed swords. Some warriors sat atop their horses ready to gallop into the masses of Incas boxed into the Cajamarca courtyard. Friar Valverde yelled. His words echoed off the buildings in the enclosure.

"Come out Christians! Come out!" The Dominican waited. He stared at the shadows on the gray walls of the Governor's Quarters. Seconds passed. Tension thickened.

"Did you see what happened? Why are you polite to this arrogant Indian?" Valverde's voice boomed the challenge into the courtyard. Friar Valverde waited; his impatience grew. Everyone in Cajamarca Square, even Gandor circling above, watched with wide-eyed anxiety knowing that within seconds a major event was about to unfold.

"This is the Antichrist!" screamed Friar Valverde, his finger pointing stiffly at the Inca king proudly sitting upon his litter. "March out against him, Christians! I absolve you!" Valverde's voice punctured the hillside silence that surrounded Cajamarca.

From inside the Governor's quarters, Francisco Pizarro signaled. Trumpets rang out signaling the planned coordinated assault. Two cannon blasts ripped into the mass of Inca warriors. It echoed through the Cajamarca countryside. With swords drawn, dozens of Conquistadores on horseback galloped into the Incas, into the nobles, and toward the Inca king Atahualpa. It was unbridled chaos. It was terror.

"This is horrible! Horrible!" screamed Potter Sims.

The Incas had no rifles, nor guns. They were too alarmed and overwhelmed to fight back with their swords. They were not prepared. Pizarro himself, with a sword in one hand and a dagger in the other, charged the litter holding Atahualpa. Reaching up high over the nobles, Pizarro grabbed Atahualpa's arm and pulled the Inca Emperor to the ground, but Governor Pizarro could not hold on. Around him, the Spanish Conquistadores hacked and butchered Atahualpa's nobles, cutting off their arms and hands. With amputated limbs, the loyal noble Incas supported Atahualpa's litter with their shoulders to keep him on high.

Though invisible, Potter Sims stayed at Jack's side and watched the massacre that was unfolding all around him. Incas were climbing atop one another to escape. Those who were not being trampled or running away were butchered like surprised lambs. Ens was calm and emotionless. He stood next to Caitlin, who was screaming, delirious with horror.

Running toward the Inca king with his sword raised was Sergeant Hicks. Several of the twelve soldiers, now Conquistadors, were with him. Sergeant Hicks was only ten feet from Atahualpa.

"No!" Jack yelled. With his battle-axe raised, he stepped in front of Atahualpa and the litter bearers, who could barely support their Inca king. The litter was beginning to dip on one side. Seeing an opportunity, Sergeant Hick's raised his sword decorated with religious and military symbols of Spain. He swung it downward with great thrust. Jack blocked it with his axe. Swiftly, Hicks raised his heavy sword again and struck another blow. Jack blocked it. Potter Sims did everything possible to protect Jack, but his presence had no effect. No matter how hard Potter Sims tried, he could not help his friend.

"Hicks!" Jack screamed.

As Jack yelled, Sergeant Hicks' sword cut through the air. Jack blocked Hicks' Conquistador sword for the third time. Hicks' sword and Jack's axe formed a perfect diagonal cross, as they stalemated in the air with a loud crack against each other. They stared at each other through their crossed weapons. Hicks' eyes squinted slightly. He recognized Jack's 24-karat gold Inca amulet. He knew this Inca musician and warrior. He knew him from the future.

"Tott?"

"Yes, it's me. It's me, Hicks!"

"My God," Hicks said.

All around them, Cajamarca Square had become a slaughterhouse, as the Conquistadores yelled and butchered the unsuspecting Incas. Jack and Sergeant Hicks lowered their weapons. They stood together watching the slaughter. From nowhere, a sword severed Jack's left arm just above his elbow.

"Augh!" Jack screamed. His arm fell to the ground. Blood gushed from the stump, where his arm once was. It happened so fast that Hicks barely had time to wonder, Who did this? Before Hicks could see who cut off Jacob Tott's arm, before Jack could fall to the ground, a sword was thrust into Jack's side. Jack's mouth opened wide in pain. He sucked in air. No sound, no scream emerged. His eyes showed his utter astonishment.

In the chaos of Cajamarca Square, Caitlin screamed when she saw Jack stabbed. Jack's scream was silent, and no one heard Caitlin. Emotionless, Ens watched her. Right next to Jack, Potter Sims yelled and fluttered his transparent wings wildly and spastically about. He made screaming sounds that were unhuman gibberish. No one heard them. Potter Sims was alone.

Dying, Jack fell into Sergeant Hicks' arms. Lying on the ground, in Sergeant Hicks' arms, Jack looked around. It was Spaniard against Inca. Incas climbed atop one another to escape death. He saw Atahualpa's litter dumped and the Inca king yanked from the litter. Hicks cradled Jack in his lap, as they lay on the ground.

Jack spotted Sebastian walking through Cajamarca Square, among the slain Inca bodies. His body was transfigured, glowing. Sergeant Hicks could now see Sebastian, Potter Sims, Ens and Caitlin. Sergeant Hicks was stunned. He stood up in the midst of the slaughter and stared at Ens, and those he could not see before. With compassion, Sebastian smiled at Jack, who smiled back at him. Jack closed his eyes and died.

Caitlin sobbed uncontrollably in despair, but no one could hear her. No one could comfort her. She looked in disbelief to the hillsides above Cajamarca, where 70,000 Incas swarmed across the grassy Cajamarca plains, running for their lives like stampeding cattle on the open range. The Incas had lost their ferocious warrior leader, saw him taken ruthlessly and mercilessly as a prisoner, manhandled and degraded. Not only did they lose Atahualpa, they saw his men slaughtered. The Incas were terrified, afraid for their hostage king, and for themselves.

Ens watched Caitlin absorb it all. They walked around the strewn Inca bodies piled upon each other in Cajamarca Square.

Encircling the square from above, Gandor flew over the fallen bodies, thousands of them, too many to count, so many that their bodies and blood covered Cajamarca Square. By Jack's side, Potter Sims collapsed with his arms lying across Jack's body as if to envelop it. Potter Sims was heavy with sadness, the greatest grief he had experienced since the death of his sister, Cordula. Sergeant Hicks and Sergeant Stone and the other Special Forces soldiers stood soberly together

near Jack, who lay on the ground with other slain Incas. Conquistadors led
Atahualpa away in chains.

Caitlin was lost. Ens pointed to Jack's fallen body.

"Do you love him?"

Sadness drew her face down; tears glazed her sparkling hazel eyes over red.

"Yes," Caitlin answered.

"Would you trade his life for an entire civilization?" Ens asked.

"As a scientist or as someone in love with him?"

"As a lover of life," asked Ens.

Caitlin took her time to answer while she stared at Jack's lifeless body. "How
can anyone compare the life of one person with the life of an entire civilization?
Or a planet?" Caitlin said.

"It is done," Ens said. He snapped his fingers, and like a great blast, a blinding
white light filled Cajamarca Square.

CHAPTER 58

ONE SHORT DAY

The blinding flash of white light exploded into a rolling wormhole of luminous color, which rotated and twisted through infinite time and space. Inside the wormhole, Jack and Caitlin, Sergeant Hicks and Sergeant Stone with their soldiers tumbled as if freefalling through the never-ending tunnel of infinity, which was made of sparkling points of light like stars and colors that hummed in assorted musical pitches. While flipping and rolling uncontrollably in the great tube, each traveler saw their destination, a dense black cloud, which was sucking in all of the stars and colors, and any matter intersecting its path. Both Caitlin and Jack noticed that the longer they tossed and spun in the wormhole, the farther they were from the dense black cloud.

Suddenly, there was another explosion of dazzling white light. As fodder shot through a great cannon, Jack and Caitlin were blasted onto the Giant Beanstalk from the wormhole. Instantly, they clung to the Beanstalk for their survival. They were shocked and disoriented. New York City was 13,000 feet below. After staring down at the city, Jack and Caitlin looked up. About one hundred feet above them, they saw the twelve Special Forces soldiers blown out of a black hole in the periwinkle sky onto the Giant Beanstalk. But this time, the soldiers were not Spanish Conquistadors, as in Cajamarca, they were a U.S. Special Forces Swat Team, just as they were when they had first assaulted the Beanstalk with Captain Jordan.

Jack looked at his left arm. It was still wood. He felt for his amulet. It was still there.

"We were in fourth dimension, a wormhole," Caitlin said.

"I died 500 years ago in Cajamarca!"

"I was there, I saw you." Caitlin said clinging to the Beanstalk. "I don't even know if we are alive or dead."

"If we were dead, we would know." Jack's voice had a certainty in it.

"Then when are we?" asked Caitlin.

Jack stared at his wooden arm. "My arm is still wooden …" His attentions turned to New York City to verify if it was the thriving New York City, which he had left behind. "Are we before we met or after?"

"It couldn't be before because we are on the Beanstalk together, unless the future has been changed. We are too high to tell if it is the same New York City which we left behind," Caitlin pointed.

Suddenly, they heard a loud rumbling. The Giant Beanstalk vibrated. They felt the vibration on the palms of their hands, and against their bodies, as they clung to the Beanstalk. The air all around them vibrated against their skin. At a distance, they saw a dark speck in the crystal cerulean sky. They watched the speck grow into a jet. An eerie feeling hung in the air, as if something momentous was about to happen. Jack looked up at the U.S. Special Forces soldiers, whose attentions were fixed on the jet. From nowhere, there was a brilliant white flash. It was followed by a crushing shock wave. A great roar filled the air. Jack and Caitlin watched, as a nuclear shockwave rolled across the Earth's landscape, as far as they could see in every direction on the still horizon.

Below Jack, Caitlin, and the twelve soldiers, Manhattan's skyscrapers crumbled like paper-mâché blocks obliterated in a blinding white wind. From more then two miles up on the Beanstalk, they watched as civilization on Earth was destroyed. Giant mushroom clouds churned up the debris of earth, the greenness of the plants and trees, the vaporized oceans, the melted sand and charred dirt, dried cement of civilization, all mixed in a great bowl by the white fire of hell. The clouds' voracious appetites ate everything as they gorged themselves on the periwinkle sky, their white sinewy necks rising, their proud and arrogant fiery red and white heads reaching to overtake the Great Green Beanstalk. These were spectacles of de-creation. Jack and Caitlin and the twelve soldiers were unable to look away.

"Oh, my God! They've done it!" screamed Caitlin.

"It's the future," Jack said.

"I feel sick. I feel like I did at Cajamarca," Caitlin cried out.

"My father told me, life is not about five years from now, or next week, or even the next minute, it's about now, this moment."

Jack and Caitlin looked out at the blackened sky, the leveled cities, and the many rising mushroom clouds as far as they could see.

"We must go back!" Jack said to Caitlin.

Jack yelled up to Sergeant Hicks and Sergeant Stone and the U.S. Special Forces swat team, "We must go back!" The twelve soldiers were paralyzed with fear and disbelief, as they watched the mushroom clouds rising into the air. One great mushroom cloud rose violently toward them out of Manhattan's bowels. Jack and Caitlin saw electrical charges arcing inside the voracious turbulent cloud, which chewed up the dead urban debris. Collectively, they thought what enormous power! How could anyone ever know unless they see it? What destruction! Jack remembered Ens' words, 'You are visual beings. You memorialize your mistakes.' Since Hiroshima, every man, woman and child on the planet who has ever watched television has seen the giant mushroom rising over Hiroshima. Then, Jack realized, we are visual beings. It is a blessing and a curse. He remembered, and heard the words in his mind, I could not take my eyes off Captain Jordan as he died. Jack thought as he clung to the Beanstalk looking down at the great mushroom clouds rising out of New York. How many times had people replayed the atomic holocaust of Hiroshima in their minds, been unconsciously drawn to and fascinated by the gigantic mushroom cloud?

Jack, Caitlin and the soldiers were rapt by the incredible spectacle.

"We must go back!" Jack yelled.

However, Sergeant Hicks and the soldiers were too high up and could not hear anything, but the great wind that was sweeping across the wasteland below them.

"Do you hear me?" Jack yelled angrily into the void surrounding the Great Beanstalk. He looked upward into the deep periwinkle sky. "Bring us back!" His face was red and desperate. "Bring us back!"

Moments passed, as the roar of the wind from the nuclear blasts filled the air and shook the Beanstalk, like a great hand grabbing onto a small tree and shaking it. There was a blinding flash of white light. It shrouded everyone on the Giant Beanstalk. Jack, Caitlin and the twelve Special Forces soldiers were gone from the Beanstalk.

CHAPTER 59

THE CHOICE POINT

It was nighttime and still in the Sacred Plaza of Machu Picchu, where the Milky Way shined. Ens waited in the Sacred Plaza with Sebastian, Potter Sims and Gandor.

"What are we doing here? Where is Jack? Caitlin?" yelled Potter Sims.

"For once I agree with Sims, we have been through a torturous amount," Gandor said. His hands shook as he tried to pack his pipe.

"Patience, patience." Ens said as he waved his arms and a burst of blinding white light flooded the Sacred Plaza. Everyone in the Sacred Plaza, except Ens, shaded their eyes.

"What you are seeing is the passage of future time," Ens explained.

"What rubbish!" Potter Sims said shielding his eyes with his gloved fingers.

"Did you not go into the past, Sims?" Ens said. "Then why not the future?"

"Because it is not normal!" Potter Sims answered.

"But it is." Sebastian said with assurance.

"How?" Gandor asked.

"If you know how, you can track the future. But the future is like clay, it can change according to the pressures that are put upon it."

Potter Sims and Gandor shielded their eyes more as the light got brighter. Gandor backed away nervously. White light illuminated the entire Sacred Plaza, Potter Sims and Gandor saw images of people as the light slowly faded. It was Jack, Caitlin, Sergeant Stone, Sergeant Hicks and the Swat team. After several seconds, the light disappeared into the darkness. Everyone was present, but dizzy and nauseous; it took them several minutes to orient.

"Is that our future?" Jack asked.

"It is one of several futures, all of which are possible." Ens answered.

"What does that mean?" Potter Sims interjected.

"Shut-up and listen, Sims, he'll explain it!" Gandor said.

"The future is always about the choices we make," Ens said.

"What year was that?" asked Caitlin.

"Around 2010 or 2012, thereabouts." Sebastian answered.

"Thereabouts?" Jack was disturbed at Sebastian for being so cavalier, and his tone conveyed his frustration and anger. "We just saw our planet destroyed!"

"We can track the future and see different paths," Sebastian said in a very low calm voice. "But we can only see events within a general time and space. If we identified a future event on a specific date, it would be coincidence if it were to happen on that date." Sebastian explained.

"You know the prophecies?" Ens asked Caitlin.

"The Hopi Prophecies!" Potter Sims blurted out.

"Just how do you know about that, Sims?" Ens asked. He was amused by Potter Sims' recent education about the Hopi Indians.

"Jack told us," Potter Sims said.

"He even drew an impressive diagram," Gandor said as he puffed on his pipe.

"What are the Hopi prophecies?" Sergeant Hicks asked.

"Many years ago, the Hopi elders predicted that men would have a spiritual conflict with material matters," Jack said. While he spoke, there was silence in the Sacred Plaza. "The Hopi prophesied three great shakings—World War I, World War II, and World War III. Those peoples who first received the light of divine wisdom or intelligence in the ancient countries would start World War 3—India, China, Egypt, the Middle East, Palestine, and Africa. The final Great Shaking would occur when the great house in the sky is complete, the International Space Station. The Hopi prophesied that the United States would be destroyed by atomic bombs and radioactivity."

The twelve soldiers were stunned.

"We saw it," Sergeant Hicks said.

"Yes, you did." Sebastian spoke with sadness and compassion.

"Glad I did not see it! I've seen enough destruction for one day, thank you!" interjected Potter Sims.

"Me, too," added Gandor. He looked at Jack, "I thought you were dead."

"I was, but it was a past life," Jack answered.

"You were Inca, close to Atahualpa." Sebastian said.

"Yes."

"You had to live it to understand it," Sebastian said. "To study the fall of a great nation and to live it are two experiences separated by a great chasm."

"The Incas have a name for the great shaking," Sebastian said. "They called it Pachakuti, like Dr. Bingham's planet. Pachakuti is a millennium moment in time of great turmoil and enormous change."

"It's happening today," a younger Swat soldier said.

Another soldier spoke up, "When we saw the atomic bombs, the ground trembled."

"Yes, it did, and it will again, depending upon what you envision in your mind and what you commit to in your spirit," Sebastian said.

"Nearly every religion and culture of your world has similar predictions about 'the end' that are recorded in their sacred texts," Ens said. "the Inca, Hopi, Mayans, the Lakota Sioux, Navajo, the Christian Armageddon in the Book of Revelations, Islam's *Yawmid Din* or Day of Reckoning, and the Jews with the Fall of Jerusalem."

"Are you familiar with the Bible Code?" Sebastian asked Caitlin.

"Yes, but I am skeptical," Caitlin said.

"What is the Bible Code?" Potter Sims asked, but Sebastian and Caitlin ignored him.

"How can the Torah written thousands of years ago, predict names and events in the 20th Century?" Caitlin challenged.

"You have a short memory, Doctor." Sebastian questioned Caitlin.

Caitlin's complexion turned crimson. Sebastian had questioned her ego, whether it was based on science or not. Even though Caitlin was a brilliant scientist, she had great admiration for the legendary shaman, so Sebastian's questioning of her bias had exposed her hubris. He had revealed something that lay far deeper in her being, namely her insistence that man had an explanation for everything in the universe. She worried that Sebastian saw this not just as a crick in her professional armor, but as a flaw in her character. Caitlin had never felt this way. *Naked. Exposed.* Nevertheless, she persisted. "I don't understand how we traveled back in time," Caitlin said. "I accept it. Einstein showed that time and space as relative. However, the Bible Code is different."

"Is it perhaps because the Torah is a religious text and not a scientific one?" Sebastian asked.

"I suppose that is the reason," Caitlin answered flatly.

"Are you saying that scientists do not have religious beliefs?" Sebastian asked.

"Some do. There are scientists who believe in a higher power, and there are scientists who believe that if something is a mystery, then it is merely a matter of time before it is explained," Caitlin said.

"You mean they don't believe in the idea of God?" Ens said.

"Yes, that's well put."

"What about you?" Jack asked. "Do you think everything can be explained?"

Caitlin took her time to answer, "After what I have seen, I am not sure."

"You must understand the extent of these predictions for your world. They are real, and they are good, if you heed them," Ens said. "Let's see."

Ens snapped his fingers and an enormous holograph of a book, twenty feet tall and fifteen feet wide, appeared in the middle of the Sacred Plaza.

"Sims, you asked what is the Bible Code. Watch," Ens said as he pointed to the huge book. "The Torah," he said, "is divided into Genesis, Exodus, Leviticus, Numbers, and Deuteronomy."

"Do you know about the Bible code?" Ens asked Jack.

"A little bit."

"Maybe you can enlighten us?" Ens asked, gesturing his opened palm toward the twenty foot tall holograph of the Torah. Jack stepped towards the great book and stood directly in front of it staring up at its huge gold embossed letters.

"Biblical scholars and mathematicians suspected that the texts of the bible, besides offering parables, contained embedded codes that were prophetic. One of the first to suspect was Isaac Newton." As Jack mentioned Newton's name, he looked at Caitlin, suggesting if she chose to believe in something unexplainable or even 'mystical' that she would be in good company. "Mathematicians eliminated every space, every capital letter, all punctuation from the text," Jack continued. "In short, they reduced the Torah to a word find puzzle, and then, they fed it into a computer."

"I could've translated it for them." Ens said with an amused tone.

"Oh! That would have been an outstanding translation!" Potter Sims interrupted.

"Ever wonder, Sims, if extinction might fit you well?" Ens said as he gave Potter Sims a threatening look. Potter Sims knew that Ens was not playing with him. "Embedded codes are like space-time states, like this holograph," Ens explained.

Ens waved his arm. Like a tornado, a great wind whirled turning the Torah's pages. The flapping of the book's pages echoed off the stone walls of Machu Picchu's buildings, off the mountain rock faces surrounding the cloud village, and like a rock thrown across a smooth pond, the flap of the pages skipped from mountain to mountain. Ens snapped his fingers. The wind stopped. The pages stopped. Everyone on the Sacred Plaza watched, as the words "World War II" were highlighted and raised from the text. Diagonally, the words cut down the page. Ens waved his hand. A series of words written horizontally and vertically in three dimension raised from the text and glowed: "Roosevelt," "Churchill," "Stalin," and "Hitler." Everyone on the Sacred Plaza was wide-eyed and still. The page turned and highlights shifted to the vertical, horizontal, and diagonal revealing the words "Germany," "England," "France," "Russia," "Japan," "United States," and the words "atomic holocaust" and "1945."

"This sacred text was written over 3,000 years ago. World War II occurred in the 1940's," Sebastian said as silence filled the Sacred Plaza.

It had become a somber gathering on the Sacred Plaza, all except for the Shaman Sebastian, whose face was alight with hope. With his hands, Ens leafed through more of the transparent pages of the Torah. He stopped. The words and phrases, "assassination of Yitzhak Rabin," "assassin that will assassinate," "Tel Aviv," the date "in 5756/1995" and the name "Amir" were highlighted.

"Yitzhak Rabin was a great peacemaker; he was assassinated in November, 1995. His name is here, as was Anwar Sadat's name, a great Egyptian peacemaker, who was assassinated in 1981," Sebastian said.

Ens waved his hand and the pages of the Torah flipped-by rapidly, and then stopped. Raised out of the columns and rows of Hebrew letters appeared the word "Twin," in a vertical alignment. Fire burned the letters without consuming them, and smoke spewed out of the letters where they touched the surface of the Torah. Just above and to the left, the Hebrew letters for "Towers" appeared in fire and black smoke, and just below appeared the letters "Airplane," all on fire with black smoke. Ens turned the page of the Torah, the raised burning letters read "Bin Laden," "Twice," "and "End of Days."

"And the finale!" Ens said, as he waved his hands in a great arch across the Books of the Torah. A brilliant white light radiated from the center of the Sacred Book. The glimmering ancient pages leafed by rapidly. They sizzled in the cool night air. The pages of the Sacred Book stopped turning. Burning flames highlighted letters and phrases, as if the sacred text was being sifted out of time and space and branded, *"Earth annihilated"* and *"Year 2012."* At the bottom of the page encoded horizontally, vertically, and diagonally, in all dimensions, a stark burning sentence appeared, "It will be crumbled, driven out, I will tear it to pieces, 5772."

The fiery words branded images of destruction and death into the minds and hearts of everyone standing on the Sacred Plaza.

"Five Thousand, Seven Hundred and Seventy-Two!" Ens said. He repeated, "The year 5772 is the Hebrew year for the Gregorian calendar date, 2012."

A golden band of light connected the words of assassination prophecy. It weaved a radiant path through the Torah and highlighted other names, which were once references to cities of global warfare. The golden luminous ribbon of light settled upon a highlighted phrase embedded in the Sacred Text. The band of light enveloped the phrase, spun around it like a cocoon of golden light, and lifted it off the page above the other words in the sacred text. Golden light radiated out from the words to the Sacred Plaza.

Jack, Caitlin, Potter Sims, Gandor, Sergeant Hicks, Sergeant Stone, and the other ten soldiers were speechless. They were transfixed by one simple phrase of four words. The golden light from the phrase reflected off their faces, shimmered through their bodies, which made them appear translucent, as if transfigured in gold.

The words said, *"Will you change it?"*

CHAPTER 60

REMEMBERING THE
FUTURE

"How can anyone change the future?" Potter Sims asked.

"Ancient cultures from all over the planet," said Sebastian, "cultures with no contact or knowledge about one another, believed that people have the ability to alter the future, literally change a prophecy by collectively choosing and willing a different path."

"It's not just ancient cultures, but science." Caitlin said. "Quantum physicists have theorized that for any one event, there are many possible outcomes. For a brief moment, every possible outcome exists as a reality, sharing the same time and space."

"This is only a theory, am I correct?" Gandor asked as he chewed on the end of his pipe.

"It is a current and widely accepted theory," Caitlin answered, "like Einstein's General Relativity was a theory."

"It is not just possible, it is a fact." Potter Sims said. "As a mapmaker," Potter Sims began to speak, but Gandor quickly cut him off.

"You were a mapmaker?" Gandor said removing the pipe from his mouth.

"Yes, I knew about the Cave, and Devastation Plain and the Thorn Maze and the Salt Flats." Potter Sims said to everyone's surprise. "I was our Tribe Storyteller, which pledged me to years of journey, and so I also made maps as a service to our tribe."

"I am impressed, Sims," Gandor said.

"I guess there is hope for all of us." Ens said.

Potter Sims glared at Ens, but bit his tongue.

"What does mapmaking have to do with quantum physics?" Jack asked.

"Let me show you," Potter Sims said as he stooped down to the blocks of stone in the Sacred Plaza. Using the point on a small rock, which he picked up off the ground, he scratched a small circle into the stone, and then scratched an 'X' in the stone about two feet away. "Let's say the circle," Potter Sims said, "is the place where someone begins their journey." He pointed at the small circle, and drew a line from the circle to the 'X.' "And the "X" is his destination. But what if during the course of his journey, say here," Potter Sims drew a triangle about three inches from the origin point, "the traveler changes his mind and decides to travel to a different destination, say here." Potter Sims drew a line to another 'X' but it was farther away than the first 'X.' "Or what if he was unsure and was considering three different destinations at the same time, like here," Potter Sims drew a third line connecting it to another 'X', each a different location from the original destination.

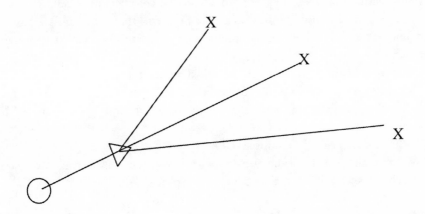

"At the point of his journey, when he changes his mind," Potter Sims pointed to the triangle, "and thinks that he might travel to any of three locations, each one of those destinations are real and exist at the same time as real possibilities." Potter Sims dropped the stone and rubbed his gloved hands together to dust off the residue from the stone etchings, and he stood.

"Sims, that was remarkable. I didn't know you had it in you!" Gandor said.

"I learned how to draw from Jack," Potter Sims said, cracking a faint smile.

Jack laughed and patted Potter Sims on the back.

"Potter Sims, that was brilliant. You are in the wrong field, you should be a scientist." Caitlin said.

Potter Sims got embarrassed and was speechless; they could not believe that he was tongue tied because no one had ever seen him so.

"This is all good," Sebastian said, pleased with a communal bond that he felt developing.

Caitlin found herself in a unique position. As the great granddaughter of Machu Picchu discoverer Hiram Bingham, she understood the Inca culture, as well as the Mayan and Native American cultures, who derived their power from the Earth. As a scientist, Caitlin also understood the basics of quantum mechanics. In this Sacred Plaza arena, these two seemingly diverse studies were merging to construct what Caitlin thought could be a new way of seeing the world.

"So, it is essential that you understand that nothing is so carved in stone that it cannot be changed." Sebastian said.

"I don't understand," a young soldier said. "What does all this mean?"

"It means we can change the future, if we have a will to," Jack said.

"Not just the future," added Sebastian, "you can change the past."

"How is that possible?" Sergeant Stone asked in complete disbelief.

"Just as there are multiple futures at one moment, there are multiple pasts at any one moment, and multiple presents." Sebastian's words were certain, unflinching.

"History is history. You can't change it." Sergeant Hicks countered.

"You can change the imprint," Sebastian said. "Even though we live our lives everyday chronologically, time and space are not linear. Your great scientist Einstein proved that."

"What did he prove?" Gandor asked.

"Einstein showed that time and space are not linear, but curved. As objects approach the speed of light, time slows down relative to objects at rest," Caitlin said.

"Let's get back to changing the past," Gandor said chewing on his pipe's mouthpiece. "You can just ask something to go away, like it never happened?"

"No. You must see it the way that you wanted the event to happen, and only that way," Sebastian said.

The Sacred Plaza was stone silent, as everyone absorbed what Sebastian had said.

"Gandor, if you could change anything, what would it be?" Ens looked at Gandor.

"I would bring Alba back."

Everyone looked at one another. The silence of the mountain filled the space.

"Then bring her back," said Ens.

"Oh, just like that?" exclaimed Potter Sims.

"It becomes of living prayer," Sebastian said. "You must think her, see her, hear her, touch her and smell her."

"How do we do this?" Jack asked the question, but everyone thought it.

CHAPTER 61

ALBA

"Make two circles, you ten soldiers form the outer circle," Sebastian directed them. "On the inner circle, Ens and I will join Sergeant Hicks and Sergeant Stone, Jack, Caitlin, and Potter Sims."

Sebastian looked at everyone standing around him.

"What about Gandor?" Potter Sims asked.

"Patience, Sims." Ens whispered. His voice was like a father reprimanding his impetuous child.

Everyone moved into two circles, except Gandor. He was nervous, trying not to show his fear. He did not want to shake and shiver in front of everyone.

"Gandor, would you please stand in the middle of the two circles?" Sebastian pointed to the center of the circle. Gandor ruffled his feathers to get a grip upon himself, and then waddled timidly into the middle of the two concentric circles. Everyone watched him. It made Gandor extremely self-conscious as he waited like a stone relic in the center.

Sebastian walked over to a large flat stone in the Sacred Plaza, and picked up a bundle of sage wrapped tightly with vines. The green bundle filled his hand as if he was gripping a thick tree branch. He then barely touched the end of the sage to a solitary nearby torch used to illuminate the Plaza steps; the sage caught fire and glowed red. Quickly, he blew the tight bundle of flames out. Whfft! As the blue smoke wafted into the air from the end of the sage bundle, the Shaman walked around smudging the front and back of each person to purify and open a person's heart.

"Open your hearts, free your minds. Let the Apu mountain guide you and give you sight."

As Sebastian walked around the soldiers, he chanted. In his left hand, he held the smudge stick, in his right hand he held a great condor feather, which he had pulled out from the sash wrapped about his waist. The soldiers watched him warily as the Shaman circled them wafting the blue sage smoke about their chests, under their armpits, up and down their arms and legs, across their shoulders and down their backs. The smoke drifted through the Sacred Plaza and hung in the air around each soldier the Shaman cleansed. As he moved to the inner circle, Potter Sims' eyes got very wide and white. He looked in Jack's direction trying to get his attention, but Jack was absorbed with Sebastian. Potter Sims made a whistling-like whisper.

"Phewt! Phewt!"

Jack heard a noise coming from Potter Sims' direction, so he turned to see Potter Sims staring at him. He turned his head away to ignore Potter Sims, as Sebastian walked around Caitlin smudging her with the sage bundle.

"Phewt! Phewt!" Potter Sims repeated his whistle at Jack.

Jack glared at him.

"I hate smoke!" Potter Sims whispered to Jack, who was about to be smudged by Sebastian. Jack was still glaring at Potter Sims when Sebastian passed the smudge stick in front of his face, down to his heart and up and down his arms. He could see Potter Sims through the blue sage smoke, as Sebastian moved the smudge stick in concentric circles around Jack's chakras. He walked to Potter Sims, faced him directly, and began incensing him. Potter Sims' eyes got bigger. He shook his head rapidly back and forth as if he was trying to shake a sticky particle off his face.

"I hate smoke." Potter Sims whispered directly into Sebastian's face.

Sebastian turned his eyes away and kept smudging Potter Sims' body.

"Quiet," the Shaman said without missing a beat. His voice was serene, but commanding. Potter Sims knew it by the tone, so he endured the blue sage smoke.

When Shaman Sebastian finished cleansing everyone in both circles, he snuffed out the smudge stick in the rocks and brought out a small rawhide drum decorated with Red Hawk feathers and painted with a bear. From his sash, he pulled a small corked bottle, opened it, sipped a small amount of the fragrant liquid into his mouth and held it. Raising his head skyward to the southern stars and mountains, he blew a fine spray mist between his teeth and his tightly pursed lips into the cool night air where the tiny droplets disappeared. He spoke.

"The winds of the South, Great Serpent."

He turned to the West, the North, and the East.

"The winds of the West, Mother Jaguar, the winds of the North, humming-bird, ancient ones, whisper to us in the wind. The winds of East, great eagle and condor who soar in the blue sky beneath the sun, and Mother Earth, Pachamama guide us."

Sebastian stooped down and placed his palm flat upon the ground. "The Rock People, the Tree People, the Fin People, of the land, in the water, in the air, all those breathers," he said.

He raised his opened palm and outstretched fingers to the sky, "Sun, Moon, Planets, Stars, and all those who look down upon us, the great spirits of the Apu, and the Great One without a name, open our hearts, hear us, guide us, and be our light. Let those who walked before us and the ancient ones join us in prayer, let their wisdom guide us and show us your way."

Sebastian spoke to each person standing in a circle. "You must close your eyes and see those close to you who have died. See them here. See them standing next to you,"

Standing across from Potter Sims in the inner circle, Ens closed his eyes. Brilliant colors, bright and dark, hopeful and menacing, calm and torrential, swirled around Ens' body. They streamed out into the air all around him.

"What is happening?" Potter Sims asked nervously.

"There is nothing to fear," Sebastian whispered.

Fading into the two circles were the transfigured, ghost-like images of people. At first, the images were indistinct, but as they grow in strength, they became more detailed. A golden light glowed through and around each transfigured image. In the inner circle, Yamqui faded in next to his son Sebastian. Gage Tott appeared next to Jack, who could not see his musician father. Captain Jordan appeared next to Caitlin, but she also could not see him. In the outer circle of soldiers, Private William 'Billy' Ketchum and the Unknown Soldier, who died in the Thorn Maze with Captain Jordan, materialized next to the soldiers in his platoon; they were also invisible to them. And last, Potter Sims' sister Cordula faded in next to him. He was filled with emotion, when he saw her, more than he had ever expressed during this entire journey.

Once Yamqui, Gage, Captain Jordan, Billy, and the Unknown Soldier had faded into the circles, the light brightened. It glowed and radiated out of each person's body. The connection between everyone strengthened. The dead joined the living.

As the minutes ticked on, the energy level rose in the circles, especially in the center where Gandor stood. Everyone could feel it. A hazy light gathered around Gandor, who stood motionless inside the two concentric circles. Light emitted by each person's energy began to touch and intertwine, connecting everyone to one another.

Ens turned toward a large pile of granite in the rock quarry shrouded in darkness just beyond the Sacred Plaza. He opened his black cape revealing his two enormous skeletal black wings, extended them eight feet above his head, cracked the air and Hranknor appeared, floating ten feet off the ground. His giant bat-like wings cut the air with power and elegance. He glided over to Ens, set his large clawed feet on the stone ground.

"Ut undig zuitat Alba kandu nräng rangut zut," Ens said to Hranknor.

"Grundig zait duit." Hranknor answered. With one flap of his wings, he lifted off and disappeared into the black night.

"What's all this about?" Potter Sims asked Ens.

"Alba."

Hranknor floated back to the Sacred Plaza with two members of The Corps carrying a turquoise mineral, six feet in length, four feet in width, and three feet thick. It was semi-transparent, cylindrical with thin crystalline sheets layered so they overlapped one another. Each layer though similar in color and translucency, was uneven in width and length. Hranknor and the two soldiers of The Corps set the translucent bluish cylinder down in the center of the two circles.

"This is Ubunite." Gandor said as he stared at the cylinder in disbelief.

"It is." Ens answered.

"Rufus is the only place where it is found," Gandor said. His voice trailed off with an unsure tone.

"The people of Rufus Island brought extinction upon themselves," Ens spoke. "Greed and power were the mates that conceived your extinction, but nature finished it with disease. That is, everyone but you—and your spouse Alba."

"Alba?" Gandor looked up.

Gandor stared at the turquoise mineral two steps from him.

"You thought she was dead from the disease that killed everyone else, but I preserved her, just for this moment. She still has the disease. If she is not healed before the mineral breaks open, she will die within minutes, right here in front of you. You and everyone here have the power to heal her before the mineral breaks open and thus choose an alternate future not just for her, but for you, and your entire species."

There was not one sound in the Sacred Plaza.

In the center of the circles, Gandor stared down at Alba. He began shaking uncontrollably.

"I can't do this," Losing his courage, Gandor feared that he would make a mistake and doom not only his spouse Alba, but also his entire species. Weighed down by what he perceived as the heaviest of burdens, Gandor became paralyzed. Standing in the circle with everyone surrounding him, he felt alone, and he could not do it alone. Just then, Potter Sims looked at his sister, who smiled at him and nodded toward Gandor. Without saying a word, Potter Sims knew immediately what his sister was nudging him to do. Be with Gandor. Give him strength. So, Potter Sims let go of his sister's hand, left his circle and joined Gandor, standing by his side, in the middle.

"Nobody knows this, but Jack. You wanted to know what I am doing out here alone. I am on a pilgrimage to reflect on my life. My sister is here, you see her. She was my best friend, I loved her more than anything in the world," Potter Sims spoke to Gandor, and as he spoke over at Cordula his sister. Everyone listened with rapt attention. "Her name is Cordula. She died of a rare disease. After three months of mourning, the tribe elders ordered me to take a pilgrimage to a land, where I had never been, where I would be open to my sister's spirit. I was afraid to go because I was alone. I knew that I could not make it alone. By accident, I met Jack and Caitlin. I met you once again. After everything that we've gone through, I knew that I could overcome anything because we were together. I see now that Cordula is here because of our unity. You have a chance to bring Alba back. You may lose her. She might die right here in front of us, but you must try. We will help you. Together, we can do this."

Gandor was visibly moved by Potter Sims. From the outer circle, Cordula stared at her brother Potter with more than tears in her eyes, she felt great pride for he was a person of love and respect.

"Does Alba look like you?" Sebastian asked Gandor.

"Yes."

"Does she have your smell?"

"Yes."

"Do you wish to bring her back to live a life with you?"

"Yes," Gandor's voice trembled.

"Let us begin." Sebastian said to the entire group. Potter Sims stayed close to Gandor in the center. "Everyone, you must see Alba alive. You must see her with no disease, as if she never had disease. See her face. Look into her eyes. Smell her. Run your fingers through her feathers. With your hands, gently reach under her wings and extend them. Feel her lightness."

From under his ceremonial poncho, Sebastian took out a rattle. It was the size of a grapefruit, decorated with Condor feathers and painted with images of the sun, moon and the stars. As Sebastian chanted, he shook the rattle. It was a life chant. Sebastian heard the music of the rattle as a beating heart. Jack also heard it, the beating of Alba's heart, of Gandor's heart, of everyone's heart gathered around the two circles. In Sebastian's mind, the rhythm of the rattle was born of nature's pulse: the moon as it revealed nightly its varied shimmering faces, the sun as it rose daily over the mountains, as the crops grew annually and were harvested, as the constellations arched nightly across the sky.

Everyone in the two circles joined Sebastian, chanting a steady drone. The Ubunite began to glow, then crack. Gandor shivered in fear.

"I am afraid," said Gandor shaking, as he stared down at the form of Alba imprisoned in the Ubunite. The translucent blue layers cracked. Potter Sims placed his white-gloved hand upon Gandor's back.

"You are afraid to bring her to life because you are afraid to lose her again," said Potter Sims.

Gandor knew Potter Sims was right.

"You are not alone!" Potter Sims desperately pleaded to convince Gandor. "Gandor, the Ubunite is breaking. Change your destiny!"

Gandor stared down at the Ubunite that was breaking apart. He took a deep breath, closed his eyes for several minutes, and then opened them.

"Alba," Gandor said, his tone was pleading. "I am here."

The Ubunite crackled and dissolved. Thin pieces drizzled to the ground, where they broke into thousands of tiny diamond-like particles. Alba was nestled and protected in the mineral's blue womb, where it hugged every curve and line of her body. She began to stir. The more the crystal cracked and dropped away, the more the color returned to her face. Her feathers changed from a stiff bristle to fine delicate hair. Her wings became supple. Her lungs filled with the cool night air. Gandor inched closer, and Alba opened her large oval eyes. Gandor moved his face to hers, and she turned her face toward him, staring into his eyes, while the crystal pieces fell in sheets to the stone, where they shattered. Completely exposed, Alba stared at her mate.

"Gandor?" Alba said.

Gandor felt a lump deep in his throat. Tears formed in his eyes. Out of joy, he trembled. His mate was alive. His species *Raphus gryphus* was saved. In an instant, the guilt that he had carried lifted.

"Alba!" Gandor's voice resonated with gratitude and humility ... and disbelief.

Ens stepped back beyond the outside circle. He read the energy level in the Sacred Plaza, like a matrix, but it was uneven and weak, unconvincing. To some, the resurrection of Alba was impossible, an allusion of some kind, a trick. The young soldier Billie, two other soldiers, and even the energy around Caitlin, showed a lack of faith. Ens raised his large hands in air and bellowed.

"Be sure!"

His voice shook like an earthquake as it reverberated against the great walls of stone in the Sacred Plaza and the surrounding mountains.

"Be sure!" Ens bellowed again.

Suddenly, Alba's face began to darken, her feathers became hard and stiff, her body began to shrivel.

"Gandor?" she cried out, but this time her voice trembled with dread. Gandor's worst fears became reality right in front of him. The disease ate into Alba's body with a swiftness that no one could have imagined. Gandor let out a whelp of pain, as he stared at Alba, whose eyes had closed and began to sink into her skull. Her beak turned purple and black, her bright, blue webbed feet blackened as they curled up and her wings crumpled. Her face had the caste of death upon it. The blue Ubunite womb had become a tomb.

"Be sure!" Ens yelled. Out his great hands that extended over everyone, a dark energy poured, like a fluid black hole. It ate the light. It encircled the blue Ubunite, seeping into the inner chamber that imprisoned Alba tightly. "You doubted in your minds. There was doubt in your hearts!" He bellowed.

Gandor moaned uncontrollably, and then, Alba died. Gandor looked at the dark shriveled form of his mate, and then abruptly turned his gaze away. The disease had eaten her beauty and life. Alba was gone.

"You and your species' insatiable greed brought this upon yourselves! The universe claims *Raphus gryphus*! It will be no more!" Ens proclaimed to Gandor.

Blind red rage rose in Gandor. He looked up from Alba's body and with his beak extended like a lance, he flapped his great wings and charged Ens. Everything happened in seconds. Gandor never saw Sebastian, Gage and two young soldiers whom he hurled violently aside to reach Ens. Gandor thrust his beak sharply into Ens' side, but with no effect. He did not move, nor did he fend Gandor off. Ens merely looked down upon the bird doomed to extinction and he smirked. Gandor repeatedly battered Ens, while Potter Sims like a bolt of lightning raced over and wedged himself between the two, pushing Gandor away, fending off Ens, who was amused by the impotent charade. Potter Sims put his face inches from Gandor's eyes.

"Gandor!" Potter Sims yelled. "Stop! This will not help. You must accept it! You have no other choice."

Gandor pushed against Potter Sims, but his body blows were weakening. Ens looked down upon both Gandor and Potter Sims, while everyone else stood helplessly by. Gandor planted his blue webbed feet on the stone ground and thrust his beak one last time at Ens, but Potter Sims blocked him.

"It is over! Surrender. You must surrender," Potter Sims said staring directly into Gandor's eyes. Potter Sims' voice overflowed with compassion. "If this is what must be, you must live with it. There is a greater purpose here; we just cannot see it now. And you may never know it."

Gandor relaxed his stance, lowered his head. *Surrender.* Potter Sims guided him to where Alba lay dead, nestled inside the heart of the Ubunite tomb.

Sebastian and Ens looked at one another, and something passed between them. Then Sebastian and his father Yamqui walked side-by-side to the Ubunite. Jack now saw his father, and touched his father's arm lightly. Gage understood. Together, the father and son, once at odds with each other, walked to an end of the Ubunite. Captain Jordan led the young soldier Billy, who was nervous and the most unsure, to the other end of the crystal. Standing in a circle around the crystal were Sebastian and Yamqui, Jack and Gage, Captain Jordan and Billie, Gandor and Potter Sims. Sebastian turned to Caitlin, who was standing with Sergeant Hicks and Sergeant Stone and the soldiers.

"Help them," Sebastian said as he pointed to the soldiers. Her eyes scanned the confused soldiers. They were lost. "Guide them," Sebastian said. She understood.

"This is Gandor and Alba's choice point. It is the choice point of their species," Sebastian said. "You must have faith. You must see her standing here with you."

Everyone looked at one another, then down at Alba's dark lifeless body inside the Ubunite.

"Pray Alba!" Sebastian shook the rattle over her body. "Pray Alba!" He rattled at everyone in the Sacred Plaza. "Pray Alba!" He rattled at the mountains, at the stars, at the stones of Machu Picchu. Inside the Ubunite, Alba's shriveled body stirred. The wrinkles of her skin smoothed out, her plumpness gradually rose. Dark spots that blotched and stained her feathers faded revealing a beautiful coat of shiny soft feathers. Deep orange and rose tint returned to her beak. Her eyes, though closed, became full and oval once again. Her chest heaved in and out with life.

As the thoughts and emotions of every soul in the Sacred Plaza merged, Alba extended her wing out of the Ubunite and touched Gandor, who began to sob. Fires traveled down from the Pleiades and chanted like a boys' choir. The Fires flitted and sparkled around everyone present in the Sacred Plaza, producing a hum that vibrated in the cool dawn air. Their song rose to the river of stars in the Milky Way and the black region in the sky, where the fox chased the llama whose steps were fading in the morning light. The Fires swirled around Gandor, Alba, and Potter Sims.

Everyone in the Sacred Plaza saw and heard The Fires. It was the first time that it had ever happened. Alba had become everyone's new destiny, the symbol of a new life. She stepped out of the Ubunite and stood next to her mate, Gandor.

When it was done, Jack and Gage stared at each other with tears in their eyes. Gage took Jack in his arms and hugged him. Potter Sims walked over next his sister, removed his white glove and took his sister Cordula's hand in his. Gandor and Alba stood wing-to-wing, humbled and strong. Courage shined in the young soldier Billie's eyes. Standing next to Ens, Caitlin found a faith in the mysterious and inexplicable as she stared at Alba. Shaman Yamqui and Sebastian stood side-by-side at their home. The soldiers were quiet. Everyone was humbled. A peace filled the air of the Sacred Plaza.

CHAPTER 62

THE RETURN

Seventeen degrees below the horizon of the Andes, the awakening sun was rising. It smeared deep rose and apricot yellow just above the earth's craggy edge. It was time for the Fires to leave. It was time for them to disappear into the periwinkle sky and return to the waning Pleiades. Slowly, Gage, Yamqui, Captain Jordan, Cordula, Billy and the Unknown Soldier faded into the morning dew of Machu Picchu. As they smiled, Jack watched his father's image slowly dissolve away. Everyone turned and looked at the center. Alba remained. She stood with Gandor. Potter Sims was close by. Everyone broke their circles, and converged upon Alba, Gandor, and Potter Sims. It was a hive of excitement.

"It is your choice," Ens bellowed throughout the Sacred Plaza. "Your destiny is in your hands."

"Why are you doing this?" Jack asked.

"Because every once in awhile, the universe just gives you a good day," Ens answered. "It's your choice point. Don't make a muck of it."

"Unchecked, history will repeat itself. Whether it is a great people like the Incas, an empire like Rome, a great nation like the United States, or an entire planet," Sebastian said.

"Now what?" Caitlin asked.

"You go back to your time and your place in history, and you choose," Ens said. "But make no mistake," Ens lowered his fist and great wing down with intent and restrained power. "Do not let the ease which you felt here leave you with the impression that I am weak. I will crush your planet like a dried piece of clay. I will turn it to ash and cinder, if you do not change your course."

"The night I was ordained a shaman," explained Sebastian, "my father Yamqui took me up to that mountaintop," Sebastian pointed to Machu Picchu Mountain. "He told me that there will be one day, one single day, when the people of your world will choose between two paths. It will be the time of your choice point, moments will determine the life or death of your world. He knew this with absolute certainty, and now that I am a shaman, I know it to be true. I am absolutely certain of it."

"I am grateful." Gandor spoke to Potter Sims with affection and respect.

"Glad I could help, but you don't have to play it up!" Potter Sims said embarrassed.

With Alba nudging his side, Gandor said more to Potter Sims, "I must say this, you taught me compassion. At first when I met you, Sims, I hated you. It was no secret. Then my hatred fell away when I started seeing you. You stayed by me. You saw me through my fear."

Potter Sims could not talk. Any antagonism and dislike he once felt for Gandor melted away. Silence hung over the Sacred Plaza because it was time for Jack, Caitlin and the soldiers to leave. Gandor spoke first waving his pipe around, as if to make a concerted point. "Thank you."

"You have great will to live, Gandor. Your courage has saved your species." Jack said.

Caitlin put her hand upon Gandor's feathery back. "Survival of the fittest in the flesh. As a scientist and a human being, I admire your incredible will to survive. Have many offspring."

"I don't know why I am going to miss you, but I am," Caitlin said to Potter Sims. "When I close my eyes, I will see those bright red patent leather boots, hear your complaining, shrieking voice. You say that you hate everything, but I am not so sure. These are strange times, and I will miss you."

"I hate all this mushy stuff!" Potter Sims turned his head away and stared at the ground. Potter Sims looked at Ens for help, "Isn't everything you have to do here finished?"

"Patience, Sims, that's the one thing you haven't learned," Ens said.

As Jack and Caitlin gave Gandor and Alba hugs, Potter Sims tightened his white gloves over his fingers and straightened the creases out of his black tuxedo jacket, "I hate wrinkles!" he said.

Jack stepped in front of Potter Sims.

"You will always be my friend." Jack embarrassed Potter Sims, whose skin turned plum with goose bumples.

"Sims, you are not embarrassed, are you?" Gandor asked as he puffed away on his pipe.

"So, what? What if I am?" Potter Sims barked.

"I will miss you, but I think that someday we shall meet again," Jack smiled.

"Fine with me! As long as it is not in the dark and I am not frozen, parched, drowned, melted, incensed, smoked, or ignored!"

"No promises," Jack grinned.

"I hope your sister Natalie lives," Potter Sims said.

"She will," Jack answered.

Jack gave Potter Sims a hug, but Potter Sims fended it off by striking Jack's wooden arm, making a knocking noise like a woodpecker.

"Don't get me wrinkled!" Potter Sims yelled, as he straightened his wrinkled black vest, white gloves, and shirt. Then he pulled up his jacket sleeve, unfastened the gold cufflink at his wrist, and handed it to Jack.

"For you, I have the other," Potter Sims said as he raised his arm which had the other cufflink. Jack smiled, and fastened the gold cufflink to his sleeve that covered his wooden arm. He held up his wooden arm with the gold cufflink for Potter Sims to see, then he looked at Ens, "Is this permanent?" indicating his wooden arm.

"I don't know. There are some things that I do not control," Ens answered.

Jack walked toward Shaman Sebastian. He removed the 24-karat Inca amulet that hung from his neck. He hung it around Sebastian's neck. "You are my brother," Jack said, and Sebastian was deeply moved.

"We will meet again." Sebastian said. Then, from a simple woolen brown and white bag that hung from his side, Sebastian took the shiny reddish-clay earthy khuya with black inclusions, the khuya that his father Yamqui had given him, and he placed into Jack's palm. It fit Jack's palm perfectly, as if it was meant to be there.

"The power of apu Machu Picchu, it is yours now. Carry it in your heart," Sebastian said.

Jack smiled pleased to the depths of his being.

Sebastian turned to Caitlin, who was standing next to Jack, and smiled. "You balance each other."

"Are you pushing that Art and Science thing in your father's diagram?" Caitlin asked joking.

"No, this time I am selling love, only love."

Jack and Caitlin smiled. They each gave Sebastian a hearty hug. Jack gave Potter Sims and Gandor a final glance.

"Choose a wise path to destiny," Ens said softly, but his words echoed like a roar off the craggy faces of the Andes Mountains, across Machu Picchu's Sacred Plaza. A brilliant white light enveloped them. As they beamed through the blinding light, Ens' words echoed all around them, "Choose a wise path to destiny." There was a brilliant blinding flash of light, as if they were inside a bolt of lightning. Jack, Caitlin, and the soldiers opened their eyes and found themselves, clinging for their lives on the Giant Beanstalk. Ens' words followed them like whispers in the wind, "Choose a wise path to destiny."

Clinging 13,000 feet above Manhattan, Jack, Caitlin, and the soldiers looked down at New York City below them. It was cold, near zero, and snowing heavily. The snow was bursting out of the clouds above them. When Jack looked up, all he could see were thousands of snowflakes, some fell in his eyes causing him to blink until they melted. Caitlin was five feet above Jack, clinging to the Beanstalk. He looked up at her.

"Are you all right?" Jack yelled to her.

"Yes," she yelled back.

Jack grabbed a large tendril with his good hand, but it was frozen and slippery. He tried getting closer to Caitlin, but it was difficult, especially with his wooden arm.

"Don't!" she yelled. "I'm okay."

Huge spotlights streamed up from Manhattan illuminating the Giant Beanstalk, carving narrow white streaks across the snowy sky. The wind howled as it blew between the leaves of the Giant Beanstalk. Jack and Caitlin listened to the wind and began to shiver, as they clung to the Beanstalk. Ten feet above them clinging to the Beanstalk were the soldiers.

"Hang on!" Sergeant Hicks yelled from above.

Belaying himself to the Beanstalk, Sergeant Hicks climbed down to Jack, who struggled to hold onto the Beanstalk. He dug his wooden fingers into the fibers of the Beanstalk, but they would not hold. Sergeant Hicks yelled to raise his deep command voice over the howling wind.

"I am going to put a rope around your chest! Hang on!"

While Sergeant Hicks tied a rope around Jack's chest, Sergeant Stone carefully climbed down to Caitlin.

"Doctor Bingham, I am going to tie a rope around you!" Sergeant Stone's fingers were freezing as he shouted and fumbled with the rope.

"Do it!" Caitlin yelled projecting her voice above the cold shrill wind.

Sergeant Stone quickly belayed a rope around Caitlin's waist, as they both swayed and struggled in the wind. Caitlin gripped a large Beanstalk leaf tightly, but snow covered the green leaf. Just above them, the other soldiers struggled to hang on to the Beanstalk. The snowstorm had thickened. The snow had obliterated New York from their view, and the wind roared so loud in their ears that it hurt.

"I'm going to put a harness around you because we have to jump. You will be tethered to me!" Sergeant Hicks yelled to Jack.

"Okay!"

Sergeant Hicks quickly fastened the harness around Jack, who struggled to hang on in the wind and snow. Just above them on the slippery stalk, Sergeant Stone buckled the harness around Caitlin's waist. They struggled in the wind and the snow; it was getting colder rapidly. Finally, Sergeant Hicks snapped the last buckle on Jack's harness. He looked up to Sergeant Stone; Caitlin's harness snapped closed. Staring up at the ten soldiers hanging above them on the Beanstalk, he squinted to keep the giant snowflakes out of his eyes. The soldiers waited in the biting wind. Sergeant Hicks waved his arm in a sweeping arch. One soldier waved his arm in a wide arch acknowledging that he understood. Sergeant Hicks turned his attention back to Jack.

"When I say 'Ready, Set, Go!'" Sergeant Hicks yelled to Jack, "On Go, push off the stalk with me!"

Jack raised his wooden arm to say yes.

"Okay," Jack yelled into the cold thunderous wind.

Sergeant Hicks took a calm deep breath. "Ready!" He yelled as loud as he could above the howling wind. "Set! Go!"

As close to perfect synchronicity as they could on the slippery stalk, Jack and Sergeant Hicks pushed off into the snowflake-filled sky. Caitlin and Sergeant Stone followed. Then, one-by-one the ten soldiers behind let go. They dropped through the sky freefalling away from the Giant Green Beanstalk. Through the blizzard of snowflakes, the howling wind bit at their exposed skin. Jack could see nothing. The wind shrilled in Jack's ear.

"Freefall for sixty seconds, sir! We may land hard, so be ready!"

Jack nodded.

Jack could barely see Caitlin next to him through the falling snow. He looked down at Times Square, Manhattan, Ellis Island, and the Statue of Liberty that began to come faintly into view through the snow. It seemed to Jack that time and space were suspended. The spotlight was a glistening white blade cutting through the cold night sky, as the wind flicked at the snowflakes causing them to swirl in a lively dance. It was peaceful. It was deadly. It was surreal. As they fell into Earth's time and space, a time they once left behind, each one remembered the exotic world, which they were leaving behind. Each one saw the faces of Captain Jordan and Billie and the Unknown Soldier and Potter Sims and Gandor and Alba and Ens and Sebastian. They saw the Great Forest, Devastation Plain, the Thorn Maze, the Salt Flats, the ice of Lake Saquasohuh. A rush of images flooded their minds. They all saw and thought the same images in unison. Linked in mind, body and spirit, they fell as one.

At the base of the Giant Beanstalk, six enormous spotlights shined their beams, tracking the green stalk thousands of feet upward. The wind whipped through the city and stirred up the huge snowflakes, as they fell through the beam of the lights.

Two thousand feet above Manhattan, from out of the cold blackness, twelve parachutes glided into the spotlights that swept across the snowflake sky. They circled and swirled around the Giant Beanstalk, as they slowly dropped closer to the ground, where thousands of people, bundled in cold weather clothing, still massed around the Great Green Beanstalk.

Sergeant Hicks pulled on his parachute toggles, but ice covered the frozen brake lines. Under the flawed parachute and out of control, Hicks and Jack were drifting far away from the base of the Giant Beanstalk. They could not slow down, nor could they maneuver and control their descent. Just above them, Sergeant Stone and Caitlin were able to control their approach, albeit sluggishly.

"Hang on, sir! We are going to land hard!" Sergeant Hicks yelled to Jack.

Jack saw the white ground rushing up fast toward them. They were above Battery Park, blocks away from police and emergency crews. As the final anxious seconds flew by, Jack got a glimpse through the thick snowstorm at the Giant Beanstalk and the hole in the ground that used to be the World Trade Center Plaza.

"Get ready, sir!" Sergeant Hicks yelled.

"I am!" Jack yelled into the wind, as the ground rushed up to them.

It happened in slow motion. They hit the ground hard and plunged into a snow bank. The crack of the fall slammed them to the ground. As they rolled hard on the ground, the chest strap broke, hurling Jack like a pendulum through the air. He tumbled over-and-over until he came to a stop.

Lying on his back in the snow, he was bleeding and broken and barely conscious. Jack opened his eyes. As the snowflakes hit his face, he heard them delicately clicking on his forehead. He watched them stick on his wooden arm, and then melt away, replaced by another, and another. He turned his head. Every-thing was peaceful. In a semi-dream state, Jack stared at the Great Green Bean-stalk through the falling snow. The approaching emergency lights of the ambulances and paramedic units glowed in the snow with reds, yellows, blues, greens, purples, and oranges. It reminded him of the Tree of Life on the Salt Flats. He looked at the gold cufflink on his sleeve, it sparkled in the rainbow of lights. Thoughts echoed in his head,

> *"It is the music of our lives, the music of life. We float like leaves falling from a snowy tree. As we fall, I wonder that at the moment of our death, if we had an opportunity to watch our planet being born with all of its magnificent peoples and its divergent cultures and its spectacular geographies, would we do it differently? How would we treat one another? My God, what a beautiful world!"*

Alone, Jack lay in the snow, barely conscious, not even wondering where everyone was, and not even caring. Slowly, his eyes closed. The Fires descended down out of the snowflake sky chanting, and they flittered around Jack, lit upon his eyes, encircled his body and settled all around his wooden arm. Slowly, his arm turned into flesh, as the tiny Fires danced and sang in the still of the snowy night. The wooden Stradivarius bridge fell out of his arm into the soft snow, where a faint red flicker grew as an ambulance approached. Sergeant Hicks reached Jack first, then Caitlin and Sergeant Stone arrived with the ambulance. Jack was unconscious. Caitlin knelt in the snow and cradled Jack's head in her lap. She rubbed his temples, but his eyes remained closed. Every muscle in his face was relaxed, the color of his skin was pure, and the tired exhausted wrinkles of his face were tranquil and soft. She stared at his left arm. She lifted it. The gold cufflink glistened on his shirtsleeve by his wrist, a wrist, she noticed, that was made of flesh and not wood. She sighed a breath of relief in the cold night air; it turned into a tiny fog cloud illuminated by the yellow and red lights of the ambu-lance, as it floated downward to the snow. It dissolved into the snow next to the Stradivarius violin bridge. Caitlin watched the cloud curiously, then smiled and picked up the bridge. She tucked it deeply in her pocket.

The paramedics loaded Jack onto a gurney and slid him into the ambulance. Caitlin said goodbye to Sergeant Hicks, Sergeant Stone and other soldiers, who had just arrived. They watched Caitlin get into the ambulance. They closed the ambulance door, and it drove off. They watched as the flashing red lights slowly disappeared in the falling snow.

CHAPTER 63

A MUSIC BORN

In an upper floor Manhattan Hospital room, Jack lay in a bed with his eyes closed. His hands lay flat on the white sheets tucked closely to his sides, an intravenous drip in his left arm. Monitors surrounded him. Out the window, the red sun was rising and bathing New York City in warm morning light. It tinted the eastern side of the Beanstalk with a shimmering red and orange light, as if airbrushed around the stalk's immense girth. The Beanstalk had a three-dimensional presence never before seen. The red morning light streamed through the window into the hospital room, cutting a line across Mattie's legs, where she slept slumped uncomfortably in a hospital chair. Arms folded, wearing jeans and a ball cap, Natalie stood healthy and strong, as she stared out the window at the Beanstalk. The hospital room door opened quietly and in walked Caitlin carrying three cups from Starbucks. Mattie awakened.

"Good morning," Caitlin greeted her.

"Good morning," Mattie pulled herself up from the sleepy slump in her chair and straightened herself.

"A double latte," Caitlin handed Mattie the coffee.

"I need this. Thank you." Mattie said smiling and sipping the hot coffee through the tiny oval hole in the white plastic lid.

"Orange blossom tea." She handed it to Natalie.

"Thank you."

"How is he?" Caitlin asked.

"He hasn't budged." Mattie said looking lost. "It has been three days. What if it's longer?"

"It won't be, Mother," Natalie said.

There was a gentle rapping of fingertips on the hospital room door. The door swung quietly open as Murland entered into the room carrying a violin case under his arm. It was the Stradivarius. With his white hair and white beard, and a watch fob dangling from his vest, he looked grandfatherly.

"Good morning to you all," said Murland with a sparkle in his eye. "You look splendiferous," he said to Mattie. He set the violin case down on the table, then took her hand, and held it warmly between his hands.

"We were wondering if we were going to see you," Mattie said.

"Oh, you couldn't keep me away! Especially now, it's a good time."

"You brought the Stradivarius?" Mattie asked.

"Yes, there it is! Magnificent instrument!" Murland said. Mattie wondered why he brought the violin. She decided to let things unfold, not press it, not yet anyway.

Murland turned to Natalie who was standing at the window staring at him, the Beanstalk in the distance out the window, and the sun behind her head creating a radiant halo. "You are looking quite wonderful, my dear." Murland gave Natalie a big hug.

"I feel great, thanks to you." Natalie said.

"No, I was just one of Santa's helpers. Jack was the one who brought the goods. So, you are Dr. Caitlin Bingham?" Murland addressed Caitlin who stood nervously by watching this eccentric man's every twitch and smile. Since he walked through the hospital room door, she was anxious to meet him. After all, he had changed everything in her life, and somehow he had the original cosmological diagram of Juan de Santacruz Pachacuti Yamqui, which she first saw in her grandfather's den at four years old. She pondered about the mysterious connection between this strange man and her grandfather.

"I'm sorry, I should have introduced you," Mattie said slightly embarrassed.

"No fret! I know who she is, and she knows who I am!" Murland said smiling reaching out with his hand to her. "I am delighted."

"Hi," Caitlin apprehensively extended her hand to shake Murland's.

Staring into her eyes, as if he was gazing into every nook and cranny of her being, he said, "You are indeed a creature of the stars. Jack is a lucky man."

Caitlin blushed, for she felt his silent study of her and it made her slightly uneasy. After a few self-conscious seconds, the curious scientist emerged, as she quickly composed herself. "How did you get the diagram of Juan de Santacruz Pachacuti Yamqui?" she asked.

Murland brushed it aside waving his hand, "Oh, that's a long story, I'll tell you about it later. Right now, I am concerned about your young man here, our young man! Everybody's young man!" Murland chuckled. His turned his attention to Jack, but Mattie was not laughing, she was concerned about her son.

With her voice cracking, Mattie spoke up, "He's not doing too well."

"Did you bring the red stone?" Murland asked.

"Yes," Mattie said.

She walked over to her purse and took out the glossy red earthy khuya, which Sebastian had given Jack, and handed it to Murland, who smiled when he held the earthy khuya in his hands Murland walked to the bedside. He touched Jack's forehead with his hand, and ran his fingers gently down Jack's cheek. Mattie's first reaction was that it was too familiar, too intimate, but her experience with Murland while he helped Natalie, gave him license to touch Jack this way, so she bit her tongue. He placed the red khuya in Jack's right hand.

"Good!" Murland said cheerfully. "Do you have the Stradivarius bridge with you?" Murland asked Caitlin.

"How did you know about that?" she asked.

"You told me," Murland said, smiling as he held out his hand.

Caitlin had never met Murland before a few minutes ago, much less spoken with him, and she knew that neither Natalie nor Mattie knew anything about her finding the Stradivarius bridge in the snow because she had told no one. It was her connection to Jack, her umbilical to him. So how did this odd white-bearded man know that she had it?

"Thank you!" He said smiling broadly.

Murland placed the Stradivarius bridge firmly in the center of Jack's left palm, then closed his fingers around it. Jack never budged. In one hand, Jack held the ancient Khuya; in the other hand, he held the Stradivarius Bridge, part of an instrument of antiquity.

"This is Jack's sacred space," Murland opened the two windows letting the outside sounds filter into the room. He walked around the bed and waved his arms in a circle at the four walls. The morning sun streamed into the hospital room creating a radiance and lightness everywhere; inexplicably, they all felt the room's lightness, it was as if particles of light surrounded them and passed through them. The sounds of New York, people talking, birds, dogs barking, traffic and horns and sirens, airplanes, music, the wind blowing, all of it trickled in and echoed off the walls, but it was not a cacophony of urban noise. It was an orchestra of urban sounds, which fit together in a strange, yet perfect harmony. The city was on its way to becoming whole.

"We have been invited here," Murland said. "True Jack is in a coma. He is dreaming, and dreaming is good." Murland placed his hands upon Jack's head.

Jack's mind became flooded with a flash of images and sounds—the organic songs of his band at the EarthRock Cafe, he and his father playing with the New York Philharmonic, the blue ice cracking inside his ears at Lake Saquasohuh while he froze, the villagers of Machu Picchu playing pan pipes, drums and zampoñas, Sebastian's incessant steady rattling during the ceremony to bring Alba back to life, the Thorns droning chant at the Thorn Maze, the Fires chanting all about him as he heard the snowflakes flicking softly on his forehead, the music of the iridescent fruits on the Tree of Life, the crack of the lightning that split the Great Oak and killed his father, the sounds of the battle in Cajamarca Square, the streams of fire burning sacred words into the Torah in the Sacred Plaza. Every sound had an image. Each sound merged with other sounds to create a symphony. Murland, Mattie, Natalie, and Caitlin felt Jack's energy. It had a flow like electricity. It connected them to Jack, and he to them.

"He needs to dream," Murland said. He picked up the small table with the Stradivarius violin and carried it over to the side of the bed near Jack. "When he wakes, he'll want it." Murland looked at Caitlin, "How about you being the keeper of the bridge?" The Stradivarius bridge had loosened in Jack's left hand; Murland removed it and handed it to Caitlin.

"Thank you," Caitlin said.

"He will be needing it," Murland said. "Mattie, let him hold the stone until he is ready to let it go, then you take it and keep it for him. You will know the right time."

Murland gave everyone a hug.

"I'll call you when he wakes up," Mattie said.

"Please do."

Even though Murland politely agreed that Mattie would call him when Jack awoke, everyone was sure that Murland already knew when Jack was going to come out of his coma. Murland walked to the door, waved his fingers goodbye to the three women, opened it and left. They turned to Jack and waited.

CHAPTER 64

PACHAKUTI

It was early April in Manhattan. The ground was wet from the warm spring rains that bred lilacs and tulips out of the cold roots that tunneled under the parks, tubers still numb from the winter. The last snows had melted and New York was sprouting, dotted with bright verdant green buds on every tree branch in the city, but the memory of the previous year's early fall mixed fear with desire in the hearts of New Yorkers.

It was forty days until Jack awoke. Three days after, he walked outside into the shining sun. He looked up and the sky was blue. He could hear the winds blowing through the corridors of the city, a touch of magic in the air, he thought. He listened while walking near the World Trade Center Plaza, which was cordoned off to keep people away from the Giant Beanstalk that still loomed over the great city. While he slept, people went about their daily business, as the Beanstalk became an accepted part of the skyline, of their lives. On the days when the sun shone brightly, it cast an enormous shadow that moved like a sundial across the urban landscape. People merely looked up, and then stared back down on their way to wherever they were going.

It was one month after Jack had awakened on a Sunday morning, when a million people gathered at a cordoned-off boundary, which was twelve blocks away from the Giant Beanstalk rooted deep into what was now the warm ground of spring at the World Trade Center site. Thousands of people surrounded a large platform, lucky fans ringside for an once-in-a-lifetime concert. The New York Police were everywhere and highly visible, as were packs of newspaper and television journalists. Dozens of news helicopters hovered above the crowd and circled the Beanstalk. Network and cable news satellite vans from the United States, as well as the foreign press, Univision and Telemundo, BBC, Al-Jazeera, and hundreds of others lined Washington Square near New York University to dazzle the planet with the century's Greatest Show on Earth.

On the podium were city officials and political leaders. Rudy Giabellini, former mayor of New York City, stood confident and bright-eyed with New York Governor George Potemki, Michael Bloomingdale, current mayor of New York, and other delegates. Jack and Caitlin sat in chairs on the elevated platform; next to them were Mattie and Natalie. Smiling broadly and wearing his three-piece suit with dangling watch fob was Murland, who stood at ground level in the crowd rubbing elbows with excited onlookers who had traveled to the World Trade Center site from all over the world.

On the ground, front and center of the podium, was the entire New York Philharmonic Orchestra dressed in performance attire, black tuxedoes and black dresses, with all of their instruments and music stands ready. The conductor Loren Fazcel stood before them, in calm anticipation.

On one side of the podium were musicians from Peru, Ecuador, Bolivia, Brazil, Venezuela, the Qero Inca nation, the Quechua Indians, and other select musicians of Latin America. Dressed in brightly colored clothing and hats, they held an assortment of instruments: charangos, tiny 10-stringed guitar made of an armadillo shell; panpipes, a series of bamboo reeds; chác-chás, rattles made of dozens of goat hooves worn around the wrist; tarkas, ancient wooden flutes used for religious ceremonies and dances; quenas, rattles, rainsticks and many more.

Next to them were hundreds of musicians from the Near and the Far East. Each musician dressed in performance costume reflecting their nation and culture, fidgeting with their instruments, an array of strings, winds, and drums.

Around the podium, musicians in full color, full performance dress, represented every nation of every continent. They were from Africa, from every European nation, from Russia, Mongolia, the Ukraine, from Australia, and even from most of the countries in the Middle East.

The musicians cradled their instruments. Some rested upon the ground. It was a marvel of instruments, of humankind's inventiveness, just as the scene was a spectacle of costumes and cultures, all with a common language, music. They tuned their instruments and conversed with one another.

Twelve blocks away loomed the Beanstalk. The million onlookers who had made the pilgrimage to the Beanstalk and the thousands of musicians, who were drawn to it, felt the electricity in the air. Everybody present wanted to be part of an event of great historical significance.

Rudy Giabellini walked to the microphone. The television cameras flickered to life, flashes from thousand of cameras lit the podium, and the helicopters hovered.

"Citizens of our planet, presidents and leaders of nations, musicians who represent your nations and your continents, my fellow New Yorkers," he said, as a roaring cheer went up. Rudy Giabellini's words echoed all through Manhattan. "Honored guests, friends all, and my family, I am honored to be here today. I welcome you to New York and our country. We have endured so much since that clear and sunny September morning. Three thousand people from over eighty nations were killed that day, and the world became forever changed. Would that we could turn the clock back to September 10, 2001, but we cannot. We must live life anew. We must dedicate this place to those who gave their lives to escort us hopefully to a better world. We cannot consecrate this hollowed ground, it is they who have unwittingly earned the right. We have no choice, but to follow with our good will, our open hearts, and our desire for world peace. We shall always remember." Rudy Giabellini pointed to the Giant Beanstalk, "Perhaps this great greenness marks a new beginning for New York, for America, and for our planet. I wish I knew."

As Rudy Giabellini spoke, he looked over to Jack, who was overwhelmed by the day's events and apprehensive about speaking to billions of people across the planet. Jack scoured the thousands of people crowding the platform looking for Murland. Then, he saw him; Murland was staring straight at Jack, his eyes were gleaming in the sunlight, and his smile was the brightest and widest that Jack had ever seen. Murland raised his hand high and waved to Jack, who returned the broad smile, but decided not to wave since he knew that probably at least two billion people were watching the event. Caitlin squeezed Jack's hand; he looked down at their hands and saw the cufflink Potter Sims had given him; it sparkled in the sunlight. They both looked at it and smiled. Just then, Rudy Giabellini called Jack to the microphone. He rose and walked to the microphone. Flashbulbs exploded all around him. He adjusted the microphone with his left hand, and then turned his head and looked confidently at the former Mayor of New York.

"Mr. Giabellini, you said that you wished that you knew. Well, I do know. Because of our unimaginable journey and the friends whom we met, Dr. Caitlin

Bingham, Captain Riley Jordan, Sergeant Daniel Hicks, Sergeant Larry Stone, the other soldiers and I know why the Beanstalk is here. We do know what it means. I am humbled and honored to be here today before you. Across our planet, New York is the great vertical city, but there are remarkable cities of every kind on Earth. You built them; you live in them. They symbolize the great achievements and cultures of our planet. The Two World Trade Center Towers reached upward to demonstrate humankind's desire to excel, our need for vision, our passion to express our aesthetic nature. Men have always built their Towers of Babel. On a most basic level, it is our need to ascend, and in that ascent to say, 'Look at me. I can do it. I stand for something.' It is in that spirit that this Great Green Beanstalk is here. It ascends to our greatness. It ascends because of our greatness. It ascends as a green umbilical of hope to a new world."

Jack took a moment to scan the crowd. Silence filled the arena, as everyone waited anxiously for his next words and the wind blew gently through the trees and down the streets of New York.

"While we were gone," Jack continued, "I learned a great many things, particularly from a man of another time and another place, and from two individuals, who are not human, but in expression, in spirit, in courage they are more human than anyone I have ever met. Actually, what we all learned from them was simple and prophetic."

In New York City's Times Square, thousands of people stood fixed on street corners, in front of stores, and outside of restaurants watching the giant NAS-DAQ television, as the words from Jack's speech scrolled along the bottom of the screen.

In Paris, France, dozens of people watched the international broadcast, as they sat in the lounge of the Hotel Montaigne. Outside the lounge window, the Eiffel Tower's pointed-arch of iron girders thrust up into the blue sky.

In Rio de Janeiro, hundreds of people sat at a restaurant eating lunch watching a television set mounted on the wall. In the background of the crowded city, was the statue of Cristo Redentor with his arms outstretched on the top of Corcovado Mountain.

On the podium in Manhattan, Jack spoke humbly as he stared out at the sea of people and cameras aimed at him broadcasting to lands far away. Yet, he felt at peace. The words and ideas flowed through him as if they were coming from somewhere else, somewhere far away, and he knew that they were sent with love and compassion.

"I am a musician and not a philosopher. The philosopher Plato said 'the unexamined life is a life not worth living.' There were many messages, which our friends from above left with us.

"Treat the world and all beings in it with kindness.
Live your life with vision and courage, not fear."

In Tokyo, thousands of people had stopped in the populous shopping district of Ginza. Like New York City's Times Square, the neon lights of Ginza created a kaleidoscope of color that glowed in the night sky like the aurora borealis. People stopped in place to watch the gigantic television screen and listen. Behind Jack loomed the Giant Beanstalk. The Japanese translation of Jack's words scrolled across the bottom of the giant screen.

"Keep your heart open," Jack said as his image filled the huge screen.

In San Francisco, at the Golden Gate Park, a handful of construction workers in orange overalls sat on a wooden picnic table eating donuts and drinking coffee. Gathered around the radio, they listened to the Manhattan broadcast.

In the Netherlands, near a row of giant windmills, a family of four—father, mother, ten-year-old boy and six-year-old girl, gathered around their television in their quaint Dutch cottage. On their television, the image was scratchy and often distorted, but they still watched Jack speak. *"Be compassionate with one another."*

Just outside of the Sydney Australia's Opera House, nearly a hundred people rode aboard a Harbor Ferry. The iridescent lights of the Opera House glimmered upon the water, but tonight on the Harbor Ferry, there was no one at the ship railing staring at the Opera House or the lights shimmering on the water. They were watching the broadcast from New York.

On the podium in Manhattan, Jack said, *"Love and compassion are the answers to all problems,"* The wave of his words rolled gently across the million people crowded in the Manhattan streets, yet for those few seconds of time and space, not even the wind fluttered the young green leaves of the trees in the park. It was completely still.

"I mentioned that on our journey, I met a man from another time and another place. His name is Sebastian Juan de Santacruz Pachacuti Yamqui. He was a great Shaman with enormous powers of healing and vision. Years ago, his father, and Sebastian saw it later, had a profound vision and a prophecy for our world on the brink of this 21st Century. 'Years from now,' he said, 'there will be one day, one single day, when the people of your world will have to choose between two paths that will determine the life or death of the planet. It will be either a time for the Earth to rise and become a great beacon in the heavens, or to burn out like a dying ember and disappear from existence.' It will be our choice point."

Jack's tone became reflective, somber. "Minutes before my father died, I was faced with two choices, to play a song for my father, or walk away. My father was the famous violinist Gage Tott. On a picnic in the Cascades Mountains outside of New York City, he asked me to play *The Lark Ascending*, but I was too proud, too arrogant. I said no. And I walked away from him."

Jack looked out to the throngs of people, his eyes tearing up as he scanned the crowd. His eyes landed on Murland, who had nothing but love in his eyes and heart for Jack. He gave Jack strength; he gave him courage. "I made the wrong choice, but it was too late. I could not go back. I was unwilling to see the pain that he was feeling, or to see the world as he saw it. Three minutes later, he was struck by lightning and in seconds, I understood the power of a choice point. Mine was gone forever."

Jack stopped and walked to a nearby table, where his Stradivarius lay in its velvet satin-lined case. He took the revered violin from its case, and quietly walked back to the microphone. Loren Fazcel stood up and moved to the front of the New York Philharmonic. He raised his baton. The musicians raised their instruments. In the glistening sunlight, each musician was poised waiting for the nod from the accomplished conductor.

"I am asking you today, right now at this moment, not tomorrow, not next week, but right now in your heart to choose love, to choose compassion. It is love and compassion that will save us. I am asking you to commit today to making the right choice at our planet's choice point."

Jack raised his violin, then paused and spoke into the microphone, "This is for you, father. I am sorry." Jack tucked the violin under his chin, set the bow gently on the strings and played. In perfect sync, as Jack played the first note, Loren Fazcel signaled his orchestra. It was *The Lark Ascending*. The gentle notes floated over Manhattan like a lark climbing high above the urban landscape. It reminded Jack of Gandor ascending the magnificent heights of the Andes. Jack closed his eyes. As he played, he saw Gandor and Alba, wingtip to wingtip, climbing through the endless blue Andean sky above the Andes Mountains.

Jack played for three minutes, and then nodded to an Inca musician, a conductor, who stood up and held his arms high above his head to signal the thousands of other musicians and conductors gathered from every nation around the world. In perfect unison and harmony, the musicians joined Jack as he played.

The music ascended. It was like no music ever played or heard in New York, or heard anywhere on Earth before. It had a harmony and intent that ascended to the top of the Giant Beanstalk. It lifted the hearts and souls of everyone there; it lifted the hearts and souls of everyone watching a television or a computer screen, or listening to the radio.

As all of musicians from all of the nations and continents played together with Jack and the New York Philharmonic, the two World Trade Center Towers became visible in the air next to the Beanstalk, but they were apparitions, translucent glowing with a rich golden light. At first, only a few people saw them. Most did not. Those who did were transfixed and overwhelmed with awe, grief and joy.

Out of the doors of the two World Trade Center towers filed people, hundreds and hundreds of people who kept coming out of the towers. They glowed translucent with a golden aura, firefighters carrying people, police officers helping the injured, office workers helping one another, caterers and waiters, cooks and more. The transparent people walked out into the bright sunlight.

Suddenly, Jack and most of the musicians saw the World Trade Center Tower apparitions next to the Beanstalk. Some musicians stopped playing, but most kept playing as the tears trickled down their cheeks. They saw the firefighters, police officers, office personnel, the men and women dressed in business suits, the waiters and cooks in white uniforms.

Of the million people gathered there, those who saw the transfigured Towers and victims of September 11 were stunned. Some cried quietly. Some prayed. Some tried to catch their breath. Some were unable to speak.

In the crowd, a mother held her five-year old daughter's hand. The daughter saw the translucent World Trade Center Towers swathed in golden light, but the mother could not.

"Mother, look!" the little girl pointed.

"I see, darling." The mother smiled and answered her daughter, but she could only see the Giant Beanstalk and the collection of international musicians.

The daughter looked up startled. She saw a New York City Firefighter walking toward her. It was her father. He was translucent, glowing with a pure golden light. It surrounded him, flowed through and around his body, as he smiled at his little girl. She looked up at him and simply smiled back. He took his daughter's small hand in his hand, it was swallowed up in his large golden transfigured hand.

Together, they stood there looking at the Great Green Beanstalk, listening to the musicians from every corner of the globe, and staring at the translucent World Trade Center Towers shimmering in the rich golden light.

The spirits of those who had worked in the World Trade Center Towers on the morning of September 11, 2001, and those who heroically entered, were transfigured that day in translucent gold light. As they exited the World Trade Center Towers, they intermingled into the crowd of people, who were their spouses, their mothers and fathers, their friends, their coworkers. They were coming home. It was the gentle music and compassion that called them; it soothed and unified them. Those who watched their loved ones coming to them sobbed openly. For everybody, it was a confusing mix of grief, joy and mystical awe. Thousands stood in disbelief.

After several minutes, Jack, the New York Philharmonic, and the thousands of international musicians finished playing *The Lark Ascending*. Jack's eyes were riveted on the translucent golden World Trade Center Towers and the people transfigured in gold, who had rejoined their families. A great silence and reverence filled the air, only the sporadic sounds of people sobbing dotted the landscape's silence.

Millions of people around the world saw the apparitions of the World Trade Center Towers, and the apparitions of the September 11 victims leaving them to join their families. At home, in restaurants and bars, on docks, on large screen televisions in stadiums, people cried.

On the Manhattan stage, Rudy Giabellini stepped forward to the podium and adjusted the microphone. On a table next to the podium, there was a black metal box about seven inches square and three inches high with a large red button.

"I have no words, but my heart is full. I believe that this Great Greenness is a new beginning for our world. May we of every nation and continent, of every religion, pray together and make the right choice. For world peace, we do this."

Rudy Giabellini leaned over and pressed the red button. A great explosion rocked the Manhattan area. As the ground rumbled and shook, Jack reached into his left pocket and held the smooth, red earthen khuya from apu Machu Picchu in his palm. As he squeezed it, he could feel heat radiating out from the stone into his hand. It was as if the khuya had been gathering a deep warmth from a fire, and it warmed his entire being.

At the World Trade Center site, the base of the Giant Beanstalk blew apart. There was a thunderous shaking of the ground. Another set of charges blew. As the Giant Beanstalk wavered and started to sway, the translucent apparitions of the World Trade Center Towers did not budge as they glowed radiant in their golden light. The Giant Green Beanstalk tipped and teetered. Then it fell, collapsing upon itself. As the Beanstalk fell, it was pulverized into millions of bright green pieces that fell with a great rumble and thunder to the earth. People watched in awe, as the Giant Green Beanstalk crumbled. People cried. People hugged one another. People shook. The ground trembled violently, as if there was an earthquake. The golden World Trade Center Towers did not budge, as the Beanstalk fell crashing down all around. It was deafening. A great green cloud of pulverized Beanstalk dust ascended hundreds of feet into the air and rolled down the streets of Manhattan obliterating the blue sky.

In Moscow's Red Square, an enormous video screen had been erected. Thousands of Russians stood in the snow in Red Square watching the screen. Silence hung in the air, as they watched the Green Beanstalk crumble.

In Tiananmen Square, Peking China, hundreds of thousands of people gathered. Huge loudspeakers broadcast the rumbling, as a large video screen projected the collapse of the Giant Beanstalk. People looked down at the ground, which shook beneath their feet.

In Manhattan, weaving his way through the crowd, Murland jumped up on the podium next to Jack, who was holding Caitlin's hand tightly. Mattie and Natalie stood arm-in-arm, trembling as they watched the incredible display. Murland's eyes were full of astonishment.

"It is *Pachakuti*!" he yelled.

"It is!" Jack yelled. His face radiated with this new revelation.

Caitlin overheard them. Her eyes filled with tears; she wiped them quickly with the back of her sleeve and looked up to the sky. To the right of the gold translucent World Trade Center Towers, high in the deep blue sky, a pinpoint of bright light shined. For a moment, Caitlin lost her breath; Jack thought that something was wrong with her. He turned to her and saw that she was struggling to catch her breath. She pointed to the sky at the point of light.

"It's Pachakutek!" she said with tears in her eyes.

Murland, Jack, Natalie and Mattie looked up.

"So, it is!" Murland laughed.

Jack gave Caitlin an enormous hug, and they held each other.

Circling in orbit above the earth, the International Space Station was directly over New York City. It picked up the rumbling in Manhattan. The shaking reverberated through every antenna, and every square millimeter of metal and high tech plastic of the Space Station. It was a rumbling of hope, an opening to an awakened life. It was the turning point. It was Pachakuti. It was recorded by the ISS antenna. It was transmitted out of the solar system into the Milky Way, and far beyond. The International Space Station passed over North America, Europe, the Middle East, and on—

In Baghdad, Iraq, Muslims gathered in a mosque to pray. The ground trembled and shook.

In Rawalpindi, Pakistan, many people were gathered in a hotel lobby watching the New York broadcast on television. On the television screen, the Giant Beanstalk was collapsing. As the rumbling rolled out of the small television speaker, the ground in Pakistan shook, like an earthquake. Everyone looked at one another in disbelief.

In Paris, France, it was near sunset when people walked under the Eiffel Tower. The ground trembled.

In Washington D.C., hundreds of people, some who were oblivious to the unfolding events in New York City, some who walked in the sun around the Reflecting Pool, were filled with trepidation when the ground beneath their feet trembled. Between the Washington Monument and the Lincoln Memorial, the water in the Reflecting Pool shimmered. The vibrations upon the water created gold sparkles of light as bright as the sun upon the Reflecting Pool surface.

In Machu Picchu, Peru, tourists and guides stopped in their tracks, as the ground trembled. The stone structures and walls shook and rumbled, but not one stone fell.

At the World Trade Center site, millions of the green Beanstalk pieces were falling. As the ground rumbled, the last of the Beanstalk came down. The pulverized pieces covered the excavated World Trade Center Plaza and three square blocks of lower Manhattan. The rubble piled up nearly five stories. What was left were the two translucent World Trade Center Towers, and they glowed in pure gold light. The music had stopped. It was silent.

For several seconds, a silence swept across the earth. People of every nation around the world looked at one another, bewildered, knowing that something great and historical had just happened.

For the next forty days, the World Trade Center Towers glowed with the purest golden light anyone had ever seen.

People traveled from far and wide across the planet to see.

EPILOGUE

───────────── ❧ ─────────────

It was summer in the southern hemisphere, one day before the Winter Solstice in Cuzco, Peru. Jack, Caitlin, Mattie and Natalie were 100 miles outside of Cuzco riding in a modern, shiny blue indigo train with bright yellow trim. The majestic Andes dwarfed the train as it meandered on a path around the river and down through the town below the ruins of Machu Picchu. Out the windows, expectant tourists from Europe, South and North America, the Middle East and nearly every country around world looked out from their red leather chairs and cappuccinos to the majestic mountains. Balanced just above the rivers, Inca stone villages that were silent and fixed to the side of the mountain for centuries passed by in the train's window glass as a blur.

After arriving in the town of Agua Caliente, Jack, Caitlin, Mattie and Natalie rode in a bus zigzagging their way up the steep side of a mountain, where they overlooked the Urumbamba Gorge. They walked through the National Park gate. In a matter of minutes, they were standing before the majestic ruins of Machu Picchu. They stood in awe before the great stone city, as zampoña music played in Jack's head.

Later that night, at 4:45 a.m., the four stood atop of Intihuatana, the grand piano shaped rock called the "hitching post of the sun" and looked through a telescope, which Caitlin had brought for just this purpose at this moment in time and this place. One-at-a-time, they looked through the telescope toward the East North East sky. Just above the horizon sparkled the Pleiades. Three degrees and twenty-seven minutes West of Maia in the Pleiades shined *Pachakutek*. They each saw it through the telescope. It sparkled with a blue shimmer against the night sky.

As the sun rose over the Andes bringing warmth to the cold stones of the Inca village, Jack scanned the ruins of Machu Picchu's temples and royal houses. Slowly, apparitions, translucent bodies of Machu Picchu's 16th Century Incas blended into the 20th Century ruins.

Jack scanned the village and found his friend, Shaman Sebastian Yamqui. The Shaman was wearing the twenty-four karat, sun-shaped Inca amulet, which Jack had given him. Jack took the shiny reddish-clay earthy khuya with black inclusions from his pocket and held it in the clear blue Andean air next to his heart.

From thousands of miles apart and centuries divided, they smiled at each other.

ACKNOWLEDGMENTS

Many people have given me support and advice during the time it has taken to bring this book to print. For my editor and friend, Jerry Gross, who encouraged and guided me to make the necessary changes that would forge *The Ascendancy* into a stronger work of fiction. For Joel Gotler, who from the first rough draft, saw its vision and potential, even when, at times, my spirits were down. For Eric Weissmann, Esq. who has over many years, with his compassionate guidance and brilliance, represented my legal interests.

I could never have brought this novel to its present form, if it had not been for three people, whose steady friendship and business expertise, gave me support and strength over the years, Michael Cahill, Esq., Bill Sheffler, and Percil Stanford, Ph.D. For their friendship, I am deeply grateful. For Tom Nelson, Ph.D., my mentor and close friend, for his brilliance and humor, his passion for film and literature that incited me to study film at UCLA; for Leonard Friedman, his friendship, support, and faith in me; for Michael Lydon, my life-long friend, for his compassion, love and his deep faith; for Bob Dean, for his steadfast friendship; for Ann Ullrich, Ph.D. for her kind friendship and her gifted spiritual guidance; for Dawan Stanford, his friendship, his unique talents, his passion for art & writing which inspire me; for Claudette Woodworth, for her friendship and the profound spiritual awakening, which she gave me that changed my life; and for John Balla, a life-long friend whom I met by invisible design in the Andes on a journey to Salkantay Mountain and Machu Picchu, who introduced me to the writings of Gregg Braden and to Joan Parsi Wilcox's book "Masters of the Living Energy."

For my friends, for their belief in this vision, Joe and Sue Cook, Kevin Thill and Shawn Weber, Ph.D. especially Shawn for her enthusiasm and editing services, Steve Butler and Gary Taylor, Cathy Oldham, Pam O'Sullivan, Pat Blankenship, Allen & Virginia Holmquist, Tami & Scott Dickerson, and Tami's late mother Lola Workman, friends who never doubted, and Ron Dale and Robin Potter, Carole Moore and the participants in the Jacob's Bean Trilogy investment group.

I am grateful to Wolfgang Peterson who told me, after reading the screenplay *Jacob's Bean* that it must first be turned into a novel, and encouraged me to do so. For Michael Barnard who helped put the Beanstalk and the World Trade Center Towers into graphic form. For Kelley Lowe, who painted the Beanstalk. For Carlos Aranaga, for his compassion, his brilliance, his love of writing and our global community. For Michael Fiedler, for his incredible support at iUniverse. For the managers at Barnes and Noble #2575, for their support and enthusiasm—Jeff, Heidi, Jeri, Linda, Jake, Jennifer, Jordan, and John S., and the staff.

I was sustained by the love and encouragement of my family, who were always interested, but often too considerate to ask about the novel because the task had become tedious and long, and sometimes discouraging. My mother, for her love and energy, especially when she asks every week about the novel, my late father John, who always took the time to read every screenplay that I had ever written and took me on a trip to New Brighton and Beaver Falls, Pennsylvania so I might write about my summer memories there, my brother Jimmy for his love and his great heart, my sister Donna, for her love and strength. For my father-in-law and mother-in-law Brooks and Emilye Hill, for their love and belief in me, for Patty Hill for her compassion, insight and love, for my-brother-in-law John Hill, who is smart, loving and kind and always asks questions. For Tony and Katrina Kern, for their faith and kindness. For Patricia Weiskopf, for her understanding and the steady presence, which she has provided for Caitlin and Sebastian.

So many people have given me support, but three have given me inspiration, my son Sebastian, who is most empathetic to people around him, a talented athlete with a great sense of humor, and always wants to know how the novel is going, my daughter Caitlin, amazingly talented and driven, who is a wonderful musician and writer, and who convinced me years ago, when I wanted to sell the story, to hold onto it until it was ready. And lastly, my wife Judy, who is brilliant, funny, does complex logic problems for relaxation and teaches elementary school science, who is the light of my life, who in every part of her being is positive, encouraging and kind, not just with me, but with her friends; she listens to my rants, reads and critiques my rewrites, and waits patiently, never doubting for one minute, knowing that the novel would be published one day and be a success.

In writing this book, I had to read numerous books and articles, so that the information contained in the novel, even though it is a work of fiction, would be based upon fact. To those writers, whose works I read, I am deeply grateful because you opened my eyes and mind; you taught me how to see the world differently. Anthony Aveni's *Stairways to the Stars: Skywatching in Three Great Ancient Cultures* and *Between the Lines: The Mystery of the Giant Ground Drawing of Ancient Nasca, Peru,* APA Insight Guides' *Peru,* Hiram Bingham's *Lost City of the Incas,* Robert Boissiere's *Meditations with the Hopi, The Isaiah Effect* by Gregg Braden, *The Mayan Calendar and the Transformation of Consciousness* by Carl Johan Calleman, Ph.D., *The Penguin Dictionary of Symbols* by Jean Chevalier and Alain Gheerbrant, translated by John Buchanan-Brown, Jared Diamond's, *Collapse* and *Guns, Germs and Steel: The Fates of Human Societies,* Michael Drosnin's *The Bible Code I and II, "The Wasteland"* by T.S. Eliot, Graham Hancock's *Fingerprints of the Gods, The Conquest of the Incas* by John Hemming, Michael H. Jackson's *Galapagos: A Natural History,* Kurt Johnson and Steve Coates *Nabokov's Blues,* Carl Jung's *Man and His Symbols,* David H. Levy's *A Guide to Skywatching,* John Maddox's *What Remains to Be Discovered,* Drumvalo's Melchizedek's *The Ancient Secret of the Flower of Life, Vol. 1,* Donald H. Menzel's *A Field Guide to the Stars and Planets, Hopi: Following the Path of Peace* by Native American Wisdom, Percy Shelley's *"Ozymandias",* William Sullivan's *The Secret of the Incas: Myth, Astronomy, and the War Against Time, Shaman, Healer, Sage* by Alberto Villoldo, Ph.D., *The Cities of the Ancient Andes* by Adriana von Hagen and Craig Morris, Frank Water's *Book of the Hopi,* Joan Parisi Wilcox's *Masters of the Living Energy,* Ruth M. Wright and Alfredo Valencia Zegarra's *The Machu Picchu Guidebook,*

—John Weiskopf

END NOTE

Ascend: 1. to move, climb, or go upward; 2. to rise to a higher point, rank, or degree; 3. to go toward the source or beginning; 4. to go back in time.

Man has always been driven to ascend. It tempts his ego. His need to touch the divine requires it; his will to dream demands it.

To challenge and touch God, he built the Tower of Babel; to survive, he constructed Machu Picchu; to observe the universe, he built Mauna Kea's giant Keck telescope; to observe astronomical events and worlds from millions of light years past, he launched the Hubble; to envision a world community, he built the International Space Station; and, to advance shared global financial visions, he built the World Trade Center, towers that dared to ascend and become a gathering place for people of eighty-six nations on our planet.

Whatever the plan, humankind searches upward to understand its place. When a person looks down from the mountaintop or gazes through a telescope into space, he or she marvels. That person will know that there are forces far greater than his or her small steps in this temporal earthly life in the awareness of this moment. Not only does the individual become part of greatness, he or she can evolve towards it, if there is the will to do so.

Therefore, humankind must ascend. If we are to survive, we have no other choice.

978-0-595-40920-4
0-595-40920-2